S U C H
A
Hope

SUCH
A
Hope

PATHS OF GRACE

SONDRA KRAAK

Trail House Publishers

Such a Hope

First Printing, 2016

Published by Trail House Publishers, Old Fort, North Carolina

Cover design by Roseanna White Designs, www.RoseannaWhiteDesigns.com

Edited by Dori Harrell, Breakout Editing

This is a work of fiction. Any references to real people, events, or places are used fictitiously. Other names, events, and places are creations of the author, and any resemblance to actual people, events, and places is coincidental.

www.sondrakraak.com

To my mom, Jeanette, with love.
A bold woman with great hope.

"Since we have such a hope, we are very bold."
2 Corinthians 3:12

Chapter One

Seattle, Washington Territory, September 1871

Anna Warren breathed the crisp air that hinted of salt. The entire voyage from Portland to Seattle, the sea air had tantalized her, but now it took on the intimacy of an old friend. It was the air of her Seattle, the place she'd come and gone from the past fourteen of her eighteen years.

"Sorry, Father." The breeze swallowed her whisper. She'd tried to find a new life in Portland at his dying request, but the pull back to Seattle had been too strong.

Wobbly legs threatened to send her tumbling as she disembarked *The Adelaide* onto solid ground, but she steadied herself. The sooner she hopped back onto the seat of that freight wagon, the sooner life would return to normal.

But she didn't want normal.

She didn't want to traverse the countryside three hundred twenty-five days a year, as had been Father's way, the way of a businessman who'd refused to say no. His death offered her an opportunity to find community. Stability. She'd discover that balance between home and the wagon seat, which had been lacking in her life for years.

Anna walked the block to the livery and retrieved Maple, her Palomino, from a stable boy she didn't recognize. Maple tossed her mane and sidestepped before nudging Anna's shoulder with her nose.

"Me too, girl." It'd been too long. A trip that was supposed to have taken four weeks had lasted six months.

Anna climbed into the saddle and urged Maple down the street. Stretched a quarter mile across the hillside, Seattle's townsite was in constant flux. Three new buildings stood conspicuous, their fresh wood yet to receive the coarsening of a wet winter. If possible, Skid Row, the road sloping to Henry Yesler's sawmill, appeared even more congested with oxen towing cedars and firs to the waterside. Seattle hadn't rested since the Denny party had staked claims twenty years ago.

A sense of the surreal crept in on her as she surveyed the changes. She'd missed much in six months.

She settled into Maple's gait and guided her up Denny's Knoll and east, past the university, whose grandeur made it look like it belonged in the midst of an eastern city, not on a muddy rise in a western territory. At the top of the hillside, the road narrowed and veered into the woods. Trees blanketed the landscape to Lake Washington and continued for miles beyond to the Cascade Mountains. She longed to be back in that wild. If she closed her eyes, she could imagine the sway of the wagon.

A Steller's jay cawed, its throaty voice like an old friend's greeting. Only a ten-minute ride home. Maple wound through the moss and fern undergrowth as if she'd walked the road yesterday. And in Anna's mind, they'd walked it every day of her absence.

When she reached the lane to her cabin, she urged Maple to a trot, rounded the last bend, and savored the sight. The cabin's brown logs wore a weathered look, same as the rock chimney flanking the left side window and reaching skyward like a steeple. She and Papa had spent far too few nights here, but it was home all the same.

How right to be back, where the presence of Father would resonate with each scratch of the branches at the bedroom window, each creak of the cedar floorboards.

"Thank you, Lord."

From the corner of her eye, she thought she saw the curtains in the front window flutter, but that didn't make sense. She dismounted, her gaze steadfast and unblinking on the window. The rocking of the boat must have left her woozy. But when a shadow crossed behind the curtains, the pulse in her throat pounded. Keeping the horse between her and the cabin, she willed her shaking hand to steady and reached into her saddlebag for her Colt. Weary as she was from the journey, she'd not allow a vagrant to plunder her and Father's belongings.

The door flew open, and a figure strode out. Anna stepped from behind Maple and raised her gun at the same moment the dark-haired man saw her and skidded to a halt, his intake of breath audible to her some twenty feet away.

"Anna Warren, welcome home."

Her surge of energy waned, and she lowered the gun. "Tristan." She struggled to smile, her lips trembling.

Tristan Porter rested his weight on one leg and beat his hat in a soft rhythm against his thigh. He regarded her in his forthright and expressionless way.

She'd never quite understood him. "What are you doing?"

"Passing by. Checking on things."

"Inside my cabin?" Father had bonded with this young farmer. She had not.

Tristan closed the distance between them with a few strides. "Rumor was you were staying in Portland."

"I tried, but I couldn't. It didn't feel like home." She tipped her chin toward the cabin. "Do you do this often? Check on things?"

"Peter was a friend."

Tristan might be stoic, but he was responsible, and he'd cared for her father. She'd understood at least that much about him.

"Sometimes I stay the night."

Her gaze jerked to his. "It's not a hotel."

Tristan shoved on his hat and crossed his arms. "If it's

evening, and I need to be back in town in the morning, I stay here. It's called hospitality."

Tristan Porter, dour-faced and taciturn, using a word like hospitality? Her fatigue leaked out as a strangled giggle. Too many emotions vied for her heart. "Looks like trespassing."

"It's not."

The sharp tone of his voice hit her like a slap, and she frowned. She'd only meant to tease.

His scowl deepened, and her impression of him as a simple plow boy vanished. Other than keeping himself clean shaven and calling her father Mr. Warren, nothing about him was boyish. Hours of farmwork had carved hills of muscle in his arms and shoulders. His broad stance boasted confidence, and with his dark eyes roaming her like storm waves, he was anything but a boy. This was a man. An angry man.

Wasn't she the one who should be angry? She'd found him making himself at home in her cabin.

Her protest died as the hardness in his eyes broke like water around rock.

"I'm sorry about your father," he said. "He was a good man."

Her heart flinched at the unexpected softness of his voice. She attempted a thank-you, but her dried throat snagged the words as the exhaustion of the past months swept over her.

He shoved his hands in his pockets. "You staying around long?"

There was nowhere else she wanted to be than on this land, in this cabin, roaming these hills in their one remaining Conestoga, and becoming part of this community. She rubbed her aching forehead. "I'm here. To stay."

His eyes narrowed. "You're going to live out here by yourself?"

She'd slept beneath a wagon most of her life; surely four walls and a nearby town wasn't irresponsible. "A fifteen-minute walk from town is hardly 'out.'" She turned her back on him, not appreciating how his eyes sought to decipher her.

Maple blew a breath, and Anna tucked herself on the other side of her mare and stashed the Colt back into her saddlebag.

"I was just leaving."

She whirled to face him standing a foot behind her. He'd always been intimidating, and now she could add stealthy. She started to step away, but a dark smudge on his face distracted her. It zigzagged along his right ear up to the ends of his wavy hair. Hair the same color as rich soil. How fitting for a farmer. Close up, with the smoothness of his cheeks, he was all boy again. She smiled, reminded of how often she'd had to straighten Father's handkerchief or fix the buttons he'd fastened lopsided. She missed him, missed looking after someone.

With one finger, she reached to brush off what looked like soot. Tristan wrenched back, grimacing at her in a way that set her face flaming and her hands clutching at her skirts. Weariness and a rich vein of tenderness was not a good combination for her.

He backed away, brushing at his face. "You have a great cabin. Well built. I'm grateful to you for letting me use it."

"But I didn't let . . ."

He strode off, purpose anchored between his broad shoulders. Arguing would be useless. And what was there to argue, anyway? He'd stayed at her cabin. Considered it hospitality.

She walked toward the cabin. Though she'd had miles to summon strength, nothing could prepare her for coming face to face with everything of Father's.

Lord, this is hard.

She poked her head across the threshold. Smells assailed her: dust that layered thick on the furniture and tickled her nose, the wood oils Father used on the walking sticks he carved. And a smell she wasn't expecting, a fire smoldering. Tristan's doing, for sure.

A chair next to the table faced her. She accepted its invitation and sank down, shutting her eyes against the crowding in of memories. She drew in a slow breath and released it with control. Eighteen was too young to be alone in the world.

Opening her eyes, she picked up *Aesop's Fables*, which had sat upside down for the length of her absence. She fingered the worn binding, earmarked a page, and closed the book. A painting of Father and Mother on their tenth anniversary hung on the opposite wall, commissioned a year before Anna was born. Joy flowed from their smiles, streaming across the room to Anna.

Life was topsy-turvy, but not void of joy.

Anna pushed to her feet, strode the short distance to the chest beneath the window, and cracked open the lid. The folded ivory material on top drew her touch, and she fingered the flowery lace on the sleeve, her nail catching on the tear alongside the stitching by the shoulder. She'd spent hours stroking Mama's wedding dress as if she'd somehow been able to touch Mama.

With a final run of her hand over the rouching along the back, Anna rose and shut the lid. Her throat stung with dryness, and the urge for tea drove her to the stove. The teakettle with the blackened bottom sat on the corner where she'd left it. She picked it up. Water that had sat all those months sloshed. No, this wasn't the same water. This water was warm, as was the stove.

"I unsaddled your horse—"

She slammed the kettle on the stove, splashing water on her gray dress.

"—and put her away. Fed her some hay."

"Thank you." She didn't turn but stared at the nail her ten-year-old self had hammered into the log when Father had refused to let her stay behind from his trips to attend school. She supposed she'd learned as much from the hundreds of books she'd read as they'd bumped along in the wagon. But that girl who'd wanted to go to school hadn't been after learning. She'd been after community.

A pursuit that had never waned.

"Let me bring in more wood," Tristan said. "It's starting to cool at night."

He left and returned with an armful and stacked it in the box by the stove. Without a glance at her, he strode back out. She'd slept outside in winter, rode for hours through chilled, wet conditions. She didn't need more wood inside during the middle of September. As grateful as she was for his kindness, she needed to be alone, to face the grief of homecoming with privacy.

Seven loads later, he brushed off his hands and eyed the pile, satisfaction easing the sternness of his rigid features. They'd never had this much wood inside, not even in January. They'd never stayed around long enough to use so much.

"That'll do." He planted his hands on his hips. "You going to be all right?" His tone held such nonchalance, as if he asked what she ate for breakfast, not inquired of her well-being.

She forced a slight nod.

He squinted at her, then in one swift movement, came near and peered into her face. The depth of concern in his eyes split her composure. Compassion like this from the reticent Tristan? She bit her lip, but it was useless. Tears fell like a spring rain, mellow but relentless. Focusing straight ahead, her gaze traced the plaid lines of his shirt and landed on his hands. They were strong, working hands, like Father's. Hands with purpose.

She wiped her damp eyes. When she looked up, Tristan's scowl had replaced the earlier glimpse of compassion.

He shifted his feet and ran a hand over his mouth. "You'll be fine."

He looked so uncomfortable that she smiled, unable to stop the swing from heartache to amusement. What a mess she was. A rainbow heart, that was what Father called her swirling emotions.

Tristan wandered to the door, then paused, looking back at her. She thought he might try showing more compassion, something she wasn't ready to experience again, but instead, he picked up a fallen book and placed it on the desk, retrieved silverware from the table and returned it to its basket, and folded a crumpled towel. And then with one nod, he left.

She lifted the curtain to view this man whom she'd known for several years. And yet, whom she didn't know at all. He'd never been outright rude, but his reticence had fit snug as his plaid shirts. Tristan had been Father's friend, not hers.

She let the curtain fall back in place, closing out the confusion, and collapsed into the rocking chair. She'd survive this season of grief by reaching out to others and finding that elusive stability.

No. She repented of the self-reliant thoughts. Nothing borne of her power would get her through the sorrow and loneliness. The presence of the Holy Spirit, His whisper that felt closer than her next breath—He would upright her lurching heart.

She'd already survived, and would continue to do so, by looking to God's strength.

Unbelievable. Arthur Denny had told him she wouldn't be back.

Tristan's thoughts smoldered as he rode from Anna's cabin. She'd written Denny to say she'd taken a position in Portland at some boarding house. A notice had been posted at Joe's Mercantile telling the Warrens' clients to find other arrangements.

Why, then, had he just been at the end of her gun?

He grunted and rode faster. So much for a miracle. Was he surprised the Lord had failed him again?

Friendship with Peter Warren had crashed into his life like a tidal wave, unsought. Two years ago, he'd hired the Warrens to transport his new plow from the ship to his land. What a fiasco. Their wagon had hit a divot, lurched, and sent his brand-new sulky plow tumbling down the hillside, or so he'd been told by an apologetic and flustered Anna. Peter had compensated him instead of insisting that risk of damage was part of the freighting contract. Tristan had formed an alliance with Peter that day. The way that man had conducted his business, not merely with honesty but with reverence, had pried into Tristan's heart. A man with a moral code deserved respect.

He pictured Anna standing in the yard, shoulders slumped, eyes fatigued, staring at her cabin. She'd looked like the last streak of color in a sunset sky, hanging on before the night swallowed it.

If she knew what her father had done . . . but she didn't. She'd been ignorant of why Tristan had been at her cabin. He'd have to tell her. Unless he could think of another way.

Chapter Two

Tristan ran a hand through his hair, wincing at the grit. He needed a haircut, but at least he didn't have soot on his face like the other day when Anna had tried to groom him.

He shoved the disastrous afternoon of Anna's return from his mind. He had another disaster in the making. The four walls of the office confined him. The stale air suffocated him. And John Henry Hall, president of the Territorial University of Washington, irritated him.

Hall tapped his fingers on the cluttered desk. The president's friendly countenance masked what Tristan had discovered to be an iron-strong layer of tenacity.

Tristan perched on the edge of his chair. "I'm not asking for hundreds of dollars." Starting an agricultural program would benefit not only the university, but the entire region. Well worth the investment. "I want academic support . . . and a little money."

"How about land?"

"I'm working on that."

Hall smoothed his bush of brown curls, then rested both hands on a stack of papers. Youthful, dark eyes stared at Tristan. "A secret, huh?" He laughed and scratched his beard.

Tristan inhaled the scent of old leather-bound books. They almost smelled like earth. Everything smelled like earth to him.

"Fine," Hall said. "Keep your secrets, but around here whatever land you acquire will need clearing."

"The logs would bring us the profit needed—"

Hall held up a hand. "We'd have to hire it done, another expense."

"I'll do it."

Hall raised a brow as he stood and paced, his shoes clapping against the wide-planked floor. Though only a dozen or so years older than Tristan, Hall's charisma and position as president demanded respect. He pulled a cigar from a tin, and a spicy aroma wafted through the air. "The university can barely sustain the programs it has, Tristan. Starting up another—as qualified as you are—would not be wise." He lit the cigar and drew a puff.

Tristan spied a map of the United States on the wall behind Hall's desk. "You're from Ohio, right?"

"New York, but I graduated from Oberlin College in Ohio."

"Where were you during the war? Did you notice how agriculture saved the North from starvation? Do you realize how essential agriculture was to the North's victory?"

The president chuckled.

Maybe Tristan had exaggerated, but his point had merit. He glanced out the window. Two boys chased each other down Union Street—boys whose childhoods would probably never hold the angst of his. "I was a boy during the war, but I helped." Tristan tore his attention from the boys. "My father owned several hundred acres of farmland in Illinois." He'd been planting seeds before he could speak. "The soil there's amazing. Rich. Eager to yield. Smells good enough to wear like aftershave."

"That's how you helped the North? Provided an army of men with the darkest, earthiest aftershave?"

A smile wavered on his lips, but Tristan didn't give it freedom to grow. "You've heard of the potato brigades?"

"Yes."

"I organized them. Collected potatoes, onions, and anything else people could spare, and delivered the food to units nearby. It's all the boys left behind could do." His voice cracked. He could have fought with his brothers, but his mother had begged him to stay, said she'd needed him, called him too young to fight.

Tristan picked up the copy of *American Agriculturist* he'd set on the president's desk. "Read this. You'll see the new inventions, the advantages of the sulky plow, the experiments with nitrogen-packed fertilizers." He had so many ideas for a program.

Hall moved around the desk and stopped in front of him. "I'll skim it, but I'm telling you, the university isn't ready for this."

They'd never be ready. Not until they saw the need. "People are coming to this area looking for a new start and settling in the valley all the way down to the mountain." Blood pounded in Tristan's temple. "Half these people didn't know a turnip from a rutabaga before the war, but they expect to turn the ground with a fork and reap its benefits. They waste time, money, and energy trying to figure it out."

"I see your point, but it's not the right time. Denny, Bagley, and the rest are focused on getting the railroad here."

The railroad. It always came back to the railroad.

Hall held out his hand, and they faced each other. Tristan enjoyed an inch advantage and wished he'd edged out on top in this conversation as well.

Riding from the trees into his northernmost field, Tristan passed the *Porter* sign marking his property line, a broken piece of wood he'd thrown up on a tree that first year to feel more like a real farmer with real land.

Hall's objections had swarmed his thoughts the hour-long ride home. Tristan didn't know how to make the university executives understand. Lumberjacks and miners swarmed the Pacific Northwest, as plentiful as tiger beetles. The half-broken, old-fashioned tools locals used would be hard pressed to satisfy demands. Maybe a man could support his family that way, but not a growing region.

Ember, his Appaloosa, whinnied and tossed her head. He dismounted and patted the mare on the shoulder. Sun warmed his back as he knelt and lifted a fistful of soil, savoring the acrid smell. On impulse, he kissed the dirt. Granules stuck to his sweaty lips, and he sputtered them away.

He settled on the ground and stretched his legs, not caring about dirtying the pants he'd cleaned for the meeting. It would take a miracle from God Himself to get the university to let him start an agricultural program.

That posed a problem. God had already refused him one miracle, the memory of which twisted his gut like the morning glory vines clinging to the north side of his barn.

Lying back, he looked at the sky. Mother had teased him about coming in for dinner with that dusting of earth still moist on his clothes. Told him he spent more time lying in the fields than his own bed. Told him she was about to toss his blanket out the door and let the fields have him.

She'd done just that. Not intentionally. She hadn't chosen to catch the pneumonia that snatched her last breath.

He squeezed a mass of dirt into a compact ball. Last year he'd grown potatoes right in this spot, a first since he'd come west in '65. He hadn't been ready to face the memories those brown roots churned. The smell of potato peelings on his mother's hands when she'd cup his face and kiss him. Those hands were always covered in something—if not peelings, then dough. If not dough, then soap.

Standing, he brushed the dirt from his clothes. He dwelt on the past enough during the moonless hours of night. No use bringing those thoughts into the sunshine. Next year he'd plant more potatoes. A good harvest was worth the memories, which lurked in his mind no matter what grew in his fields.

His boots tramped the soft earth as he made his way toward his homestead. Ember trailed behind, tail swishing. At least someone followed him, trusted him. His eyes squinted against afternoon sun as he rounded the corner of the barn. He shoved open the broad doors, and the smell of hay welcomed him.

"Where you been hiding?"

Tristan jumped and knocked his elbow against the door. He spun to see Lazarus sitting on a barrel, leaning against the planked wall. A piece of grass protruded from the black man's mouth, and he looked as relaxed as a gopher snake in the sun.

"Lazarus." Tristan kicked the door. "I told you not to do that to me."

"Do what? Come talking?"

Tristan scowled and walked deeper into the barn. He heard Lazarus behind him.

"I got news." Lazarus's soft-spoken words leaked excitement.

Tristan pitched hay into Ember's stall.

"You gonna ask me, or do I have to tie you down and make you listen?"

"Tie me down, Laz."

Lazarus shuffled his feet, one boot swirling a lazy circle pattern in the dirt.

Tristan rolled his eyes and sighed. "Fine. What's the news?"

"Just thinking of how to say it."

"Didn't have enough time to think while you were perched on that barrel?" Tristan set the pitchfork aside and picked up a hammer that had been left on the ground. He hated clutter.

"Expect visitors."

Tristan stared at Lazarus, the hammer half lifted to its peg. Sounded like a warning, not an announcement. "Who?"

"Luther Collins, Henry Smith, Baldwin brothers, maybe Phelps."

Prominent farmers, some of whom had been farming since the initial influx to the valley. Tristan put the hammer on its peg, aware of Lazarus's amused expression. The man loved stringing this along like meat before a dog.

"You wanna know why they're coming?" Lazarus spit out his blade of grass and rubbed the graying hair at his temples.

"Yep." Best to let Lazarus get it all out.

"Saw the new man in town, Captain McRedmond. He's farming east of the lake. Told him you were talking with the university about a program. Frank Baldwin overheard. They're both interested."

Tristan growled and snagged the horse brush. "I hardly know what I'm doing. Why does everyone else have to know?"

"They're on your side. Fact is, they want you to start an association."

"An association?" Tristan brushed Ember with long, quick strokes.

"Don't know what they have in mind."

"I don't want an association." He'd enough to worry about with the university and Anna. Her brown, teary eyes had been like a weed in his mind. He shoved away guilt. So what if he'd been a friend of her father's? Did that require him to look after her?

Lazarus laid a hand on Tristan's arm. Tristan ceased brushing. Lazarus had lived with Tristan's family for longer than Tristan had been alive, and the only time he touched anyone was when he wanted to be heard. Tristan calmed his foul mood and lifted his gaze to the man he respected like a father.

"I 'member you trying to start that potato brigade. Asking all children to bring in a potato or two for the troops. You 'member how you visited each home?"

Lazarus had better hurry and make his point.

"You got yourself some gift as a leader. Those children came to school next day wild for the cause. Brought in the most of any brigade in the state of Illinois. You was the potato boy after that, and only thirteen years old."

"That was a lifetime ago." He was twenty-two, and he'd

already lived several lives.

"You listen to these farmers."

Tristan stepped back from Lazarus and removed the hand, which felt more like a prod on his heart than a touch on his shoulder. He didn't want to listen to them, to organize their harvest socials or whatever else they expected an association to provide. His father had worked years to get the Morrill Act signed by Lincoln so that agricultural education would be recognized as essential for the health of the country. Tristan needed a university setting to teach agricultural topics in depth.

Lazarus took the brush from Tristan. "I like this McRedmond. Seems like a man of influence."

Who didn't Lazarus like? "What's so significant about him?"

Lazarus smiled, revealing the gap in his teeth along the upper right side of his mouth. "He a captain, ain't he?"

Tristan shrugged. The soreness of his shoulders and upper arm muscles reminded him of the demands of harvest season. "He's a farmer now."

"He still a captain."

Lazarus tossed the brush onto the table by the door. Tristan glared at him and waited until Lazarus, grinning, picked the brush up and hung it on the tack wall.

They walked out of the barn together, but Tristan hurried to put space between them.

"Boy!" Lazarus called as Tristan walked away. "You be nice when those farmers come."

Tristan knew Lazarus was looking for a promise, but he couldn't give one. The only promise he could make was to work harder, sweat more, and to hound the university's decision makers until they realized the necessity of a program.

Chapter Three

From the crest of the hill above Seattle, Anna uttered a prayer for acceptance, a plea for friends, and then nudged Maple into the descent. Scows bobbed on the water, and workers unloaded steamers at Plummer's Wharf. Those months in Portland, she'd longed for a vision of the waterfront. And oh, those mountains. She basked in the beauty of the snow, how it draped like a shawl across the broad shoulders of the mountains on the far side of Puget Sound.

In front of Yesler Hall, Anna slipped off her mount. She'd missed many of the celebrations the meeting house had held. No longer.

She rounded the building and stopped where Mr. Wyse's plaque, *Attorney at Law*, hung askew. She hoped his sign wasn't indicative of his ethics. He'd taken over the practice immediately before the fateful Portland trip, and Anna wasn't well acquainted with him.

The door swung open as she approached. Stepping back, she silenced a groan. "Hello, Mr. Roberts."

"Miss Warren." Mr. Roberts pulled the door shut with a bang. Wiping a hand across his beard, his gaze traveled from her head to her toes. "Mighty surprised to see you."

She'd never been able to read Mr. Roberts, either his age or his intentions, though her impression of the portly, unkempt businessman was far from positive.

He gestured to Mr. Wyse's door. "He's in a nasty mood today. Fidgety as ever. You'll not get anything done."

Mr. Wyse strode out, flicking the door shut behind him. His wiry body hunched forward, and his brows drew tight. When he looked up and saw her, he halted. "Miss Warren." His eyes bulged. "I'm afraid I can't discuss your father's will right now. I assume that's why you're here."

"Yes."

Mr. Wyse wrung his hands and scowled at Mr. Roberts. "Things have come up."

Heaving out a breath that fluttered his whiskers, Mr. Roberts rolled his eyes. Even from four feet away, Anna cringed at the smell of stale tobacco from this man whose habits appeared not to include a comb or bar of soap. Ironically, rumor was, this man had money.

She backed up. "I'll return later."

"How long are you visiting?" Mr. Wyse shoved his hands in his pockets but drew them out seconds later.

"I've come home to stay."

Mr. Wyse's movement ceased, except for a tick along his cheekbone. He offered a fleeting smile before marching around the corner.

Mr. Roberts stepped closer. "Thank you for not pressing him today. You've always been understanding, Anna."

His words were too quiet, his tone too sweet, and his use of her name too familiar. He reached for her elbow, and her body tensed as he escorted her around the building to Maple.

His eyes smiled more than his mouth. "I trust you will adjust to being home alone and that you'll have the wisdom to make the hard choices and deal with any surprises."

She shrugged from his touch. "Thank you for your concern."

"Good day." He coughed and rushed down the street.

She followed his progress until he turned in at the bank. Father had somehow managed to maintain a polite demeanor with Mr. Roberts, and she'd endeavor to do nothing less. Kindness, generosity, selflessness—those were Father's ways. An ache traveled through her chest.

She mounted Maple and crossed from Yesler Hall toward the livery. Having sold their team of drafts in Portland, she was ready to barter for a new pair.

"Watch out!"

Anna jerked on the reins, moving Maple to the side. A wagon lurched around the corner of Union Street, the sound of pounding hooves accompanying it. Cries of alarm rang out as the wagon tore recklessly down the street.

"Jones!" An older man shook his fist at the driver of the wagon.

Urgency mushroomed in Anna's heart, a sense she'd become familiar with as a call to prayer, though not since Andy had it manifested in regard to an individual in need. And in the case of Andy . . . No time to think of that now. She kneed Maple to follow in the cloud of dust. The wagon passed Yesler's Wharf, sending workers diving for safety, and veered west, following the waterline onto Maynard's land before it stopped in front of the doctor's clinic.

The man called Jones ran to the door and fumbled with the latch.

Anna pulled Maple beside the wagon, coughing at the grit swarming the air. Swatting the dust clear, she peered at the young man sprawled on a pile of blankets, his bloody head wrapped with a sawdust-covered shirt. Bruises encircled his swollen right eye, and a piece of skin with eyebrow on it flopped loose. She reached for his hand, hoping to feel some response, but his cold fingers were limp and sticky, like dried seaweed.

Dr. David Maynard rushed through the door, Jones close behind. Doc's glance passed over her, then snapped back. "Miss Warren . . ." He stepped onto the wheel and reached to check the man's pulse.

A sense of expectancy pushed Anna off Maple, and she hurried to clear the way as Doc and Jones carried the unconscious patient inside. She couldn't believe it was happening again: the inner swelling of prayer, the sense that God was about to do something and she was to have a part in it.

SONDRA KRAAK

"What's going on? David—" Mrs. Maynard gasped. "Anna Warren. You're home."

"Catherine, boil some water." Doc didn't even look at his wife, continuing down the hall into the exam room.

They set the patient on the fresh-made bed. The man's arms fell limp on the white sheets, and his head rolled to the side. Fresh blood soaked through the bandage on his head. The yearning to pray overpowered the queasy feeling in Anna's stomach. She'd seen injuries before, but never so much blood on someone's head.

"Twenty-one." Jones breathed heavily. "He's only twenty-one. Axe-head flew"—he motioned with his hands—"right into the side of his head. I—" He gasped for breath, sagging into a chair at the foot of the bed. "Careless." Jones put his head in his hands and pulled at a thatch of matted gray hair.

Anna stepped around him and moved to the front of the bed. Careful to stay out of the way, she reached for the patient's hand while Doc gathered supplies.

He laid a roll of bandages on the table and looked at her with a frown. "Anna?"

She'd never assisted Doc before and had no intention to medically assist now. But she wasn't going to ignore the command of the Lord and leave, no matter the consequences later. And there had been consequences with Andy. "I'd like to stay and pray."

Doc paused only a moment before nodding.

While Doc worked and Jones babbled, Anna considered the broken man before her. His dark hair was made darker by the paleness of his skin and the white sheet beneath him. His lanky form didn't resemble the build of a lumberjack, nor was he wearing cropped pants. But his face drew her in. Round, open, and uncommonly whisker-free—which reminded her of someone else.

She shoved Tristan from her thoughts, letting her prayers

take over as Doc administered medicine, washed the gash, and stitched it. By the time he'd finished, Anna had prayed through Psalm 91 three times. With each utterance, the intensity of the warmth waving through her body had increased. She was supposed to be here, praying for the Lord's intervention in the life of this stranger.

Doc stood back. "Jones, the boy's lost a lot of blood, and until he wakes, if he wakes, I won't know the extent of injury to his brain. Pulse is fainter now than when you brought him in."

Doc's words silenced Jones's mumbling.

"I wish I'd seen him sooner." Doc wiped his hands on a cloth.

"My camp's five hours out. I made it in four. Probably cracked a wheel."

"It's not your fault." Doc paced to the bed and checked his patient's pulse again. "Hmmm." He wiped his hand over his eyes. "I don't see how he's going to make it. How long has he been out?"

"Most of the trip. I heard a few groans, is all."

The three of them stared at the man, the silence of the room increasing the weight on Anna's heart. God wanted her to speak, wanted her to act. Now.

"Pardon." Her voice shook.

Both men looked at her as if they'd forgotten her presence.

"May I say a prayer?" She didn't understand why, but the words had to be spoken.

At Doc's nod, Anna placed her hand, which felt on fire, over the patient's forehead. His clammy skin flinched. Her lips parted, and she waited for the words to come. "Almighty God, thank you that you are the giver of life. In the name of Jesus, your Son, grant your healing to Michael."

Surprised by her boldness, her breath caught. The words flowed unrestricted, with a directness she couldn't have mustered herself. She looked up, expecting to see critical glances from Doc and Mr. Jones, but their attention was fixed on the patient. The blanket covering his legs rustled, and his hand moved toward his head.

Doc rushed forward. "Easy there." He grabbed the man's hand before he disrupted the bandages. Doc fingered the patient's wrist, and his lips twitched. "His pulse is strong."

The patient tried to sit up on his elbows, but Doc pushed him down. "What's your name, son?"

"Michael Riley." His clear eyes connected with Anna's.

Mr. Jones rushed around the bed, finger pointed at Anna. "You healed him."

"No, sir. God restored him." But even as she assured Mr. Jones, nausea stole into her middle, and memories of Andy stirred her need for escape. She stepped toward the door, but Mr. Jones cut her off.

"How did you know his name?"

"I'm not sure what you mean."

"You spoke his name, when you prayed."

She remembered now. "It was the Lord's doing." Unable to take the praise beaming from Mr. Jones's eyes, she glanced at Michael. His gaze searched the room, then landed on hers and intensified. She turned again to leave.

Mr. Jones snagged her sleeve. "Please, your name?"

"Anna Warren."

"Anna Warren, you're an angel."

Good gracious. What purpose was a healing if God didn't get the glory? "What you saw was the power of God, not the work of an angel."

"Either way . . ." Mr. Jones paced to the door. "This is news for the town. A miracle worker." He rushed from the room.

Anna's head throbbed. She needed to escape.

"Anna, a moment." Doc ushered her into the front room. Outside, at least a dozen people mingled by Jones's wagon as the man's animated retelling of Michael's healing resounded through the closed door.

Doc stepped in front of her, blocking her view. "That *was* a miracle, you know. Michael was minutes from death."

She studied his earnest expression. "Yes."

"Thank you."

Soft lines framed the doctor's eyes. She respected this founder of Seattle and admired not only his medical skills but his tenacity. Smiling up at him, she placed her hand on his arm. "Thank God."

He squeezed her elbow and returned to the exam room.

Anna stared out the window, her legs rooted in place. Walking through the front door to retrieve Maple meant risking questions or unwarranted admiration, as with Andy. That had been six years ago, and Father had been her defense.

Mrs. Maynard entered the room, a pile of folded sheets in her arms. "It's good to see you again. I'm sorry about your—" She surveyed the commotion outside. "What's all this? Can't a man be healed at a hospital?" Mrs. Maynard frowned as she met Anna's eyes. "You look exhausted."

One day back, and already her plans to meld into society in a quiet, gentle way were ruined. "I'm fine. I could use a bit of solitude though."

"Say no more. I'll bring your horse around. While I'm at it, I'll tell these loiterers to scat." She dropped the laundry on a chair and moved to the door. Her hand paused on the latch. "Do you need food?"

Anna's breath hitched as she shook her head. Home. She needed home.

"Of course you do." Mrs. Maynard disappeared and in less than a minute returned with a basket. "Come back for more if you need it." She pushed the load into Anna's arms and exited onto the front porch.

Anna stared at the generosity before her. Fresh bread, a hunk of cheese, Mrs. Tolliver's blueberry preserves, and eggs wrapped in a tea cloth. Anna blinked her eyes against the gathering tears.

The backdoor slammed.

"Doc!" A man's voice.

Her chest tightened, and she girded herself to answer whatever questions were thrust at her. Best to meet the curiosity before rumor had her raising the dead.

"I can explain—" She spun around but choked on her words.

Tristan's frown mingled with surprise. "Explain what?"

A stray tear slipped down her cheek, accompanied by a ripple of emotion she didn't understand. "I thought you were someone else." Sullen eyes studied her, and she spoke without thinking. "You have something on your face. Again."

He wiped the back of his hand across his cheek. Twisting sideways, he edged between her and a rocking chair, but before he'd gone ten paces down the hall, he pivoted. His perpetual scowl was locked in place, though his expression seemed more concerned than angry.

Not what she expected.

"Are you all right? Why are you here?"

She didn't have an answer, only the barest nod. With several steps, he was beside her, his hands on her shoulders.

She jerked back. "I'm fine, really."

The furrow of his brow deepened, and then he broke eye contact and peered into her basket. He reached into his pocket, pulled out a potato, and tossed it in. "A meal's not complete without one of these."

This man was never without a dirty face, a scowl, and evidently, a potato. She studied him, trying to decipher the mystery that waved throughout his countenance. His brown eyes challenged hers, with a hint of suspicion. On closer look, they offered more than a hint of suspicion, along with a few golden flecks that added texture . . . and attractiveness.

She looked away, heat invading her face. This was not the time for such thoughts. And with Tristan the gloomy, it would never be time for such thoughts.

Doc hastened into the room. "Tristan, here's the ligament. Twice a day on the shoulder."

Tristan shoved the tube into his pocket as Anna glanced at his shoulders. They were broad, weight-bearing shoulders accustomed to a day's work. He didn't appear in pain. Was he? She could offer to pray for—

Tristan caught her scrutiny and frowned.

Prayer was the last thing he'd appreciate. She suppressed her spiritual senses, still heightened from the stimulation of the past hour.

"You missed the excitement." Doc clapped Tristan's shoulder, but Tristan didn't seem to flinch. "Anna prayed a lumberjack back to life."

Tristan's face darkened, and he stepped back.

The strength of his disapproval, coming so close to his apparent concern for her, cuffed her heart. "I didn't heal. God healed."

Tristan grunted through a clenched jaw.

Looking away, she whispered, "I need to go." She paced through the kitchen and out the back door.

Resting the basket of food on the front of the saddle, she climbed onto Maple, which, thankfully, Mrs. Maynard had been able to bring around.

"Wait." Tristan plowed through the door.

She swallowed around the boulder of dread in her throat. If he'd followed to deride her, she'd break down, her emotions frail as a single strand of weathered twine.

Without meeting her gaze, he reached up and rubbed Maple's withers. "Let me get Ember and lead you east across the spit."

He wanted to help?

Before she could respond, he stalked around the side of the house. Anna scanned the waters, recognized low tide, and relaxed. She'd not have thought of the spit, a circuitous route, but much quieter than riding through the heart of town at midday.

Tristan rode around the corner, hat pulled low enough to shadow his eyes. She nudged Maple forward and followed his lead to where the land dropped down to the mudflats, an inlet that filled during high tide. Their horses waded across the narrow strip of swampy beach that marked the opening of the flats and reached the finger of dry land.

Once on the spit, she drew alongside him. His fierce profile reminded her of an Indian brave. Tristan was on the warpath of something . . . something to do with God. He'd not win a battle against the Almighty. Then again, to lose oneself to God, was to win, wasn't it?

When they sloped up to the edge of the woods, creating distance from the town, her fingers loosened on the reins. She glanced back toward the Maynard's. The crowd had dispersed, and once again things appeared normal.

"Thank you."

He nodded.

She expected him to turn south and angle home, but instead he rode north with her along the periphery of Seattle until she reached her turn. She swiveled in her saddle. "Again," her voice came out thick.

He shook his head. "Don't." He rifled through his coat pockets. "For good measure." He pulled out another potato and tossed it the three feet distance into her basket.

She smiled, wanting to meet his gaze, but his head was bent, and the rim of his hat barricaded her vision. He turned Ember and rode down the hill into Seattle, not looking back. But she couldn't look away, not until buildings hid him from view.

Anna rubbed the noses of the two horses Ben Johnson had hooked up to the wagon. Thankfully, the livery owner had several drafts to spare at short notice, even if they did sport dull coats and tired gazes. Anna's fingers stopped as they passed over a bump next to Clover's eyes. Clover sneezed, and Anna drew her hand back.

"Don't be fooled." Mr. Johnson stepped behind her. "Clover and Iris will get the job done."

His reassurance did little to convince her the team could make it to Green Lake and back, or at least not in a half day, which was as long as the trip to Mr. Kellman's camp should take. "Thank you, Mr. Johnson." She climbed up to the seat.

"I can have a team of drafts here for you within the week. Got a friend down by Auburn has some for sale. Strong and young, not like these two here. But like I said, they'll get the job done."

"I'll take good care of them."

She'd been home four days and already had three requests to freight. One she'd turned down because it'd been an overnight trip. The thought of sleeping in the wild by herself didn't sit well. Even so, she had a hunch she'd have plenty of day trips to fill her schedule, a schedule that could easily get too frenzied, leaving no time for building community.

Intentionality, Anna. Think through every choice.

She gripped the reins and commanded the team forward. The horses left town with an eager step. Maybe she'd underestimated them. An easy first trip was what she needed.

Easy? Not her first trip without Father, even with capable horses.

After the initial incline, the team's enthusiasm seemed to slip away with the sounds of the town. So much for exceeding expectations.

Anna settled into the steady motion, fighting the loneliness of an empty seat beside her. Her body knew the routine, and traversing the ruts felt heavenly. She couldn't remember her mama, but she imagined the gentle sway of the wagon to be like a mother's arms rocking her to sleep. Except she couldn't relax. Not while in charge of the team or with the absence of Father oozing fresh.

A songbird called from a cottonwood, but Clover's cough cut off the sweet sound. Anna slowed the team until Clover's wheezing eased. At this pace, the roundtrip would take till sundown.

There's no rush.

Anna gloried in the changing colors of the foliage. Morning sun filtered through thin clouds, and already, warmth bathed the right side of her body as the horses trudged north. Soon the dense shade of Douglas firs, cedars, and hemlocks would dull the light.

"Oh, Father." Her uttering was half a prayer and half the call of a grieving daughter.

She attempted to hum, but the sound wavered. With a lungful of air, she tried singing. Her voice smoothed the longer she sang the hymns Father had taught her, the hymns that had introduced her to Jesus. Echoes of his baritone resounded with each verse of "Immortal, Invisible." By the time she sang "Amazing Grace," the memory of his voice nearly overpowered her own.

Rustling brush cut off her song. Squinting into the sun, she prepared to shoo off a coyote, but she saw no animal, and the sound had ceased.

She refocused on the team. Clover's gait seemed labored.

The whinnying of a horse, followed by a loud thrashing, sent her pulse spurting. Jerking her attention back to the woods, she reached beneath the seat for her rifle.

Tristan emerged from behind a thicket of devil's club.

"Whoa." He pulled his horse to a stop.

Considering his full-fledged grimace, aimed directly at her, his shoulder must still bother him.

She spoke past her pounding heart. "You almost had the pleasure of being at the end of my gun. Again." She tucked the rifle back in its place.

His mare side-passed, but he steadied her. "Let's not make that the pattern."

She wanted no pattern with Tristan, gun or otherwise, at least until he learned to smile.

"Where are you headed?"

"Smith Cove."

The home of Henry Smith, homesteader, horticulturalist, doctor to the natives—and neighbor of Mr. Kellman. She'd have to endure two hours of stilted conversation with this man, who pried through her friendliness and accessed her rare, flustered side.

"What takes you to Dr. Smith's?"

"Grafted fruit trees."

"Really?"

He nodded once.

Strange. Tristan's heart was potatoes, beans, peas, hay. But how well did she know him? She'd read her books in the wagon while he and Father had discussed every aspect of farming imaginable.

Tristan brought his horse alongside the wagon, and they rode in silence, except for the rattling of Mr. Kellman's stump remover in the back, and Clover's wet cough.

She had to break the silence or go deaf by her thoughts. A comment about farming should set him off. "Tell me what you love about farming."

"Everything."

Tristan's eyes focused ahead. Apparently he wouldn't help the conversation along. She'd stare at him until he elaborated.

He squirmed, flexed his hands on the reins, and squared his shoulders. "I love the planting most. There's nothing like the burden of promise to make a man work hard."

A farmer who talked poetry. Considering the mystery of Tristan, this shouldn't surprise her. "Burden of promise?"

"An entire field awaiting attention. You sow seeds, and they depend on you to bring forth harvest. That'll pull a man out of bed every morning."

"And the Lord."

His eyes captured hers, dark in the shadows of the evergreens. Or maybe the darkness came from behind his eyes, from the bent toward cynicism she sensed in him.

She smiled past the intimidation twining her heart. "Harvest depends on the Lord too. The One who ordained the seasons."

He looked away.

This would be a long two hours. "What about the burden part?"

He raised his brows as he glanced at her. "Do you know anything about farming?"

"I guess not."

"The responsibility weighs. I don't sit and twirl my thumbs."

She imagined him sitting on a fence, whistling, thumbs twirling. Not a chance. She chuckled but silenced the outburst when he frowned. The responsibility must push on his sense of humor as well.

"Tell me what you love about freighting."

She caressed the rein between her thumb and finger, surprised he'd initiated conversation. Perhaps he felt as awkward as she did. "The time with my father." She shifted her attention to the road. "And I love being outside and meeting new people, seeing new places, helping others."

"In other words, you love everything about it."

Like he did with farming? No. Her community stretched

broad, but it didn't burrow deep. She didn't love living on the fringe of Seattle, and by that, she didn't mean the outskirts of town.

"Tell me what happened the other day," he said, his voice taking on a quieter, yet harder, quality.

She didn't need to ask for clarification. "I was in town when a wagon tore through. I followed and assisted Doc."

"Truly?"

"By assist, I mean I prayed."

"For a miracle."

"No. I prayed because I felt led to pray. I prayed Scripture and whatever else came to mind." She'd not been seeking a miracle. She'd sought the Lord in prayer, at the prompting of His Spirit.

Tristan shifted the reins from one hand to the other. "Has this happened before?"

She smiled. "My praying or a miracle?"

"You admit it was a miracle?" He didn't shy from her gaze.

"It's happened once."

He grunted again and veered his attention to the bushes alongside the road, where a squirrel with bulging cheeks pawed another nut in its mouth.

"We were up north and met a boy who had frequent asthma attacks." The need to defend herself caused her to speak quicker. "He could never run and play outside. He had an episode while we were delivering supplies to his father's store. Started turning blue. I felt God telling me to lay hands on him and pray."

"And?"

"His wheezing stopped. As far as I know, he's never had a spell again. He runs around and plays outside like any normal child."

Tristan laughed, but there was nothing happy in the sound. "Doesn't that beat all?"

What beat all was the fascination the healing had ignited in

Andy's community, as if God had never answered a prayer before. She didn't want such a fixation here in Seattle. The admiration, the questions. It had pushed her from that community, whether they'd intended it to or not.

"What's magical about your prayers?"

She swiveled toward him. "Nothing." All she'd done was pray for Andy, yet they'd dubbed her *the healer*. A shy twelve-year-old couldn't handle that pressure. And all she'd done for Michael was pray. "God is the one who heals. Why do people have to make something big out of something small?"

"A miracle—or lack thereof—is no small thing." Bitterness edged his tone.

She'd not continue to feed whatever resentment had a hold on him.

"How's your shoulder?"

"Pardon?"

"You know, the ligament from Doc."

"Oh." The intensity of his expression melted into a form of amusement. "That was for Ember." He rubbed his mare. "But thanks for the concern."

She fought against the heating of her cheeks as he held her gaze.

"In other words," he said, "no need for your prayers today."

She felt her flush deepen, and with it, a frustration that went beyond being humiliated by a misunderstanding. She hadn't expected that the farmer Father had most respected would have a spiritual chip on his shoulder as large as King County.

They approached a stream, and Tristan edged ahead of the wagon. Anna eased the horses into the water. The roughness of the riverbed bounced the load, forcing her to slow. Clover paused and pressed her nose to the water. A minute passed, then two, as the mare licked water between bouts of wheezing. The trip would take more than a day at this rate, and Anna wasn't sure she could last another hour in Tristan's presence.

Clover sneezed, and Iris jolted forward, pulling Clover with her. On the other side of the stream, the road zigzagged up a hill covered with Queen Ann's lace. The horses bent their heads as they strained, their breaths short and quick. Clover tossed her mane and stopped, jerking Iris back. Bending her head low, Clover coughed a wet, rattling sound.

Tristan dismounted and moved to the horses. He reached for their bridles, and a scowl shadowed his face.

"What?"

He flicked a glance at her, then shook his head. "Let's get to the top, then stop and let them rest."

A freighter didn't let horses rest after four miles, not when she'd kept the pace slow. Then again, a freighter didn't drive horses better suited for munching grass. "Fine."

She had to control her grumpiness before it curdled what little peace remained in her. As Tristan gripped the bridles and pulled, she offered up a prayer and searched the moment for natural beauty, remembering Father's advice to counter negativity with praise. Sunshine penetrated the fir branches, speckling the road with dots of light. The scents of moss and fern haunted the grove. God was good to lace His creation with beauty.

Iris tossed her head and neighed. "Come on." Anna breathed the words, as much a prayer as a command to the horses. They surged forward, and Tristan slipped before them, sending Anna's heart into her throat, but he regained his footing, and pulled them up the rest of the hill. Potential disaster averted.

At the top, Anna tugged the reins and was down before Tristan could offer help.

She rubbed Clover's muzzle but drew her hand back at the stickiness. Red covered her palm. Her widening eyes darted to Tristan. He'd moved to his mare and was rumbling through his saddlebag.

"She's bleeding."

Tristan didn't look up. "She's old. Sounds like tuberculosis. Should never have come on this trip."

Him or Clover? Keeping her touch light, Anna caressed the side of Clover's face. Mucus dripped from the mare's mouth. "Can we continue, do you think?"

Tristan pulled his gun out and walked over.

"What are you doing?"

"Anna, Clover was tromping around these hills years before I arrived. She's as old as Seattle."

"What are you implying?"

"I'm suggesting she's ill and needs to be put down." Tristan stared at her.

A new disaster threatened, one over which she had no control. Anna shook her head. "This isn't my horse."

"This horse should never have left the livery. I don't know what Ben was thinking."

"I told him I'd take good care of the team."

"This is good care. Trust me."

Trust a man who seemed to have more secrets than manners? Clover coughed again, a rasping sound that drowned out the innocent chatter of birds. Tristan's stoic face hinted no emotion. In their twelve years of freighting, Father had only put a horse down once while on the trail.

"I have a delivery to make." Anna turned back to the wagon.

"You can at least pray for her healing."

Tristan's caustic tone drew her gaze back to his. "Maybe I should."

"Come on, Anna. She's suffering."

"And who will pull this wagon to Kellman's?"

"Ember can do it."

Anna raised her brows. "Ember, with the wounded shoulder? We're wasting time." She climbed on the wagon seat.

"The Anna I know is compassionate."

He didn't know her. Only Father had truly known her. Her

jaw shook, and she mustered a glare to keep the tears from falling. The sound of Clover's coughing grated on her ears and sunk the truth into Anna. "Fine. Do it quickly and away from Iris and Ember." She'd lost the strength to argue. And deep down, she was compassionate. The horse was sick. Ben would understand.

As Tristan led Clover into the woods, Anna covered her ears, closed her eyes, and sang "A Mighty Fortress." She was on the fourth verse when something shook the wagon. Opening her eyes, she looked over at Tristan, who leaned with both hands on the edge of the box.

"Thank you."

Her frown relaxed at the gentleness in his voice. She faced forward, signaling him to get Ember in position.

What a fine welcome back to freighting this morning had been.

Chapter Four

The next day, Anna steered Maple along the wooded road toward town. Considering the crowd on Doc's porch the other afternoon, she feared her involvement in Michael's healing might shroud her return. If Tristan's response was any indication of the community's, finding that quiet sense of belonging would be more challenging than she'd expected. She'd already fielded questions from Ben when she'd rented horses yesterday.

The day Tristan had shot Clover.

The day she'd embarrassed herself senseless by showing concern over Tristan's perfectly fine shoulder. More so, the day she'd allowed his pessimism to slice through her joy. Had he talked to Father with such candid attitudes? Had he taunted Father's faith like—

Put it aside, Anna.

Whatever burden Tristan carried wasn't hers to take up. At the end of the day, she'd had to admit, it'd been nice to have company, to not have to make that first trip by herself.

Stopping on the ridge above Seattle, Anna let her eyes drift over the town. Praise God she had the cabin, had clients who needed her. She couldn't expect to be invited into ladies' societies and clubs in one week's time.

Sticks snapped to her right, and Anna drew her gaze from the bustle of Skid Row to Lorna Caine. Of all the things rapidly changing in Seattle, one thing remained the same: Lorna's beauty, a loveliness delicate as butterfly wings but certain as the sunrise.

"Good morning." The petite blonde shielded her blue eyes as she gazed up at Anna. "I'm sorry about your father. We'll miss him."

"Thank you."

Like Anna, Lorna had lost her mother at a young age. Perhaps this seed of a friendship could grow.

Lorna twirled a bouquet of wildflowers in her hand and shifted her weight. Glancing up quickly, she offered a shy half grin. "Have a nice day." She hustled down the path toward town.

Anna's smile faded as she nudged Maple a little too hard. Maybe next time she could draw out the hesitant blonde.

At the bottom of the rise, she rounded the corner of Front Street and slipped off her horse, intending to check in with Mr. Wyse.

"Miss Anna Warren." Michael strode toward her, vigor punctuating his steps. His friendly singsong call warmed her heart.

"You're looking well, Mr. . . . ." His last name slipped her mind.

Michael scratched around his bandaged right eye. "Itches like crazy." With a shake of his head, he clasped his hands behind his back, striking a formal pose, and bowed. "Mr. Riley, but please, you've earned the right to call me Michael."

His joy sprouted her smile. She heaved aside worry about the miracle. Michael looked well, his pale-blue eyes reminding her of forget-me-nots. She'd rather embrace his friendliness than stew about the future.

Michael grasped her by the elbows, and the surprising touch rendered her motionless. "Thank you for saving my life."

She laughed. "I only prayed for you. God saved you, and He deserves your gratitude."

"Yes, indeed. Please don't misunderstand."

"You can thank Doc as well." Seeking an appropriate distance, she stepped back, and he dropped his hands from her elbows.

"I've already done so. He's the one who told me your name. But I offer you my gratitude too. No arguing."

He reached out and plucked her arm. Tucking it into the

crook of his elbow, he resumed walking down Front Street. Thankful to have made a friend, Anna ignored his forward touch and towed Maple behind, letting Michael lead. It was, after all, not uncommon for a man and woman to walk arm in arm through town. Nonetheless, after a minute, she dislodged her arm.

"May I treat you to an early meal at Railroad House?" Michael looked down at her, his youthfulness begging her affection.

Something uninhibited and merry burgeoned within her. "I'd be delighted." Hadn't she been praying for friends?

Tristan watched Anna walking arm in arm with Michael, and something stirred within that could only be likened to the blight that had annihilated his barley two years ago. Ugly and pervasive. Not only had she returned and upset his plans, but she was throwing in her lot with preacher Michael? No disrespect to Michael—or maybe a little—but the Irishman's zeal for proselytizing could also be likened to the fungus that had consumed Tristan's barley field in one week.

A healing.

The entire town talked about it. Tristan scowled. One small bandage above Michael's eye didn't mean he'd knocked at death's door. Let the rest of Seattle gossip about Anna, but Tristan would remain grounded. He'd walked the road of false hope, and it led nowhere he cared to go again.

The bell above the restaurant door jingled as Anna entered ahead of Michael.

"Morning, Mr. Riley. Welcome back, Miss Warren. We sure missed you." Matthias dipped his head. "And Peter, God rest his soul." He lifted his eyes. "This meal's on me, miss."

"Thank you, Matthias."

Matthias's charcoal-colored suit looked freshly pressed, and as usual, he sported his wide grin, the one that drew customers back. The black man gestured to a table by the front window, and Michael pulled out her chair.

"Be right out with the special. First lunches served today."

Michael set his elbows on the table and leaned forward. The bruise on his forehead and around his eye had lightened into a yellowish green. "Your father has passed recently?"

"Yes." Anna rushed on, warding off the pity in Michael's eyes. "He was a freighter in Seattle, fourteen years."

"He must have been well respected."

"He cared for his customers, not just their business. That's why we traveled so much. He couldn't say no." She ended with a giggle and bit down on her lip, curtailing the urge to babble. Talking about Father was surprisingly awkward.

"Did you enjoy the travel?"

Bless him for feeding her impulse to talk. "It's all I've known. Arthur Denny gave Father a loan in '57, and we started trekking. Our only competition has been the Mosquito Fleet prowling the rivers and the Sound, but some things work better hauled by wagon."

She looked out the window at Yesler, Denny, and Company Store. Yesler and Denny had contracted with her and Father from the beginning. They were good people, these founders of Seattle and friends of Father. If she could secure their continued partnership, she'd . . . have way too much business. She'd committed to less travel, build more community.

Her thoughts fizzled as Tristan strode by the window. The man never went anywhere without a large dose of purpose fueling his steps. It prodded her fear of aimlessness during this unexpected season of life.

She looked at Michael. "Seattle's full of progress, isn't it? Change, aspirations."

He smiled, and she wondered if she could say anything at which he wouldn't smile. Secure men like Michael or Tristan couldn't possibly understand feelings of uncertainty.

She looked out the window again, taking in the colorful lines of water, trees, and sky. "It's beautiful here, rain or shine."

Their food came, and Michael blessed it. He picked up his fork and dug into the mound of shredded roast. The sparkle in his eye more than amused her—made her feel as if they shared a secret. But she hardly knew a thing about him.

"Where are you from?" she asked.

He pushed the mashed potatoes and gravy around on his plate. "I came last spring from Kansas. Hired on at Mick Jones's camp. I love the smell of the cedars, the sound of a cracking tree, its resounding crash. As for the work, look at me." He gestured to his chest and arms.

He didn't resemble a lumberjack. He was tall and gaunt and looked like he'd spent most of his years studying at a desk or playing checkers. On the other hand, he was carefree and cheerful, and she was drawn to him.

He slapped his hands against his chest. "Maybe another few years and I'll earn my chopping muscles."

If he hadn't strengthened up by now, he wouldn't.

"Actually . . ." His cheekiness disappeared. "I'm the lonely cook."

"The cook?" Anna scraped her fork across her plate. "You seem"—she shrugged—"a bit animated to flip flapjacks each morning."

He laughed. "I suppose that's a compliment."

"What does your family do back in Kansas?"

He swallowed wrong and coughed. She should know better than to ask about family so soon after a country-dividing war.

"Banking."

She raised her eyebrows. He'd left banking for a job as a cook at a logging camp?

"Miss Warren." Michael leaned back and crossed his arms, eyeing her with a slight grin.

Anna braced herself.

"Have you done other miracles?"

"God does miracles." She squirmed, searching for words, for a Scripture to deflect the admiration she sensed in Michael. "Didn't Jesus say that He did what He saw his Father doing? I try to do the same."

Michael held up his hands. "I didn't mean to imply you were some miracle worker. I just . . . I've never been so scared. I woke to hear the commotion at Doc's, and then my breathing . . . I couldn't breathe." His hand gripped his chest. "I felt myself dying."

She waited to see if he would say more. He didn't. "I felt the urge to pray for your healing, and I did." The burning in her chest that had compelled her seemed unexplainable and private.

He placed his hands behind his neck and stretched. "You're right, and that's why I've changed my mind."

"Pardon?"

"You've inspired me. I'm going to seminary."

She stared at him.

"God has given me a second chance. I won't pull a Jonah this time."

Anna set down her fork, caught up with Michael's revelation. "There's a story here."

"For another day." He stood, and Anna shoved down disappointment. "That is, if you don't mind sharing another meal with me."

A rush of giddiness took her by surprise. She'd never been flighty around men. Then again, a man had never sought to spend time with her. "I'd like that."

"Then it's a plan. I'm heading back to camp tomorrow, so it'll have to be next time I'm in town."

They bid farewell, and Anna left the restaurant lighthearted.

While they'd dined, the October day had turned warm, the last punch of summer. Only noon, and yet beads of sweat tickled her neck beneath the long hair that hung down her back. She turned toward Mr. Wyse's office, catching several quizzical glances of passersby.

Please, Lord, not the fascination with me as when I prayed for Andy.

Tristan entered Joe's intending to grab some nails before he met with Arthur Denny. His request for a meeting with the university board hung unanswered. He blew out a breath. If he wanted to start a program by next spring, conversation needed to happen. Decisions had to be made. Work started now.

When Anna's name rose above the hum of customers, his ears perked, like Ember's when the oat bin opened. Tristan paused by the kitchen goods and pretended to examine a piece of earthenware. Thoughts of Anna had carved off a few hours of his sleep each night since she'd returned.

He slanted his gaze toward the conversation. Two aisles over, Mrs. Webb inspected the seams of a shirt. "Doc's calling it a miracle. I didn't dare ask Anna about it this morning though. I kept my conversation to a simple 'welcome back.' The last thing the girl needs is to be accosted by questions."

Not accosted, but foolishness, like praying for healing, should be questioned.

"She arrives in town and immediately performs a miracle?" Mrs. Johnson's shrill voice carried. "How do we even know this man was close to death?"

His thoughts exactly.

"I saw him with Anna before coming to Joe's. He was talking, laughing, and glowing like he'd just married."

"Can you see a scar?"

"He's got a whole row of stitches, but he's thinking clearly."

Tristan peeked over the aisle.

Mrs. Webb refolded a shirt. "Anna mentioned meeting with Mr. Wyse, then purchasing some chickens from Elmer." She paused and sighed. "I wonder what she'll do now, all alone."

Tristan picked up an eggbeater and halfheartedly flipped it over. His gut felt like someone had beaten and fried it for breakfast. Whether Anna wanted the attention or not, she was getting it. If that attention found its way to him because of . . . He replaced the gadget he'd scrutinized for too long and walked out of the store.

Anna mentioned meeting with Mr. Wyse . . .

The thought nailed his heart to the wall of his chest.

Tristan looked toward the lawyer's office behind Yesler Hall. Anna talking with the lawyer. Desperation spurred his legs into motion.

Anna paused outside Mr. Wyse's office. Was she ready to do this? Reviewing Father's will seemed personal, like sharing a meal with him and hearing his voice.

The door squeaked as Anna swung it open. A mahogany desk and its surrounding chairs filled most of the cozy room. The upholstered chair on the opposite side of the desk sat empty.

"Mr. Wyse?"

He popped up from behind the desk, papers fluttering in his hand. His spectacles slipped to the bridge of his nose, and he pushed them back. With a flick of his hand, he motioned her to sit. "Miss Warren, like I said the other day, terribly sorry about your father."

He hadn't said that the other day. He'd all but told her to go away. "Thank you. Have you been well?"

He fussed with papers on his desk and laughed too loudly. "Yes. I'm always well." He scratched his head and then reached for a document protruding from beneath others. His hand shook. "Busy, you know, what with Henry Yesler suing Joshua Morrison."

"The top mill suing the wealthiest lumberjack?"

He rubbed his hands over his face. "Yes. Then there's the issue of Mr. Arnold's pigs eating half of Tristan Porter's barley, but I don't think Mr. Porter will press charges, angry as he was." Mr. Wyse fiddled with the inkwell. It tipped, and he groaned as the black liquid splattered across a document.

Restlessness shot through Anna's legs, and she had to fight against adopting the lawyer's nervous attitude.

"I took the liberty of acquiring copies from the bank to add to your father's file. We can go through his will and his estate." He reached into a drawer. "It's a good thing you came today. I'm leaving town to visit my sick uncle east of the mountains." He shoved a paper across the desk. "Your father was a generous man, but he also managed to save quite a bit." Tapping a figure at the bottom, he sat back.

The amount stopped her half-inhaled breath. Putting a hand to her chest, she leaned forward to read it again. How come she had no idea? Though should she be surprised, being that Father and she had freighted round the calendar and for the area's top businessmen?

Mr. Wyse placed the paper back in a drawer. That was it? What about the other papers? Information about property and assets? She swallowed and forced out the question that had awakened her last night. "A woman can inherit land, correct?" She couldn't lose that cabin.

Mr. Wyse glanced at the clock and smoothed his hair. "Yes, of course."

Anna's heart exhaled its long-held apprehension. Then it was settled. She had her cabin and a cushion of money.

"However, I should mention—"

The door swung open and crashed against the wall. Tristan entered like a gust of wind, his eyes wild.

"Mr. Porter." The lawyer stood. "Have you decided to take action against Mr. Arnold?"

Hands on his hips, Tristan's eyes darted between her and Mr. Wyse. "No. I wanted to make sure you remembered our earlier conversation."

"If you're referring to not taking action against Mr. Arnold, yes. I haven't begun paperwork."

"I trust you remember much of what you do is . . . confidential." Tristan diverted a glance in her direction before locking stares with Mr. Wyse again.

Anna attempted to read the silent conversation.

Mr. Wyse broke eye contact first. "Mr. Porter . . ." He sank into his chair. "Of course I adhere to confidentiality standards. However—"

"Is Miss Warren here?" A freckled boy, half out of breath, poked his head through the still-opened door.

"Yes?" Anna stood.

"My ma says for you to come quick."

Chapter Five

Anna ran behind the boy, struggling to keep up. The heat, her skirts, and his youthful energy wore on her strength. He turned up James Street and stopped at a yellow-painted house with Victorian trim. The curtains were drawn. He didn't wait for Anna but burst through the front door, leaving her to stumble up the porch steps after him.

"Mama." The boy stood, one hand on the banister, deep breaths racking his hunched-over body.

A woman scurried down the stairs, hair disheveled, cheeks flushed, and a jar of medicinal syrup in her hands.

Anna had been sought out to pray, she was certain.

No sooner had the woman reached the bottom step than she waved at Anna to follow, and ascended again. The question of who needed prayer and why would be settled in a moment.

It was a girl, small and blond.

"She came down with fever last night. Said her tummy hurt." The woman's crisp British accent contrasted with the featherlight way she stroked the hair away from the girl's face. "Doc treated her but thought it would pass. Said there was no need for concern. But this morning . . ." Her voice trailed off, and Anna felt like she was expected to know just what this morning had brought.

"Has Doc seen her today?" Anna spoke to the mother, but her heart prayed wordlessly for direction.

"He and Catherine left at dawn. They won't be back for a week. I've sent my oldest son north for Dr. Smith, but it will be this afternoon before they return."

The mother's eyes pleaded, and Anna squirmed at the expectations. "Mrs. . . ."

"Nellie Simms."

"Mrs. Simms, I can pray. That's all. I don't know much about medicine." Anna placed her hand on the woman's, stilling its stroking of the child's hair.

"Please. That will be enough. I know." The woman drew back and prodded Anna into the chair beside the bed.

The brother crowded close to Anna's left shoulder, his breath puffing in her ear. She took hold of the girl's hand resting outside the quilt. It burned like a hot kettle.

Lord, what do I do?

The same warmth of the previous day began to simmer in her, but this time, instead of peace, it brought apprehension. What would people think? What if she prayed and nothing happened?

The presence of mother and son pushed on her from behind. She'd pray now and digest the questions later.

"Gracious Father, in the name of your Son, Jesus, we ask you to fill this child with your Spirit and right her body with your healing. Cast out this fever and grant your wholeness."

"Hallelujah!" Mrs. Simms's cry rang out from behind Anna, and Anna startled.

The child's skin still burned. Her breathing still labored. *Now what, Lord?*

Let the little children come to me.

Anna felt the Lord's delight as she scanned the blonde's face. In spite of her illness, the girl's beauty burgeoned.

Anna turned to speak to Mrs. Simms, but she'd stepped out of the room. Father's words tickled her memory. *Wait, Anna. God's answer often includes the word "wait."* She'd sit and pray, repeat the verses she'd memorized, and wait on the Lord.

Humming, she folded her hand around the child's. Peace streamed into her. A compelling fullness filled her mouth. She obeyed the urge to pray, whispering Scripture, personalizing the cries of the psalmist for the Lord to hear, answer.

The girl released a sigh, turned over, and curled her legs. A smile swept her features. Her breathing deepened into a steady, easy rhythm.

Anna's entire body felt flushed as the heaviness of God's presence filled the room. The theological questions that had nagged her seemed inconsequential compared to the display of God's glory.

"What's happening?" Mrs. Simms rushed through the doorway. Her son pushed around her skirts and came to stare down at his sister.

"She's all better." Wonder and the simple acceptance of a child filled his voice.

Mrs. Simms covered her mouth with both hands, tears filling her eyes. Turning to her son, she gripped his shoulders. "Britton, fresh water. Hurry."

Anna stood. "I think her fever has broken. She seems peaceful."

The mattress shook as Mrs. Simms settled next to her sleeping child. She stroked the girl's cheek. The moment of tenderness cusped Anna's heart, and she withdrew, unsure if she should stay or leave.

"Her name is Julia." Mrs. Simms's voice shook.

Julia looked like an angel with her pale skin, bright lips, and rounded cheeks.

Mrs. Simms patted the chair Anna had vacated. "Please, stay. And call me Nellie."

"Thank you. I'm Anna."

"Yes. I've heard. Anna, the healer." Tears cut off Nellie's whisper.

No. Not the healer. Anna, the freighter's daughter, now alone. The woman who sought companionship and a normal life. "I'm not a healer. I'm a woman who loves Jesus, who prays."

Nellie glanced back at Julia. "You know, Julia's not really mine." She shook her head, a tinge of a blush adding beauty to her smile. "I mean, I came from England four years ago to the

San Juan Islands. I'd been jilted, and my uncle was stationed on the main island. I wanted an adventure, I guess. I met Jared when he was stationed with the Americans on the other end of the island. He was a widower, and his children, they needed a mama."

"How many?"

"Four. Julia's the youngest."

Julia stirred, and Nellie's attention whipped from Anna to her child. "Honey, are you okay? Speak to me, darling."

Julia murmured and reached for a stuffed bear.

Nellie fingered a truss of her hair. "It's a miracle."

Prayer had been answered, but that didn't make it a miracle, did it?

"We've been here three months, and Julia's energy hasn't seemed normal. I thought she just needed time to adjust. But this, the suddenness of it . . . I thought it was the plague." Nellie straightened, smoothing her skirt and meeting Anna's eyes. "This isn't quite the conventional way to make a friend. I should have offered you tea."

A friend. The words were a balm to Anna's heart. "I'm thankful for a new friend, regardless of the circumstances."

Nellie escorted her down the stairs and to the front door. "Wait here, please." She dashed to another room and returned with a loaf of bread. "This is so little compared to what you've given us, but I—" The woman's voice broke.

"All I did was pray. God heals."

"Don't belittle your gift."

A gift that made her stand out, raised eyebrows, and seemed more like a burden than a blessing.

The cabin creaked at the gentle breath of wind. The night was warm, and Anna shifted in bed. Sleep stalled somewhere in her muddy thoughts as faces flickered through her restless mind:

Michael's, welcoming; Mr. Wyse's, twitching; Tristan's, stony; Mrs. Simms's, relieved; Julia's, angelic. They swirled together as she sought to process all that had happened this past week.

An owl hooted, loud and near. She rose and padded across the wooden floor, enjoying the coolness against her sweaty feet. The owl released its solitary cry again. Anna paused, holding her breath, straining to hear the response of its mate.

Silence.

She stepped out to the wide porch. Bypassing her smaller rocker, she sank into Father's larger one. Her hands traced the smooth arms as she waited for the owl to call again.

She closed her eyes, and this time, only one face appeared: gray eyes, curly white hair like sheep's wool, angular cheeks. She missed his stories: *I came stumbling into the Lord's throne room,* Father had told her numerous times, recounting his conversion, *and that's the only way to come.* Though she could recall his stories, his inflections grew difficult to remember. *October 3, 1830, in Rochester, New York, I bowed my knee to Jesus after Charles Finney's sermon. A love like burning liquid rushed through me.*

Had he stressed *burning* or *liquid*? He'd been her link to a mother she couldn't remember. But he'd given her more than stories. He'd passed her his faith.

She sat straighter and opened her eyes. A love like burning liquid. That was what she'd felt while praying for Julia. She'd known the Lord's holiness before, in the song of creation, in the solitude of the wagon at night, reading God's word, listening to a sermon. But until yesterday, she'd not felt anything like burning liquid.

You're gifted, Anna, gifted with His gifts. Use them.

Father hadn't allowed her to shrink away from the urges to pray.

"*. . . to another gifts of healing. . .*" Verses she'd memorized and forgotten, now danced in her mind. Certainly she believed the Spirit of Jesus healed hearts. Father had been an underhanded businessman of twenty-three when he came to Jesus. *Anything to make money* had been his axiom. He'd been deserted by his parents at thirteen, and then the girl he'd first loved had married another.

But his life after Christ had focused on serving others, giving his best even when taken advantage of.

How could she not believe the Lord healed? But did He have to use her? She wasn't a preacher. Nor a teacher. Educated on the underside of a wagon by firelight, she wasn't a theologian either.

I'm willing, Lord, but I don't understand.

The owl hooted again, close this time, and she looked up to see its darkened outline gliding over the yard. She'd sleep outside tonight, out from under the confines of a roof. She walked back into the cabin to grab her blanket, the stuffiness of the air confirming her decision. It was a night for memories.

One more day of harvesting dried peas. At least, he'd work harder than a mule to make sure it was one more day. Tristan rolled his shoulders, stretching the taut muscles, and walked out to the porch to lace up his boots, having finished his breakfast of fried eggs. His limited homemaking skills were a dismal disgrace to his mother.

He bent to tug his laces a final time. The sound of approaching horses pounded in the distance, drawing a groan from him. He glared into the sun until the riders rounded the bend. Of the four, he recognized only the Baldwin brothers, his nearest neighbors to the north.

Expect visitors.

Tristan had disregarded Lazarus's warning, hoping the idea for an association had either fizzled or lacked support—or that they'd realized Tristan wasn't the right person for it. They'd be correct. But now it looked like he'd have to convince them.

Gray, the younger Baldwin brother by some dozen years, jumped down from his horse and smiled ear-to-ear. Enthusiasm that couldn't be held back roused Tristan's suspicions.

"Hey there, boy." Frank Baldwin spoke his greeting with a mix of respect and fatherly care.

That only made the "boy" slightly more tolerable. How ironic that according to Lazarus these men were interested in him leading an association, yet many referred to him simply as "boy." A boy wanted to drop from a rope swing into a creek, dangle frogs in front of pigtailed girls, or roll around in the dirt. Tristan didn't have time for creek play or teasing. Only for dirt. Dirt needed to be tamed, and it required a man to pull a yield from the earth.

"Captain Luke McRedmond." A tall man with dark hair and a bushy mustache held out his hand.

Tristan shook it.

Frank gestured to the last stranger. "This is Jimmy Jorgensen."

The youth shoved his hands in his pockets and jutted his chin forward in a subtle greeting. An expression fit for a funeral draped his beardless face, and straight blond hair hung low, shadowing pale-blue eyes.

"Have a seat." Tristan gestured to his porch. His mother would have served biscuits and cool, mint tea, but he didn't have that sort of thing. Correction. He had some stale biscuits. The better choice for hospitality was chairs and the shade of the porch. Another reason he wasn't fit to be their leader. He could work a farm, but he couldn't entertain.

The Baldwin brothers sprawled in his two chairs, McRedmond leaned against a post, and Jorgensen slumped on the steps, his back to the group.

Frank crossed his arms and looked out at Tristan's field. "You harvested more this year than I did the past two years combined."

Tristan smirked. Buttering him up would get these visitors nowhere. "You need a sulky, Frank."

Jorgensen grunted. "Sulky's a lazy man's plow." The southern accent was thick.

"Nothing wrong with riding behind your plow." Tristan forced the rush of words to come out slow. "Conserves energy. Goes faster. It's the smart man's plow, and the plow of the future. At least until they release the steam plow."

"Yeah, right."

"It's been tested."

Jorgensen hung his head and plucked a twig from between two porch slats.

Tristan had limited patience for men skeptical of farm innovation. Men like that were content to farm just enough to scrape by. Forget diligence—they were satisfied with mediocrity.

"Speaking of the future"—Gray took off his hat and scratched his head—"you doing something with the university?"

"Trying."

Frank waved a hand and chuckled. "They're distracted with the railroad issue."

Who wasn't?

"What'd you have in mind?" Gray rocked back like he didn't have a care in the world.

Tristan's gaze flitted to the field of peas. Some people had word to do. "Experimentation with fertilizers. Cross-germination. Efficiency studies." Tristan glanced at Jorgensen, whose attention stayed on the recently harvested barley field. "Maybe even come up with a better method for clearing land. These trees are enormous. The roots go deep." The list of needs for an agricultural program went deeper.

The men nodded with blank expressions, seeming unimpressed.

Captain McRedmond stepped away from the porch post.

"It's good to finally meet you, Tristan. I've heard much about you."

What was there to hear? *There's this man who likes to farm.* That could be anyone.

"I've settled on the east side of the lake by Coal Creek, plan to do some farming, open an inn with my wife, start a settlement." McRedmond's eyes glowed. The intensity settled some of Tristan's doubts and drew his respect. "I have to admit when I heard about your success, I didn't expect to be meeting a boy."

Was that all anyone could see? "There are no boys out here, sir. Only people who work hard."

"No offense, Porter. Age doesn't bother me."

The old rocking chair creaked as Frank pushed to his feet. "Tristan, we'll get to the point. The university's got enough to worry about trying to survive financially. What's needed, what we want you to consider, is an organization. A farmers' association that would provide not just support for us farmers, but opportunity to try new things, like you mentioned."

Tristan's gaze circled the group. The Baldwin brothers were dependable settlers who'd farmed this valley for at least a dozen years, and McRedmond seemed influential. Jorgensen—well, he had equal measure grit and stupidity, it seemed.

Gray and Frank took turns laying out ideas. Listening to them spurt plans like they were watering crops, a throb started behind Tristan's right eye. An association hadn't worked for his father, and it wouldn't work for him either.

Tristan stalked to the end of the porch. "Why bring this idea to me?"

"You don't have a family to worry about. You're motivated." McRedmond's cheeks rounded above his smile. "You're young. Successful. You look for new ways to do things. You're willing to get your hands dirty, not just talk."

McRedmond hadn't been lying when he'd said he'd heard

about Tristan.

"Think of it," Frank said. "You can search out the newest farm toys, and we'll give 'em a try. Like the hay press. We're ten years behind this innovation."

Twenty years. Not to mention other innovations. That was Tristan's whole point. These farmers saw it—why couldn't the university? Forward thinking would carve the future of the Northwest.

He didn't need to waste more time with this conversation. He had work to do. "I don't have an answer right now. If you want to go ahead with plans, that's fine. Get a list of interested names." He looked each man in the eye. "But I'm not ready to commit."

Tristan sat on the edge of his bed, bare feet aching from hours in his boots. His yawns came, one after the other clearing his mind. Though he'd washed his face and upper body, he still felt the grime clinging to his scalp beneath his wet hair.

No thanks to the delay, he'd finished his dried peas.

He shook his head. He couldn't settle for an association. Not when Peter had given him the gift of hope.

With three steps he reached the small table by the window. Placing both hands on the surface, he stared at the unfolded letter. *Why, Peter?* Tristan picked up the torn piece of paper and returned to sit on the bed.

The edge caught on his calloused finger. Heaviness plagued Tristan's heart, and he put his hand across his chest. Peter had been wise and generous, but what he'd done . . . it didn't make sense.

I'm sorry, Anna. I've got to do this. You'll understand eventually.

Chapter Six

Anna donned her brown knit shawl and laced her boots. She rocked on tiptoes, easing her antsy legs before grabbing her walking stick. As she set out for church, the ground seemed to lift under her, urging her forward. Morning sun filtered through trees, warming her back, but the air she breathed tasted cool. The first leaves to drop spread on the forest floor, color tingeing their edges. Nature suspended between summer and autumn.

Lord, I need a good conversation. No stilted condolences. No questions concerning Michael's or Julia's healings. A good, normal, unpretentious conversation.

Yet as she entered the churchyard, people expressed condolences. New families nodded greetings. And in both familiar and unfamiliar eyes, she couldn't miss the fascination. Any doubts that news about Michael and Julia had spread, dimmed.

She ascended the steps to the front door, cautious of the broken plank, but frowned at the new piece of wood across the third step. Six months was a long time. Before entering, she lapped in one last sight of the water. The God who created sea and sky was with her. Had a plan for her. She trusted Him, despite the perplexities of her first days back.

She paused, hand on the cedar doorframe. Tristan rode up on Ember. He hadn't been a churchman until he'd met her father, and though he was the type she expected to enter services late, sit near the back, and have one foot out the door as the amen rang out, he wasn't. He was seldom late, sat in the same pew each week, and one could watch the back of his head all service and never see it move.

She tore her gaze from the mystery of Tristan and entered. Mrs. Tolliver played the piano, which sounded less musical than the horns the ships blasted as they entered Elliot Bay, as Anna slipped into the third pew from the back on the right. Moments later, Tristan and Lazarus marched directly to the second row, left. It felt like she hadn't missed a Sunday.

She laughed to herself. She'd missed more Sundays than she'd attended.

Ten minutes into the service, her mind took flight like a butterfly, and she lost the battle of concentration. Tristan's dark-brown hair curled at the ends above his white collar, and she wondered if he cared, if he was paying attention to the reverend, Daniel Bagley.

Despite Tristan's reputation as an honest, overachieving farmer, she couldn't push the questions away. Why he'd been at her cabin. The nature of his relationship with her father. Father hadn't talked of Tristan much, and Anna hadn't asked. She should have asked.

Now she was left to ponder her obsession to understand this aloof, intense, and—fine, attractive—man. If only he didn't have to have such a powerful presence, even in her memory. She recalled his smile, that time she saw it. How it crinkled his eyes and brought out the boy in him. She liked his sturdiness, the way he'd loaded those barrels of apples into their wagon last fall as if tossing up feathers.

She kicked herself, feet tucked beneath the pew. Even if she couldn't focus on the sermon, she could think of something other than Tristan. Like Michael. She searched for the gangly man with fluffy black hair. Not present, and not altogether surprising considering the camp's distance from Seattle.

Her gaze darted back to Tristan. She leaned her head sideways, stretching her neck and forcing her vision elsewhere. In front of her, Nellie doted on Julia, fingering the child's pink hair ribbon.

When the service dismissed, Anna hustled out of the pew row before Tristan could turn, catch her eye, and wonder if she'd watched him the entire service. Not that he'd have any reason to suspect her of doing such.

Martha Johnson grinned. "I've wanted to welcome you back but thought you might need a break from all the excitement." She wiggled her eyebrows at Anna.

"Thank you, Mrs. Johnson."

"I won't ask you to retell the stories because I've already heard from Mrs. Webb and Mrs. Simms."

Mrs. Webb twisted away from another conversation and spoke across several congregants. "It was quite remarkable, Anna."

Others turned their attention her direction.

Addressing the obvious seemed the best approach to quelling suspicions or rumors. "I'm not sure what you may have heard about Michael's and Julia's situations."

Those who hadn't yet tuned to the conversation stopped their discussions.

The hushed anticipation heightened her desire to get the explanation out of the way. "The gist of it is this: the Lord prompted me to pray, and I did. I asked for His healing work in Michael's injury and Julia's sickness—"

Mrs. Johnson gripped Anna's hand.

"—and the Lord answered."

A chorus of amens punctuated Anna's comment. Mrs. Johnson squeezed her hand, and people pressed closer.

"What did it feel like?" Mrs. Webb asked.

Anna frowned as her lips parted.

"You know," Mrs. Webb said, "when you were praying, did something happen inside you?"

She'd melted. Burned right up. But she couldn't tell about the weight of God's glory that had squashed her chest. That intimacy had been between her and the Lord. The wonder of it had no words. But she had to say something. "I had a strong sense God wanted to act with power."

Mouths gaped. A woman gasped.

Anna tried to back up, but someone pressed from behind. "It wasn't dramatic, and it's not magic. Anyone can pray for healing."

"Some aren't so sure this is appropriate." An unfamiliar man edged his way through the crowd. His stylish suit boasted no wrinkles, and his face appeared youthful despite the gray hair edging his temples.

"I'm not sure what you mean."

The elderly Mrs. Tolliver marched down from the chancel, hymnal under one arm. "Nonsense, Mr. Foreman. What's so inappropriate about praying?"

Mr. Foreman's eyes shone like pewter. "It's not the praying. It's the presumption of it all."

"Start talking straight. No one knows what you're trying to say." Mrs. Tolliver shuffled between two people and rubbed shoulders with Anna.

"It's arrogant to consider oneself a healer."

"Excuse me." Anna held up a hand between Mrs. Tolliver and Mr. Foreman, whose sparking glares were a fire hazard. "I believe I was clear in both situations that God is the healer. Are we not to pray in Jesus's name for the things we need?"

"We are not to ask for miracles. Those are things of Bible stories." Mr. Foreman shoved his hands into his pockets. "God's work is to save people from hell. As for our other struggles, does the Good Book not say, 'In this world we will have trials?'"

"Clyde Foreman." Reverend Bagley entered from his position of greeting outside the front doors. "This is Miss Warren's first Sunday back. She's due a welcome, not an interrogation."

Mr. Foreman's expression lightened as he turned a smile toward the reverend before looking back at Anna. He tipped his hat, but his voice remained stiff. "Pardon me."

Mrs. Johnson patted Anna's arm as Mr. Foreman strode

from the building. "Don't pay him any mind. Being in the banking business causes indigestion." The livery owner's wife winked.

Anna snuck from the church as others resumed conversations. Letting the sunshine sluice the image of Mr. Foreman's scowl from her thoughts, she descended the stairs. She'd not wanted to invoke controversy by obeying the Holy Spirit.

At the bottom of the steps, Anna halted at the sight of Tristan standing next to his mount, talking with Lorna. Talking and laughing. She'd remembered right. He was handsome when he smiled.

"Just look at her." Nellie's hushed voice came from behind Anna.

Anna didn't need to look to know Lorna was beautiful. Blue eyes the color of sunshine-lit water and a figure that read "woman" with only a quick glance.

"It's as if she's never been sick," Nellie said.

Anna startled. Nellie spoke of Julia, not Lorna. Anna reached behind, grabbed Nellie's hand, and squeezed. Julia chased a dog around a wagon, her squeals robust. Peace flooded Anna as she watched. Here, before her eyes, was the fruit of God's healing work.

She rotated to face Nellie. "God is good, is He not?"

Nellie nodded, emotion wobbling her smile.

"Miss Warren." The man who'd sat by Nellie, undoubtedly Mr. Simms, approached and held out his hand. "My gratitude."

Anna grasped his hand between both hers. "It was my pleasure to pray for your daughter, and God's pleasure to heal her."

"Yes. Yes, indeed. His pleasure."

Someone understood. Bless Mr. Simms for making this about the Lord and not her.

Anna didn't understand why God had used her in these

healings, but she didn't need to understand. She trusted God, and that was enough.

Tristan cinched Ember's saddle. Another trip to town. He was dragging harvest over a ridiculous stretch of the calendar, and his crops risked frost.

The barn door slammed against the wall. Tristan jerked around as Lazarus paced across the threshold. One look at his farmhand's determined expression further soured Tristan's mood.

"Why'd you say no to McRedmond?"

"Said I'd think about it."

"You done thinking?"

Tristan didn't answer.

"Why you so hung up on the university? God hasn't opened that door."

"I shouldn't need to defend myself for wanting to do something to help others." Being passionate about his vocation was no crime. Farming was more than a way of survival. The satisfaction of drawing life from the ground, sustaining yourself and others with earth's bounty, it was the essence of thriving.

Lazarus stepped closer. "You want this for your father."

"Is that wrong?"

"Selfish is what it is."

Honoring the family legacy was not selfish, and Tristan wouldn't allow Lazarus to convince him otherwise. "So I'm supposed to do the things I don't want to do?"

"You's supposed to do the things God wants you to do."

Tristan shrugged. "Maybe He wants me to do this. What makes you God's best friend?"

Lazarus's eyes narrowed, and Tristan felt conviction at his rude speech. The left side of Lazarus's mouth twitched, and then he turned away.

He'd let down Lazarus, again.

Tristan walked Ember to the opening of the barn and swiped the letters from the work table.

"What you trying to do with those?"

"Trying to get some help." He waved a letter at Lazarus. "This one's to a man in Portland who was involved with Ohio State's Morrill grant."

Lazarus nodded, an ambiguous response. Not argumentative. Not encouraging.

Tristan shoved the letters into his saddlebag and mounted. He didn't need to look back as he rode away to know Lazarus watched him and would watch until Tristan rounded the bend. And when Tristan came back, he wouldn't be surprised if Lazarus was standing there waiting for him.

Waiting for him to come back to God.

He'd be waiting a long time.

On Wednesday, Anna returned from Seattle with a pile of library books weighing heavy in the Duwamish-woven basket slung over her arm. Mr. Foreman had talked to Reverend Bagley about "that girl who prays for miracles," or so Mrs. Webb had told Mrs. Johnson, who'd told Mrs. Yesler, who'd taken Anna aside and counseled her toward subtleness.

Was this what it was like to be part of a community? To pass around the latest news and gush about it? No, thanks. She'd been wrong to assume that community would mirror the deep conversations she'd had with Father while they'd traversed miles in the wagon.

Anna hurried into her yard, head bowed to shield her eyes from the drops starting to fall from the sky. Ten feet from the door, she glanced up—and dropped her basket.

Freshly chopped wood mounded high along the north side of her cabin. She hadn't needed more wood. But she did need the encouragement that someone cared. That someone was on her side. "Thank you, Lord." She grinned, giddy over wood.

The rain fell harder, but her smile didn't dim. She picked up her basket and rushed into the cabin. Kicking the door shut, she wiped water from her face and set her basket on the table. A paper rustled, and she pulled the scribbled note from beneath her basket.

Hope this makes up for my infringement on your space. Welcome home. Tristan.

Her wet smile settled firmer on her face.

Last week he'd referred to his use of her cabin as *hospitality*, but now it was *infringement*. And then there was the irony that he'd come inside her cabin to leave the note. Tristan had been an enigma since that day she'd begged his forgiveness for the plow, and the riddle wasn't getting any easier.

Anna put the can of peaches back on the shelf. Joe wouldn't budge on price, and although she could afford them, she couldn't stomach paying that much, not when she was used to negotiating. She'd tried bartering with Joe in the past, but he had more willpower than a mule.

Unfortunately, the dried beans were a fair price. Not her favorite. She scooped a bagful and set them on her mound of items. The handles of her basket pressed on her forearm. Yesterday books, today groceries. Tomorrow, when her arms ached, she'd regret her commitment to walk when not freighting.

Rounding the aisle, she collided with Mrs. Tolliver and bounded back. Though standing only five feet tall, the elderly woman possessed a sturdiness that rivaled the mountains.

"Pardon me." Mrs. Tolliver brushed flour from Anna's sleeve. "I'm too much in a hurry."

"No, I should be more careful."

She frowned as if pondering a theological conundrum.

"First week of October and already so cold."

Anna held back her grin at the serious declaration. Until the end of time, Mrs. Tolliver would have a comment about the weather. "The air is chilly at night."

"I've been chopping wood every day to keep my strength up." Her solemnity passed, and she winked at Anna. "Were you in town, dear, six years ago when it snowed in October?"

"I don't remember it."

"Feels like it might do it again, and I'm going to be ready."

Mrs. Tolliver reached into Anna's basket and shuffled items around, perusing the contents. She picked up the volume of *Grimm's Fairy Tales*, opened it to the middle, chuckled at something, and returned the book to Anna's basket. "Tell me how you like it."

"You've read it?"

"Every edition." She patted Anna's arm and released a short sigh. "Best be on my way." She took a step but paused, a frown drawn across her wrinkled face. "You have enough wood to cook with and stay warm?"

Anna pictured the stack against her wall, or rather, the man who'd put it there, and hoped the heat in her face didn't show. "Yes. Don't worry about me."

Mrs. Tolliver let out a laugh that sounded more like a whoop. "I won't be worrying. It's not what I do." She headed toward the counter, patting another customer on the back and tugging on the braid of a redheaded girl.

Anna had never known her grandmother, but she envisioned her to be like Mrs. Tolliver. Vivacious, looking out for others, content.

Shaking off the invasion of loneliness, Anna added candles and matches to her basket. Even though she instructed herself not to look at the ribbons as she passed the sewing counter, she snuck a peek. Unable to stop herself, she fingered a piece of blue-and-white-trimmed ribbon. She had an entire box filled with ribbons Father had given her. If she tied them together and wrapped herself in them, it would feel like his embrace.

"Anna?"

Anna wiped away a tear and turned to hug Nellie.

"The pain, is it still raw?"

Thank God for this new and unexpected friendship. "No, but it pounces on me sometimes."

"Someday I'd be honored to hear about your father. Perhaps over tea soon?" Nellie studied the ribbons. "Which one were you looking at?"

Anna pointed, her hand shaking.

"Scalloped edges. I like it." Nellie snatched the spool and pulled Anna to the end of the counter, where Joe was folding muslin. "How much do you want?"

"Nellie, you don't have to, really."

Nellie turned to Joe and held her arms wide. "This much."

He cut a generous amount and handed it to Nellie.

"Turn around." Nellie twirled her finger, and Anna obeyed. Quick, sturdy fingers braided her hair and then twisted the mass close to her head. With a few loops of the ribbon, Nellie wrapped the bun secure and tied. "Magnificent."

"Thank you. I . . ." Another tear slipped out, but Anna dug for control. No longer was the sorrow a river carving new paths. It was now the sediment on the riverbed, present but at rest. Crying roused the sludge she wanted to leave behind. She cleared her throat. "Thank you."

"A small price to pay for the gift of a friend."

Anna didn't attempt to hold back the tears.

A crash sounded from several aisles over, followed by a host of squeals. Nellie cringed. "If those children knocked over Joe's walnut bin again, there'll be extra chores tonight."

Anna nudged her. "Go tend your children, friend."

Ten minutes later, Anna left Joe's, her basket in the crook of her right arm. Her tired mind ticked off each step. At least the encounter with Nellie made the weariness of Father's loss seem less oppressive than it had this morning.

She touched the bun pulling at her exposed neck. A perusal up and down the street confirmed she was the only one preoccupied by the different hairstyle. For someone accustomed to wearing her hair down, the exposure felt odd. The breeze grazed the back of her neck, tickling her.

Rounding the corner onto Columbia, she started up the incline. Footsteps hastened after her, and a moment later a figure appeared in her peripheral vision.

"Let me carry that for you."

Tristan's voice. Her hope for a quiet walk home plummeted.

"Thank you." She handed him the basket without pausing, but after ten steps realized she walked alone. Tristan stood back, examining her. So she was conspicuous to one person.

When he caught up, he reached out and tweaked the bun. "Going grown-up today?"

Her ears burned, and she flicked his hand away.

"It looks nice."

For all the warmth in his voice, he could have been talking about Joe's freshly painted sign.

He slowed his pace to hers as they ascended. The mill hummed, and men yelled, but the quiet between her and Tristan droned louder. Silence with Father had been like holding one's breath for a glorious sunset. Silence with Tristan was like waiting on a sentence from a judge.

Anna distracted herself by reflecting on Julia's healing. Every detail was as vivid as the mountains across the bay. The smell of fresh bread that had permeated the Simms' house. Nellie's anxiety and subsequent joy. The fullness of God's Spirit within Anna.

"Did you see Julia Simms at church last Sunday?"

If her face hadn't been slanted in his direction, she would

have missed his slight nod.

Anna's fingers went to her neck, and she fiddled with a piece of loose hair. "She looked radiant. That smile. Even with those missing front teeth, I'd exchange my smile for hers. Nellie glowed as well. She couldn't keep her hands off Julia—smoothing her hair, rubbing her back. With all that commotion in front of me, I couldn't focus. It was—"

"What if she'd died?"

Anna stared at Tristan. "She didn't."

"She could have."

"She didn't." Why had she spoken about Julia to a man who seemed to question even the promise of a sunrise? "We don't choose if someone lives or dies. The Lord does what He does. I choose to rejoice, not question, when He extends His hand of mercy and heals."

"Sure you do."

That Father had managed a civil conversation with this man seemed like no small miracle itself. She dug her hands into her pockets and marched forward. At the top of the street, debris from an old, collapsed building blocked the path. Boards lay crisscrossed, jagged edges protruding. Tristan offered his free hand. She placed hers in his and studied where to set her foot, but when she lifted her eyes, the intensity of his gaze froze her step.

A muscle in his temple twitched. "And when He doesn't extend His hand?"

Despite the soft way he'd spoken, the words attacked her calm.

Anna yanked her hand back. "I feel blessed to be a part of His work, no matter what the result."

She stepped through the rubbish, careful to avoid any nails, while he bounded through the web of wood with three steps. Let Tristan ask his critical questions. She'd stay quiet. Whatever bitterness he harbored was his issue, and nothing she could say would pierce that resentment.

But how she wanted to say something. The right thing that would give God glory, free Tristan from his sour questioning. She glanced sideways, hoping to see a softening on his face, but all she noticed was the stubble shadowing his chin. Her face prickled at the memory of Father burying his face into her neck when she was small and rubbing his whiskers against her smooth skin.

Her throat swelled. Memories of Father ambushed at the most unsuspecting moments.

As a diversion, she focused on Tristan's furrowed brow. How different from Julia's face. "Julia has the sweetest face. I'll never forget. When Nellie led me up those stairs and I saw Julia, I almost forgot I was there to pray. She was like an angel. Her hair fanned on the pillow. Although she was sleeping, I almost thought she was—"

"Will you stop talking, please?"

". . . smiling." Anna finished at a whisper. Father had never asked her to stop talking. And he had never interrupted. "I'm sorry you find my conversation irritating." She swallowed. "You know, I am capable of walking myself home. I did not suggest—"

"I know you didn't. Don't be so easily offended."

An interruption, again.

He sped up, and she practically had to run to keep pace with him. If he regretted his offer to help, it was mutual. In another ten minutes, she'd be home. Or at Tristan's pace, seven. His stride seemed as long as his height.

She was breathless when they reached her cabin. He set her basket on the porch steps, and she grimaced as his eyes wandered to the pillow and blanket folded on the rocking chair. The dubious look he directed at her pulled for an explanation.

"I prefer sleeping outside." She smiled to reduce the awkwardness of the confession. "It's familiar. And peaceful."

With a snort-like laugh, he stepped off the porch, and strode past her. "Anna Warren, you do beat all."

She rushed after him, not sure his words were a compliment. "It's almost more like home than inside."

He stopped and looked over his shoulder. She expected a snide remark, but he kept his mouth closed. She sighed as he shook his head and resumed walking.

"Thank you for carrying my basket." Her words chased his back. "Tristan."

He swiveled, hands on hips. "What?"

Her mind churned. She'd called his name without a thought of what she'd say. "Are you thirsty?"

"No . . . thank you."

His brooding expression bored into her, and even though his stare possessed a hardness she knew was borne from woundedness, she had to admit Tristan wore intensity well. He didn't need a smile to look handsome.

He scratched the back of his head and eyed her woodpile. "You have enough?"

Was he serious? "You took care of that. Thank you."

He spun around and walked a few steps before halting. "Anna?"

She focused on the back of his shaggy head of hair.

"What if Julia had died? Would you have felt like a failure?"

The question unlocked a vulnerable place inside her. "Probably."

"Why—if it's the Lord who chooses to extend His hand or not?"

She studied his shoulders, admiring their sturdiness. He was all man, from the strength of his arms to his composure. Yet he looked more boy in this moment than he ever had, his slumped posture suggesting defeat. She couldn't see his face, but the presence of a scowl wrapped around him.

"Would you feel like a failure if your seeds didn't grow?"

He fisted his hair with one hand.

"God has given me a gift, Tristan, like he's given you a gift. I don't want to be presumptuous, but I do expect to be used by Him."

"Healing and farming are hardly comparable."

She stepped around him, wanting to see if his eyes were as numb as his voice. His glazed stare didn't break from the forest, even when her gaze lingered on his face.

Fearing the sudden swell of compassion in her heart, she spoke slowly. "Farming is a gift nevertheless." And then, because the urge to see beyond his self-imposed veil cut off all common sense, she probed further. "Where in the Midwest did you come from?"

"Worley, Illinois." He smiled.

The day warmed ten degrees.

"It's easy to be good at something that's been as much a part of your everyday life as eating and breathing."

She was getting somewhere. "Men farm years and never get the production you do."

He shrugged, and stoicism resumed dominance. "My father was good at it."

"Are you like your father? Is he as solemn as you as well? Or do you get that from your mother?" She meant to joke, but his face tightened.

He brushed past her. "I've got things to do."

A family issue. She should have suspected.

Chapter Seven

Each step Tristan took drilled her words a little further into his gut: *The Lord does what He does. I choose to rejoice.*

His entire life testified to the truth of that statement. His father and brothers, dead at Gettysburg. Mother, dead from pneumonia. Where was the rejoicing in that?

The Lord does what He does.

The *why* left his head aching and stole his sleep. He operated his homestead on the principle of cause and effect. If he left his machinery in the rain, it rusted. If he planted late, he risked losing his crop to frost. If the spring dumped days of rain, his fields flooded. So much about farming was out of control, but at least it made sense.

Unlike the Lord.

His steps slowed, and he leaned against the trunk of a maple. Bark scraped along his forearm and through the thin cotton of his shirt. The brightness of his mother's laugh seemed so real he could hear it, her smile so sweet.

Why, Lord?

And why did Anna have to remind him of his mother? He'd thought so from the moment she'd calmly said to him, "There's been an incident with your plow." Oh, there'd been an incident all right, in his heart, as he'd encountered the joy anchored in her warm, wheat-colored eyes.

Today, when he'd seen Anna walking, hair knotted, he'd stared at her white neck thirty seconds before offering to take her basket. It seemed indecent to see a neck normally so well hidden. Nothing hidden about her joy, though—so steadfast not even grief had disrupted it.

And there was the rub. She deserved to be bitter.

He pounded his fist into the tree.

Anna's joy exasperated him. It looked past the questions and ignored the circumstances. It didn't seem right.

He shoved off the tree and steadied his hat, the swell of frustration providing new energy to his overworked body. Dwelling on the past could suck hours from a man's production, if he let it.

Once back in town, he stopped at the post office, hoping for good news. Mr. Thorpe handed him three letters, one from delegate Garfielde. Better than good. Tristan's case for a program was building. Storing them in his pocket, he paced toward the *Puget Sound Dispatch*. Time to take his plea to the public.

As he approached the office, a surprise urge to pray sent a simple "Please, Lord" rippling through his heart. Habits died hard, and Mother had instilled in him the "present your requests to God" verse. He'd done that for the first fifteen years of his life, and where had it gotten him? His gaze drifted up the hillside to the prominent white university building.

Disappointed and in Seattle.

An hour later, Tristan headed south out of town. The grinding noise of the mills dissipated as he turned the first bend on the Seattle-Black River Road. He had two days to write his editorial. Two days to come up with the words to win the support he lacked.

At the sight of another rider approaching, he pulled his horse to the side and took in the bedroll, dirty clothes, and ragged lines on the young face of the man coming toward him.

The face registered. "Jimmy Jorgensen. How goes it?"

Jorgensen nodded, avoiding eye contact.

Tristan gestured to the pack of belongings behind Jimmy. "Headed somewhere?"

"Finished my work with McRedmond. Thought I'd see what Seattle had to offer." Jorgensen played with the reins, his apathy thick as the fern underbrush on the adjacent hillside.

"Lumber camps, mill work, or coal mines. Take your pick. Or you could check with the Seattle Coal and Transportation Company. They're building a tram from the mine to the lake."

"No thanks."

Tristan hesitated only an instant. "I've got a month of hard work left. I could use another hand."

"You'd hire me?"

They hadn't made good first impressions on each other, but Tristan thrust that aside for the sake of an extra pair of hands. "I don't know what you've heard about me, but I'm fair."

"People say you're picky."

"Picky?" The accusation stung like nettles.

"You like things done a certain way."

Of course. The efficient way. The right way. "I have high standards and require hard work. But I pay well."

"I didn't mean to offend." Jorgensen steadied his roan, meeting Tristan's gaze for the first time.

Tristan connected with the deep undercurrent of . . . what? Raw confidence? Held-back determination? Maybe it was the way Jorgensen sat tall in the saddle, but Tristan saw himself when he'd first arrived in Seattle, trying to appear self-assured, eager to make an impression, and yet not letting anyone have an advantage over him.

Maybe it was more like looking at his current self. "No offense taken."

Jorgensen scanned the trees, and Tristan let him have his space. That first summer Tristan arrived from Illinois, he'd camped in these woods, worked odd jobs, and bathed in the river while Lazarus had stayed at the Occidental Hotel and worked in the livery. Tristan couldn't have stopped that man from following him from Illinois any more than he could have stopped himself from leaving.

"It's not plowing season, so you don't have to worry I'd

make you ride a sulky," Tristan said.

Jorgensen smirked. "All right. I can give you a month." He turned his horse around and fell in beside Tristan.

"How old are you?"

Jorgensen shook his head. "No questions."

"Fine. But you have to agree to talk to me if you ever have a problem with my methods or don't understand why I do something the way I do." Everything was an opportunity to learn.

"Sounds reasonable."

The sun split the cedars and cast shadows across the road. Tristan pulled his jacket from the bag behind him. He never knew how to dress when one day the sun came out but lacked warmth, and the next day, despite cloud cover, thick air induced a sweat.

"You ever take suggestions?"

Tristan whipped his head around. "For what?"

The barest hint of amusement roamed Jimmy's eyes. "If I'm supposed to talk with you if I don't understand your reasons, do I get to make suggestions?"

This boy was more like him than he'd first anticipated. "Yeah. Make suggestions."

As long as Jimmy worked hard and accepted his authority, Tristan could handle some attitude. If Jimmy had ideas, he wanted to hear them. Maybe they could sound each other out. Maybe this was a God-ordained—

Tristan sucked in a breath and scowled. He blamed Anna that lately thoughts about God were as natural as thoughts about eating whenever his stomach growled. Like now. He put his hand to his belly. Somehow he managed to care for his fields with excellence but hardly seemed able to feed himself.

They rounded a bend. A fallen branch sprawled across the road. Tristan jumped Ember over the limb, but Jorgensen stopped. He dismounted and dragged the thick branch to the side, clearing the way for any wagons.

Perhaps Jimmy Jorgensen had more to offer than his first impression implied.

The freshness of the October morning bristled Anna's toes as she stuck them out the end of her blanket. From high in the hemlock, crows yammered, adding an edge of harshness to the otherwise peaceful morning.

She'd been back one month. Families had opened their tables to her. She'd attended the library association meetings, the knitting circle, and had been invited to celebrate the births of two babies.

And she remained an outsider, a curiosity.

The healings of Michael and Julia had become epic. She'd recounted them so often the words rolled off her tongue like school recitations. In one instance, she'd corrected the assumption Michael Riley had been dead.

Anna tightened the wool blanket around her shoulders and tucked her toes back beneath the fraying end. Fall continued its tug-of-war between summer and winter, one week warm, the next cold. She'd slept outside since Julia's healing, her own heart's tug-of-war exhausting.

Three minutes later, with her courage finally as awake as her overactive thoughts, she thrust the blanket off, rushed into the cabin, and stoked the stove. The dark-blue dress she slipped on felt as worked in as the pair of boy's boots she wore. Tying an apron around her waist, she perused the shelf above the dry sink. Cornmeal, gone. Mrs. Tolliver's fruit preserves, gone. Dried beans, almost gone. Flour and sugar, low. Potato bin . . .

Overflowing. Clearly Tristan had helped himself to her hospitality once again, perhaps when she'd freighted to Mr. Kellman's yesterday.

She shook her head, a smile prying its way on her lips, and

started to turn away, but the corner of some papers caught her eye. She shoved aside the bin of tubers and picked them up. Their smooth texture and lack of dust conveyed they hadn't been hidden long.

Write J. v. L. Ask about Law of the Minimum experiments

Present plan to board: plant one-third of each crop with nitrogen-enriched fertilizer, one-third with sulphuric acid treated manure . . .

She flipped to the second page.

What does too much nitrogen do to a crop?

How do you balance nitrogen, phosphorus, and potassium?

She scanned the third paper, but the foreign terms looked like art to her. At the bottom was one note of English, something about soil analysis and a device that removed carbon dioxide.

Tristan.

She stared at the words as if they would lead her to make sense of the man behind them. Despite knowing Tristan had come from an agricultural tradition, the technicality of the papers surprised her.

Turning a circle, she looked high and low, searching for anything else he might have left behind. She walked the perimeter of the main room, running a finger along the dust-free shelves, even shifting a few books to peer behind. She paused by the door to her room. Those nights he'd used her cabin as a hotel, surely he'd slept on Father's mattress in the corner of the main room. She viewed her tidied bed, small chest of drawers, desk, and wash stand. Of course it remained as she'd left it. He'd not slept in her cabin since she'd been back from Portland.

Last week at Joe's, he'd asked if God healed in proportion to the faith of the sufferer. The week before, he'd asked if God healed only those who believed in him. Tristan sowed more than seeds in a field. These questions he'd planted in her reaped a load of frustration. She'd not water those seeds today by taking him his papers. She'd drop them at Joe's, and he could pick them up at his leisure.

Then again, she'd yet to ride south in the month she'd been home. The hazelnut trees along the Duwamish River would be beautiful, their color crisp against today's blue sky.

She'd go to Tristan's. His cynicism attempted to hide what she sensed was an earnest desire for truth. And that was attractive. That, she could handle.

After eating a piece of smoked ham and a few slices of bread, she hurried to the barn to complete her chores. A nippy breeze swept through the open doors, disturbing the blue handkerchief on the hook between the stalls.

My goodness.

She whipped it off and stuffed it inside her pocket.

When she'd noticed it the morning after returning from Portland, she'd thought it had been Father's. Sentiment had kept her from removing it, and most mornings as she entered the barn she imagined him placing it there.

No wonder she hadn't recognized it. Father's? No. She was beginning to feel out of place in her own home.

Anticipating the surprise on Tristan's face when she showed up with his items, she mucked three stalls and readied Maple. If she didn't tarry at Tristan's—and why would she?—she could be back for the library meeting, post her letter to Mrs. Ford in Portland, and purchase food staples. She might even have time to check on Mrs. Hattie, whom she'd prayed for last week.

As she was about to mount, a wagon rounded the bend into the drive. A couple sat next to each other on the front seat and, Anna craned her neck to count: four children rode in back.

"Ma'am." The father tipped his hat. "Would you be Miss Warren?"

Oh, Lord. "Yes."

"We're relatives of Ben and Martha Johnson. We've heard about how you pray for people and heal them. See 'the healer,' they said."

She prays and heals. *She*, "the healer." With a slow breath, she summoned sweetness and smiled. "I pray when the Lord leads."

"Our son here"—the father jutted his head toward the back, and a boy about twelve waved one arm—"he's had a lame hand since birth . . ."

She invited them inside. The trip to Tristan's would be delayed. She didn't have time to analyze her disappointment.

Anna skirted east of town and headed south. She'd prayed with the Johnsons, and they'd left. The son's hand still appeared lame, and—God help her—she was relieved. Maybe now the townsfolk would see her as normal.

Or blame her for failure and reject her.

Anna urged Maple on, fighting back the temptation to despair and focusing instead on the trail before her. She knew the Seattle-Black River route like she knew Wesley's hymns. Large sections of farmland stretched between the tree-covered hillsides. Most of the fields had been harvested, leaving dark, churned-up dirt.

She held her breath as she approached her favorite bend where, on a clear day like today, she'd round and be greeted by the slap-in-the-face glory of Mount Rainier. Slowly, the mountain came into view, a towering white statue with a sash of evergreen across its base. Majestic. Because its Creator was majestic. *Her* Creator, the giver and sustainer of all life. The giver of gifts.

Fifteen minutes later, the mountain remaining a powerful backdrop, Anna viewed the first of Tristan's fields. His fenced pastureland had maintained its green, even this late in the season, and several brown spots indicated the grazing of horses and mules.

The road dipped, and Anna said good-bye to her mountain

view. Minutes later, she rode onto the northwest corner of Tristan's land, passing through a grove of cherry trees. She scanned the fields for signs of people, but they were empty. Faint traces of smoke spiraled from Tristan's chimney. She dismounted, secured Maple, and stepped onto the porch. The door stood ajar.

"Tristan?" The fluttering of leaves answered her call. She placed a hand on the doorjamb and leaned forward. "Tristan?"

Remembering the barn, she whirled around as if he'd emerged and caught her peeking. The doors were open, beckoning. She strode across the yard and entered. Her call was cut off as the first impression registered. Tack hung on evenly spaced pegs, organized by function. Shovels leaned against a wall, grouped by size. Two pitchforks rested against a support beam. Bundles of hay were stacked in the near corner on a raised platform, the space in front swept free of straw wisps. Buckets and kerosene lamps hung from hooks on a crossbeam, and an uncluttered table sat to the left.

Her smile blossomed. Yet another layer of Tristan revealed. No wonder Father had liked him, and she couldn't help but like him too. Maybe his orneriness was due to the pressures of harvest. Would Father have given his prized hand-carved chess set to an irritable, ungrateful boy? And he'd done just that.

"Tristan?"

Ember raised her head. Anna patted the Appaloosa, admiring the pure white coloring and dark oval spots. "Where's your master?"

Ember snorted and leaned into Anna's hand.

From behind, a wet nose pressed into her neck. She whirled to face two draft horses, their necks craned halfway across the aisle. These horses were more welcoming than the man who'd touted hospitality.

She left the barn and reentered the sunlight, shielding her eyes. Still no sign of Tristan. She walked behind the barn, where morning glories climbed the wall and bridged the distance to the neighboring storage shed. She peeked inside. Farm equipment, but no Tristan.

She returned to the front porch. She remembered Tristan strolling out of her cabin as if it were his own. And he'd been inside at least two other times since she'd been home. If Tristan could partake of her hospitality unbeknownst to her, couldn't she do the same? *People do things like this, you know*, he'd said. She pushed the door open and entered.

Her steps stuttered as she tripped on a boot. Shirts slumped over the back of a chair that was losing its stuffing. The edge of a quilt protruded from the lid of a trunk. Books and papers sprawled across a writing desk, and several pencils had rolled onto the floor. Dirty dishes remained on the table next to a rumpled tea towel.

Two doorways led off the main room. Through one, she glimpsed a bedraggled white bedspread half slung on the floor, with a pair of pants mounded at the bottom. Her face grew warm as she stared at those pants. Tristan was not prepared to offer hospitality. Perhaps she should leave.

No. She closed her eyes and pictured him straightening items in her cabin. Putting back the book like it belonged to him, replacing the silverware.

Opening her eyes, she marched to the stove, threw in some wood, and moved the kettle over the lingering warmth. While the water heated, she'd bring in the handkerchief and papers. Outside, she looked around. The fear of being caught stuck like a barb. No matter how she justified the infringement on Tristan's space, it still felt intrusive.

From her tether, Maple strained to reach grass. Her horse deserved more than dusty grass scraps. "Here, girl." She untied the golden mare and led her to the barn. "Enjoy some hospitality." She forked some hay and served a scoop of oats.

She crossed the yard with confidence this time, sailing up

the steps and ready to work. She poured warm water over the dishes and then fumbled through a cupboard for a rag. Her fingers pulled out a torn shirt scrap.

Really, Tristan?

An apron hung on a hook next to the dry sink. She sucked in a breath at the feminine large sunflowers stitched against a backdrop of white fabric. The material, soft from years of washing, folded easily in her hands. She tied the beautiful work around her body. She doubted he wore it, but even so, the wrapping of its strings around her waist seemed intimate.

She sank her hands into the dishwater and scrubbed food bits off the crusty dishes. The contrast of barn and cabin riveted her mind. A diligent farmer ruled over the barn, but the cabin was the realm of a boy struggling for independence, not knowing the difference between an apple parer and a pea sheller. No wonder Tristan succeeded as a farmer. He tidied his fields before his house.

When finished with the dishes, she situated the papers and handkerchief in the middle of the table. She scrawled a brief note, grinned at her cleverness, and hung the apron on the hook before surveying the transformation. How she'd love to be one of those stitched sunflowers and see the look on Tristan's face when he came home.

Anna retrieved Maple and grabbed the apple from her saddlebag. She was too late to make the library meeting, so she might as well make use of the trip south by visiting one of her favorite spots in the territory: twenty square feet on the edge of Tristan's land where one could see the Duwamish River in the foreground and Mount Rainier standing guard in the distance.

She circled a harvested field and passed another with corn standing high. Following the ridgeline, her eyes kept watch for the owner of this land. He had to be nearby.

Maple pushed through the trees into the opening. Anna dismounted and sat on a rock to let the beauty of the vista sink in. Down in the glen, the river snaked through tall grass and deciduous trees, some of which had lost their leaves.

A lick of breeze struck cold against the wetness of her cheeks. She withdrew Mama's rose-colored handkerchief from her pocket and pressed it against her face, imagining the lavender fragrance was Mama's and not her own.

She hadn't even known she'd been crying.

Father's passing, the unexpected healings, the desire for companionship, being called "the healer"—it all melted into one emotional strain.

Anna knew who the Healer was, and it wasn't her.

Oh, Lord. She sank to her knees, opened her hands, and let her posture do the praying.

By the time Anna returned to town, the library meeting had ended. She'd evidently missed another grand debate between Mrs. Bagley and Mrs. Maynard concerning the library's inventory, or so a woman had reported as she'd passed Anna on the street.

"Mrs. Foreman, Mrs. Mercer." She greeted the women exiting Yesler Hall.

"Anna, dear." Mrs. Mercer took her hand and squeezed. "We missed you. Our conversation might have been more exciting had you been present."

Anna smiled. "I was detained somewhere."

"Another healing?" Mrs. Mercer leaned closer.

Anna's smile evaporated. "No. I had to return something to someone."

"Well"—Mrs. Mercer cleared her throat—"how kind of you, dear. Good day." She waved at someone across the street and left Anna standing with Mrs. Foreman.

Mrs. Foreman shifted, and Anna sensed that more than the load of books she carried caused her discomfort.

"Are you well?"

"Most certainly." Mrs. Foreman laughed, glancing around. She leaned closer. "And no. I wondered if you might pray for me sometime." She'd lowered her voice as if asking for prayer was shady business.

"We could pray after church on Sunday."

Mrs. Foreman dipped her head, and Anna touched her elbow.

Worries about belonging faded with the uncomfortable way Mrs. Foreman shrugged from Anna's touch. Despite the stilted responses of others, she loved to pray for people. *Like butterflies to coneflowers*, Father had once said about her attraction to those in need.

"I'd love to pray with you."

Mrs. Foreman cleared her throat. "It's not important."

"I can come to your house if you'd rather have privacy. Small issue or not, the Lord cares."

Mrs. Foreman's lips pressed into a tight smile. "He does, doesn't he?"

Faith tunneled through her doubt, and Anna straightened. "More than—"

Mrs. Foreman gasped, her gaze caught on something behind Anna. With a twitch of a smile, she stepped away. "We'll talk later." She turned and bolted.

Was now the time to pray? Anna searched her heart for the warmth of the Spirit, but it was absent.

The Territorial University sat on top of Seattle's hill like a judge. Tristan rode up University Street toward what he hoped was a gracious ruling from the board of trustees.

"Come on, Amos." He rubbed the mule's shoulder, encouraging the sluggish animal. Ember had pulled a tendon that morning. Perfect timing. Amos abided being ridden about as much as Tristan tolerated outdated farm equipment.

Tristan stopped in front of the university. Some of Seattle's most influential men sat inside this building, waiting.

"Let's do this." He nudged Amos, who lugged across the treeless lawn like he was towing Anna's Conestoga behind him.

Four white columns stretched from the portico to the apex of the two-story building. A rounded tower crowned the impressive structure. Arthur Denny, Daniel Bagley, Thomas Mercer, and Asa Mercer had built this university as if surrounded by a city, not a fledgling town—a tribute to their dream for this frontier community.

The oversized doors groaned and swung open at his push. Tristan stopped inside the entryway. President Hall waited for him, dressed in a brown-striped suit, with his curly hair combed down. Tristan had worn his nicest clothes, a pair of wool trousers and a white shirt Lazarus had ironed, and he still looked dressed to farm compared to the flamboyance of the man before him.

"Good day, President." Tristan nodded once.

Hall greeted him with a full-fledged smile, as if he and Tristan were old schoolmates, and clapped Tristan's outstretched hand between both of his. "Tristan. Great to see you, as always."

They were waiting for him when he entered the room. Arthur Denny, formidable with his customary stare. Daniel Bagley, relaxed and pleasant. Dairyman Thomas Mercer, the man who'd named Lake Washington and Lake Union. And Dexter Horton, owner and founder of Seattle's bank.

Where was Maynard? Tristan had been counting on Doc's easygoing nature and entrepreneurial spirit to lighten what was sure to be an intense meeting.

"Tristan." Denny's voice, though not loud, commanded respect. He gestured to the same rickety chair Tristan had occupied during his first meeting with Hall.

Tristan edged onto the seat.

"John here has been telling us some of your ideas," Denny said.

Tristan glanced at Hall. "If I may"—Tristan met the eyes of each man in the room—"I'd like to outline my idea for a program."

Denny nodded. Tristan inhaled, the deep breath rattling the faint nervous sensation in his belly, and gave the overview he'd rehearsed, ending with the basic logistics. "Students will enroll in January, study for a month, and then get dirty, farming with both traditional and experimental methods. We'll finish in November after completing harvest. The school can sell the crops to support the program."

Mercer crossed one leg over the other. "You've got vision. And you're qualified. But I'll be honest—we got to get the terminus here."

Not five minutes into the meeting, and already someone had mentioned the railroad issue. Even if the Northern Pacific chose Tacoma or Olympia, Seattle promised to be a city of the future. A city of the future needed a strong university.

Denny stroked his well-trimmed beard. "Everyone has an idea of something that must be taught right now."

Tristan wasn't everyone. "Haven't I proved myself through hard work and high yields?"

"We're struggling to stay grounded with our main program."

If the trustees wanted to be grounded, how about providing a solid business foundation for the future of this town? How about feeding the community?

"Starting an agricultural program," Tristan pressed, "shows Congress we're serious about statehood, that we're planning for increased population."

Afternoon sunlight spilled through the window. The dust flecks caught the rays and seemed to dance to the annoying tick of Hall's pocket watch, which not only filled the silence but increased Tristan's sense of urgency. "The Morrill Act proves that agricultural education is essential. Schools are being founded with the purpose of teaching agriculture. Iowa State. Rutgers, Cornell, Brown. The University of California. They're all a direct result of the Morrill Act."

Denny held up a hand, and his lips twitched, which was about as close to a smile as he came. "And these schools are doing what?"

"Soil and organic plant analysis. Testing of chemical fertilizers. Studying plant nutrition and the crop and climate relationship. Some schools are engineering farming machines."

Interest sparked in Denny's eyes, and Tristan knew the businessman was thinking of investment opportunities.

Mercer cleared his throat. "Back to the issue of timing. It doesn't need to be perfect. But you would agree it should be prudent."

The interest faded from Denny's eyes as he nodded. "Sensibility dictates we wait at least a year. It's mid-October already. Entirely too late for this year."

Tristan's hope timbered. Denny was looking for the safe, profitable way above all else.

Tristan rose from his chair and paced to the window, wishing for one breath of the fresh air on the other side of the glass. "We only need a handful of students. I can provide the tools. It's important we start doing something."

"If the university could secure land, the bank might be willing to offer a loan." Horton spoke for the first time.

If . . .

"Whether we start this January, next, or even five years from now," Denny said, "what's most important is how we do what we do, not that we do something, anything. Action without planning is chaos."

Tristan had been planning for this his whole life, since his father had said, *People study philosophy and religion, why not something practical?*

What was more practical than farming?

Hall walked to Tristan and slapped him on the back as the others stood. "Well, this is a good start."

Tristan didn't want a start. He wanted action.

Chapter Eight

Tristan exited the building before the heavy ache in his spirit leaked out into an action he'd regret.

They'd taken their scythes to his vision. Not only his, but his father's.

Tristan snatched Amos's lead and led the mule down the hill to the post office. He needed to post his letter to Ronald Aitken, science professor at Rutgers. Next time Tristan met with the board, he planned to have at least five convincing letters from leading agriculturalists and scientists. He'd plunge those into their hesitant hands and then see what song they sung.

He frowned. The papers he'd wanted to give them today had disappeared. Even after searching every cranny of his cabin, he'd turned up empty handed.

Rounding the corner onto Front Street, he collided with a woman. Strands of long, feathery hair blew into his face, and he leaned back, sputtering, while reaching to steady her.

A flush blossomed on Anna's cheeks.

"Pardon, Saint." He bit his lip, not having planned to ever let that name slip. Distraction from the meeting had numbed his judgment.

"Tristan." Anna's eyes widened, and he didn't know if she was upset, surprised, or plain unhappy to see him. Likely the latter.

"Good day." She averted her gaze, stepped past, and rushed away, a fistful of skirts gathered in one hand, hair flapping in the breeze like sails of a ship.

Where was the chatty girl who'd handled his questions with the grace of a heron, albeit the noise of a gull?

Then it hit him. He'd left the papers at her cabin.

"Hey." He chased after her. "Anna."

She turned, suspicion cloaking her features.

"I left some papers at your house. I need them."

She smiled.

Finally, a sign of her customary friendliness.

"Oh?"

"Farming notes."

"I don't have them with me."

So she'd found them. "Can I stop by this afternoon?"

Her smile faltered. She shook her head. "It's not a good day."

"Tomorrow?"

"Tristan . . ."

Should he apologize for calling her Saint? Was it that big of an issue? Maybe it was his offer to come to her cabin. Understandable if she wouldn't welcome him, given the hospitality to which he'd helped himself. A few more days without them wouldn't hurt.

"Bring them to church?"

She nodded, and her smile reappeared, warm enough to heal frostbite. Almost warm enough to melt his anguish from the meeting. He put his hands on his hips. "All right, then." Since he'd misspoken already . . . "See ya, Saint. Go do a good deed."

Tristan walked off before he could see if it was possible for Anna to twist her sweet face into a scowl.

Tristan entered his house and sucked in a breath. "Hello? Lazarus?"

He dropped his wool jacket; it slid off the chair to the floor. In two strides he was at the table, where this morning, three days of dishes shouted for attention.

Someone had played servant.

The note caught his eye as he turned away: *You were right. Hospitality is a good thing. Anna.* Next to the note, his papers.

He grinned as if barley prices had doubled.

And then he panicked.

He clambered past a chair, knocking it over, and rushed into the bedroom, his heart pounding. He searched for Peter's letter.

It was in the top drawer, as he'd left it. He noted the lopsided bedspread and heaped pants. She'd left his room alone.

Returning to the main room, he surveyed his cabin. It hadn't looked this clean since . . . ever. Everything was in its place. No, not everything. His mother's apron hung askew, not on its usual hook. Anna must have worn it.

Struggling for breath, he pictured Anna with the apron snug around her small waist, saw her moving about his kitchen. Heard her singing. The ache started in his throat and expanded to his chest. He walked over and fingered the worn material. It was soft, as Anna's hair had been when it'd blown into his face.

The intimacy of such a thought throbbed. He missed his family. Missed a full house. No amount of farm work could overthrow the sense of emptiness at the end of the day.

And yet he couldn't deny the fullness resonating in his cabin tonight. He liked to believe it was the cleanliness that brought such peace, but he knew better.

Peace had stolen in on the shoulders of a brown-haired, plain-to-the-eye girl whose all-present spirit in his life was becoming harder to ignore.

Tristan sat at his desk, the light from a lantern reflecting off the glass window and illuminating the words on his paper. His sore fingers clenched the quill, and he wasn't sure he could unbend them. Two more letters. The stack beside him was growing. Three letters to congressmen, one to the Kansas State Morrill Grant Director, and another to delegate Garfielde in Olympia.

He opened a drawer and pulled out papers, yellowed and

torn. Original ideas for the Morrill Act. He studied his father's writing, as messy as his own. What would have happened if the war hadn't interrupted life? Father might be a congressman, head of the agricultural committee. No, not Father. Nothing could pull him from the fields. Father had only wanted to be part of the brainpower behind the Morrill Act, not a political enactor.

What do you want, Tristan?

The question that whispered in the dark, shut-off area of his heart slipped into the light with an occasional surprise attack.

He wanted dirty hands, blistered feet, and dried sweat on his face that tasted salty when he licked his lips.

Opportunity.

He wanted the chance to show others how to farm, as his father had shown him. Maybe he needed sons, not students.

Tightness gripped his calf muscle. Tristan stood and stretched. From the moment the sun had risen, and even after the sky had darkened, he'd bound hay. He wiggled his fingers, and the cracked skin stretched like new leather. Those bindings had etched the smell of twine into his palm.

He loved it.

He wasn't a businessman like Arthur Denny, nor an entrepreneur like Henry Yesler. He had no skill with dairy cows, like Thomas Mercer. And finance was out of the question. He couldn't manage a store, like Joe, or bind wounds, like Doc.

He couldn't heal, like Anna.

What else could he offer the world besides a day of hard work? And maybe—*please, Lord*—the equipping of others.

The image of Anna in his mother's apron barreled into his thoughts, and he wondered if he'd ever have anything to offer her. The fleeting and formless desire passed, and he half laughed. He'd already offered his skepticism, and the pity pouring from her eyes was nothing he needed.

No. Hard work was what he had to offer. Hands in the earth, coaxing life to rise heavenward. That was about it. All he needed, and all he had to give.

The third Sunday in October boasted brilliant color on the maples, partly cloudy skies, moderate temperatures, and a foul mood for Tristan. This week he harvested corn, and next week, his second harvest of potatoes, the last of his fields. He should be rejoicing that his storehouses were approaching full. Instead, irritability penetrated.

The trustees were reluctant. Lazarus pestered him about a farmers' association. And how could his mood lighten with all the comments he heard about Anna, *the healer*, every time he was in town?

Tristan turned a warning glare on Lazarus as they entered church. Laz didn't know a stranger or enemy, and Tristan didn't want him talking his way to the third pew. Lazarus grinned back, quirking an eyebrow, then commenced to greet each family they passed. Tristan kept his eyes forward, his jaw tense enough to crush a walnut.

Seating himself, he tried to calm down, but a bony finger poked his shoulder, notching up his tension again. He spun around, prepared for a fight.

"Five reasons Seattle needs a university-sponsored agricultural program." Mr. Foreman quoted the title of Tristan's first editorial, printed last Wednesday. "Strong words from a young man without much money to back them up."

Tristan leaned an arm on the back of the pew. "Those strong words are intended to educate and motivate. No backup money necessary."

"Money means influence."

Tristan smirked. Well spoken from a man with deep pockets.

"Your reasons were good though. I support your gumption." The banker smiled, lightening Tristan's mood a shade from black to dark gray. "But good isn't good enough, not when politics are involved. Money reasons are the reasons that stick."

How quickly the mood swung black again.

Mr. Foreman glanced over his shoulder toward the back of the sanctuary. "I'll tell you what. This town could use an agriculture program far more than a wacky healer."

Tristan's gut burned. He followed Mr. Foreman's gaze, though he didn't need to. He already had the subject pictured: wispy hair that waved down her back like ripened wheat, a smile that outshone the sun, soft eyes.

What was he, Wordsworth? *Back to earth, Tris.*

Anna laughed, and the sound lilted through the church. Her brown skirt and simple green blouse brought to mind the moss-covered stump north of his house. The stump that refused to be uprooted.

He feared the same with Anna.

Ridiculous. He hadn't feared coming west, nor when an early frost nipped his harvest the first year. He wasn't fearing a five-foot-six-inch woman, even if her tender spirit drove a spear through his defenses.

His eyes narrowed as he looked to Mr. Foreman, but the man had started another conversation. His gaze strayed back to Anna. She smiled at him.

He could have smacked himself for the grin that pulled his lips up in return. She wheedled more out of him than he wanted to give. Maybe next year he could hire her to try her magic on his bean crop, his worst producer this year.

When the music started, he dragged himself up, hymnbook in hand. Two stanzas in, her clear voice pealed above the others. No one sang hymns like Peter and Anna. Pain cut a slow path through him, and he dropped his head as tightness strained his eyes. He missed Peter.

How much more must Anna miss him?

Yet, whenever they were together, all Tristan cared about was defending himself against her gentleness. *What a selfish nut you are.*

"Welcome to the house of the Lord." The blacksmith's voice resounded powerful as his mallet. He waved a sheet of paper. "I want to share an answer to prayer. Some of you met my brother and his family when they visited. His oldest son has had a lame hand since birth. Miss Warren prayed with them, but nothing happened at the time." He waved the letter again. If his smile widened any more, it would stretch off his face. "That boy is now reporting movements in two of his fingers."

Mumbled amens swept the congregation along with a few gasps and a solo "hallelujah." Tristan forced himself not to stare at Anna like the rest of the members surely did.

Three healings, and she'd been back a month.

He closed his eyes, each breath a weight against his throat. He'd only ever asked for one healing in his twenty-two years, and he'd been denied.

Since that first Sunday after Julia's healing, Anna made sure to veer from Clyde Foreman's path. This morning after Mr. Johnson's announcement, Mr. Foreman had deflated her Sabbath joy with one look.

Tristan hadn't looked at all. The only person not to turn her direction. What a stiff neck.

Though she didn't like the curiosity or excitement spurred by the healings, she could live with the whispers, questions, and odd looks. She couldn't live with the open hostility of Mr. Foreman. And Reverend Bagley's silence percolated her fear. Why wasn't he addressing the issue? Did he disapprove?

She exited the church to find the morning's scattered clouds had thickened into a gray shield. The gloominess darkened the water from blue to slate. A kingfisher flew overhead, royal with its yellow beak, puffed chest, and gigantic wingspan. Anna warmed at the sight, and a speckle of her lost joy returned.

Lorna stepped beside her, wrapping her cloak tight around her petite frame. "Are you coming to the library meeting this week?"

"I plan to."

Lorna's blue eyes searched Anna's, a quiet summons Anna couldn't ignore. "Are you okay?"

"I'm fine." Lorna's defensive tone betrayed her words.

"Would you like to go for a walk?"

"I've got to serve and sing for the noon meal."

Anna reached over and squeezed her hand. "We'll talk some other time."

But even as she watched Lorna hurry down Madison toward Conklin House, the likelihood of an intimate conversation with her seemed slim. Anna had yet to find that common ground with the beautiful singer.

"That girl's a mystery."

Anna twirled to see Nellie squinting after Lorna and wondered at the glint in her friend's eyes. "It's permissible to have secrets."

Nellie drew back. "Of course. It's . . . sometimes I wonder what she really does."

Condemnation overshadowed Nellie's words, and Anna bristled. Just because Conklin House had a salty reputation didn't mean Lorna participated in the saltiness.

A scuffle erupted in the back of the Simms' wagon. Nellie sighed. "An hour of sitting still, and now this tomfoolery." She patted Anna's arm and headed for the wagon.

"Miss Warren!"

Mrs. Foreman descended the church steps with such pounding Anna feared she'd punch a hole through the old wood and end up head over heels with her skirts in the air. She all but ran across the yard, an awkward image. The banker's wife didn't seem the type to push the limits of propriety.

"I'm glad I caught you." The woman gasped a breath, her broach jiggling on her collar. "Please excuse my husband's grouchiness. He doesn't mean anything personal. The pressure of becoming a new partner at the bank—"

"Mrs. Foreman, it's all right."

"Oh." Mrs. Foreman gasped, her eyes closing, hand placed across her chest as if to stem off heart pains. When she opened her eyes, she smiled. "That's wonderful to hear. You know we've been in Seattle four months, and I'd hate to make a negative impression when we're starting to feel settled. I've been asked to organize the new quilting circle. That is, after Mrs. Mercer saw the quilts I'd made, she insisted I recommence the group."

Anna dismissed the disappointment that sought to commandeer her heart. Of course the friendly and cultured Mrs. Foreman would root into the center of Seattle society after only four months.

She fought for gracious words. "People here are forgiving. If you reach out to them, they'll reach back." Or so she encouraged herself.

She waited for Mrs. Foreman to invite her to the circle, but instead Mrs. Foreman leaned forward. "I saw you and Mr. Riley at the bakery the other day."

If there was a problem with that, Anna didn't know what it could be. "We enjoy a meal together when he chances to be in town."

"I don't think there's any chance about it."

Anna shifted her feet and stepped back, ready to politely excuse herself, but the solemn look on Mrs. Foreman's face froze her retreat. Perhaps the woman was ready for that prayer she'd been hesitant to ask for.

"I wish we could have met your father," Mrs. Foreman said.

Anna's heart squeezed.

"We've heard great things about him." Pity washed over

Mrs. Foreman's face. "It's wonderful you're allowed to stay in that cabin now that he's gone."

That cabin, as in my *cabin?* But of course. Why would—

A branch snapped, and Anna whipped her head around. Tristan mounted Ember, his gaze scrutinizing. Was everything she did, even talking with a churchgoer, going to be questioned by this farmer?

Anna turned back to Mrs. Foreman. "Actually, the cabin and land are mine. Mr. Wyse assured me women can inherit."

"Dear, have you not heard the rumor?"

The way Mrs. Foreman looked around and hesitated to meet her eyes slit the clouds of fear wide open within Anna.

"My husband heard that your father left the land to someone else."

Anna stared at the woman while the rumor registered. Sudden relief dissolved her apprehension, and she giggled. "No. I'm sure that's incorrect."

"If I were you, I'd look into it. I wouldn't want to find myself without a place to be this winter. You let us know if you need any help."

Sure. "Thank you for your concern. I'll stop by Mr. Wyse's tomorrow." The whole idea was preposterous.

"Yes, do that." Mrs. Foreman patted her arm and hurried away.

Anna walked up the hill, a smile still tickling her lips at the absurd things that became rumors. She glanced up, startled to see Tristan watching her from atop Ember. She tilted her head, girding her heart for his questions. *How many people have you healed since I saw you on Friday?* or *Is the miracle worker enjoying her Sabbath?* Or—her heart stopped as she remembered his cabin. *What gave you the right to come into my cabin and do my dishes?*

She squirmed beneath his inspection and then hurried past him to the path toward home.

It *was* her home, wasn't it?

She traipsed on, cringing as the sound of hooves followed. That he'd follow her without speaking or announcing why seemed so characteristic of him she could laugh, except the silence weighed heavy. She turned to face him, skirts twirling wide and rustling against the ferns. "How did harvest go?"

"High yields. Weather held nicely." He focused straight ahead. "I need it to hold one more week."

It seemed late to still be harvesting. "Then you're done?"

A cross between a grunt and a laugh came from him. "A farmer's never done." He pulled the reins, holding back the eager horse. "Then I store for winter, sell my surplus, perfect my fertilizer blend, sharpen and repair tools, decide which new products to try next year. Keep up with chores." He brushed a twig off his shirt. "And in my spare time, I've got to talk some sense into the leadership at the university."

"No luck?"

"They're worried about start-up costs, acquiring the land, though that—"

He cut himself off and swung down from Ember with such speed Anna wrenched back to avoid getting stepped on. Her foot caught on a root, and she steadied herself as he faced her, eyes assessing her like crows stalking corn.

"Mrs. Johnson's nephew can move his fingers?" Tristan spit out the first thing that came to mind, anything to change the subject.

"This morning was the first I'd heard." She squared her shoulders.

Everything about her was square, honest, down to earth. From the genuine joy that lit her eyes to the fear he'd seen flicker across her face when Mrs. Foreman had mentioned that rumor.

"No generous thank-you letter from the indebted family?"

"Thanks is due God." She eyed him in a failed attempt to look stern. "Healing is cause for celebration, not skepticism."

"It's cause for something." He started walking, leading Ember behind.

He heard the swish of skirts as Anna hastened after him.

"What vexes you so much about healing?" The swishing stopped, and her small intake of breath found his ears. "Or is it me?"

Flinging both hands out to the sides, he turned and locked eyes with her. "Saint, you don't have to try so hard to be liked. You're likable. Like a sunny day in January." He had the poetic muse going today. "Even when you're angry."

Uncertainty rimmed her wide eyes. "What about Mr. Foreman?"

"Mr. Foreman is a power-hungry man on a mission."

"What has that to do with me?"

Did she truly not know? "You have a strong faith. The peace about you is powerful. People are drawn to that, which can be threatening to some."

She shook her head. "Nothing about me is powerful. I'm . . ." Her brow tightened. "Compassionate, and I like to talk."

She saw herself as a weak, chatty gal who liked others. Incredible. He saw so much more. "Don't mind Clyde. You've got to get over trying to please everyone."

Her mouth gaped, and she stepped back. "I do not try to please everyone."

He bit back a laugh. "Say what you want. My sister denied her pleaser instincts as well, but we knew the truth."

She stilled, and he regretted the slip. He'd never talked of anything personal since his move west. Except with Peter.

Tristan marched forward, Ember in tow, and held his breath, waiting for her to move the conversation on, to come up with a way to nudge him spiritually. He'd welcome one of her theological slaps.

"Is your sister older or younger?"

He released the air, and also his hope to avoid family talk. "Older. And I was never allowed to forget it."

Anna drew alongside and peered up at his face. He knew he'd see expectancy if he made eye contact with her, which he didn't.

"My brothers bossed her around, and she bossed me around. The sibling chain of command, I guess." Noticing how she rushed to keep up, he slowed his steps. "One time my mother asked my brothers to polish the dining room table. They shrugged it off on my sister, and of course she agreed in order to please them. But then she told me to do it. I didn't know what polish was, so I went to the barn, found the ligament, and rubbed it all over the table."

"Oh." Anna's gasp ushered out his grin.

"I'm sure you know what happened." He glanced over at her.

She shook her head. "I have no memories of noisy evenings or sibling arguments."

"Mother made my brothers fix it, and we all laughed about it later over a game of marbles."

Light sparked in her eyes. "You played games as a family?" She said it as if he'd had a privileged childhood.

"Marbles, jacks, string games, checkers, trivia."

"Your mother must have had her hands full."

He'd never paid enough attention to how hard his mother had worked. Never cared about how his mother was first to rise and last to go to bed. The fields had called him, and he'd answered. He should have answered more to the needs of his mother.

He breathed deep, unable to get enough air to quell the dizziness. "Hey"—his voice sounded too cheery—"I should thank you for doing my dishes."

"I let Maple lounge in your barn and munch oats. I suppose

that's payment enough."

"Nah, that's hospitality."

The width of her smile surprised him.

"Your barn is like a work of art. I've never seen such organization, though I did notice a misplaced shovel. And there's not even a usual barn aroma. It smells like chopped cedar . . . or wildflowers."

If Lazarus had left his shovel—

His barn smelled like wildflowers? What type of nonsense was she rambling? His mouth pulled into a grin. "You're exaggerating."

"Maybe. But compared to that house of yours. Dirty dishes. Papers and books scattered like weeds. Dust taking up residence like field mice. I mean, you didn't even pick up your clothes."

He stopped walking and stared at her until the flush started up her face.

"I . . ." She fumbled with a thread on her sleeve. "Didn't your mama teach you to pick up after yourself?"

His mama *had* taught him better, and thanks to Anna for reminding him. He frowned, biting the inside of his lip until the pain matched the angst inside.

Tristan's hard countenance restricted her breath, and Anna struggled to maintain an even expression. The relaxed conversation seemed to be over, thanks to her prattling about his clothes. She could apologize, but what would she say? *I'm sorry you're so messy. I'm sorry to have availed myself of your hospitality.*

She wasn't. She was just sorry she'd compared the aroma of his workspace to a meadow in full bloom. Sorry she'd referred to his crumpled clothes. Entirely inappropriate.

She looked up, seeking his gaze, but he swung onto Ember. "Tristan—"

"You freighting this week?" He focused ahead. "Green Lake? Coal Creek?"

Did it matter to him? She didn't need anyone managing her schedule, or escorting her home, for that matter. Tristan had made it his mission not only to probe her spiritually, but evidently, to play watchdog.

"Tuesday." She sighed, not wanting to admit how nice it was to have someone know her plans.

He tipped his head as if pondering something, then nodded. "Good day, Saint." He turned Ember and rode toward Seattle, moving with his horse, relaxed and self-assured.

He flustered her every attempt to understand him. Just when she thought she'd achieved a sort of camaraderie with him, he shut that door with a frown. Father must have looked past Tristan's moodiness. He'd had such long conversations with Tristan, enough that she'd once taken a nap in the wagon. And Father had made frequent stops at Tristan's homestead if they happened to be passing.

Strange. Her business-minded father had suspended his work to converse with Tristan. Why had she not realized the peculiarity of this before?

Tristan's heart climbed into his throat, pounding in time with Ember's hooves as his mare traversed the meadowed shortcut.

Where had Mr. Foreman heard that bit of news about Anna's land? It didn't matter. That news was trouble. A kindhearted Anna healed people. But a curious Anna . . . He imagined a path of questions and actions that would wreak havoc on his plans.

Give her the letter.

Not yet.

An urge to pray slipped into his heart, and a wordless

entreaty swelled in his mind. He gritted his teeth and slowed Ember, coming back to the road. He made appearances at church to honor his mother and heritage, but he was done with prayer.

Which was why this push and pull in his heart infuriated him. Eventually, something would snap.

Chapter Nine

Anna took the cookie Mrs. Tolliver offered and set it down on her plate before gently lifting her cup and sipping the steaming liquid. Tea with the warmhearted Mrs. Tolliver, the woman who could stand up to a grizzly or nurture a sick hummingbird, had become a regular occurrence Anna refused to miss.

Anna set her cup on its saucer. "The rumor is all over town."

"I've heard."

On Monday, Anna had gone to Mr. Wyse's office. Still locked and empty, and no one knew his expected return date. What everyone *did* know was the issue concerning her land. Her initial laughter at the outrageous idea that Father had left the land to someone else had subsided, and in its place a trail of questions had kept her mind trekking half the night.

"It can't be." She spoke the line that had circled her thoughts relentlessly.

"Child, stranger things have been true. Maybe he thought you didn't need acres of woods and fields."

"But I need somewhere to live." Anna traced the gold rim of her cup, which was moist and warm from the tea. "Besides, it's not the land. It's the place." The place where Father's memory cocooned her.

"He didn't plan to have a stroke. He probably assumed by the time he journeyed on you'd be married. That is, if he did leave the land to someone else."

"Father *was* generous." But still, she couldn't fathom him giving their land away. Not without telling her.

"No one has asked you to leave your cabin?"

"No. And Mr. Wyse never said anything when we first met.

Surely he would have." Anna set her cup down and rubbed her hands together.

Her copy of the seventh edition of *Grimm's Fairy Tales* sat untouched on the table. She wasn't in the mood to talk wolves, witches, and morals, as was their custom, not when she was in the midst of her own mystery. She tapped her fingernails on the unopened book. "It makes no sense."

Last night she'd stood on the porch, wrapped in her buffalo skin, staring into the black woods. She could no more make out the animal skittering in the bushes than the source of this rumor. But she knew one thing. Father had integrity. Secrecy wasn't his way.

Tristan, on the other hand, hid within secrecy like a knight behind armor. Each conversation between them seemed laden with things held back, things hidden. Though, she couldn't fault him for being born reserved, same as he couldn't fault her for being born with a knack for chatter—even when that urge to ramble embarrassed her, as it had the other day.

"Suppose it were true . . ." Anna voiced the what-if that seemed absurd to even consider. "Who would he have left it to?" Her mind scrolled through their list of acquaintances and clients and came up with nothing.

She lifted the cup again to her mouth and swigged. An image of a middle-aged couple flitted into her mind, and she choked. Liquid seeped out the side of her mouth and dribbled onto her dress. She lunged for her napkin. "Mr. and Mrs. Wilton."

"Who?" Mrs. Tolliver handed her another cloth, and Anna wiped at the front of her dark calico.

"Three years ago a couple from San Francisco were visiting Seattle. I don't know how Father met them, but they wanted to buy our property."

Mrs. Tolliver frowned. "Whatever for?"

"Science, I think. They were studying herbs and medicine.

Father rejected their offer, and they left." She fidgeted with the wet napkin. "I'll send them a letter." Anna scooted back her chair and set her napkin on the table, her glance roaming to Mrs. Tolliver's corner desk and the letter-writing supplies stacked neatly.

"You're anxious, dear." Mrs. Tolliver's hand rested on Anna's.

Anna forced her hand to relax and offered a tight smile. "I'm confused."

Mrs. Tolliver raised a wrinkled brow.

"All right, I'm confused and anxious. I'm going to write that letter tonight, before I even know where to send it."

"Your father was taken with their vision?"

He'd been curious, but *taken* would be too strong a word. "It's the only lead I have." The cabin was her anchor for remaining in Seattle. If that were taken away . . .

The thought that had lingered in the shadows of her mind slipped to the front and fortified itself, begging to be spoken. Tested out loud. Anna's lip trembled. "I'm not sure I belong here."

Mrs. Tolliver drew back her hand from atop Anna's, and her elbow bumped her teacup, rattling it on the saucer. "Nonsense."

"People are fascinated because of the miracles. Or mad. I never get a normal *How do you do?* The other day at Joe's, I couldn't even join a discussion on bread recipes, because as soon as the women saw me, they issued suggestions for who needed my prayers. They were making a schedule for me without even asking, and I only wanted to know why my bread wasn't rising as it should."

"Human nature." Mrs. Tolliver grunted and brushed strands of pepper-colored hair from her brow. "If people aren't doubting the supernatural, they're trying to get a glimpse of it."

Or trying to manipulate it.

Anna paced to the window. "I'm simply obeying the stirring of the Spirit to pray. It's nothing more complex than that." She drew a line through the condensation beading along the bottom of the pane. "Can't people trust the Lord enough to believe He wants to heal?"

"It's more than trust, Anna. This is the age of reason."

Anna spun around. "Is it not reasonable to expect a great God to do great things?"

Mrs. Tolliver's cackle ended with a cough. "No, dear. People want logic. Unless, of course, they're hurting. Then they want a miracle." She poured more tea and motioned to Anna. "Drink."

Anna sat, but the allure of tea had fled. Not even the hominess of Mrs. Tolliver's cabin—lavender curtains, a wall of bird paintings, and shelf of books—could ease the threat of failure that mocked her calm.

Oh, for the spunk of Mrs. Tolliver, who'd chosen to remain on her own after her husband had died. Stepping onto that boat outside of Portland, Anna had expected she'd have such tenacity. How then had a crisis of faith and a rumor defeated her? Here she sat with a woman who drank an herbal concoction for her aches and then traipsed outside to chop wood.

Then there was Tristan, the embodiment of perseverance and diligence. But even those qualities couldn't mask his bleak spirit, a dreariness that clung to Anna long after he'd left her presence.

"Tristan is so skeptical."

Mrs. Tolliver's cup paused midway to her lips.

Anna bit the inside of her mouth, not delighting how Tristan had woven his way into her thoughts. Not just his questions, but his pensive stare, brooding eyes. Now he'd managed to embarrass her without being present. Her eyes lifted to Mrs. Tolliver's, and Anna felt her blush deepen.

"I feel like I'm God's lawyer, defending why He heals or doesn't."

"Child, God defends Himself."

Then He had much to stand up for where Tristan was concerned. "I wish I knew why God is using me and not someone else."

"Do you need to know?" Mrs. Tolliver reached again and clasped Anna's hands. "Or is obedience enough?"

Anna closed her eyes, remembering the moment at Tristan's Mount Rainier lookout with her hands open. Obedience was enough, but how far would her surrender have to stretch?

Anna strolled south along Front Street later that afternoon, taking in the beauty of Elliott Bay. Ships crammed together along the wharves, waves lapping at their sides. White clouds floated above, pushed by a strong breeze, and she imagined the Spirit pushing her, taking her places, whether she felt ready or not.

"What kind of amazing things are going on inside that head of yours?" interrupted a cheery male voice.

Anna shifted her attention forward and smiled as Michael approached, dark hair jutting all directions from beneath his brown wool cap.

No doubt he'd think her silly for making a spiritual analogy from clouds. "It's Thursday. How come you're not at the camp?"

When he reached her, he reversed directions and shortened his strides to match hers. "I've got work to do, and it's not logging."

"Oh?"

"The Lord's work." The smile that so comfortably dressed his face deepened. "I've been looking for you all week."

Pleasure coursed through her and sweetened some of the earlier frustration she'd felt at Mrs. Tolliver's.

"You going to tell me where you've been?"

"All over. I went to Green Lake yesterday." Four day trips in a row. She'd missed Mrs. Foreman's birthday tea, and she'd probably been the only woman in Seattle not in attendance.

"I must admit I'm surprised you're still freighting."

"Really?" She squinted against the bright afternoon sun. What was she supposed to do, sit at home and knit? "I promised myself to keep a light schedule." She stopped walking and studied what seemed to be displeasure in his eyes. Why did he care if she freighted? "When I was in Portland, I missed the travel. The miles of quiet." She resumed walking. "Many times, it was just us, the woods, the birds, and the squirrels."

"And the Lord."

She stopped again and faced him. "Yes, the Lord. Exactly."

Michael seemed to understand, and the camaraderie warmed her heart.

"Anna, are you sure about freighting? It's . . ."

"A man's job?"

Michael held up his hands. "No. I wasn't thinking that."

"Freighting's what I've known. I like it. I'm good at it. I feel needed when I do it."

"You are needed, but not with freighting." Michael rubbed his forehead. "Pardon me. I'm getting ahead of myself."

He nudged her shoulder, and they continued down Front Street. At the intersection with Skid Row, he veered them toward Maynard's Point, away from the chaos of Yesler's log-covered hillside.

"I was looking for you," he said, "because I have a proposition."

Whoa. Even if he did seem to understand her desire to walk with Jesus and follow Him, she didn't want to hear talk of propositions from a man she hardly knew. She needed a friend, not advice. Time to retreat from his forwardness and learn more about him. "I think you promised to tell me your Jonah story."

He laughed and led her toward the water. "Shall we walk by the shore?"

She nodded and followed him onto the tidal flats.

Michael reached down and picked up a shell, rubbing it between two fingers. "I was eleven when I made a commitment to Christ." He squatted and drew in the wet sand with the broken clam shell. "Already I'd planned to become a banker. It wasn't something I'd thought about but something I knew I would do." Michael's eyes danced as he looked up at her. "I wasn't going to turn down good money."

He dropped the shell, tipped over a rock, and picked up a coin-sized crab. Its tiny legs clawed the air. "During the war, everything changed."

"You fought?"

"No. But for a boy on the verge of manhood, the world seemed so chaotic, out of control. I was scared to walk from our home to the bank. I was scared the bank would be robbed, burned . . . something."

He handed the crab to her, and she smiled as it crawled a ticklish path across her palm.

He rescued the crab from falling off her hand and set it down. It scrambled into the safety of a nearby pool. "One night, looking at the stars, trying to make sense of why people were killing each other, I heard God say to me, 'Michael, tell these people of my love.'"

Anna's breath stuttered. "You actually heard his voice?"

"His whisper, yes."

"But you ran." That must be the Jonah part.

"No. I said, 'Yes, Lord, I will tell them.' Then the war ended. My father returned to rebuild his business, and I got caught in the frenzy. I worked alongside him, and he was proud of me. I ignored the call to ministry. I had a duty to my family. I had to think of my future." He grinned at her. "That's when I ran."

"But why did you leave if you wanted to help your family?"

He stared at the algae-covered rocks by their feet. Lines

creased his forehead. "I fought with my father. I thought he'd demand my loyalty to the family, but he wanted me to go to seminary. He said if I was going to disobey the Lord, to do it somewhere else, not in Kansas. So I left—because by then I thought I might have made up the call from God. Nothing seemed certain anymore."

Anna covered her mouth, but not before a chuckle slipped out. "Your father took God's side and pushed you out?"

Michael's solemnity broke, and he laughed, freeing her to do the same. "Yeah. But the Lord has given me another chance, and I want you to help me."

Anna's smile faded. "How?"

"I want to start preaching. I don't want to wait for seminary. People are dying now."

The curled ends of Michael's hair waved in the breeze, out of place. He shifted his eyes from the water to hers. Those soft blue orbs glowed. "Let's hold a revival. We'll call people to truth. We'll heal them. You've got that power."

A warning surged into her chest like a too-quick gulp of steaming liquid. Who was man to claim the wisdom and power to heal? She didn't have all her questions answered, but her belief in God's sovereignty remained solid. The power to heal was His alone.

A sigh shivered through her as she sidestepped a puddle. "Excuse me a moment." Waves foamed over the rocks, reaching inland, and she walked to meet them, seeking a moment's solace from Michael's intensity. His footsteps behind her erased that hope.

"Anna." He came around front of her. "Did I say something wrong? Forgive me."

He ran a hand through his hair, an action that made her think of a certain farmer who had already caused her one slip of tongue that day.

"I want to proclaim truth, that's all. And I sense the same

passion in you." Michael searched her eyes.

She smiled, but her lips felt tight. Turning, her gaze sought the opposite shore. The land on the far side pulled at her, and a curiosity for the other side, a longing to be there and experience what seemed just out of reach, filled her.

A revival might be such a journey, an adventure. Even if she couldn't accept Michael's statement that she had a power, she would admit God had gifted her. And with the displays of enthusiasm and persuasion she'd seen from Michael, God had definitely gifted him as well.

What would their gifts be like together?

If God had used her in three healings since she'd been back, what would He do at a revival where people actively sought Him?

Obedience is enough, she'd told Mrs. Tolliver not even an hour ago. "I'll come and pray. But, Michael . . ." She turned back to him. He poked the toe of his shoe in a clam hole and watched the water squirt out. "A gift. That's all I have." His gaze lifted to hers. "A gift God uses when He wants. The power is all His."

He held her gaze while he jumped across the pool and came to stand next to her. "Where is your faith, Anna?"

The gentleness of his tone and his smile conveyed approval, not condemnation, as one might take his words. Heat rippled through her heart. "Right where it should be, in Jesus Christ."

His laughter rolled from deep inside. She wasn't sure what to think of this man who changed from somberness to petition to laughter quicker than an exposed crab clambered under a rock.

And she felt like that crab. Chased down by Michael's friendship and eagerness, which was what she wanted, right?

He took her arm and led her back toward town. "We'll wait a week or so. Make sure all the farmers finish their harvesting. We can set up a tent, build a platform."

"The revival will take place outside? It'll be November by then."

"There's not a big enough building. We'll set up fire pits around the tent. People will dress warm. It's always a good time to be saved."

"I suppose." Trying to hold back the fervor within Michael would be like trying to keep the tide from coming in.

"I've talked with ministers in Auburn, Tacoma, Olympia, Port Townsend, and everywhere in between."

Had he mentioned her by name? Advertised her as the healer? Heaven forbid. "I'm praying, Michael." She eyed him. "Remember, that's all."

The excitement in his grin swelled over her, and she feared she'd already been washed out to sea.

Chapter Ten

Michael Riley's "Come to Jesus" Meetings.

The canvas sign stretched between two trees. Anna grinned. A simple *Revival* would have sufficed.

"It's a great sign. Don't you love it?" Michael's exuberance pushed the boundaries of humility . . . but in an endearing, boyish sort of way.

"No one can accuse you of doing something halfheartedly."

He cuffed her gently on the shoulder, a gesture that had become familiar the past weeks as they'd met to discuss the meetings. She bit her lip at the thought he cherished her—for some reason, a feeling more disconcerting than wonderful.

The revival had given the people of Seattle something new to talk about. If only she could shut the issue of her land out of her mind as quickly as they had. She'd meandered by Mr. Wyse's every day in hopes that the lawyer would materialize and put her heart at rest.

"Anna?"

Michael had spoken, and she'd missed his words. "I'm sorry. What?"

"Have a seat while we discuss tomorrow night." Michael gestured to the benches lined beneath the tent. "Here's the plan. Mrs. Tolliver's going to play some hymns on the piano—"

"Piano?" This was a new development.

"Of course. There's got to be music. The boys will bring the instrument out from Hermit's in the morning."

The saloon owners lending their piano to the revival?

Hopefully it wouldn't be their only representative.

"After Mrs. Tolliver plays, you'll give an opening prayer."

She bolted from the bench. "In front of everyone?"

"Yes, Miss Warren. In front of lots and lots of everyones."

"But I'm—"

"Don't say just a woman." He stood and drew close. "We're all one in Christ."

She shook her head. "I agreed to pray with individuals, not push the limits of propriety by praying over an entire congregation."

"Think of the Lord and what He wants you to do."

Despite the slight manipulation of his words, Michael's grin and the brightness of his eyes persuaded her. Michael believed in her. And she believed the Lord wanted her to help Michael. Where did that leave her? She conceded with a smile and a sigh.

"I will then give a convicting message about God's grace, after which a flood of people will rush forward to renounce sin and surrender to our great Master."

He had a fairy-tale revival all planned. She wished, for his sake, at least some would respond to his invitation, but she couldn't fathom a flood of people attending, much less, surrendering.

"You, dear Anna"—he took her hand—"will be available to pray with people up front."

"All right. I can pray."

His laugh barked out, surprising her. He squeezed her hand. "Yes, you certainly can pray." He started whistling "Amazing Grace" as he turned to leave. "I've got some things to do. See you tomorrow."

Anna reached for his arm. "Michael, you're thinking these meetings will last only a week?" The way he acted, he could be planning a lifetime of tent ministry on the hillside of Seattle. She'd read Father's accounts of Charles Finney's meetings: weeks of preaching, businesses closing so people could attend, people falling prostrate. Michael carried the same enthusiasm Father had described of Finney.

Maybe she shouldn't have agreed to this.

Michael grinned. "We'll see how the Lord leads. The second evening, God willing, there'll be someone able to give a testimony of healing."

Fear twined through her, and she groaned. "Michael. I'm praying. That's all. We don't know what God has planned."

"I said God willing." Something intense and intimate glistened in his eyes. His voice softened, along with the lines around his mouth. "God willing . . ." He took her hand, encasing it between both of his, and placed it against his heart.

Was he repeating himself or starting a new thought?

"Anna, God has great work for us. I do hope you know how honored I am that you would join me."

His words were getting too personal. "I'm only helping." The shift in Michael and the talk of *us* was about as comfortable as a day's ride in the rain.

His eyes narrowed. "You're beautiful, you know that?"

She took a deep breath. Time to regain control and shut down this enamored side of Michael.

He lifted her hand toward his lips, but she yanked it away and stepped back. "You . . . you mentioned things to do."

His intensity dried up, and the liveliness she'd come to adore returned with a lopsided grin. "That I did. Good-bye, for now." He tipped his hat, resumed his whistling, and walked away.

She rubbed the back of her palm, remembering his breath warm on her skin, as she studied his sign. The letter strokes were strong. The red coloring bold. That was Michael's way, and even if it made her wary of his personal attention, anticipation hitched itself to her heart. Michael was right. God had great things to do.

"Michael Riley's *Come to Jesus* meetings."

Tristan's voice punctured her thoughts.

She wheeled and looked him in the eye. "Are you coming?"

"Coming to the meetings or coming to Jesus?" His grin masked the cynicism she knew simmered beneath and waited to spew like a geyser.

"Both, I suppose." Both, she prayed.

"Not likely, and . . . not sure."

His sharp gaze circled her like a hawk.

"I hope you do. Both."

She left him, walking down the gentle slope on her way to the smithy where Maple was getting shod. For a moment, she was alone, her footsteps the only footsteps crunching the dirt. Then she heard his heavy footfall come after her, and her heart struck a hard rhythm.

She spoke over her shoulder, not liking how he trailed behind her when she knew he could catch her easily. "I heard Lazarus has a cough. I missed seeing him in church on Sunday."

"He's fine."

As always, a man of many words. She slowed, forcing him to come alongside her. Though she felt his gaze on her, she didn't return it.

"You offering to come pray for him?"

His reference to healing tempted her to banter. She wouldn't engage today. Her mind overflowed with thoughts of the revival, and on the heels of that, her land. No room for Tristan's negativity or a bristling discussion.

Keeping her head down, she pressed on toward the livery. How like Tristan to trail along without an obvious purpose. That was what made him intimidating.

Laughter intervened and snatched her attention. Samuel Walters, fresh back from San Francisco, and Alice Derrick were the picture of fellowship, sitting outside Matthias's. They'd lived the normal frontier life, learned under Catherine Blaine's tutelage, dug clams on the beach, and played hoops along Front Street. All the while, Anna had ridden about in a wagon, studied by lantern light, and laced her brown work boots in the cool of morning.

She'd begged Father to allow her to attend Mrs. Blaine's classes. She'd gone three times, not that Father was to blame. They'd lived a nomadic life, plain and simple.

"Old friends of yours?"

Tristan's question jarred her thoughts. She'd forgotten his presence, ironic since nothing about him was easily ignored. "People I grew up . . ." How could she finish her sentence and say *with*? ". . . knowing." She snuck another glance toward the couple.

"You don't have to be suspicious about everyone's attitude toward you."

She blinked, looking up at him. That kind of insight wasn't what she expected from him. She hated how it made her feel exposed. "I'm not suspicious." Cautious, discerning, realistic. She loved others, cared that they loved her back.

The twosome glanced over as Tristan and she passed. Anna returned their waves, unsure if recognition or mere politeness brightened their countenances. What reason would they have to remember the quiet girl who'd hardly shown up at community events?

Same reason Tristan had for finding her company interesting: none. And yet he appeared at odd times, pestered her, showed concern for her, and left behind squirrely feelings that wrestled within her.

She felt those feelings swirl, and her thoughts stammered for distraction. "Who is J. v. L.?"

Tristan remained silent, and she looked over at him.

"On your notes, the ones you left at my house."

He ran a hand through his dark hair, winced, and brushed out some dirt. "Justus von Liebig, a professor from Germany. He established the world's first major school of chemistry."

Chemistry. How lucky she'd steered the conversation toward something so . . . boring. Once she'd had a conversation with Tristan about nitrogen. His eyes had blazed as he'd spouted the science behind new farming techniques. Such excitement she'd hardly seen in anyone. And all because of nitrogen.

She fortified herself for another such occasion. "Do you know him?"

Tristan laughed, a happy and relaxed sound that sent Anna's heart leaping. Maybe chemistry wasn't such a bad subject after all.

"No. I've never been to Germany." He grinned. "I've read his writings. My father wrote to him, and he wrote back. Von Liebig created this five-bulb device that uses a potassium hydroxide solution to remove carbon dioxide. It's incredible."

She had no idea what he was talking about, and hoped the wideness of her eyes didn't give away her ignorance.

"He's all about soil analysis and finding the mineral component within soil that's least present. It's called the Law of the Minimum. A plant's growth is hindered by the one essential mineral in shortest supply, usually nitrogen, which is why manufactured fertilizers are going to be the thing of future farming."

She stared, not realizing she'd stopped walking, until he paced back toward her. She'd never heard him speak so many sentences at once.

"Impressive, huh?"

Yes, he was. Aside from his spirituality, nothing about him was lackadaisical.

"Have you ever wanted to go to a university? Study chemistry?"

The skin around his eyes tightened into a scowl. "I'd rather have my hands in the dirt."

"But you care about science and agricultural improvement."

"Yep."

He started walking again, and she rushed to be next to him, not wanting to miss an expression on his face. "Why don't you want to study more?"

"I do study. All the time."

Tristan was a mystery, one begging to be understood, but a mystery so delicate that if touched, might disintegrate like the wings of a dried-out moth. What wasn't nearly so fragile was the realization that she wanted to touch that mystery, finger the conundrum right out of him.

Tristan's brows drew together, and she felt herself flush as he caught her examining him.

A hint of amusement shadowed his dark eyes. "The people in my family are doers, Saint."

His nickname for her rolled off his tongue like they'd been childhood chums—as if she'd had the benefit of such friends.

"I don't want to take time from the field to sit in a classroom," he said. "I do my own research and take that knowledge to the field. People learn by doing, not sitting in a classroom—that's what my father taught me."

Ah. The door of the mystery opened an imperceptible crack. So his father was the motivation behind the university push as well as the pull to get dirty and do the work. Surely the trustees could see Tristan's intelligence and fervor. His love for faming went beyond a drive to provide food. It was a zeal for perfection, a thirst for success, a quest for innovation.

Father must have seen this in Tristan.

"You knew my father well," she said.

Tristan's walk stiffened. She could feel him shutting down. The door closing to the mystery.

Even if he didn't want to talk about her father, she needed to know some things. "What did the two of you talk about?"

He blew out a breath. "Theology. Farming. My family."

"That's it?"

"There's a lot to talk about there." He glanced over at her. "We didn't talk about you, if that's what you're asking."

Her face heated. She'd not been asking that. Thinking it,

perhaps. "Have you heard the rumors?"

"What rumors?" Tristan's scowl could have stirred dust into a funnel cloud.

She rolled her eyes. "About my land." Certainly he'd heard.

"Yep."

"It's silly, really. You don't think my father could have done such a thing, do you?"

Tristan's mouth firmed.

He still hadn't uttered a sound as they arrived at the smithy. Was he recalling a conversation he'd had with her father?

"Tristan?"

He shook his head. "We never talked about it. I'm sorry, Anna."

She stepped in front of him, lifting a hand but not daring to grab his arm. "Does it sound like something he'd do?" She needed his opinion, considering how close he'd been to Father.

Questions swirled in his unblinking eyes. Turning from her, he fiddled with the top button of his shirt and leaned his head back as if the sky contained a secret. "No, Anna. It doesn't."

The steady stream of people gathering at the tent proved her wrong about a November revival. Should she be surprised Michael's advertising had been successful? The man could succeed at anything, or so it seemed.

At present, she only wanted to succeed at one thing. An opening prayer. It didn't have to be long. It didn't have to be eloquent. Which meant her anxiety was an overreaction. God forgive her, she wanted to make a good impression. Wanted this prayer to push her toward the graces of others, not further into their suspicions.

By the time the sun sank down and splashed orange on the mountains across the bay, Anna had wrapped herself in her coat. The hum of voices cluttered her mind, and the question of whether a certain someone would appear refused to leave her alone. Even more distracting was the question why his presence mattered.

Michael wove through the rows of benches and mismatched chairs to where she stood by the platform. Lanterns hanging from wooden posts swayed with the breeze and illuminated the joy in his eyes.

A family jostled her from behind, knocking her toward Michael. He reached out to steady her, but his eager grip lingered. If Michael's energy increased any more, he'd be able to pull her Conestoga.

Anna smiled. "Are you ready?"

"Absolutely." His gaze darted around. He pointed to a chair. "Take this up on the platform so you can sit with me."

"Michael . . ." No matter how many times she underscored her role as a helper, Michael wanted to propel her into more.

"All right." He smiled. "Maybe tomorrow."

No. She would not sit up on the platform looking like Michael's—what?—assistant. Wife. Oh, no.

Anna took a seat on the end of the first row while Michael walked to the pulpit and gestured to Mrs. Tolliver at the piano. Though dragged over stones and ruts, and now sitting on the uneven platform in cold temperatures, the piano sounded moderately in tune. The first miracle of the revival.

The loud proclamation of "Praise Ye the Lord, the Almighty" rattled the tent, juxtaposing with the nervousness knotting her stomach. Anna sang the familiar words out of habit, but her mind moseyed to the whispered comments she'd overheard about her land as people had gathered. Her voice faded.

Don't think on that right now.

Her mind turned to what Michael had asked of her, what these people were expecting. Healing. An encounter with the living God.

Questions threatened to pinch every part of her until she bled worry. What if people disapproved of her prayers for healing? What if others thought her gift bizarre? What if she prayed and nothing happened?

The lilting melody of "My Shepherd Will Supply My Need" rang through the tent, slowing the raging of Anna's thoughts.

Every need supplied in Jesus.

She repeated that truth to herself while the congregation sang through seven verses.

By the time Michael stood to speak, anxiety had loosened its grip on her. Michael's strong voice didn't waver as his eyes sought out each individual during his welcome.

His confidence encouraged her. His joy, her spiritual strength. She'd been right to agree to help. What could be so difficult about bringing the needs of others before the Lord?

"How can I pray for you?" Anna took the woman's clammy hand in hers.

Wispy blond hair curled from beneath the woman's bonnet, and guarded hope draped her tired brown eyes. "I'm dying."

Short, shallow breaths accompanied her words, but the woman's color was strong, and she didn't appear pained.

"It's my heart. It's erratic." The woman paused to take in several breaths. "I can't walk more than twenty feet without losing breath."

Anna squeezed the trembling hand in hers. "What's your name?"

"Abigail Turner. My husband's over there with our children." She jutted her chin toward a man in a ragged jacket. He looked wide eyed at Anna and stroked the head of a small child asleep on his lap. Two other children flanked his shoulders, huddling close.

A mother, dying. A swell of compassion replaced any fear

left in Anna.

"Every day of ours is numbered by God." Anna leaned her head close Abigail's to be heard over the murmurs of the crowd. Heat traveled down her right arm, and she placed her hand on Abigail's head and spoke the words of Romans chapter eight that floated into her mind. "'If the Spirit of him who raised Jesus from the dead is living in you, he who raised Christ from the dead will also give life to your mortal bodies because of his Spirit, who lives in you.'"

A sob slipped through Mrs. Turner's tightened lips. Anna kept her hand on Mrs. Turner's head, silently seeking the Lord's will. She'd been praying prayers of blessing and healing over people for an hour, but instead of the weariness she feared, energy filled her.

She'd had nothing to worry about after all. Those who'd asked for prayer had been grateful, willing, seeking the Lord.

Mrs. Turner's body jerked beneath Anna's hand, and Anna stepped back, startled.

The woman opened her eyes and gasped. "I'm healed."

Her loud proclamation silenced those nearby. Heads turned. Eyes stared.

Anna didn't know whether to shrink from the attention or offer a hallelujah.

"My, oh my." A young man with a mop of shaggy hair grinned at her.

Michael wove through spectators to stand by her side. He squeezed her shoulder, and the affection brimming in his eyes offered encouragement.

"Praise the Lord." His words rushed forth a little too loud.

Echoes of *praise the Lord* rippled through the crowd as cheers erupted. Anna focused on her hands wringing together in front of her. Even amid exclamations of praise, she had the horrible fear the cheers might be for her.

Tristan stood in the middle of the field, the afternoon sun a hot whip across his back. For heaven's sake. This was the first week of November. Was this Seattle, or had he awoken in Texas? What had happened to the cold temperatures of the last days?

Of course, all this sweat could be the result of his frenzied pace. He'd ravaged through more rows of potatoes this hour than last, wanting only to be done with harvest. And he was so close. Tristan wiped his arm across his brow. Next to him, Lazarus guzzled water. On the opposite side of the field, Jimmy and the two seasonal hires sprawled by the wagon, taking a short break.

Tristan rested his forearms on the wheel of the wagon, resisting the urge to groan at his aching stomach.

He'd tried to befriend Anna, to care for her like he had Peter, but these healings brought him headaches. Jimmy had returned from the revival two nights ago worked up over the woman with cancer that Anna had healed. Really? And how did everyone know she was healed? Maybe she wasn't sick to begin with. Maybe she'd die next month.

"What you thinking?" Lazarus paused his water guzzling to breathe, the ladle resting against his lips. "Thinking of clearing another field?"

Tristan blinked, his gaze unmoving from the distant tree line. Yeah, he wished he'd been thinking of that. "I was thinking of Anna."

Lazarus chuckled, took a hasty last drink, and brought the bucket to Tristan. "I can't imagine anyone letting their woman kin stay out west by herself. She only eighteen."

Tristan shrugged, taking the ladle from Lazarus.

Lazarus sighed. "I pity that girl."

Tristan focused on the hawk looping the blue sky. "Don't." He drank long from the sun-warmed water, turning his back on

Lazarus. Just because he'd admitted to thinking of Anna didn't mean he wanted to talk about her.

"You got something against her?"

"No, but she doesn't need pitying."

"Sure she do. You should of seen how upset she was last night when some women were talking 'bout her land." Lazarus plucked a piece of straw from the ground and shoved it between his teeth. "Oh, she try to hide it with that sweet smile, but her eyes, they were wild."

Nothing about Anna was wild, except her notions of healing prayer. Tristan took another long drink, ignoring Lazarus. The water traveled into his empty stomach and sat heavily.

They were a few days from completing harvest, the hardest work of the year. His favorite work. Blisters that delivered a reward. Aching muscles that meant he'd brought forth life from the land. Oats, barley, hay, beans, corn, turnips, and soon, potatoes, garnered from the earth.

Tristan poured water over his filthy hands. The dust turned to grime. He wiped his palms on his pants and saw skin again. If only the problem with Anna could be wiped away so easily.

"Who'd take land from a young woman left alone?" Lazarus gnawed the piece of straw like it was a meal.

"No one took it."

"Why ain't it hers, then? It's not right, a woman not knowing if she got a place to live."

"She has a place to live."

"Who knows when some no-good fella gonna say, 'Honey, move on. This land be mine.'"

"That won't happen."

Lazarus's eyes narrowed. "Why you so sure?"

Tristan groaned and flung his hands out. "I own it, Laz. Are you happy now? Will you leave me alone?"

Lazarus dropped the handkerchief he'd been using to mop

his brow. They stared at each other until low rumbles of laughter rolled from Lazarus and turned over Tristan's heart like tines of a plow.

"How'd you get that land?"

Tristan shook his head. He dropped the dipper in the bucket. "Break's over." Moving to the far side of the wagon, he motioned across the field to the shade of the cottonwoods for the men to resume working. Out of the corner of his eye, he saw Lazarus unmoving, staring.

"You gotta tell her."

Tristan straightened and blew out a breath.

"You gotta."

"I can't believe Peter left it to me."

Lazarus laughed more, the piece of straw dangling. It fell to the ground, and he sobered. "This ain't good." He bent and picked up his handkerchief, brushed the dirt off, and shoved it into his pocket. "This ain't good at all. When you gonna tell her?"

"We got work to do."

"You heading down a bad path. This ain't good."

Yes, he knew *this ain't good.* "Would've been fine if she'd stayed in Portland."

"She gonna be on fire when she find out."

"No." Tristan turned to meet Lazarus's searching eyes. "She's going to be hurt."

Tristan reached for his shovel and pushed it into the ground. He turned over the earth and bent to pluck the potatoes and toss them into the wagon. Hiding his ownership from Anna was a bad path, but it was too late.

He pictured Anna holding that gun out, terrified, then confused. He should have told her that first afternoon she'd found him at her cabin. But how could he look a grieving daughter in the eyes and tell her that her father had left all he owned to another? Well, not all. He supposed she had a good deal of money. Peter Warren knew how to run a business.

He slammed his shovel into the ground again. Sweat streamed across his brow. Tristan needed that land for leverage with the university. The land was manna, falling from heaven, nourishing his dream—and it was spoiling, just like Israel's manna had spoiled when they'd held on to it. Manna used wrong turned rancid.

They finished their day's goal as the sun dropped below the horizon, fading the western sky to a pale blue. The air had cooled considerably, and though Tristan felt the chill of dried sweat, nothing had cooled within him. What an idiot to blurt out such a secret to Lazarus. He'd never hear the end of it.

They walked in from the field, Lazarus following a step behind. "That why you been totin' her stuff around, goin' into town when I know you got nothin' there to do?"

If he weren't so frustrated, Tristan would have grinned at how Lazarus picked up their conversation from hours earlier. "She's the daughter of a friend. It's the least I can do." He quickened his pace, ready to hang up the day along with his shovel.

"She can be your friend too."

"Anna, the daughter of Peter Warren, I can handle. Anna, the healer . . ." He spun on Lazarus. "I heard about that woman healed from cancer."

Lazarus grunted. "Not cancer. A woman with heart issues claimed she was healed. Said she felt a burning hand on her when Anna prayed."

Tristan smirked and continued walking. Not only was the woman's healing questionable, people weren't even clear what that healing was.

"And Anna, the woman?"

"Not now, Laz."

Lazarus's persistence was welcome in the field, not in Tristan's private life.

Anna, a woman. He supposed eighteen constituted womanhood, although the innocence of her face and the way her hair hung down all the time, well, she looked more child than woman. And her silly peace. Good heavens, the girl had just lost her father. But no, Anna oozed grace like . . . like he oozed grumpiness when he was around her.

You can do better.

He needed her land, but at least he could be polite.

Anna, a woman.

And he, a man. Somehow, in these years of building his homestead and of dreaming about an agricultural program, he'd ignored the fact that he, Tristan, the boy who'd come west, was now Tristan, the man. He'd always seen himself as Tristan, the farmer, but he was still a boy with so much to learn.

Again, you can do better.

Lazarus nudged his elbow, and Tristan shrunk away, letting out a huff of air. "I guess I am a man."

Lazarus looked up, mouth parting before turning up in a grin. "Yes, you is."

"When I'm with Anna, I see *her* face . . ."

"Yep, Anna be like your mama."

Tristan squirmed. He'd definitely made a mistake letting his secret slip.

They reached Tristan's porch, and the older man sank into a rocking chair. "She innocent, willing to help others. Maybe too willing."

Meaning? Tristan narrowed his eyes and claimed the rocker next to Lazarus.

"She need to know. Sooner, not later." Lazarus laid a hand on Tristan's arm.

Tristan brushed the touch away. For a man who usually kept his hands to himself, Lazarus was doing a lot of elbow nudging and laying on of hands today.

"She vulnerable out there. Some people might got more demands for her than prayer."

Tristan felt the indirect challenge as Lazarus peered over at him, dark eyes focused.

"If I wanted somethin'," Lazarus said, "like to claim her land, or something' else, I'd hide in that cabin of hers, wait till she come through the door . . ." He shrugged. "Just saying."

"What *are* you saying, Lazarus? You can't guilt me into telling her by spinning some crazy scenario."

"If you care for her, tell her about the land before she do something stupid and get herself in trouble."

If Anna got in trouble, she could pray for deliverance. He had a program to think about. Peter Warren might have been her father, but he'd still been Tristan's friend. A friend who'd believed in Tristan's dreams. Peter wouldn't mind his land being used for experimental farming, and Anna would get over it.

He leaned forward and put his face in his hands.

You're acting like a boor.

He never should have let the secret go on so long. But what could he do? If he confessed now, he'd ruin . . . what?

A friendship? Yeah, right. What with the way he plagued her with questions and his suspicious attitude toward healing, she likely cringed at the sight of him.

An obligation? No, Peter hadn't commissioned him to look out for Anna, not in such plain words, at least. The compulsion to watch over Anna stemmed from his own guilt.

Whatever it was, he'd ruin something he didn't want to ruin.

Best to deal with the consequences later. The land and the opportunity with the university were first priority. Hadn't his father said as much?

Tristan, agrology is the future of this country. There's a nation to feed, and if we're going to do it right, it's going to take more than hard work. It's going to take skill.

And skill was honed at a university, through trial and error and experimentation. His father might not have lived to see his work with the Morrill Act pay off, but Tristan would ensure that every leftover ounce of strength, after tending his own land, went to fulfill his father's vision.

Chapter Eleven

Anna walked down the boardwalk, swinging her basket in time with her steps. After a day of unseasonable warmth, the morning had dawned with a bite. Clouds hung heavy over the bay, looking as though any minute they would release their moisture. Typical November, playing tricks with the weather.

Typical Tristan. He'd been absent the first three nights of the revival. The energy she'd focused on his presence—or lack of—disturbed her as much as the reverent looks directed at her by those with whom she prayed.

Father would ride to Tristan's and ask him to come.

She wasn't Father.

She quickened her walk and shoved thoughts of Tristan, Michael, and the revival out of her mind. Not difficult, considering the land rumor that hung over her as dreary as the sky above.

If Mr. Wyse didn't return soon, she'd considered traversing the pass eastward. The seed of unease, fed by the whispered concerns of others, refused to be uprooted. Why hadn't anyone come to claim her land or cabin?

She frowned as a new thought took over. Maybe Mr. Wyse hadn't notified the mystery owner yet. Maybe there was still hope that if this rumor was true, for some bizarre reason, she could sort out the mix-up with Mr. Wyse before facing the supposed inheritor.

The tail of her worn purple scarf blew up and tickled her cheek as she crossed the street and rounded the corner of Yesler Hall. A piece of paper was tacked to the door of Mr. Wyse's office. Hastening her steps, she steadied herself for the worst.

Dear Clients of Mr. Wyse,

We regret to inform you Mr. Wyse has been delayed

and will not return until spring. Please see U.S. Deputy Marshal Jude McGrath for your legal needs.

Anna pressed on the door with the weight of her frustration. Father's will was filed in this office, mere feet from her. Confidentiality aside, didn't his daughter deserve to see the document that dictated her future?

"May I help you?"

Anna straightened and pulled her gloved hand off the door.

The man before her possessed a height and breadth that rivaled the size of the biggest lumberjack. Feeling like a fawn next to an elk, she took several steps back and noticed the star pinned to his leather vest, smudged with dirt and bent on one edge.

Hope beat a direct course to her heart. "You're a marshal."

"*The* marshal." He nodded to the note. "Jude McGrath."

His clean look of short sandy-brown hair and whiskerless face, combined with an open expression, put her at ease. "I need to know who owns my land."

His smile seemed effortless. "You're Anna Warren, the healer."

Despite the title, she returned his smile, appreciating that only kindness inhabited his voice.

"I've heard about you," he said. "I just came from the east side." He tapped the note. "Not a good situation."

Her smile faded. "Did you see Mr. Wyse?"

"Briefly." A shadow overtook Mr. McGrath's hazel eyes, and he shifted his weight. "He won't be returning for a while. Did you need to speak with him?"

"Have you heard the rumor about my father leaving our land to someone other than me?"

He shook his head, a frown turning down the edges of his eyes, and she sensed genuine concern. "You want to know if it's true?"

"Mr. Wyse and I were interrupted while discussing my father's will. He left town before we could finish, and now I'm not sure how to find out who owns my land. Could you let me inside his office?"

The corner of his mouth twitched. "Sorry. Can't do that."

"I only want to see my father's will."

"I can't let you in without authorization. You'll have to travel to the courthouse in Olympia and check the records. See if a transfer of ownership has been filed since your father passed. Perhaps the new owner has paid taxes already."

She still hadn't heard from the Wiltons, and a trip to the territory's capital and back would most of a week. "Could I write a letter?"

"They might not release that information through mail, but you could try." Mr. McGrath rolled his shoulders back and folded his arms across his chest as he studied her. "You've got rights of occupation. Someone can't foist you off your land without proof. I wouldn't worry if I were you."

He wasn't her, because the thought of living on land owned by someone else burned her mind like an August sun.

She tightened her grip on her basket. "Thank you."

"Let me know if I can help." He tipped his hat, and she watched him walk away.

You can go for me and find out who owns my land.

She sighed. Onward to Joe's to shift two delivery dates. She'd agreed to help with this revival, but she hadn't expected people to request to meet with her during the day. Her entire schedule was out of control. Make that her entire life.

Mr. Foreman exited Joe's and approached without looking at her. He would have passed without acknowledgment, but she swallowed and forced a greeting. "Mr. Foreman. How are you?"

He jerked his head up, and she smiled as a peace offering.

"We are not all fooled by you, Miss Warren." He stepped around her and rushed down the street.

Her mouth wobbled, smile disappearing, as tears swarmed her eyes. Today had been nothing but a string of failures. Mr.

Foreman despised her. Mr. Wyse had left her helpless. And sometime in the next months she had to set aside freighting to travel to Olympia.

And where was Tristan?—nearly the only member of the community who had not showed up at least once during the revival. For all his dour-faced arguing, she missed him. Needed the strength and determination he so easily emanated.

Biting the inside of her cheek, she turned up an alleyway and let the tears fall.

Tristan climbed the bitter cherry tree and settled onto a sturdy limb, letting his legs straddle. He'd told Anna *not likely* about attending these revival meetings, and he'd meant it.

But *not likely* had happened.

He leaned back and waited for . . . what? Memories to awaken? Anger to kindle? Deliverance? Yeah, right. He'd be waiting years. *Been* waiting years.

He twisted, back against the trunk, trying to get comfortable. So what if he'd come. It wasn't out of curiosity. Not because a certain brown-haired, sweet-faced girl had looked into his soul, singeing his conscience with the purity of her faith.

He wouldn't sit in the tent. He wouldn't pretend to be swayed by Michael's preaching. He wouldn't allow himself to be manipulated. Again. He'd trusted Jesus when he'd been younger, at an event not unlike tonight's, but God had driven a wedge in their relationship the day He'd failed to answer Tristan's most important prayer.

Tristan was here simply to prove the ridiculous nature of these meetings, to confirm to himself how right he was to reject the emotional fuss. People would get tossed high on the waves of religion only to crash down when the reality of everyday life left them washed ashore. The singing, preaching, praying of tonight would be a short-lived glory.

He closed his eyes as Anna's tender, sturdy voice projected in prayer. Her words scraped his heart more than the bark digging through his thin jacket. Her sincerity shallowed his breathing. Even after she'd spoken the amen, he couldn't pry his eyelids open lest the warm liquid behind them slip out. His cynicism didn't have a chance against the tenderness of her spirit.

And he hated it.

A softening crouched around the bend of his future, waiting to wrap around his heart, and the thought of such vulnerability—that maybe he couldn't keep God at arm's length much longer—terrified him. His lower lip trembled, and he thrust his hand over his mouth to still it.

Then Michael began to preach, and like a tourniquet, hardness cinched his spirit again. Tristan didn't hear the voice of the youthful man on the platform but rather the baritone of another preacher. He heard former words as if he were back in the canvas tent in an Illinois field. His frail mother, wheezing, holding his hand as he'd helped her down the aisle for prayer.

Such hope. Stupid, misplaced hope.

The preacher had prophesied healing, had pronounced health for her sick body. A miracle promised but undelivered. A boy of fifteen didn't recover from something like that.

And a man of twenty-two didn't let a Spirit-filled woman peel away the scabs of his past.

The energy under the tent on Saturday, the sixth night of the revival, surpassed the previous evenings. At least the energy of the people. Anna rubbed the ache beneath her temples as the crowd pressed toward the front of the tent. Some knelt, others stood. Michael walked back and forth on the platform, speaking Scripture over upturned faces, interlacing prayers with exhortations.

Anna backed away from the scene, thankful for the break

from praying with others. Michael was in wonderful form: a broad smile across his face, lively hand gestures. He loved Jesus. He loved people.

He loved her. She'd seen it in his eyes. Michael was unguarded. His lips in speech, and his heart through facial expression.

Tension churned her stomach. Michael's expectations were larger and more intimidating than the cedars. He was going places, and although the excitement of ministry pulled her, she didn't appreciate feeling directed by him.

She looked away from Michael, needing more than a break from praying with others. She needed fresh air. Beneath the canopy, the air was thick and warm, and the heat from strung lanterns mingled with the stuffiness of the crowd. Yet the brusqueness of early November hovered around the edge of the tent, inviting her out.

She eyed her coat, slung across the back of a chair. She'd have to weave through people to retrieve it, and that might draw her into ministry. She stepped out from under the tent, willing to withstand the coolness.

Her boots crunched stones and sticks, a calming sound, as she walked from the light farther into shadow. Not twenty feet from the edge of the tent, darkness surrounded her. She reached out a hand to touch the cover of night, which held both a wideness and an intimacy she'd always loved as a girl. It created a feeling of boundlessness. And yet it pressed close like a whisper. Her mind honed in on the stillness.

"Does Michael know you're out here?"

Anna wrenched her head back and peered up into the branches of a bitter cherry. Tristan had spoken from above, perched somewhere, but the night hid all but a faint outline of a body. His presence painted a smile on her face, a smile that quickly dimmed, thanks to the negativity of his comment. "He's not my keeper."

Tristan laughed, a short and humorless sound. "Perhaps he is."

"Perhaps not." Anna's neck cramped, and she dropped her gaze.

She heard a thud, and the ground shook. She sensed Tristan standing beside her, his nearness overpowering the darkness.

"How are the meetings going?"

Was that genuine interest in his voice? "Wonderful. Michael's been bold with the Gospel, and people have responded. It's like nothing I've experienced, though Father did talk about Finney's revivals. He might have told you about them—" She cut her rambling short. Tristan didn't need a history lesson. "Michael can draw a crowd. More come each evening."

"They come for you."

She wished she could see his eyes to tell if he was teasing.

"They want you to pray for them."

He said it matter of factly, a hush in his voice that matched the shroud of night. But he was wrong. "I'm not sure about that."

A soft chuckle, this time full of humor and something else. Tenderness. "I am."

"Is that why you've come?"

"I'm certain you already pray for me." A twig snapped as he shifted. "And I'm grateful."

Pleasure filled her. "You know my father prayed for you."

"He prayed *with* me."

"With you?" How she wanted to see his face, as if by seeing his face she could see her father again. She inched closer, but when her arm bumped against his, he yanked back.

"I shared my idea for an agricultural program, and he said, 'Let's pray about it,' so we did, right then. Rather, he did."

She held her breath. *Tell me stories, Tristan. Tell me why you loved my father, why he loved you.* His relationship with her father bonded them—him and her—in a strange, untamed way of which she couldn't get enough.

Voices drifted from the tent. A child's cry, the sound of a chair falling, and a man's deep laugh rose above the noise of the crowd dismissing. Michael marched to the back of the tent and peered into the darkness, probably looking for her. She didn't want to be found.

"He prayed with me another time," Tristan said.

Anna turned toward his voice.

"About my mother."

Was she sick? Father had never mentioned anything, and Tristan had only spoken of his family once.

"Your father was a good man. Unassuming, unlike some." Tristan faced the tent.

"What do you have against Michael?"

"Nothing."

Which was why there was poison in his voice when he spoke of Michael.

"It's not Michael," Tristan said. "It's the whole idea that God heals."

The honest admission offered her a glimpse further into him. She'd have to tread with care. "Do you not believe Him capable?"

"Oh, He is." The words launched like a rock from a slingshot aimed at God Himself.

"Do you not believe Him willing?" She knew she poked dangerously close to Tristan's wound.

The rustling of his clothes indicated squirming. If she poked again, he might strike at her.

She could take the bite. "Is it an issue of God's sovereignty?"

"God doesn't heal, Anna."

At the sound of Tristan's raised voice, Michael stepped in their direction.

Tristan turned and receded into the darkness. A sense of

separation closed around her. The sound of his steps halted, and Anna held her breath until his voice sounded through the grove. "God doesn't heal. He just doesn't. It's as simple as that."

By the middle of the second week, Michael's voice rasped, weakened by the hours of preaching. His intensity, however, only strengthened. His forehead glistened with perspiration, and King David's words rushed to Anna's mind: *Zeal for your house consumes me.*

Guilt snagged her as she viewed Michael's fervor and compared it to her own apathy. Her excitement had waned, sunk like the falling sun. Night after night of praying for others had suffocated her spirit. Her soul needed to breathe.

"Come." Michael's voice carried the weight of conviction as he spoke over the congregation. "Come, all you who are weary."

People sat forward in their chairs. People who'd been there every night. People who'd rolled into town that morning.

"Jesus has promised rest. Jesus has promised new life." Michael paced to the far side of the platform. "But you must have faith. You must make your choice."

Anna had chosen obedience, so where was the promised rest? Shouldn't those who serve Him feel revived by their obedience? She closed her eyes, cutting off the ache that traced the lines on her forehead.

Tristan hadn't been back since the sixth night, and disappointment had dimmed Anna's enjoyment of the past evenings. She'd hoped Michael's preaching might smooth Tristan's sharp edges.

An absurd thought.

A man like Tristan didn't respond to imperatives ushered from a flamboyant preacher. Her gentleness would more likely be effective, and so far, she'd failed.

"If you hear Him calling, Scripture says do not delay. Come

now. If you live in sin, repent. If you have strayed, return. If you are hurting, be healed. You need only have enough faith."

Anna straightened, some of her weariness shocked away by Michael's bold statement. Enough faith? As if God was waiting in heaven with a measuring stick?

"Come claim your salvation. Take hold of your healing."

Amens rang out. Anna tensed. Michael hadn't been one to stay in the boundaries, but this skirted the borders of presumption. Quantity of faith? Such craziness set people up to feel like failures if their prayers went unanswered.

"God's reordering of the world through the victory of his Son over death has made a way for you to know good things. For you to know healing."

True, but not in the way Michael portrayed it.

He looked down at her, his gaze intense, inviting. He wanted her to stand at her place in the front corner, but her feet felt rooted to the ground. She wasn't handing out healing like peppermint sticks. She wasn't promising people God would give them whatever they asked.

"Come forward and pray with me for your salvation. Receive eternal life today." Michael looked at her again. "Come forward and pray with Anna for healing for whatever ails you. Receive wholeness for your soul and your body."

He motioned her forward with a flick of his hand, and somehow she found the strength to take her place. Several people lined up, waiting on her to bless them, to pray God's wholeness over their brokenness.

Lord, I will be faithful to do what you have called me to do.

She didn't know if God would heal their aching backs, their rheumatism, or their failing vision. She did know God promised peace and joy for His children.

You know their hearts and needs. Provide your abundant life for them tonight.

The crowd dispersed. Fires burned low, a deep orange. Though Anna needed to talk with Michael, she didn't have the strength for such a confrontation tonight.

She gathered Father's Bible and tugged her coat around her shivering body. She could be home in ten minutes if she rushed Maple. She marched from the tent toward the hitching rail before remembering. She stopped, covered her eyes with her hand, and moaned. Maple was already home. Anna had walked to town this morning, planning to return to the cabin and rest for the afternoon. Interruptions had rescheduled her day, and now she was without Maple.

Not that she'd never been in the woods at night, but she'd experienced too many visits from coyotes and raccoons to enjoy a stroll after dark. Everything within her tensed at the thought of asking Michael for an escort home. Confrontation would be unavoidable then.

She'd borrow one of the lanterns and walk.

"Anna."

No, Michael. She'd paused too long. Forcing her feet to move, she turned. His blue eyes appeared black in the dim light.

"You didn't seem yourself tonight," he said.

"Your message troubled me." So much for waiting for a confrontation.

He crossed his arms, and the defensive look he offered didn't fit his open nature.

"What was different about my message tonight?"

"Healing is not about having enough faith or claiming God's promises."

Michael uncrossed his arms and shoved his hands toward the warmth of a diminishing fire. "Scripture says without faith it is impossible to please God."

"Faith in Jesus Christ for salvation, yes. We cannot please

Him with our faithless law keeping. But saying that healing depends on our faith ignores the very source of healing, Jesus Christ. What happens if a person isn't healed? Does that mean he didn't have enough faith?"

"Maybe. The confidence of one's faith as he asks for healing is an important component." Michael stepped toward her. "And in your prayers, too, you need to exert more confidence. You have a gift."

Movement caught her peripheral vision. A man stepped from the shadows into the light at the edge of the tent. Tristan. She ignored the shock, focusing on Michael, who'd yet to notice Tristan's approach behind him.

"Don't be afraid to use the power of your faith," Michael said.

Frustration burned her throat. "Faith isn't something we use to get what we want."

"Yes and no. God gave us faith to use. A tool. Faith can move mountains."

"You've misinterpreted Scripture." She took a few slow breaths and riveted her gaze on Michael, shutting out the distraction of Tristan standing in the shadows like an animal poised to attack. "Jesus said to the disciples, 'If you have faith as small as a mustard seed, you can say to this mountain, 'Move from here to there,' and it will move. Nothing will be impossible for you.' Faith, however small or big, is in a person, Jesus Christ, and *Jesus* is the mountain mover, not faith."

Firelight glimmered in Michael's eyes as he stared at her. He smiled, and she felt herself blush under his amusement, not seeing the humor.

"I'll have to remember not to question your knowledge of Scripture."

She kept silent as he studied her, wondering what pushed through his mind. Michael wasn't upset, that was for sure, and his ease furthered her irritation.

"People have responded well to your prayers." Michael closed the three-foot gap between them until their coats touched. "If you claim healing for people, they'll receive it. If you don't . . ."

She recoiled.

"So now it's Anna's fault if someone isn't healed?" Tristan stepped forward.

Michael spun, his expression a mixture of surprise and displeasure.

Breaching the short distance, Tristan entered the light, and the hardness in his eyes sent her pulse reeling.

"Don't be like Job's friends." Tristan stressed each word to Michael.

Michael frowned. "What do you mean?"

"They blamed Job for his suffering. Told him he'd sinned and deserved what he got."

"That has nothing to do with what we're talking about." Michael looked at Anna, a sideways glance that didn't hold back any annoyance.

"Wrong," she said. "We're talking about faith, healing, why God answers prayers sometimes and not others. We're talking about who is responsible for divine intervention. God or us? That was Job's issue: Who was responsible for his suffering? We are too quick to blame ourselves for not having enough faith, or for doing something to bring about bad things, as if God's decisions depend on us."

Michael reached a hand toward her arm, but Tristan advanced, and Michael drew his hand back.

Anna's breathing faltered. Judging by the way Michael and Tristan glared at each other, this conversation had moved beyond faith and healing.

She stepped between the men. "You are partly right, Michael. Faith is important for healing, but healing doesn't depend on human conviction. Nor do we need to claim God's work, as if we're even certain of what that work is."

Michael shook his head. "Sometimes we need to reach out and grasp for Him, Anna. We can't accept sickness and death."

Her head ached, and she willed the stupor to lift. "Sickness and death are part of this broken world."

"We've been redeemed. We're not to live in the brokenness."

"So everyone who is redeemed shouldn't experience sickness or death?" How she wished that were true.

"God wills for people to be healed," Michael said.

"Yes, but . . ." Anna stepped back. "Ultimate healing is reconciliation to Him." Her eyes pleaded with Michael. "Some healings may never be complete until heaven. Bodies might remain broken. Illnesses will take lives. Accidents will happen."

Michael's face sobered. "You're resigned to letting people hurt?"

She winced as though he'd struck her, and Tristan moved between her and Michael, his back in front of her face, a protective wall. She wanted to lean forward and rest her head on him, just close her eyes and wake up in another place and time where all the questions would be answered.

The silence stretched, inviting her to imagine the war between glances going on between Michael and Tristan. Her head bobbed, heavy.

"I'm sorry, Anna. That came out wrong." Michael's voice sounded muffled, and she realized she *had* leaned her head against Tristan's back and her ear was pressed against the warmth of his shoulder blade.

"And if it came out right, how would it sound then?" Tristan's voice vibrated against her ear, and she forced herself to pull back, though all she wanted was to sag deeper into her defender.

Michael huffed and stomped several paces away.

"Good night." Anna walked toward the path that would

lead her home. Low tones sounded behind, and she glanced back from the protection of darkness. Both men stood with arms crossed, not a foot between them. Tristan spoke into Michael's face, an angry expression causing her to wonder at his words. She turned away.

If she hadn't been so tired, she would have laughed at the irony that the man who so opposed healing had defended her position, or at least had defended her right to hold that position.

A sigh tumbled from her, and she marched on, remembering the warmth of his shirt against her cheek and the muscles flexing in his back.

Chapter Twelve

Tristan left Michael staring after him and went in search of Anna.

The past five nights he'd sat in that bitter cherry, each night telling himself it would be the last. The Gospel flowed from Michael as natural as breath. No wonder Anna admired him and respected him.

Each day after sweating out his irritation in the field, Tristan found himself riding Ember to town and hearing that Gospel again. A Gospel he'd believed since childhood. A Gospel that had started to tug at him like a too-tight scarf. Even through his layers of anger, it tugged, but he wasn't ready to let go of the hurt. Extricating grief wasn't like pulling weeds or digging out rocks. You couldn't yank out grief with one firm tug.

Except for the night Anna had wandered beneath his perch, he'd been invisible to everyone. A man had to fight some battles on his own.

But not a woman. The tree couldn't hold him when Michael had started harping on Anna. Sweet Anna. Michael treated her like an asset, a feature of his self-promoted revival. It'd been no small feat to restrain from pummeling the mouthy Irishman.

He scanned the darkness. She couldn't have walked far, not with the weight of exhaustion slowing her down. She looked like his mule at the end of a long day, not that he'd tell her so.

Tristan strained his eyes but saw no movement ahead on the trail.

He was a get-it-done guy, from the potato brigades during the war, to his homestead, to his struggle with the university. He had to escort Anna home. He couldn't tell her about the land, not yet, but he could make up for it by ensuring she had what she needed. And right now, she needed to get away from Michael. She needed sleep.

A flickering light twenty paces ahead caught his attention. The light was lower to the ground than if she'd been on a horse. Crazy Saint was walking.

He untied Ember and caught up to Anna after only a minute. "You're tired."

She didn't even look at him. "Yes."

A gentle breeze tossed around her feather-like strands of hair, and she brushed them back from her face. Even the simple motion appeared burdensome.

"What did you say to Michael?"

He could tell her about the threats, but she'd be upset. She'd likely defend Michael even after he'd questioned her motives. What an insensitive lie that Anna would resign herself to watching another's pain. Anyone who spent an hour with her could see that compassion streamed from her with the strength of spring runoff.

"Tristan?"

He took the lantern from her hand, ignoring her question. "I know it's hard for you to see people hurting."

The soft pad of her boots on the dirt filled the quiet.

Then her words started, a melodic sound in the hushed night. "It *is* hard for me to see people hurting, but it's harder on the Lord to see His children hurting. Especially those who want to seek Him but have blocked the path."

He kicked at the trail. Even in her tiredness, she'd found a way to thrust a charged statement at him. *God cares about you, Tristan*—she might well have said. *God cares about your hurt, your past, your distrust.*

"Let's get you home." He pulled on her elbow, and she stopped. Her eyes bled vulnerability, and something about her made him want to break down and weep, and at the same time take up sword and shield to defend her. He wanted to offer comfort, but what would he say? She demanded too much from him concerning God.

He nodded toward Ember. "Climb on."

Instead of the expected argument, she put her hand on his arm, stepped in the stirrup, and slung her foot over. The oil in the lantern burned lower as Tristan walked beside and led Ember through the trees. Maybe the oil would burn out and he wouldn't have to look in her eyes again and face the questions she stirred in him.

An owl's cry pierced the night, long and hollow.

"A great horned owl. Father's favorite."

The joy in her voice lightened the darkness.

Another owl hooted from the opposite direction, and Anna gasped. "It's not alone. When I heard it a few weeks ago, its call went unanswered."

In spite of her tiredness, he sensed a new vigilance about her, thanks to the owl.

She nudged his shoulder with her foot. "Blow out the lantern. It's fading anyway."

He did as she asked.

"Stop the horse."

Again, he obeyed. Without the tread of the horse and his boots, the silence of the night came alive. Moist air rested against his cheek like a tender hand, and he found himself holding his breath. A dark shadow broke through the tree line in front of them and coasted above their heads. A call echoed through the evergreens, hollow and deep. He shuddered. After another minute of stillness, he turned to Anna. He could just make out her form, head bowed, arms wrapped around herself.

He clicked his tongue at Ember, and the horse followed him.

They came to the cabin, and Tristan helped Anna down, her shaking unmistakable. Here she'd been praying for the health of others, and was about to fall ill herself.

He relit the lantern and entered the cabin first.

"Thank you."

Her voice pulled his gaze around. She stood on the threshold, wiping a tear from her cheek.

Don't fall apart on me, Anna.

He'd never seen his mother cry, not even at the news of his father's death. She'd been tough like that. Too tough. He appreciated Anna's sincerity, the openness of her emotions, but he'd rather admire it from a distance.

"Thank you," she said again.

He sensed her gratitude extended beyond his escorting her home. "Don't let Michael's words bother you." Emotion husked his voice, exposing him in ways he didn't like.

Her attempted smile trembled. "No. He means well."

"Maybe." Probably not. Definitely not.

He set the lantern on the table. Anna remained in the doorway but moved to the side to let him pass. He shifted his shoulders to fit through the narrow opening without bumping her. He'd almost passed when she reached out and tugged his coat sleeve.

He averted his eyes. He couldn't let her look in his eyes now, when every secret posed on the edge of his soul.

"Tristan?"

"Yes?"

The lantern hissed.

"How's the view from the bitter cherry?"

He exhaled and swung his gaze to meet hers. Her smile made him believe he could lead an association, start an agricultural program, and farm twice as much as he did. All in one week.

What about Anna, the woman?

Tristan had been doing a good job holding God at arm's length, but wasn't sure he could hold back Anna anymore.

He scanned her face another moment before seeking relief from her penetrating eyes in the darkness outside the cabin, but when he peered into the nothingness that stretched across the yard, the withdrawal left him empty. His gaze shifted back, and he drank in the fullness of Anna. "View's fairly good. Excellent, in fact."

He left her in the doorway, mounted Ember, and rode away from his cabin, his land, and what was starting to feel too much like his woman.

Tristan glanced over to the stall next to him, where Jimmy pitched hay. The youth's movements were fluid, quick, and proficient. Jimmy had mucked three stalls in ten minutes. For standing an inch shorter than Tristan, and with arms like saplings, Jimmy worked with an intensity Tristan hadn't expected. He'd fill out soon enough, with a work ethic like that.

Lazarus strode through the open barn doors and tossed a rake into the corner by the shovels. Metal clattered against metal.

"Lazarus." Tristan crossed and set the rake on its hook. "A little respect, please."

Order and cleanliness led to production; sloppiness led to mediocrity. Wise advice from his mother, who'd allotted extra chores to anyone who had dared misplace a cooking utensil. He could imagine the horror on his mother's face if she entered his house. He could only master so much, and the choice to rule the inside or outside domain was no choice at all. He lived and died for his fields.

Naturally, it'd be nice to have someone ruling the inside. Who wouldn't prefer tidiness over bedlam? After Anna had straightened things in his living quarters, the peace of her presence had lingered for a few days. But that peace had been lost, covered up by more dishes, a stack of agriculture references he'd taken off the shelf and hadn't put back, and dirty shirts he'd piled by the door after coming in dusty each evening.

Lazarus walked over and slapped him on the back. "You

letting that boy outwork you?"

Tristan glared, refusing to let his mouth turn up at the corner. Only Lazarus got away with teasing like that. "Finish packing the potatoes. We'll drive them in on Monday. We're getting a good price this year."

Whistling "Go Down Moses," Lazarus left the barn.

"He always like that?" Jimmy placed the shovel on its appropriate hook.

"Yep." Tristan nodded toward the shovel. "Thanks."

Jimmy wasn't at all like the grouchy boy who'd kicked up dust at that first meeting when McRedmond had presented the association idea. Nonetheless, the hardworking, quiet youth had a secret.

Who didn't?

"Why don't you join Lazarus?" Tristan asked.

Jimmy walked to the doorway and turned. Morning light framed him as he pushed a thatch of blond hair off his forehead. "You heard of crop rotation?"

"Sure. We started practicing it in Illinois, but the war . . ."

Jimmy settled against the doorjamb and stared at him, a bit of that initial defiance in his eyes. "What about the war?"

Jimmy's drawl reminded Tristan of all the war had severed, not only on a personal level but a national level as well. And since working together was about trust, and half of leadership was being an example, Tristan felt compelled to offer a piece of his background, and maybe in doing so, mend a fragrant of the brokenness the war had left behind

"I was twelve when it began," Tristan said. "My brothers and father left to fight. The hands left. I stayed to care for the farm and my mother. My sister, whose husband joined up, came to live with us. Lazarus and I ran the farm those first two years, but we only planted a tenth of our fields."

They'd worked hard as ants, lifting what was too heavy for two to carry, harvesting more than two people could reap, working longer hours than the sun. Tristan rubbed his hands together, remembering the rawness that had marked those days and the ache of those seeping blisters.

Tristan snatched his axe. He'd shared enough. "It's not easy to lose your family."

Jimmy looked away but not before Tristan saw the smirk. "At least you had family to lose."

That was telling.

"But about crop rotation"—Jimmy looked back—"I was thinking that maybe division of crops is too ambitious for a start-up association."

Even Jimmy had been taken in by the idea of an association, dropping comments here and there about getting farmers together.

"I know Frank and Gray are pushing it," Jimmy said, "but I think they just want a break from growing wheat. Someone new to the area isn't going to want to be told to grow only potatoes or peas. Specializing—that's something for a more developed region."

Well thought. Jimmy should lead the association.

"Teaching others to switch around the position of their crops," Jimmy said, "that's an easy concept to grasp. It's been well received in the South."

"Any other ideas?" The Baldwin brothers had gotten commitments from thirty-three farmers to attend the informational meeting next week, and Tristan needed ideas. Not that he had any intention of accepting the position. But he could advise.

"I do have several—"

"Come with me to the meeting. Help me present."

"Really?" Jimmy pushed off the doorjamb.

"Sure." Tristan walked from the cool barn into the sun, motioning behind him. "Grab the short saw." Lazarus could pack potatoes on his own. Served him right for pestering Tristan about Anna. Tristan would take Jimmy and prune his cherry trees.

Tristan waited as Jimmy snatched the saw and hurried from the barn.

"Point the sharp side away from you, Jimmy."

Jimmy turned the saw around.

Tristan smiled. Here was a young man with a keen mind but not a lot of experience. The perfect candidate for the program Tristan wanted to institute with the university. Tristan had land. He had a student. The letters from congressmen and from professors at Morrill Grant universities stacked high on his dresser.

Maybe he'd get that miracle after all.

Anna rubbed the dull ache in her lower back. The air under the canvas tent was cold, and she shivered. "How many more nights?"

Michael held up a finger, putting her off, as he thumbed through his Bible.

She hadn't meant for the question to sound rude, but she needed to know how much longer she had to survive. She yearned for a tree-lined road and the chatter of squirrels and birds. A little time on the road would help her sort out the theological conundrums that had risen between her and Michael.

Michael looked up and shrugged. "Hard to tell."

He'd been withdrawn this evening as they'd tidied the tent, filled the lanterns, and overseen the wheeling of the piano out from Hermit's.

She picked up a rag and began wiping the cedar pulpit.

"You don't have to do this, Anna."

The quiet confession stilled her dusting. Did he refer to the cleaning or her continuing to work with the revival? This pensive Michael was hard to read. "Are you upset with me?"

He grinned sideways at her and winked, the exuberant Michael peeking through. "It's impossible to be upset with you."

Anna relaxed. "I didn't mean any disrespect last night."

He closed his Bible, paced to her side, and grasped her hand. His touch was firm, bearing his usual confidence. "You have a gift. It's beautiful, and I want to see you satisfied with it."

"I am satisfied." She glanced from his impassioned eyes and withdrew her hand. He was always advancing, and she was always retreating. "I've enjoyed praying with people and seeing God work, but I didn't expect to be so tired by it." She focused on the revival sign, which had loosened from yesterday's early rain and now hung limp. "And I didn't expect us to disagree on something as foundational as the role of faith."

"We can get past this."

We, as if Michael were making plans for her life. Advancing again.

Michael crowded closer and reached for her hand, but footsteps interrupted them.

Mrs. Foreman approached the tent. "Am I intruding?"

Anna stepped back from Michael. "Of course not." Anna gestured to a bench. "Please, sit and visit."

Mrs. Foreman shook her head and shifted her weight like a nervous filly.

Anna walked to her side. "Is everything all right?"

"I haven't had an opportunity to come for prayer," Mrs. Foreman said.

Or to come at all. "That's all right."

Mrs. Foreman collapsed onto the nearest bench and smoothed her skirts with shaky hands. She drummed her fingers on her lap. Her look was the same as usual, tidy chignon and handkerchief folded in the pocket of her vest, but the composed mannerisms were absent.

"Does Mr. Foreman know you're here?" Anna covered Mrs. Foreman's hand with her own, already knowing the answer.

Mrs. Foreman shook her head, and a tear trickled from her eye. "If he knew, he'd laugh and call it balderdash."

Anna prayed for direction as she kept hold of Mrs. Foreman's hands. The woman sniffed, scaring a chickadee from the ground into a tree.

"Hope deferred makes the heart sick, but a longing fulfilled is a tree of life." Anna spoke the wisdom of Proverbs 13:12.

Mrs. Foreman shuddered and laid her head down on Anna's lap. Her shoulders shook, and Anna felt tears wet her hand.

"I want to have a baby."

Anna soothed her hand across the woman's firmly pinned hair. "Frustrated desires are like quills of a porcupine to the heart."

Mrs. Foreman looked up. "Is that Proverbs, too?"

Anna smiled. "No, but it's truth." She knew it from experience. The quest for community. The striving to maintain success in Father's business. The need to discover the truth about her cabin. Yes, unfulfilled—even uncertain—longings left one struggling for breath.

The familiar warmth of the Spirit stirred her as she prayed silently for the heartache of Mrs. Foreman.

"It's like I've a weight hooked into my chest." Mrs. Foreman spoke around ragged intakes of air. "The longing is so heavy. Clyde says I've done something to upset God."

That was the same faulty theology of Michael. That God responded to people according to their actions.

"Do you see God's withholding a child as punishment?" Anna asked.

"I don't know." Mrs. Foreman sat up and pulled her handkerchief from her pocket. "Have I not been a good wife? Am I harboring jealousy? Perhaps I've been discontent about our move to Seattle."

She was searching for connections, but connections weren't always available. Cause and effect might work with some things, but not with God.

"Do you love God, Mrs. Foreman?"

The woman stopped her sniffing. "Oh yes."

"As His child, you live under His grace, with His favor. Do you remember Gabriel's words to Mary? 'Greetings, you who are highly favored! The Lord is with you.'"

Mrs. Foreman nodded.

"We who love Jesus are all those highly favored, and we live in that favored place as those who belong to God, not in the place of striving, as if He will punish us if we fail to please Him."

"Favored . . ." Mrs. Foreman dabbed the wet splotches beneath her eyes and stood.

When Anna rose as well, Mrs. Foreman pulled her into a hug. A dusky rose scent filled Anna's senses, a soft and gentle aroma that seemed contradictory for this woman of rigid formality.

Mrs. Foreman pushed back. "Thank you, Anna. I should have come sooner. I don't know why I didn't." She smiled faintly, ducked her head, and left the tent.

Anna was praying peace over Mrs. Foreman when the image sparked her mind. Her pulse quickened. "Mrs. Foreman," she called.

The banker's wife turned.

The Lord hadn't given her an image during prayer before, and doubt encouraged her to rethink sharing.

But the image was strong, persistent. And Mrs. Foreman waited.

"I see a picture of a seed pushed deep in the ground," Anna said. "Except it's not in earth. It's in flesh, and that flesh is moving."

Mrs. Foreman pressed her hand to her chest, tears slipping fresh down her cheeks. "It's my heart." She rushed back to Anna. "I can feel it."

Mrs. Foreman threw her arms around Anna and drew her

into another embrace. A throat cleared, and Anna jerked back.

Mr. Foreman stood on the far side of the tent, as expressionless as a cow chewing its cud. She'd bet he was chewing a few choice words. Mrs. Foreman whipped out her handkerchief again and wiped her face before turning and walking toward her husband. Mr. Foreman took her by the arm, and with a final glare at Anna, led his wife toward town.

Twenty paces away, Mrs. Foreman looked over her shoulder and poured out a peaceful smile.

God had healed, again.

Anna forced her attention to the line of people waiting for prayer and repeated the imperative once again. *Don't look toward the bitter cherry.*

Though darkness prohibited any view, her eyes disobeyed and strayed toward the blackness.

"Anna."

She straightened and looked at Michael, but at the slight frown creasing his brow, she moved her gaze elsewhere. He'd announced that tonight, the tenth night, would be the last.

He rested a hand on her back, and her muscles stiffened. With the other hand, he motioned for the woman approaching to wait. He leaned close to Anna's ear. "There's a couple I'd like you to pray with."

The spicy scent of Michael's aftershave unsettled her empty stomach. "Others have been waiting."

He glanced at the line. "Remember our conversation. Be bold." The light from the lantern caught his grin. "But do so in a hurry."

His eyes challenged her before he broke contact and moved on.

Thirty minutes later, with most of the crowd dismissed, Michael rose from the back row and led a young couple forward.

The man hobbled, leaning on the woman next to him.

"Let's sit," Michael gestured to the front pew.

Stand.

The word slammed into Anna's mind. "Michael, I'd like us to stand."

Michael paused, half lowered to his chair. "He needs to sit."

Stand.

"Michael . . ."

With a heavy look, Michael sat and helped the man down beside him. The woman took a seat on the other side of her husband. Michael's eyes glanced toward a chair, and Anna pulled it up and sat in front of the threesome.

She closed her eyes and exhaled. The Spirit had said stand. And here they sat.

"It's his leg," the woman said. "Never been good. But lately, it's worse. He can't hardly go ten steps without having to stop. His back hurts all the time from the uneven gait."

Anna looked at the husband for confirmation. "What is your name, sir?"

"This is John Crane," the woman said, "and I'm Susan, his wife. We've come from Bellingham because we've heard of your gift."

Bellingham, nearly a week's journey.

Anna looked again to the husband, wanting his story. "Has there ever been an accident? A childhood illness?"

He shook his head. Beside him, Michael motioned her to pray, but Anna ignored him. She'd not rush ahead of the Lord to ease Michael's impatience.

"Does your leg hurt more at certain times?" Anna asked.

He shook his head again.

Mrs. Crane reached over and grabbed her husband's arm as he opened his mouth to speak. "It doesn't work right," Mrs. Crane said. "And it gets worse each passing year. Really, Miss Warren, there's nothing more to say. We just need you to pray."

"Have you confessed Jesus as your Savior?" Michael's first words.

"Yes, sir."

"Well, then." Michael looked at Anna, one brow raised. "Let's pray."

Anna closed her eyes, taking Mr. Crane's hands in her own. *Oh, God, what's going on here?*

Tristan listened to the quiet murmurs of Anna's prayers from the shadows. Like the other nights, he hadn't meant to come. Then again, he hadn't meant for many things to happen, like this ache that burned his chest whenever Anna was around. He leaned his head against the sugar maple he'd chosen in place of the bitter cherry in case Anna wandered out.

Anna sat back, released the hands of the couple, and stood. The woman's muffled sobs carried on the night air as she leaned her head into the shoulder of the man. In the muted firelight, those revival participants who remained shifted their gazes between the couple and Anna.

The couple left, the man hobbling.

One woman whispered to another, frowning toward Anna.

She'd failed. That was what they thought, but Tristan knew better. God had failed.

Michael laid a hand on Anna's arm and started to speak, but she pulled from his touch and retrieved her coat. Slinging it over her shoulder, she hurried to Maple. Tristan held his breath. If Michael followed . . . but he turned and greeted the last congregants.

Anna mounted her mare, and unaware of Tristan's presence at the edge of the woods, approached. He leaned closer to the trunk of the tree. Even in the moonlight, he noticed the web of tension woven across her features. As she rode past, no farther than ten feet from him, a tear trickled down her cheek.

An unexpected wave of compassion drowned the skepticism he worked so hard to feed. He bit his tongue, resisting the compulsion to call out her name. She'd gotten what she'd asked for, not that he was glad she'd been hurt. Not at all.

He hung his head. One tear snuck past his squeezed-shut eyes.

Why, Lord?

Chapter Thirteen

The next morning, Anna slid her feet over the bed. Coldness from the plank floor seeped through her wool stockings. With the revival finished and many prayed for and healed, she should feel joy. But her heart didn't respond to the *shoulds* of her mind.

She'd ended the revival a failure.

She tucked the gingham curtain behind its peg to reveal dull, gray light. Even the sun seemed hesitant this morning, offering its light but not its brilliance or warmth.

Relentless drizzle accompanied her walk to church. Fitting, considering the dampness of her spirit.

After sitting through the service in a haze, Anna wandered into the churchyard while families meandered down the hill to Yesler Hall for potluck. She berated herself for having no appetite for food or people. This draw to seclusion was why she had trouble fitting in. Her lack of community was her fault.

Breathing in the salt air, she slowly crossed the yard, undecided. If she had a family, they'd walk hand in hand, laughing, to join the others.

She glanced down at her hands. Mostly smooth, a bit of a callus from pulling ropes tight on the wagon and wielding reins. Rubbing them together, she veered from the direction of Yesler Hall toward the water. She couldn't face a chattering, jubilant church crowd with the failure of last night so fresh.

Her steps halted as she noticed John and Susan Crane speaking with Mr. Foreman. Had they been in church? Anna dropped her head and circled wide of the group.

"I should have warned you about praying with Miss Warren." Mr. Foreman's words seemed too loud for a close conversation in the emptying churchyard.

They coiled her heart, and though she told herself to keep

walking, they slowed her step.

Mrs. Crane responded, but the words were too quiet for Anna to understand.

"Nothing but claptrap. That's what it is."

Anna choked on her gasp. Mr. Foreman's accusations were not only uncalled for but a direct affront against the living God. Praying was not claptrap. Asking God to restore the broken was not hogwash.

She clenched her coat and rushed down the street. By the time she reached the cliff on the north end of town, her tears fell freely.

Echoing the psalmist's words, she stared at the water. "Why are you downcast, my soul?" People had been encouraged, healed, and saved. Yet her soul chose to focus on one prayer time at the end of the revival and a few harsh words from Mr. Foreman?

Tristan's words *God does not heal* rolled unbidden into her thoughts. When he heard about the Cranes, it would feed his resistance to God. He'd been oddly absent this morning, and she wondered if he'd have defended her to Mr. Foreman as he'd done with Michael.

She sighed aloud, letting the waves wash the sound away. A gull answered with a caw. He waddled closer. She held up empty hands. "Nothing to give you."

Shooing the bird away, she moaned again. "Nothing to give anyone, apparently."

The hum of conversation inside Yesler Hall competed with the arguments grinding inside Tristan's head. With a force of will, he planted his feet on the dusty floor. He'd made a commitment; he'd not leave.

"The reason for this meeting is simple." Frank Baldwin eyed Tristan, raising up a hand to quiet the men gathered. "To convince you to be our leader."

Tristan pulled his lips into a smile. "I want to be your leader."

Murmurs rippled through the room. Men straightened in their chairs, stared.

"But I can't."

The excited whispers fell silent. Rain splattered against the windows, the steady drone mimicking the pounding of Tristan's heart. He knew each of the thirty-two men in attendance. He'd helped them during harvest. Farming was like that, a community ordeal.

Which meant he was letting down the community by saying no.

He winced. Standing here in front of them—well, he wanted to help, wanted to be their leader. But he'd be helping the community more by starting a program with the university.

The door opened, and the sound of rain intensified. Heads turned as Arthur Denny entered. If it were possible, his solemn face looked more severe than usual, cheeks pinched, mouth taut. Water dripped from his felt hat. He shook it. Men sitting nearby, Jimmy included, wiped the spray from their faces.

Leaning against the wall at the front of the room, Tristan measured Denny, a surprise attendee. He wasn't a farmer, didn't have capital in agriculture. He could be here for one reason. To encourage Tristan to take the association position and thus be distracted from the university. Tristan firmed his mouth. Why did this have to be such a fight?

"Gentlemen." Denny stood at the back, crossed his arms, and jutted his chin out.

Tristan stared over the heads of the others straight back to Denny.

Frank cleared his throat, and Tristan broke eye contact with Denny to look at the eldest Baldwin brother.

Frank shuffled his feet. "Tristan, why don't we begin with

you telling us what a farmers' association includes."

Tristan glared. "Why don't you share your thoughts first?"

Frank evidently thought that getting Tristan talking would be a surer way to gain a commitment from him.

"Well . . . we might split up who grows what, try planting different things. You know, I've always had a hankering to try beets, and I sure do hate growing peas . . ."

Frank mumbled on. Even Tristan couldn't track with the clumsy phrases. Frank made the whole endeavor sound like a boys' schoolyard club. The only thing left to discuss was how to prank the girls.

Mr. Tulley, a man with more facial hair than a bear, raised his hand. "Would we have a monthly party or something?"

A party? What type of man wanted a party—let alone used the word *party*—when there was work to do?

"Gatherings would be part of it." Frank turned to Tristan. "Anything to add?"

Tristan narrowed his eyes. He didn't want to give a lecture, to appear too interested, but Frank's presentation had been a lazy effort. "Listen—"

"I'd like to add something." Jimmy strode to the front.

Here was a man with leadership potential. Amazing that only three months ago Jimmy had exhibited about as much interest in farming as a squirrel in swimming.

"I've worked for Tristan the last seven weeks. I've seen firsthand why you all want him for your leader. He's my top choice as well."

Oh, come on, Jimmy. He was supposed to share ideas, not lobby for Tristan's leadership.

Frank raised his brows. "That's what you wanted to add?"

Thank you, Frank. Keep the kid on track.

"We already know he's the best fit." Frank clapped Tristan on the back. "No one else cares as much for all this new machinery. No one else works hard as a badger. No one else is as thorough or successful."

If I'm so great, why won't the university give me a chance? Tristan glanced at Denny, who remained settled against the back wall.

"How about an association with different levels of membership?" Jimmy asked.

Tristan whipped his gaze back to Jimmy. This was a new thought.

"The majority of men are interested in a basic support group," Jimmy continued. "You know, a small entrance fee, a voice with legislature, camaraderie with other farmers, a newsletter about agricultural developments. But some of us want to experiment, try new things, invest a little more time. That could be a different level of membership."

Jimmy hooked his thumbs into his belt and turned to Tristan. "Someone like Frank can organize the basic group, and Tristan can focus on the experimental group."

A great idea, except it still required leadership from Tristan.

The door opened again. Two men slipped inside, collars raised high on their overcoats and hats pulled low. The wind slammed the door shut. Dexter Horton shrugged out of his slicker and placed his hat on one of the hooks by the door. Mr. Foreman did likewise.

Interesting. All latecomers were those not in agriculture.

"Sorry to intrude." Mr. Horton brushed a hand down his suit. "I hope I'm not too late to contribute to the discussion."

This'll be good.

Two bankers come to weigh in on agriculture. Probably to offer some business deal, which Tristan wasn't prepared to accept or decline.

"Please." Frank, always accepting and never suspicious, waved the men to the front.

Tristan's jaw tightened, and he wanted to question the meaning of the interruption, ask the men to wait until the end, but wouldn't that be exhibiting the kind of leadership he was trying not to accept?

"Thank you." Mr. Horton clasped his hands in front and addressed the group with a confidence borne from years in the seat of influence. "Starting an association is tricky. There are expenses—"

A loan. The bankers were here to pitch for business. Tristan could've ground his teeth through his jaw.

"—so I'd like to offer a fifty-dollar gift."

Tristan frowned. The farmers stared at Mr. Horton as if he'd offered an extra month of growing season. The gift must be a trick though, and Tristan still hadn't breathed.

"Well, Dexter, that's generous of you." Frank looked at Tristan, the pleasure in his eyes showing he'd fallen for whatever the banker had in mind.

"Thank you, Mr. Horton," Tristan said. "We're still working out the details of the association . . . like who will be in charge." Tristan looked right back at Frank, noticing a bit of the sparkle dim.

"Would there be stipulations on how that money could be used?" Frank asked.

Mr. Foreman stepped forward. "Not per se, but naturally, the money will be used for farming issues. Perhaps to purchase some fancy plow?"

Was he kidding? A *fancy plow*, as the banker had so articulately mentioned, cost a heap more than fifty dollars. What a way to fish for favor, as well as show ignorance. A banker should know better.

Mr. Foreman scanned the room, looking too pleased with himself. "While I'm up front——"

Tristan had the premonition he wasn't going to like what was coming next.

"I'd like to take a moment," Mr. Foreman said, "to encourage those of you who are clients of Dexter Horton and

Company to refrain from using Anna Warren as a freighter."

Tristan's heart plummeted. What did Anna have to do with anything?

"Miss Warren has been the center of some controversy," Mr. Foreman continued, "and we prefer those of you with loans from our bank, as representatives of our company, and therefore our community, to guard your reputations by refraining from hiring her services."

Tristan spotted three of Peter's former clients. Furrows lined their brows, evidence of the confusion palpable in the room. Anna still freighted for two of them.

"Well now, I suppose that finishes our business." Mr. Foreman turned to Mr. Horton and motioned him first down the aisle.

It finished Anna's business as well.

And his, here in this crowded, stale-smelling room.

"Thank you, gentlemen." Frank addressed the farmers. "Tristan and I, along with a few others, will draft a mission statement and post it at Joe's. Another meeting will be announced soon. Let's dismiss."

That was it? Wasn't anyone going to stand up for Anna? "Hold on." Tristan's voice shot out, silencing the murmurs. Horton and Foreman turned, midway to the door. "Whether you're clients of the bank or not, you're all part of this territory. If the company one keeps is any indication of reputation, you can't go wrong with Miss Warren. You all knew Peter. He was a good man." He pleaded with the eyes of those listening. "Let it be known I don't support Mr. Foreman's suggestion." Or threat, as it was.

Tristan flung his slicker over his shoulder and whipped his hat from the spindle of a chair. He plunged out the side door before anyone could hail him with questions. Rain pelted him, but he didn't stop to put on his slicker until he'd ridden several blocks. How dare Foreman interrupt the meeting and manipulate the farmers with a monetary gift. Buying support. How pathetic.

But as pathetic as it was, it would work. Money had power. Hadn't Foreman said as much to Tristan weeks ago?

Tristan's anger drained, replaced by something more feral and confusing. He feared for Anna.

"Having you along is such a blessing." Anna smiled at Nellie as the wagon rumbled over the ruts to Newcastle, carrying not only her freight but friends.

Nellie reached around Julia and squeezed Anna's arm. "So you've said, several times."

If she was going to build community and freight at the same time, she'd have to be creative. And inviting friends to join her was her most creative idea yet.

Now if that creativity could extend to dealing with Michael's attraction to her. She needed some way to deter it. Even if part of her relished the attention, she didn't feel for him the same as he did for her.

They'd shared breakfast yesterday at Conklin House. He'd been full of charm and compliments, as expected, but when she'd mentioned the Cranes, reserve had curtained off the affection in his eyes, so she'd changed the subject. They couldn't hide their differences on faith forever.

The wagon wheels creaked as the horses climbed the last ridge to Newcastle. Crates of groceries and fresh produce weighed down the back. Goods to Newcastle were frequently floated up the river system or across Lake Washington, but Drake Mercantile had endured a falling out with the captain and thus had hired Peter three years ago.

At the top of the ridge, Anna scanned the view to the west. The lake rested directly below in the foreground, then Puget Sound farther out, and finally the jagged mountains. Three large black birds circled the valley.

"Look, Julia." Anna pointed to the turkey vultures.

Julia glanced up from her buttoning the dress on her rag doll. "Herons!"

"Vultures," Nellie said.

"Yuck." Julia laid her head against Nellie's shoulder.

"Are you tired? It's been a long trip." Nellie stroked the girl's hair as she spoke to Anna. "I can't believe you did this for days upon days throughout years and years."

"A body gets used to sitting so many hours." Maybe inviting friends wasn't such a creative idea after all. "You can walk alongside if you'd like."

Nellie eyed the pair of drafts. "I don't think I could keep up." She shifted, rubbing a hand along her backside.

"It's just another twenty minutes or so to the settlement."

They followed the ridgeline as it angled to the river. The rough town, nestled at the bottom of a hillside, made Seattle look like a distinguished city.

"Tell me about your last moments with your father."

Anna's gaze jumped from the road to Nellie. No one had asked her for details from her time in Portland. She supposed they wanted to give her space.

The simple question carried her back to those days that seemed like last week, and at the same time, years ago. Focusing ahead on the smoke drifts rising above Newcastle, Anna sought for a steady voice. "I read to him hours each day. Jonathan Edwards's sermons, Scriptures, Dickens. He insisted I get outside and walk, but other than those walks, I stayed by his side. He told me the stories I'd heard hundreds of times, about New York, Mother, and Finney's revivals—although his voice was slurred and difficult to understand."

Anna gripped the reins tight, not letting the sadness loosen her concentration from the horses. "I knew, Nellie. I knew he wouldn't get better."

The horses snorted, and the steady, familiar clop calmed Anna.

Nellie reached for her hand. "When you pray for people, do you have an idea what will happen?"

"The first time I prayed for someone, the urge of the Spirit came so suddenly, I just placed my hand on the boy's head and started praying. I didn't have time to think. I was only twelve. A child's faith is so simple, unquestioning."

Was it the questioning now that bred anxiety, or was it the feeling that what she was doing was not fully accepted by the community?

"God speaks to me," Anna said. "Not with a voice, but with a subtle knowing. I feel his desire for people when I pray for them. With Father, I knew it was God's desire to take him home."

"Did your father agree?"

Anna nodded. "I'm not sure he did at first, but quickly his condition weakened, and he became peaceful with the thought of going home. Then . . ."

Anna pictured his eyes, the way they'd pleaded with a depth greater than words. She turned to Nellie. "He asked me to stay in Portland."

"Why?"

"Because he wanted me to have a fresh start in a larger place, I guess. He felt guilty about me being different than the other children here, not attending school and such."

"But why a new place? You know so many people here."

Anna frowned, not having an answer. Wanting to please him, she'd agreed to try. She'd not wasted time sorting through his reasons. Why would he want her to stay and work with Mrs. Ford instead of returning to the place he knew she loved, the cabin—

Anna gasped. "Nellie!" She squeezed the hand holding hers. "He *did* give our land away."

"What?"

It seemed so obvious now. "That's why he wanted me to stay in Portland."

His desire for her to stay in Portland had been more than a father looking out for his daughter. It'd been a father hiding a secret.

"After I agreed to give Portland a try"—Anna's words stuck in her throat—"he told me he'd written a letter, some final business. I didn't look at it, just handed it to Mrs. Ford, who said she'd post it."

The rumor was true. She knew it now, deep inside where people knew things they didn't want to know. Why hadn't Mr. Wyse said anything? She gasped again. He'd tried, but Tristan had interrupted. And then she'd run off to Nellie's, and Mr. Wyse had left town.

"Who owns your land, then?" Nellie asked.

"I . . . I don't know."

"Oh, Anna. I'm sorry."

The band of green trees blurred together in one line as Anna stared ahead.

Julia coughed, and Nellie stirred. "That's the fourth time I've heard her cough since lunch." Nellie cupped Julia's face and examined the girl's eyes. "Are you hungry, Jules? You didn't eat much."

"My tummy hurts."

"Are you warm enough?" Nellie looked at the sky. "I shouldn't have brought her out in the cold for such a long trip."

Anna couldn't concentrate. Her mind ran circles. The day before yesterday she'd received word from the Wiltons that they did not own her land, and now, suddenly, she could think of many people to whom Father might have given the land. Mr. Mercer wanted to expand his dairy. Mr. Thatcher loved the location between Seattle and Lake Washington. Mr. Roberts had asked to purchase it and had made generous offers. The Seattle

Coal Company had hinted they would be interested if Father wanted to sell.

Tristan.

The more she learned about his relationship with her father, the more it seemed like father-son, not businessman-client. But if Father had left the land to Tristan, Tristan would have said something. The man who had no qualms about sharing his opinions on healing, why would he remain silent about owning her land?

It couldn't be Tristan. He had more than enough land. Fertile, cleared, flat land. Father was too practical to leave the land to someone who didn't need it.

Oh, God, it's true. My land is gone.

Chapter Fourteen

Anna's heart quickened as the woman in bed moaned, a hollow sound rending the silence of night. Moisture beaded on Anna's lip, itching, but her tired arms couldn't lift to scratch. The circle of light from the lamp barely reached the clock on the far wall. A quarter past three. Two hours had passed since Mrs. Maynard's pounding on the cabin door had jarred Anna from sleep.

The door creaked open, and Doc slipped through. "You don't have to do this." He looked at Anna as he sat on the bed and took the ill woman's hand.

The summons had come so unexpectedly, she'd jumped from bed and rode Maple through the cold without a prayer to the Lord for discernment. Now, in the fog of sleepiness, she doubted her decision. Tristan had said she couldn't please everyone, and maybe that was what she was trying to do.

"If I'm not in your way, I'll pray." She'd not risk being disobedient because she was too fatigued to think straight.

"I'm no fool, Anna. I can only do so much. You can pray anytime you want."

"Thank you."

As she prayed, Anna examined the pale woman in bed. Lines edged her closed eyes, but a pure skin tone spoke of youth. Tangled red curls matted thick to her forehead and neck. And right below her neck, protruding from the top of the gown borrowed from Mrs. Maynard, the gash Doc had sewn appeared puffed and discolored.

"Have you checked her belongings?" Mrs. Maynard stood in the doorway.

Doc shook his head. "Doesn't have any."

Anna leaned forward on her chair and patted the woman's

pockets.

"I've already searched." Doc walked to a drawer and replaced a vial. "I've done what I can for this stranger. I'm going to rest before checking back." He paused at the door, looking at Anna with narrowed eyes. "Don't wear yourself out. It's in the Lord's hands. It won't help to beg."

Anna nodded and grasped the woman's limp hands. One last prayer, then she too had to sleep.

Her mouth opened, but words stalled. She'd already prayed Psalm 91 and Ephesians 3:16–21. She'd sung hymns. She'd let the yearning of her heart offer wordless petitions.

Tristan's words pummeled her thoughts. *God doesn't heal. God doesn't heal. God doesn't heal.*

"You heal. You restore. You mend what sin has shred apart." Confession of truth rose from within her. "You created the earth from nothing. The heavens, you stretched out like a canopy. Your arms you stretched out surrendered to death. And now, you reign over death, the first fruit of resurrection."

Fingers flitted in her hand, a touch so light against Anna's sweaty palms she wondered if she imagined it.

God doesn't heal.

Anna wiped a hand across her eyes and moaned. "Tristan, you're killing me."

The woman's head shifted.

Anna released the patient's hands and dug into the bag at her feet until she felt her Bible. She pulled the book out and flipped through I Chronicles until she found the passage on the building of the temple, and read, "'Yours, Lord, is the greatness and the power and the glory and the majesty and the splendor, for everything in heaven and earth is yours.'"

Everything. Anna's life, this woman's life, Tristan's, Michael's, Nellie's. She couldn't stop the flood of names and images swarming her mind. Clyde Foreman, crusty demeanor and all. And more so, the things for which they all fought to do and be: Tristan's program, Michael's ministry, her freighting business.

Her land. *Oh, Lord.* Her land—no matter who held the title—was the Lord's.

She stared at her hands, fingers clutching her Bible with white-knuckle strength. Concentrating on the words, *everything in heaven and earth is yours*, she loosened her grip, relaxed her body. She closed her eyes, but instead of sleepiness, watchfulness overtook her spirit.

The healer. She could no more heal a person than she could hang the moon. How easy to be deceived and think her gift was something special. That with the strength of her will—or according to Michael, her faith—she could make a person live or die. How foolish.

She opened her eyes and continued reading. "'Yours, Lord, is the kingdom; you are exalted as head over all. Wealth and honor come from you; you are the ruler of all things.'" Her eyes scanned ahead, caught the upcoming words, and she reclaimed the stranger's hands. "In your hands are strength and power to exalt and give strength to all."

A whimper sounded, and tears leaked from the woman's closed eyelids. Anna's pulse quickened. The woman's lips moved, but no words sounded. Her eyelids fluttered, then jerked open. Dark eyes, glinting in the lantern light, looked directly at Anna.

"He tried to kill me." The woman's voice rasped. She sat up and scanned the room. "Oh God."

Anna sprung from her chair and put her arms around the woman. "You're safe now." The wound peeked from the woman's gown. A knife wound? Mercy.

Doc burst through the door. "What's going on?" He took one look at Anna's arms around his patient. "I see."

When the woman's cries subsided, Doc sat on the opposite bedside from Anna and pried the woman's arms from around

Anna's neck. "And what do we have the honor of calling you, young lady?"

"Alive. Call me alive."

Doc raised his brows. "Well then. First things first. Lots of rest. You've sustained internal injuries the likes from which I wasn't sure you could recuperate." Doc smiled and patted Anna's arm. "But this is Anna, and she has prayed you back to health."

"No." Anna shook her head. "The Lord has strengthened you."

The woman sank back. "Strengthened, yes. But I still feel weak. I ache from my head to my waist." She closed her eyes and let out a groan. "I'm Amelia." She paused, and the two breaths she took sounded of pain and sorrow. "Just Amelia. That's all."

Anna squeezed Amelia's hand and stood. "Welcome to Seattle, Amelia." The clock read five past four as she slipped from the room. Anna leaned against the closed door, hand resting on the handle. "Yours is the kingdom, O Lord."

She grinned, almost laughed at the strangeness of which God moved within his Kingdom. What tired joy.

Yes, let joy swell tonight when fatigue licked at her soul. Tomorrow she'd face the questions.

Anna rubbed her eyes, the burning evidence of the short night. Sitting up, she surveyed the Maynard's crowded guest room. With its boxes of medicine and sterilized equipment stacked in the corner, the room served more as overflow from the surgery than a welcome respite for others. She yawned, weariness spanning from body to spirit.

The approach of this first Christmas without Father had brought fresh depression. Combined with her lack of sleep, the uncertain relationship with Michael, and Julia's new stomach pain, it was too much. She stretched her arms above her head.

The enigma of Tristan didn't help. Until the past weeks, she'd not paid heed to his frenzied work effort, his discipline, and his knack for leadership.

Nor the depth of his cynicism.

Light snuck through the curtains and beckoned her to join the half-passed day. She glanced at the clock. No, not half-passed. Only nine in the morning.

She brushed the wrinkles from her dress and walked to the kitchen, where Mrs. Maynard hummed as she fried eggs.

Mrs. Maynard pushed a warm cup into Anna's hands. "Apple cider."

"Thank you." The steam swirled warm beneath her nose and pricked her with a measure of alertness.

Doc entered the kitchen and grabbed his own cup of cider.

"How's Amelia?" Anna asked.

"That gash was deep. Definitely a knife wound." Doc sat at the table and leaned forward on his elbows. "But she says the throbbing is gone. It's a miracle, Anna."

"Will she be safe?"

Mrs. Maynard tried to refill Anna's plate, but Anna pushed the spoon away.

"Don't really know where she came from or where she'll stay, but the marshal will take care of the safety issues," Doc said. "You don't need something else to worry about."

"What about Julia?" The child had grown worse since the trip to Newcastle.

Doc chewed long before swallowing. "It's not good. I need to do more research."

Anna's food stuck in her throat, and she reached for her cider.

"More, dear?" Mrs. Maynard stood, teapot ready.

"No, thank you. I'm supposed to meet with Mr. Yesler this morning."

She bid the Maynards good-bye, returned to the guest

room, brushed her hair, and splashed water on her face. She looked like a wilted moonflower, not that Mr. Yesler would notice. She'd be lucky to get five minutes of time from the businessman who had as much to do with Seattle's success as the Denny brothers and Doc.

The walk around the edge of Elliot Bay to Yesler's Wharf seemed twice as long to her sleep-deprived body. Machinery purred, crowding her thoughts as she drew near the mill and entered Mr. Yesler's office. Dust plastered every surface, and the stuffiness of the air stung her nose.

Mr. Yesler buzzed through the back door and halted at the sight of her. "Anna." He tossed some papers on a desk and checked his pocket watch. "Ah, ten already."

"Good morning, Mr. Yesler. About the special order for next week. I'd rather take it Tuesday—"

"There's been a change." Mr. Yesler held up a hand, and with his other hand, scribbled a note on a scrap of newspaper. "I no longer need your services."

"That's fine."

He smoothed his beard. "No, it's not. I do hate to cancel once a deal's been made. And you offered the best price."

Which meant Mr. Yesler saved money, and for a man driven by profit and industry, that was a deal maker. Evidently, something had changed his mind.

Anna bridged a heap of sawdust and stood beside the short man. "I'm not offended."

"I've put you out of a job."

"I'm getting all the business I need."

Mr. Yesler's eyes narrowed as he stared at her. "Let's hope that continues." He checked his watch again and glanced out the window.

"I'm not worried." She'd never lacked for customers. "Good day, Mr. Yesler."

"And to you, Anna." He was halfway out the back entrance

before he'd finished his farewell.

If Seattle continued to prosper, it needed men like Yesler, like Father. Men who rushed and worked and clattered like tomorrow's sun was in danger of not rising, thus leaving a task undone. Forbid such a thought.

Men like Tristan.

The door slammed shut behind her as she exited. She paced Front Street, pushing herself in spite of her lack of energy. Home sounded like heaven. She needed a fire, a bath, and a nap.

"Miss Warren."

Mr. Kellman sauntered up, a grizzly of a man with his face half covered with whiskers and the hair on his head looking bushy enough to conceal treasure.

The sight of this loyal customer drew out her smile. "Mr. Kellman. It's nice to see you. You're due for more supplies." She frowned. "Unless you're picking them up today yourself."

"Yes." He stared at his feet. "Doing it myself this month, I'm afraid."

"Is everything all right?"

"Anna, I've known you since you were this high." He marked his waist with his arm. "What a dear thing you were." He smiled briefly. "I hate to say this, but I'm going to need to secure a new freighter."

Her jagged breath triggered a cough. "I—I'm not sure I understand." Not at all. "Have I done something to upset you?" She'd make it right, as Father had taught her.

"No. It's nothing like that. It's . . ." He looked away. "Mr. Foreman has sent a letter to the customers of Dexter and Horton, advising those of us with loans not to, well, not to . . ."

"Hire me?" Anna cringed at the stinging tone of her voice.

Mr. Kellman sighed. "Yes, that's about it."

More than three-quarters of her customers banked with D&H. How many of them had loans?

"Miss Warren, I'm sorry. I can't afford to challenge Mr.

Foreman's wishes."

"No. You need to protect your business." Mr. Kellman would lose a hefty logging enterprise if Mr. Foreman foreclosed his loan. "Good day, Mr. Kellman. Thank you for explaining to me. Best wishes."

"And to you, Miss Warren."

She tried to smile. Best wishes to her, indeed. After a number of her customers left, which they'd be forced to do, she'd need those good wishes.

Anna scanned the crates in the back room of Joe's Mercantile, hugging herself to ward off the chill. The warmth of the stove failed to reach from the main room beyond the curtain to the storage area.

"Would you like some help?"

Anna flinched at the familiar voice and turned to greet Mr. Roberts. The gleam in his eyes combined with the tone of his voice seemed more like an offer of marriage than an offer to cart crates.

"No, thanks."

He wiped a dirty hand across his brow. She couldn't believe this man was rumored to be rich. Scuffed shoes, pants too short, unkempt beard. The only indication the rumor might be true was his generous offer to buy their land three years ago.

Had Father . . . Not possible.

He eyed the mess across the storage area. "Looks like a lot to haul."

"I'm not taking all this." She donned a polite look, recalling Father's phrasing when dealing with a difficult customer. "I appreciate your offer, Mr. Roberts, but you are a busy man, and I insist you attend to your business."

Cocking his head, he snickered. "Very well, Miss Warren. I see not much has changed." He exited the rear door without a backward glance.

Anna sighed and hoisted a box of groceries. Good thing she knew every lip of wood on Joe's floor, every obstruction loitering out back, because she couldn't see where she was going. She could walk this route blindfolded or in her—

She stumbled on a rock and fought for balance.

"Let me take that."

The voice was young, male, and unknown. Surrendering the crate, she glimpsed a gangly youth as he swung away. He shifted the load to one arm and pushed the other crates on the wagon bed until he had a space. Fine blond hair fell in his face when he maneuvered the crate among the others, but he blew out a breath and tossed his head, clearing the bangs away.

"Any more?" he asked.

She liked the honesty of his face, and even though he didn't smile, friendliness shone in his eyes.

"Three." She led the way to the back room and pointed to hardware supplies and fabric bolts.

Joe pushed a sewing machine in from the main room. "Take this, too." It looked cracked and ready to snap.

Anna puckered her brow. "Whatever for?"

"Mrs. Borst wants it. Said if Frieda was ever getting rid of it to send it her way."

"Forty miles of rattling might bust this wheel off."

"Regardless. Here you go."

Father had said, *Accept the surprises like they aren't a big deal, and customers will remember you.* With Mr. Foreman's actions against her, she could use all the favor she could get.

She nodded at her helper. "You can start making the trips, but I'll have to rearrange a few things."

He followed her out, carrying two crates.

A deep voice started singing, and she jerked to a stop. The youth knocked her from behind. "Sorry," she muttered, moving out of the way, still focused on Lazarus's rich voice.

"We are climbing Jacob's ladder. We are climbing Jacob's ladder."

His was the only voice she loved as much as Father's, thick and smooth as shredded cedar bark. He unloaded a barrel of apples from Tristan's wagon, which was wedged between hers and the bank next door. Never mind Tristan had blocked the road. Efficiency at all costs. Lazarus caught her gaze and smiled.

The black man yelled past her. "Jimmy, when you done helping Miss Anna, ask Joe how much for three barrels of apples."

Anna's smile faded. Her helper was part of Tristan's operation?

He'd rearranged some boxes and retrieved the sewing machine and now awaited her direction.

"Thank you," she said. "Let's tie the machine to these crates. Maybe that will keep it from bouncing too much."

He intertwined the rope between the crates and the spinning wheel twice as much as she would have. A Tristan find all right. Thorough and diligent.

"All set." Satisfaction shone in his blue eyes, though he still hadn't smiled, also confirmation he was a Tristan find.

"Thank you, Mr. . . ."

"Jimmy. I'm not old enough to be a mister."

"If you're old enough to work hard"—Tristan's voice came from behind her—"you're old enough to be a mister."

Jimmy straightened his shoulders and thrust his hand out to her. "Mr. Jorgensen. My pleasure to assist."

Anna smiled at the way Tristan commanded respect. And he thought he wasn't a leader. She shook Jimmy's hand. His grasp was quick and his shake weak.

Jimmy turned to Tristan. "I'll see about those apples." Hands in pockets, he ambled away.

Evidently, Tristan hadn't worked on Jimmy's stride yet. Before meeting Tristan, she hadn't known it was possible to admire a man's walk. Yet when she'd stepped from the wagon to apologize for that broken plow, the way he strode across his field had made her want to get on her knees and beg forgiveness.

He had that same commanding presence now, looking at her in a way that made her want—no need—to step back and seek space, which she did.

In turn, Tristan leaned against the wagon and folded his arms, staring after Jimmy. "I'll have to work on his handshake, but he's coming along."

Leadership seeped from Tristan. Even if he didn't want to run an association, or if he didn't get his opportunity with the university, he'd find a way to pass on knowledge.

"His handshake was fine."

"Lacks confidence."

"A shake's a shake."

Tristan held out his dirt-coated hand. His eyes locked on her hand until she reached out. He gripped her fingers loosely, wiggled his wrist several times, and let go. Her arm fell to her side.

"Not good," he said.

He held out his hand again. She reached right away.

He grasped her hand and shook it with precise movements. "Better."

He held out his hand a third time. She reached to grasp his hand firmly and do her part of the shake, but he intercepted her hand, placed his fingers beneath hers and his thumb on top. He brought her hand to his lips and kissed it.

"Best."

Anna snatched her hand back as the weight of his glance struck her heart. It wasn't every day a woman received royal manners from a potato-packing, somber-faced farmer with dirt, not a crown, on his brow. She managed the slightest twitch of her lips, nodded, and stepped around the wagon, where the air felt cooler, more breathable. A rope dangled from the corner of the wagon box. She grabbed it and yanked.

"It's secure. I checked."

She jumped, the weight of awareness traveling from her heart into her stomach, making it feel like she'd eaten rocks for lunch. He'd charmed her, then followed her when she'd sought space. She'd not have thought it possible of him to be so . . . agreeable, friendly? Though by now, she should have learned to stop connecting *impossible* to Tristan and to anticipate the unexpected.

A wagon rolled by on Front Street, and a boy stood up in its bed. "Hey, Miss Warren!"

Anna waved at Colt Johnson. Though she couldn't see it from this distance, she was sure the twelve-year-old wiggled the four fingers that had begun to recover movement. She'd prayed with him three times now, and each time they prayed, she felt new joy that God would bring healing.

Tristan shuffled his feet next to her, and Anna looked up at his stony face. The charming man had taken leave.

"People think prayer is like medicine. Some magic cure."

The bitterness of his voice strangled her joy.

"There's nothing magic about prayer," she said.

"I know."

She wanted to ask how he knew, but she couldn't imagine him pouring out his story like a hospitable glass of tea. For all his talk of hospitality, Tristan Porter couldn't be classified as open. Confident, yes. And as today proved, intimidating even when amiable.

Tristan stalked to his wagon, reached up to the front, and pulled an apple off the seat. With one chomp he devoured half the green fruit.

She drew alongside him, as close as she dared—about three feet. "Maybe there is a bit of magic in prayer."

His gaze snapped to hers, as she'd hoped.

"Not magic as in we get what we want, but the magic of

intimacy. We get what we need. Closeness with our heavenly Father." She gripped the top of the wheel. "Healing happens when there's intimacy. But intimacy can't happen without trust."

He sighed. "Spare me the sermon, Saint."

"It's no sermon." She inched closer. "It's truth."

"Truth or not, keep it to yourself."

She'd pushed too far.

He tossed his apple core into a bush. "Don't you have a delivery?" With those husky words, he turned and walked away.

She tried to ignore the tripping of her heart.

How was she to reconcile the Tristan who defended her with the Tristan who, at times, couldn't stand to be around her? Like chicken gravy on fresh berries. A colossal mismatch.

Chapter Fifteen

Tristan fisted his hand, the money Joe paid for the apples digging into his palm. Anna's words quarried a hole in his heart: *the magic of intimacy, the closeness of the heavenly Father*. He knew how close God could be—or rather, how far off. When his father and brothers had died at Gettysburg and life plummeted, he'd called out to God. And what did he get? A dead mother.

People had tried to comfort him. Friends. Church members. They spoke of providence, of God working good things from bad. A boy didn't need theology. He needed to be held. He needed to know the trembling earth beneath him wouldn't open and consume him.

He shoved the money in his pocket and pushed around the few remaining crates in his wagon. Spying a crate of apples, he frowned. "Jimmy!" He'd sold three crates to Joe, and three had gone to Mrs. Tolliver. Had he loaded seven by mistake?

Jimmy rounded the corner by Dexter and Horton Bank. "Yes?"

"How many crates did you load into Mrs. Tolliver's wagon?"

"Two."

"She paid for three." The roundtrip north to her cabin and back would take an hour, and then he'd have to go south to his homestead. Too much time.

Anna's wagon was gone. "Find Anna."

"You mean Miss Warren?"

"Yes, Miss Warren." Was there another Anna? Not a chance. Not in name or personhood.

Lazarus walked from Joe's, that constant whistle streaming from his lips.

"Laz, you seen Anna?"

"She long gone."

Tristan jumped up to the seat, reached underneath, and pulled out two pieces of paper, one of which had a footprint square across the middle. Oh well. He thrust the sheets toward Jimmy. "Take these to the *Puget Sound Dispatch*. My next editorial."

Jimmy looked down and read a few lines, then grinned. "Nice. Challenging the importance of the railroad. Should go over well."

Lazarus laughed. "You know better. A railroad terminus means we plant more, harvest more, sell more, earn more."

Rolling his eyes, Tristan huffed. "It's not about the money. Besides, what good does a railroad do without people who know how to grow things?"

Lazarus and Jimmy stared at him like he'd lost his mind.

"Lumber. It's about the lumber," Jimmy said.

Everything was about the railroad and the lumber. "People need more than trees. You can't civilize a region with trees. You can't eat trees." He released the brake on the wagon. "You two relax. I'll pick you up in an hour."

Keeping the pace steady, he drove north. Damp air snuck between the open flaps of his coat, and he cinched the wool tighter. Solid clouds mantled the sky. In the six years he'd been in the Pacific Northwest, he'd gotten good at predicting weather. Now to master predicting how Anna might react *if* he told her about . . . no, not an option.

He had that letter hidden away, the one Peter had enclosed with his—*in case Anna returns*. She'd get her letter eventually. He just needed a bit more time.

He turned up Pine Street, passing half-cleared lots. Angling toward the woods and the road to Lake Union, he pushed his team as much as he could without being irresponsible.

Michael rode from the trees, sitting tall in the saddle. Not in the mood to argue, Tristan searched for an escape, as if one could easily veer a wagon into the woods and hide.

Michael looked up, and his countenance faltered. He reined in his horse near the wagon. "What brings you north of Seattle?"

"Apples for Mrs. Tolliver."

Michael studied Tristan and seemed to be pondering his next comment.

Did they have to play at civility? What did a preacher and a farmer have in common?

That was the problem. They had nothing in common but a fascination with Anna. God help him, Tristan *was* fascinated. She dominated his thoughts, and not only because he owned her land.

"I'm sorry you didn't make it to the revival. Other than that one evening."

That one evening, as in the evening Michael had accused Anna of being heartless, willing to let others suffer because she didn't assert more faith in her prayers.

"Listen, Tristan." Michael scratched the back of his neck. "If it makes you feel better, I've apologized to Anna several times. I meant to encourage her in her amazing gift."

The idea of Michael groveling at Anna's feet made him feel better. And worse. He didn't want Michael spending more time with Anna, filling her head with thoughts of ministry and miracles. Couldn't a person live a simple life, serving others through friendship and hard work? Wasn't that good enough? Everything with Michael was extravagant, superspiritual. And next to Michael, Tristan felt lame. Like the horse that couldn't keep up.

Tristan grabbed the reins.

Michael reached his hand out but refrained from touching Tristan. "Whatever's eating your spirit, know that the Lord cares. More than cares. He—"

"Did Anna put you up to this?"

Michael's posture stiffened. "Up to what? Telling you God

cares? I know the two of you squabble, and she's told me her concern for you—"

Marvelous . . .

"—but Anna's not the type to put someone up to something."

Touché.

"Telling people about Jesus's love is who I am. That's why I'm telling you, because you may have heard it, but you don't believe it." Michael started off, but turned his mount back. "You know what your problem is?"

Tristan caught the widening of his eyes and squelched it before Michael had a chance to notice the surprise. Michael was meting out a bit of what Tristan had that *one evening*. Except Tristan had been inches from Michael's face and had laid a hand on Michael's shoulder. It had either been a hand to Michael's shoulder or a fist to his face. Tristan grinned. "I'm waiting."

"You rile Anna with your questions, but you don't take her answers seriously."

"Doesn't seem like such a bad problem to me."

"It is a problem. She's intimidated by you, and it holds her back in ministry."

Anna had more strength of presence than he could ever hope to possess. If someone was holding her back, it wasn't him. "Anna's not intimidated by anyone."

"I can see it in her eyes."

Tristan poured all the hardness he could muster into his glare. Two could play this game. "You want to know what I see in her eyes? In her face, and even in her heart? She's weary with you. With your expectations. She doesn't know how she's supposed to act around you. Like Moses wielding his staff or like Elisha chasing after Elijah, seeking the double blessing."

Michael wasn't so lucky to catch the widening of his eyes. "You know your Scripture."

"I'm not a heathen." Tristan raked his fingers through his

hair. "I'll tell you who I am. I've had my 'thank-you Jesus' experience. And now I'm a desert-wandering, disillusioned disciple."

"Since we're being honest, this is who I am. A preacher. If I get preachy with you, put up with it." He drew his horse one step closer—close enough Tristan could reach out and grip his shoulder.

"And you know who else I am? I'm a man who cares for Anna. Deeply." Michael's jaw twitched. "Deal with it."

Before Tristan could respond, Michael kneed his horse and rode away. Which was for Michael's benefit. Tristan would not have put a hand to the preacher's shoulder today.

If Michael cared for Anna, fine. As long as he didn't crush her faith with his enthusiasm. They belonged together. Both charismatic, obedient to the Lord, trusting, joyful. If Michael married Anna and took her away, Tristan's problem with her land would be solved. He might not ever have to confess.

He tried to make the idea sound enticing.

It wasn't.

By the time Tristan returned home and put the wagon away, his stomach was growling worse than a cornered badger. And it was raining. Water dripped on his face, irritating more than his skin; the annoyance went soul deep, at least today. Man, he wished he had a meal waiting for him. He didn't do rain well, not like a seasoned freighter like Anna.

Jimmy tromped across the field with Lazarus, and Tristan entered his cabin, aware for the first time in years that being alone could actually be lonely. Homes were supposed to smell of spices and fresh bread and soap. Not old, dried earth crusted onto shirts piled over the back of a chair.

He hung his dripping coat by the door, shrugged out of his boots, and splashed fresh water on his face, rinsing off the grime.

The contents on his kitchen shelves looked about as exciting as his boyhood rock collection of, backyard stones. He chose a jar of Mrs. Tolliver's blackberries and three leftover biscuits, one with a protrusion of mold. No problem. He tweaked it off.

He grabbed a blanket, sat on the porch, and ate, trying to ignore the smoke drifting from Lazarus's chimney. He'd heat up some of his famous bean and rutabaga stew, and he and Jimmy would laugh and chat. Maybe even comment about how grumpy Tristan had been.

Tristan forced down the last bite of stale biscuit and rose. He used to love the solitude after a hard day, but ever since the day Anna'd come and cleaned, the cabin had felt different. Empty.

He went out to the barn and began sharpening tools. He needed a distraction before his mind settled on Anna by default, which would lead to the spiritual questions, which would lead to the ache.

Footsteps sounded, and he recognized Lazarus's approach.

"Brought you some leftovers."

Charity. It churned his insides, or maybe that was still hunger pains. He looked at the stew. When charity tasted good, he could live with the slap to his pride. He set down his axe and took the offering. Not caring about the sawdust on the stool by his worktable, he sat. "Thanks."

Lazarus nudged his side. "You told her yet?"

Shoveling in a bite of food, Tristan shook his head.

"Needs to be done."

Needs to be done about as much as he needed to lead the association.

"What you got against her?"

Tristan swallowed. "Nothing."

Lazarus chuckled. "Then I guess the question is, what you got for her?"

"Nothing." What had Lazarus put in this stew? Seemed

spicier than usual. "Not like Michael."

"Oh, I see." Lazarus settled on a crate.

"No. You don't see." The strength of his voice surprised him. "It's like this. Anna is everything good and pleasant and trustworthy and spiritual. Which of those things applies to me?"

"How does a seed grow?"

Tristan growled. The man changed subjects faster than thunder followed lightning.

"Tell me how a seed grows."

"A seed gets plunged into the ground." Impatience flattened his tone. "Warmth, moisture, light, and oxygen trigger germination. The plant sprouts, and rain and sun bring harvest."

"No." Lazarus shifted, reaching for a piece of straw and shoving it between his lips. "A seed breaks. Cracks open."

"That's called germination. Which I mentioned."

"Not germinate. That's fancy jargon." He worked the straw around in his mouth. "Breaks. That's soul jargon."

"Sure."

Lazarus could play his semantics game all he wanted.

"We plunge that seed into darkness," Lazarus said, "and it's gotta crack. It's gotta break its shell and push toward light. That's how a seed grows." He grinned.

"Fine, Laz. That's how a seed grows."

"You don't know what I'm talking about."

Tristan tossed the tin plate down on his worktable. When he stood, it felt like three barrels of potatoes were strapped to his back. "I know what you're *trying* to talk about." He whipped his hat off and squeezed the worn felt. "You're trying to tell me I have to break open before God. I know a sermon when I hear one. And yours is the third today." Tristan paced to Lazarus and leaned close. "How's this for an analogy? Some seeds don't sprout. They fail to break soil and see sun. They remain hidden in darkness." The tears that threatened had reduced his voice to a husky moan. Stupid, pathetic weakness.

Lazarus stared back at him. "I gets it. I gets it, son." He stood from the crate and brushed off his hands. "My life ain't been peaches 'n' cream neither. Just thought that if Anna be causing you so much discomfort, might be the Lord's way of saying 'time to break.'"

Or it might mean time to avoid Anna. Tristan put his head in his hands, waiting for Lazarus to leave. A minute later, receding footsteps punctured the silence.

Lazarus was right. A seed had to be broken. In order to grow, in order to give life, a seed had to crack.

But, oh Lord, the rain. Where is the rain?

Rain softened the seed, coaxed it open.

And his soul hadn't seen rain in seven years.

Later that week, Tristan entered Arthur Denny's office with a lightness in his step he hadn't felt in months. In his coat pocket he carried the needed letters to convince Denny that a school of agriculture was crucial. Now.

"Good morning, Tristan."

"Morning, sir."

Sunlight slanted through the window, shafting across Denny's desk and revealing its dust-free surface. As usual, Denny dressed casual. Tristan wasn't fooled. Nothing about Denny's attitude was ever casual, which was why Tristan had great respect for the man.

"You've got something for me." Denny scanned the words of the first page Tristan gave him. "This Jonathan Turner, creator of the Illinois Industrial League . . . interesting observations."

Tristan fought the urge to roll his eyes. Interesting observations? Professor Turner had been the initial force behind the Morrill Act and championed any effort from a university to increase its impact on the working class. The man's words were more than observations.

Denny shuffled the pages to Delegate Garfielde's letter. After a few seconds, he chuckled and set it aside. "Of course Garfielde's in favor. The man's always looking for something new."

Denny frowned as he perused the third letter, the one from Illinois senator Lyman Trumbull. "He says there's no chance for a Morrill grant. Our population is too small, we're not a state, and the university is an established institution."

"Keep reading."

Denny's brow furrowed, his lips moving soundlessly as he finished. "Oh." He chuckled again.

Tristan leaned across the desk and motioned halfway down. "'Every institution hoping to make a name for itself should have an agricultural program.' And see this line?" Tristan pointed to the bottom of the page. "Prudent. He says it's prudent to start now, while Seattle is still in the stages of formation."

Prudent, a word that defined Denny and should delight the cautious man.

Denny straightened the letters into a pile on his desk. "You've done your research. I'm impressed."

Sensing an impending *but*, Tristan intervened. "You've missed a letter."

Denny searched and pulled out a wrinkled envelope. "Justus von Liebig?"

"A professor from the University of Munich."

"Germany."

"Yes. A chemist."

Denny stroked his beard, read a few seconds, then shook his head. "This is too technical for me."

"Here." Tristan pointed to a paragraph. "Von Liebig says the most important thing an institution can do is build its chemistry program as it relates to the industries of the community." Tristan sat back and crossed his arms. "In our case, agriculture, logging, mining. We need a program that teaches about plants, trees, soils, minerals."

"And that can't be done in an association?"

Was Denny listening? This wasn't association material. This was fodder for academia. He fought to keep his voice conversational. "The focus of an association is different than that of a university."

"The focus of an association can be what you want it to be."

The room closed around him, and if the roof collapsed, he'd feel no less squashed.

Denny stood. "In five years we'll be more ready and capable for a venture like this. I admit, though, your enthusiasm is contagious. However, in the past decade the school's had to shut down twice for lack of students or funds, and we've yet to graduate a student."

Maybe if they had a good program, they could graduate a student.

"There'll be a day for this. In the meantime . . ." Denny perched on the edge of the desk. "If you could find some acres of land near the school, start clearing and grooming the land . . ."

Tristan's heart stopped. Acres near the school? Anna had those. Correction. *He* had those. "I can find acres."

"Hmmm." Denny nodded. "That's the next step. If you start farming acres nearby, it'd be a simple transition to add a few students when we're ready."

Hope cut off Tristan's ability to speak. This was the closest he'd gotten to a positive response.

"Focus on the land first."

How could he not focus on that land? It'd consumed his thoughts. Tristan cleared his throat. "I'll find those acres."

Finding the courage to tell Anna was something entirely different.

Anna drove her wagon through town, the afternoon light skimming the water like a long arm. Despite the clearing skies, the air kissed cold on her cheeks. Her body sagged. How she didn't want to freight again tomorrow, but she couldn't turn down a trip, not when trips were becoming scarce as sunny days.

Maybe she should quit the business. Mrs. Tolliver could teach her how to make preserves and harvest honey. Anna could start an orchard—

Her land. Her stomach turned over, reminding her of the low-grade nausea that had plagued her since her epiphany with Nellie on the way to Newcastle.

Nothing made sense.

She parked the wagon behind Joe's and climbed down. She needed to load the crates for tomorrow's trip if she wanted to avoid backtracking.

Entering through the rear door, she called Joe's name. She snaked around the mess of the storage room in search of her load. He could take lessons from Tristan on efficiency.

And there was that farmer, invading her thoughts again.

She pushed through the curtain into the main room, and the sharp aroma of peppermint nipped her nose. The floor creaked, announcing her presence, and the woman in front twirled around.

"Nellie." Anna moved to hug her friend, but the look on Nellie's face stopped her midstride. "What's wrong?"

"What's wrong?" Nellie's tone bit like a wild dog. "Julia has a tumor in her stomach. Doc thinks it's cancer." Her voice broke, the last words a whisper.

Anna gripped the shelf nearby to still the room from spinning.

"I thought you healed her."

"Nellie." Anna propelled forward and wrapped her arms around Nellie, the noises of customers nothing more than a dull ringing. Sweet Julia. Cancer. And what exactly was cancer anyway?

Nellie pushed from Anna and stared at the floor. "You've got to come pray. I can't lose my Julia."

Anna glanced beyond Nellie to Mrs. Mercer, who hurried down the aisle, basket over her arm.

Mrs. Mercer laid a hand on Nellie's shoulder. "Terrible news. We're all praying." She wove around Nellie and met Anna's gaze. "We're counting on you, dear."

Good heavens. Far more wise to count on a mighty God. Her eyes circled back to Nellie, but the burn in her friend's expression was more than she could take. Anna diverted her eyes.

The gaze she met was no friendlier. Mr. Foreman.

A pull on her arm brought Anna's attention back to Nellie, whose trembling hand encircled Anna's upper arm with desperation's strength. "Please, will you come?"

Caution snagged Anna's spirit and warred with compassion. Her friend wanted a miracle, and what mother wouldn't? But Anna couldn't promise a miracle. She couldn't set Nellie up with expectations that might end in disappointment.

She couldn't not pray either.

"I'll come and pray." Tears stung Anna's eyes as she took Nellie's hands. "Whatever God does or doesn't do, He is good." Words of truth, even if they sounded like a platitude in this moment.

"Nellie." Mr. Simms's voice carried from the front of the store. "Are you ready?"

Nellie locked eyes with Anna, searching, pleading. "Come tonight."

"I promise." She walked with Nellie to the front.

Mr. Simms didn't try to mask his anger. "Our girl is sick again."

"I'm so sorry." Anna's voice trembled. "I'd like to come pray for her."

"Lot of good that did last time."

"Prayer is about more than healing, Mr. Simms." She curled and uncurled her toes against the lining of her boots. "It's about seeking the Lord's presence. I don't know what He has planned for Julia, but healing or not, she needs His presence."

The anger drained from Mr. Simms's face, leaving a residue of uncertainty. "We all need His presence." He grabbed Nellie's elbow and escorted her out.

Anna stared through the window into the dusky light. *Oh God*. What was she to do? Warmth pulsed in her throat, and the trembling of her chin indicated imminent tears. She squeezed her eyes, but tears slipped beneath her lids. Opening her eyes, she kept her gaze floorward as she slid around a display and down the aisle toward the back.

Joe called after her. "I'll be right there to help you load, Anna."

Nodding, she pushed through the curtain into the storeroom. She scanned crates, looking for a label. She had no idea what among this mess was hers to take to Captain McRedmond. Heavy footsteps sounded behind.

She spoke as she turned. "Joe—"

Tristan measured her with a concerned look, stilling her movements. She didn't know whether to be glad for his presence or to prepare for an argument.

He edged forward until he stood a foot before her. She tipped her head back to look into his face, pushing aside the urge to banish control and weep. His eyes narrowed, and for a moment she recalled the look on Father's face before he'd admonish her. She couldn't take admonishments, not now.

"Are you all right?"

His question, hesitant and gentle, filched the breath from her.

"I . . ." She grasped for words, for command over her cracking emotions. "I'm fine." Her gaze skimmed the room. Didn't she have something to look at? Anything but him.

"You know, Saint." He tugged on a strand of her hair. "It's permissible to be something other than fine."

She swiveled and met a gaze so tender it pushed her a step back. "But I am fine." Her voice broke. She clamped her jaw. She was ten seconds away from launching herself into his arms like a helpless waif.

"Anna . . ."

His whisper sent a wave of weakness through her. "Don't."

Don't what? Comfort her, make her feel like she needed his arms sheltering her?

Joe burst through the curtain. "Sorry I made you wait." He stalked over to three crates in the corner. "These here, and . . ." He surveyed the room. "Where did I put that trough?" He disappeared behind a row of shelves. "Must be in the main room still. Tristan, will you help?"

Tristan backed away from Anna, intensity firing his eyes. When he reached the curtain, he exited the room after Joe.

Anna exhaled, steadied her shaky legs, and loaded the first of the crates. Darkness had cooled the air, and by the time the men loaded the remaining items, all Anna wanted was to hurry home.

"That's some news about Julia, huh?" Joe climbed from the wagon bed. "Not good at all. Sure is hard for parents to hear something like that."

Tristan looked at her, a hard glint in his eye. Apparently, he'd used up his moment of compassion, and just as well, because she'd used up her moment of weakness.

"Thanks, Anna." Joe patted her shoulder and returned to the store, leaving Tristan and her to spark gazes under the stars.

Tristan advanced, his countenance fierce. "What do you do now?"

"Now I pray."

"You can't be serious."

"Why?"

Tristan cocked his head, hands on hips.

"I need the Lord to heal her."

"So you can prove God heals? So people will like you?"

How dare he accuse her like Michael had.

Climbing onto the wagon, she thought only of escaping Tristan, escaping this day. "I have no need to prove anything. Take your anger out on the Lord, not me."

The moon winked through the trees as Anna flicked the reins and drove her team up hill. She was to the edge of the woods before Nellie's pleading face flashed into her mind. Groaning, she turned the wagon around and headed to the Simms' home and to expectations she knew she couldn't meet.

Ascending the Simms' stairs felt more like climbing a mountain. Anna heard his voice before she saw him. Michael. He stood when she walked in Julia's room, took her by the elbow, and ushered her back out. "Just a moment," he called over his shoulder.

He led her down the hall. "This is it, Anna. Time for boldness. You need to ask now for complete healing. Jared and Nellie are beside themselves."

Anna frowned. "I'll do as the Lord leads."

"The child is dying. Speak healing over her. Any doubt might prohibit a miracle."

"Michael."

Britton tugged on her sleeve. "You gonna heal Julia again, Miss Warren?"

The confidence in his eyes burrowed into her heart, nailing down the pressure to produce a miracle. She took his face between her hands. "I don't heal, Britton. The Lord does."

Britton nodded. "We'd best ask Him, then."

He tugged on her hand and led her into Julia's room. She didn't have the courage to ask.

She sank into the chair next to the bed and took Julia's hand.

Watching the girl sleep, she tried to summon a prayer. No use. She silently spoke verses over Julia, but by the time Nellie entered with a tray of tea, frustration had seized Anna by the throat. Perhaps she wasn't being bold enough. Perhaps Michael was right—her faith wasn't strong enough.

Or perhaps the father of lies was shrouding her with confusion.

Excusing herself, Anna nodded a farewell at Nellie, stepped from the room, and followed Michael down the shadowed hallway. She'd taken the first stair when Nellie's soft calling of her name caused her to look back.

Nellie posed outside the door, hands gripping her apron. "I need a miracle."

"You can trust the Lord, Nellie. He knows what you need."

Nellie whirled, and with a swish of her skirt, disappeared into Julia's room. Anna stared into the dim light before plodding down the stairs. Michael likely waited for her—to discuss faith, reprimand her lack of boldness, and who knew what else.

More so, the town would now be waiting. Expecting her to do something. Holding their breaths to rankle her when she failed.

Chapter Sixteen

Fifteen minutes later, Anna rounded the bend of her driveway, lantern in hand, and entered her yard. Moonlight glowed pale blue on the grass and silhouetted the outline of an animal grazing between her cabin and barn. She slowed until she noticed it was a horse. A strange, unfamiliar horse. Then she saw him. Mr. Roberts sat on a rocker, legs crossed, head back, hat over his face. Asleep on her porch? Of all the nerve.

As if sensing her presence, he sat up and pulled his hat from his face. "About time." He stood and stretched, eyeing her wagon. "Heard you haven't been freighting much lately."

"How are you, Mr. Roberts?"

"I'm confused." His dark eyes churned over her like she were cream to be whipped into butter. "I'd like to know what game you're playing."

Anna frowned, her foot feeling under the wagon seat for her gun. "I don't follow you."

"This land, who owns it?"

"The issue will be settled soon enough, when Mr. Wyse returns." Or when she finally made it to Olympia. Her letter to the court had gone unanswered.

"Nah. Wyse's not returning." He descended the porch steps and advanced toward the wagon. "You know I've wanted this land."

As well as about a dozen other properties, and no one knew why.

"I'm still interested." His gaze swept her.

She reached down and lifted the gun to her lap. "I'm in no position to consider selling."

"Is that so?"

"Mr. Roberts, I've had a busy week, if you don't mind

taking your leave. I'd be happy to discuss this some other time . . . in town."

He stared, and she considered cocking her gun, but finally he put on his hat. "I'll look forward to it." He mounted and left.

His cigar smell lingered, a nauseating sweet aroma, and she waited until he'd rode off before rushing to put away her wagon and team. Then she entered her cabin and locked the door.

Only a miracle can save Julia.

So Doc had said to Nellie and Jared on Friday when Anna had stopped by the Simms'. Gazes had turned on her.

Doc suspected Julia's tumor had been present for months. With its recent growth, symptoms had elevated. Julia's appetite had shrunk.

So had Anna's.

She'd woken this morning with a sense of dread, and for the first time, she did not want to attend Sunday service. It would be her first morning to face Mr. Foreman since last Monday, that horrible day when the bad news of his threat had dumped on her like hail. If she'd been a wheat field, she'd have bowed to the mud and surrendered all hopes for harvest.

By the time Anna entered the church building, her doubts about Julia, Mr. Foreman, and her land had increased twentyfold. And along with those doubts, a sense of disappointment that her faith had to be so weak, that grief had been a constant burden, sapping her strength.

Choosing a seat in the back, she closed her eyes. Mrs. Tolliver's piano music filled the room, a lilting melody Anna hadn't heard before. *Thank you, God for Mrs. Tolliver's friendship.*

I am making all things new.

Please, Lord. She opened her hands, having nothing to offer but trust.

All things new.

Those around her stood to sing the opening song, but she couldn't move for the words of the Lord mantled upon her. Her breathing quickened as hot tears deluged her eyes. All things new, and she was so thankful. But still, why did it have to be so hard?

The promise of all things new butted against the circumstances of her threatened land. The loneliness etched on her heart. Michael's confusing attention and Tristan's skepticism.

She bowed her head. *God, forgive me.* What was the approval of man when she had the love of a Savior? What was a piece of land in relation to eternity, compared to the inheritance awaiting her? Nothing. And yet, she ached, in spite of the trust.

All things new.

She opened her eyes to see Tristan step into the pew next to her, cleaned up, handsome, and with an unusually relaxed expression on his face. He turned to remove the hymnal from the seat, and his gaze connected with hers. She looked down, not wanting him to see the redness rimming her eyes.

The singing ended, and the sounds of shuffling feet and rustling pages filled the narrow chapel. Anna opened her Bible and waited for Reverend Bagley to announce the passage.

Tristan sank to the pew beside her. "Are you all right?" His whispered words were tense.

She didn't need him questioning her sanity every time he saw her. "Yes." A straggler tear slipped down her cheek, and she wiped it away. At least, she would be all right.

God, help me be all right.

Her fingers drummed the pew. She rested her palm on the smooth, cool surface. The stuffiness of the room choked her. She was so lonely. Desolate. God had ripped from her the one strong relationship in her life.

Reverend Bagley's voice carried as he read the passage, and

Anna closed her eyes and listened.

"Now Moses was tending the flock of Jethro his father-in-law, the priest of Midian, and he led the flock to the far side of the desert and came to Horeb, the mountain of God. There the angel of the LORD appeared to him in flames of fire from within a bush. Moses saw that though the bush was on fire it did not burn up. So Moses thought, 'I will go over and see this strange sight—why the bush does not burn up.' When the Lord saw that he had gone over to look, God called to him from within the bush, 'Moses! Moses!' And Moses said, 'Here I am.'"

A hand folded around hers. Her body stilled. With one touch, Tristan had bolted her to the pew. His calluses brushed against her knuckles, reinforcing to her his work ethic, his strength. Any thought of loneliness seemed absurd with her hand tucked into his fierce grip. Her face felt on fire, and breathing required effort. She wasn't hearing a word of this sermon.

If this was what it felt like when his hand held hers, what would it feel like to be fortressed in his arms?

She'd never know.

He'd reached out today, but she wasn't harboring illusions. He questioned her, shushed her, squirmed when she spoke of healing. Though he'd defended her, it was only his relationship with her father that caused such kindness.

There would be no fortressing.

The service ending, Tristan rubbed his fingers in his palm. What had possessed him to hold her hand as if she were a child in need of comforting?

Because she *was* a child—at least had the innocence of a child—and, well, he'd just had the urge to hold her hand. There was no sin in that.

He entered the aisle and collided with a young woman.

"Pardon, Miss Amelia."

She dismissed him with a wave of her hand. "I've been stabbed. Being bumped doesn't bother me."

He continued around her. Strange woman. And tight lipped. Jimmy had said he'd barely gotten a greeting from her during a fifteen-minute conversation, which meant Jimmy had done a lot of running of his mouth.

After a short conversation with President Hall, Tristan left the warmth of the chapel and stepped under the cloudy canopy.

Mr. Foreman was engaged in a heated discussion with Reverend Bagley, and Anna stood nearby like a cornered kitten.

"Such utter nonsense." Mr. Foreman wagged a finger at Anna, then turned to Reverend Bagley. "This is witchcraft. Sorcery."

Could the man be any louder? Heads slanted their direction.

"Those are extreme accusations," Reverend Bagley said.

At least Bagley stood up for Anna.

"But, Anna," Reverend Bagley continued, "your actions have stirred controversy, and unity in the church is essential. It'd be best if you reserve your praying for the privacy of your home."

Tristan strode across the churchyard and into the midst of the threesome. "Anna has every right to pray when and where she wants."

Foreman stared at him as if he'd sprung from the ground like a weed.

Come to think of it, he had. What was he doing intervening? Too late. "You can't tell Anna not to pray any more than you can tell her not to breathe."

He ignored the widening of Anna's eyes.

"We're not suggesting she stop praying, only that she do it privately," Reverend Bagley said. "Prayer pleases the Lord."

"I *am* suggesting she stop praying." Foreman glowered at Bagley. "One wonders if the church was better off when only those who were ordained prayed and read the Bible on behalf of their congregations. Things have become too lax, as evidenced by Anna's trying to play God."

Tristan cringed as Anna turned and walked away. The breeze tossed her hair about her shoulders as she headed up the hill.

"Something's got to be done." Foreman's words were low and menacing.

Tristan smirked. "As if you haven't already done something."

"And what would that be?" Bagley frowned.

"If Mr. Porter's referring to my business practices, that has nothing to do with church matters."

No, of course not. Foreman was a law unto himself. "So I guess the unity of Christ has conditions? Like when it benefits you, it's permissible to encourage discord?"

Bagley gripped Tristan's arm. "Let's be civil."

Tristan clenched his fist. The whole affair stirred so much aggravation, he wanted to go plow a field, since knocking Foreman down wasn't an option. Not in the churchyard.

"I can't have my clients entrusting their livelihoods to a mere child, and a girl at that. If something should happen, I would be out money, not just clients."

Tristan rolled his eyes. Could Foreman come up with anything more ridiculous? "First, Anna is a woman, not a child. Second, she's grown up on the seat of that wagon and knows this territory better than you. And third, should she need to defend herself, I'm sure her shot is as good as yours."

Foreman stared him down. Tristan was two seconds away from open-firing his fist, but Jude McGrath sauntered up and sliced Tristan with a warning look. Tristan tried to relax. "Why can't she just do her thing?"

"She's caused a stir," Mr. Foreman said.

"You'd know about causing a stir." Tristan stepped into Mr. Foreman's space.

"Tristan." McGrath wedged his arm between him and Foreman.

"All right. Sorry."

Clearing his throat, Foreman backed up and shoved his hands into his pockets. "I suggest excommunication."

"Oh, come on." Tristan ran a hand through his hair. Just when he thought things couldn't get more absurd.

"I've made my decision," Bagley said. "Anna is welcome to pray how she wants in her home, but she is not to traverse the county at the beck and call of the wounded. We have Maynard for that."

"And how will you enforce this?" Tristan could imagine Foreman hiring someone to shadow Anna.

"Anna's honorable. She'll do as I ask," Bagley said.

Foreman looked smug as he tugged on the bottom of his vest. "It's a start at least."

The start of heartache for Anna.

Frustrated that it mattered so much to him, and finished with the nonsense, Tristan turned his back on the men and headed for home. This healing business had been trouble from the start.

Chapter Seventeen

Bells and mistletoe garnished doorframes, and tinsel draped a twelve-foot fir.

Inhaling the heady evergreen scent, Tristan tried once more to deck his heart with a joy to match the spruce boughs and red ribbons, but the only thing his spirit scrounged up was more determination to make this Christmas gathering count in his fight for a program.

"So do we have a deal?" Tristan eyed President Hall across the white-linen-dressed table. Empty dishes stretched the length of the tables set up in the university's front hall for the community celebration.

"Another piece of pie each?" Hall smiled, and Tristan couldn't hold back his grin.

Dinner sat happily in his stomach, but he could squeeze in another piece of Mrs. Tolliver's cherry pie. Better yet, he needed Hall's word to push this program with the trustees.

"I'll take care of the land." Tristan set his fork down. "And you put in a word with the trustees. You've got that charisma."

"I'll do my best." Hall lowered his voice, and Tristan strained to hear over the din of voices. "These men are hard nuts to crack."

So it seemed.

Hall grabbed two pieces of pie from Mrs. Tolliver's tray as she passed, and set one in front of Tristan. "Work on this. I'll work on that." He nodded toward the corner where Arthur and Mary Ann Denny conversed with Arthur's brother David and his wife, Louisa. Founders of Seattle, all of them, and tight fisted on what they expected for this community.

Tristan forked in a bite of pie, the sweetness lost as his eyes wandered to the end table, where Anna served cups of punch.

He'd committed to tell her. Today. It'd be like a Christmas gift. Apprehension claimed the leftover space in his stomach, and he pushed the pie back from his place.

Tones from Mr. Kellman's fiddle pierced the room, causing a momentary lapse in the other noise, except for that coming from the children who huddled around the perimeter of the room, their knucklebones jangling and their marbles rolling. When Joe and Mrs. Tolliver started dancing, despite the disapproving frowns of the Methodists, people returned to conversation.

Michael approached Anna and took her by the elbow, and though she shook her head, Michael smiled, whispered something to her, and led her toward the dancers. Tristan bit the inside of his cheek and turned his focus on Julia, who lay wrapped in a blanket, sleeping on a pile of coats against a wall.

When the song ended, his gaze wound back to the dancers. Michael released Anna, who smiled halfheartedly and walked to the corner nearest the Christmas tree. She leaned her head against the wall, scanning the room. He'd hardly seen her the past few weeks, and she seemed even more worn than previously. Carrying the responsibility for a freighting business while grieving her father had taken its toll. Not surprisingly.

When her eyes locked with his, she stood straighter.

Now's the time.

Tristan grabbed a cup of cider and joined her.

She accepted the cup without meeting his eyes. "Thank you."

"You know you can stand up for yourself."

She raised her gaze. He was right. Her eyes lacked their usual shine.

"If you don't want to dance, don't," he said. "And if you disagree with Mr. Foreman's censure, go after your customers. Get them back."

She swallowed wrong and coughed. "It's not that simple."

She collapsed her shoulders against the wall. "Losing customers isn't the issue as much as being shut out of the community. Though I've never really been a part, have I?"

The voice of self-pity sounded terrible on her.

"You can't be serious," he said. Anna and her father were loved by most everyone. "I don't know what you're expecting from these people."

"I want to belong."

"What makes you think you don't?" Because from his viewpoint, she did. From his viewpoint, belonging didn't mean that everyone liked you. It meant you were welcomed within a community, and Anna was certainly welcomed.

"People like me for what I can do for them, not for who I am."

"People like me because I farm well, and I'm not offended." He chuckled at the skepticism painting her face. "I'm honored they trust me enough to ask my help with an association."

"Then why don't you help them?"

A challenge thrust from her eyes and jousted his conscience. He angled his body and studied the crowd. Pursuing the university had taken over his dreams. With Anna's land, it seemed a reasonable hope.

Anna's land . . . He felt the clamp tightening his heart, squeezing off the courage. He needed a bit more time. There had to be a solution that would benefit them both. "I have other plans to help people."

"Of course you do." She smiled, and that sweetness of hers wiggled past his attempts from the last weeks to hold her back from taking over his thoughts. "You're a leader."

Seemed to be the unanimous decision, but because he had leadership tendencies didn't mean he wanted to lead just anything. More than anyone else, he wanted her to understand why the university was so important.

"What do you know of the Morrill Act?"

"Everyone knows how much you love it, but I think it's the land you really love, and any means that gets your hands into the earth makes you happy."

Any means. He flinched. "My father helped craft the act, years ago, before Justin Morrill presented it to Congress."

She tilted her head to the side, her eyes softening as they looked at him. "My father mentioned your father was killed in the war. I'm sorry."

His throat thickened.

"What happened to your family's land?"

"My sister and her husband live on it and run the farm."

She frowned, and he read her confusion.

"I didn't leave because of a falling out." Not a falling out with his family. A falling out with God had forced him away. Leaving had been instinct to survive.

"They'd welcome you back?"

"They'd embrace me." His voice cracked, and he wiped his mouth.

Her questions were derailing his attempts to explain his dream. He'd only wanted her to understand why an academic program was so important to him.

"Do they have children?" She laughed softly. "I'm trying to picture you as an uncle."

"Hey, it's not that hard to imagine." Coaxing the land to produce required a gentle touch and a lot of wisdom. Surely rearing a child couldn't be much different. "I want children someday. A pair of boys who aren't afraid to work hard."

Ann stilled. Yeah, he'd not meant to make an admission like that. Women talked about those things, not an eligible man with an eligible woman.

"What's new with you these last weeks?" He palmed the back of his neck. "How many people have you healed this month?"

Her mouth gaped before a pathetic attempt at a scowl

crossed her face. What a pretender. She gave up the pretense and sighed. "I don't heal. The—"

"Lord does. I know."

She sipped her cider, slow and careful. He held her gaze over the cup's rim, enjoying the way she shifted her feet. She rolled her eyes and set the cup down. "One."

"Who?"

"Not Julia."

He wished he could pull the wistfulness out of her tone.

"A family staying at the Occidental asked me to pray for their deaf baby."

"And?"

"He hears now."

Tristan's breath rammed to a stop like a hoe against a rock. No one came close to commanding his respect like Anna—and it cut him. The healing cut him until he felt his heart bleed longing. He didn't want to be back there, in that position of wanting something. He'd only been disappointed last time.

"Tristan."

He still couldn't breathe. She set her cup on the windowsill and took a timid step forward, though it felt more like a giant leap into his space.

"Healing's not a puzzle we solve. As much as He's revealed himself to us, He's still a mystery."

She saw beyond the topsoil into the bedrock of his heart, and it unsettled.

"You're fine with that?" If God was going to do something like refuse a fifteen-year-old boy's prayer, at least He could be clear about why.

"I'm at peace with that." She fidgeted with her dress. "What I'm not at peace with . . . Reverend Bagley asked me to stop praying with people."

He'd failed to warn her. As much as she pried his opinions from him, he wasn't able to tell her the things that mattered.

Like about her land. Like what Reverend Bagley had said after she'd left the churchyard.

"Will you?" he asked.

She turned and peered out the window into the darkness. "I can't. It's who I am." She whirled to face him.

He met her unguarded gaze. The intensity in her eyes reached inside him and yanked every cord of compassion he possessed. How he wanted to solve all her problems.

Then tell her.

"Thank you," she said.

He drew back. "For what?" He could do no more than whisper the words.

"For being a good friend."

"I'm not a good friend, Anna."

A smile tugged at her mouth. "You can be a grump, even a cynic, but you're honest about it."

Tell her now.

Her friendship invited transparency. She deserved the truth. For the sake of privacy, he could ask her to step outside. Her compassion would be generous. She'd forgive him for holding back. But how could he tell her after she'd referred to him as honest?

How could he not?

His tongue stuck to the roof of his mouth. He grabbed her abandoned cup from the windowsill, swallowed the last of the cider, and set it down again.

Anna was wringing her hands, prattling, "I know we have our differences. This healing stuff drives you crazy, but that's your issue with the Lord." Her eyes searched his. "I do thank you for your friendship. It makes me feel more connected to my father."

She was burying him alive.

She brushed hair away from her flushed cheek. "It probably seems silly to everyone that I even wanted to come back and keep freighting. It's a great amount of work for one woman. Yet you haven't challenged that decision, and I'm glad. Thank you."

Anna lifted her cup and peered inside. She frowned, and her gaze questioned him.

He shrugged, and a smile broke across his face, despite the sour feeling in his stomach.

Anna began to smile, but Nellie's voice drifted from the opposite side of the room, and Anna's lips tightened.

This healing business was no good for anyone. Reverend Bagley's censure had bothered Tristan at first, but it was best to cut the healing nonsense off before Anna drowned in her perception of others' expectations. She was building herself up to feel like a failure.

But cutting off her prayers for healing would suffocate her spirit. And strangely, that would suffocate him.

Tears filled Anna's eyes as she watched Nellie.

"She likes you, you know." Tristan almost lifted his hand to touch her arm.

Anna bowed her head, and strands of hair fell in front of her face, blocking her expression. He wanted to brush them away, and along with them, her sorrow.

Something was wrong with him. The sentiment of Christmas had messed with his mind. The sooner he wrapped up this issue with Anna and her land, the sooner he could get on with building an agricultural program and serving the world the way he knew how.

He took a deep breath. "Anna—"

"Excuse me." She dashed through the room toward the front door.

He swallowed bile, ashamed of the sudden relief seizing his heart.

The four turns Anna took around the building should have

eased her anxiety, should have relaxed her spirit, not wound it tighter. But standing now inside the front door, at the edge of the room, her angst seemed twice as strong.

I don't know what you're expecting from these people.

She didn't know either anymore. Everywhere she looked, community. Conversations. Debates. Games. Belonging came so easy for others.

Mrs. Tolliver looked up from her place within a circle of quilters and caught Anna's eye. She set aside her squares and shambled through the townsfolk to Anna, by the door. "You look fatigued."

Warmth from the older woman's expression embraced around Anna.

"I suppose I'll head home."

"You do that. Enjoy a nice fire. Think of your father." Mrs. Tolliver squeezed Anna's shoulder. "But no pitying yourself, now."

Anna tried to chuckle, but it sounded more like a groan. "I wouldn't think of it. It's not my way, as you would say."

Mrs. Tolliver laughed, really laughed, like the happiness needed an outlet from her heart. She embraced Anna. "Merry Christmas, dear."

Anna took one last look at the community. Michael joked with Amelia. Mrs. Maynard read to the children. Nellie sewed with Mrs. Mercer and Mrs. Denny. And—she frowned—Tristan laughed with Lorna?

She swallowed hard. Even Tristan had found a merry heart. And why not? Lorna was Seattle royalty. Talented, beautiful. Quiet but friendly.

Stepping from the overheated building, Anna tried to cast the image into the winter air, but it followed her home.

Tristan's body moved with the rock of the wagon. The

lantern hung out front, lighting the way along the well-traveled route south of Seattle.

Jimmy climbed from the back up to the buckboard. "Talked with McRedmond and the Baldwin brothers tonight."

Course he had. Jimmy had talked with everyone, Anna included. Tristan had seen them laughing. His jealousy had made for indigestion, or maybe that was the constant whisper of his conscience to tell her about the land. His conscience had been on the loose tonight, had almost gotten the best of him. He'd corral it by the next time he saw her. He had reasons to stay silent and had preached every one of them to himself, since he'd nearly spilled it all to Anna before she'd fled the room.

Jimmy settled by Tristan, hands rubbing the arms of his thin coat. "Since things are progressing with you and the university—"

"No, they're not." Lazarus spoke from his seat in the back. "Not until he talks—"

"Quiet." Tristan swiveled and glared into the darkness.

Jimmy looked from Lazarus to Tristan. "Anyway, they've asked me to be the leader of the association."

"What?" They'd asked a boy with barely any farming experience to lead? A desperate move.

"They like my enthusiasm." Jimmy grinned and slapped Tristan on the back.

If Jimmy weren't careful, such enthusiasm might get him pummeled.

Jimmy shifted under Tristan's steady stare. "All right, so I'm more the organizer than the leader. Don't take it personal."

Tristan had no words. He'd asked for this, pushed the men to leave him alone. He should be relieved to get them off his back, but instead, the weight on his shoulders seemed even heavier.

"You know"—Jimmy stood and straddled the buckboard— "if you change your mind, it won't bother me to share the leadership with you." He plunged to the back, shaking the wagon as he settled by Lazarus.

"I won't change my mind." Not about the association. Not about Anna.

Two weeks later, he'd changed his mind—at least about the association. Only mid-January, yet here he rode to visit Captain McRedmond. Tristan hadn't needed to eat any breakfast thanks to the lump of pride he'd swallowed and digested.

He didn't know what he wanted anymore. Too often when he pondered that question while lying on his bed, moonlight slanting across his room, the answer included a brown-haired woman with big eyes and soft smile.

No. It was her peace he wanted. The peace that remained even through the struggles with grief and the healings. The peace that surpassed the weariness, that placed others' needs before her own.

Jimmy rode behind Tristan, his humming floating along the breeze and contrasting with Tristan's sober mood. Tristan knew if he looked back he'd see a silly grin on Jimmy's face. That boy had known Tristan would say yes.

Tristan had known as well. And it heightened the sense of defeat. He'd caved on his own dream with the university.

No. Not permanently. He'd just redirected for the moment. Caving permanently would mean he'd failed. Himself and his father.

Several weeks later, Tristan paced Front Street's planked walkway, hand lifted to shield the afternoon sun sparkling off the water. McRedmond and the Baldwin brothers had called the first official association meeting. And what a meeting it had been.

Behind him, men joked and conversed, speaking thoughts from the meeting. Tristan stared at the water and felt like throwing himself in and shocking out the past hour of gossip and agricultural balderdash. Livestock invading neighbors' fields. That had dominated the discussion. Could it get more mundane? Gray Baldwin argued with Luther Collins like they'd been in front of a jury.

Lazarus came alongside and clapped him on the shoulder. "We're going to Matthias's. You coming?"

"No." At least ten men from the meeting had entered the restaurant. Tristan wasn't about to hold another judicial session.

"I guess you prefer a cold, hungry ride home and your own fine cooking." Lazarus grinned.

With a scowl, Tristan crossed James Street. The white-painted front of the bakery beckoned. A piece of pie, or a whole pie, ought to ease the disappointment of the meeting.

He opened the door to the bakery, and the yeasty smell of bread transported him to another kitchen and into the presence of a woman with a sunflower apron. He strode to the counter and surveyed the items. Hunger pains stirred his soul, a longing for the days when he and his brothers and sister read from their primers as tarts baked. Father would come in from the fields, and Mother would spread her baked goods before them all.

"The sweet rolls are on sale today."

Tristan raised his head. The school-aged girl behind the counter waited, and for a moment he stared at her, picturing his sister instead. "Um . . ." Sweet rolls, why not? "Three." He laid the coins on the counter. The girl's braids swung as she turned and grabbed the rolls.

"A new batch. Still warm." She smiled and shoved the wrapped rolls toward him, an air of innocence and delight in her simple gesture.

His throat constricted. "Thank you." With his eyes down, and not daring to inhale another scent of his past, he exited.

Maintaining a staunch focus on the ground, he paused to breathe the cold air and let the past three minutes drain from him. Footsteps approached, and then someone stopped beside him. He knew the hem of that dress. The tips of those sturdy boy-sized boots. An acute awareness of his failure niggled him as he raised his eyes.

Anna gripped a basket in her gloved hands. Always that basket. Always walking. Her cheeks flushed pink from the chill. Of course she smiled, and he hated the softening that apprehended his heart.

"I'm proud of you," she said.

"Whatever for?"

"You know."

She probed him, her eyes awash with a respect he couldn't accept.

"Ah. The association."

Her smile widened.

How he wanted to deserve that praise. "Have you stood up to Foreman yet?"

Her smile faltered, but before she could answer, Michael rounded the corner. When his gaze clashed with Tristan's, his smile died. Too late Tristan realized he'd squeezed the package of sweet rolls. He'd have to enjoy them as pancakes, if he could enjoy anything after this encounter.

Michael's scowl lasted a brief second. He grasped Anna's elbow and talked to her as if Tristan wasn't present. "I say you do it now. It's already the beginning of February."

"Michael." Anna glanced back to Tristan.

Tristan edged closer to Anna.

Michael's eyes challenged Tristan's only a moment before he cupped Anna's chin with his hand. "You can't avoid this. You're being unfaithful to your calling."

Anna's brows turned in, but she seemed transfixed on Michael, unable to move.

Tristan wanted to drag Michael away and mete out justice. "Nothing about Anna is unfaithful." The word *unfaithful* didn't belong in the same sentence with her name.

Michael glared at him, then looked back to Anna, whose chin he still cupped. "Anna, if you want, I can—"

Pulling from Michael's grasp, she stepped back and looked to Tristan. "Would you please escort me to the Simms' house? I'd like to check on Julia."

"Anna, that's not necessary," Michael said. "I'd—"

"Sure." Tristan flanked Michael and took Anna's elbow, steering her up the street even as she glanced over her shoulder and offered an apologetic smile. Leave it to Anna to feel guilty for not wanting to be with someone. Leave it to Anna to loop him into another situation where the past was sure to spit more pain and regret at him.

One oil lamp lit the Simms' parlor. Anna peered at Tristan. His shadow loomed on the wall behind where he sat, stiff backed, on a chenille settee.

Nellie rounded the doorway and resumed her seat next to Anna. "She's asleep." Nellie's chest heaved, and the depth of emotion in her eyes offered Anna a warning. "Do you think Julia will die?"

The answer burned on Anna's tongue, but she couldn't get the words out.

Nellie must have read the hesitancy in Anna's eyes, because she covered her face with her hands. "Oh, God." When she looked up, tears dripped down her raw cheeks. "You said you feel God's desire when you pray for people." Nellie grabbed Anna's hands. "Tell me—what do you feel when you pray for Julia?"

Anna couldn't drag her attention from Nellie to look at Tristan, but her peripheral vision caught him leaning forward. If she looked over, the force of his eyes would bore into her soul with pain, not the tenderness that had started to break into his gaze in recent days.

"I feel . . ." Anna's pulse throbbed in her throat. "I feel . . . Nellie . . ." Tears threatened. "I have the sense that Julia will be going home . . . to heaven." That last word choked her, releasing her tears.

Couldn't she hold herself together at least for Nellie's sake? Her chest stuttered with uneven breaths. She sucked in air and held it, willing her emotions to compose.

Nellie stood and paced across the room. Her whimpering stung Anna's ears. What a terrible mistake to invite Tristan. He must be ready to explode, sitting here and listening to her fail at offering Nellie hope. Fail at friendship. Could there be any more proof that she didn't belong?

Spinning around, Nellie's gaze pierced hers. "I'd like you to leave."

"Nellie—"

"Please, Anna."

Anna's voice stuck amidst the swelling lump of her throat. She rose, and for the first time since entering the Simms', looked at Tristan. He withdrew his gaze, confirming she'd failed at another friendship.

"Nellie." Anna waited for her friend to turn, but she didn't. "I had to speak the truth."

The pressure of a hand against the top of her back uprooted her. Her feet felt heavy as Tristan's gentle prodding ushered her to the door. When he opened the door, a gust of cold air slapped her from her stupor.

Twisting around, her heart sought for one more moment of grace. She sped to Nellie and pulled her into an embrace. "You know I love you, but my anguish is nothing compared to the Lord's. I'll leave now, but He will never leave you nor forsake you. Please, Nellie. If you can't believe anything else right now, believe that."

Anna squeezed Nellie, wishing she could inject peace into her heart, but the woman in her arms remained motionless.

Although not late, the cold, the darkening evening sky, and the brooding of his mood made the hour seem so. Mist chilled him head to toe, heart to mind. Tristan walked beside Anna down the hill from the Simms', toward the water. Her tension rubbed against him as real as the occasional bump of her shoulder.

When she'd told Nellie she thought Julia would die, a hardness had broken within him. Broken in a good way, like his fever had when he'd been sick with measles as a six-year-old, not like when he'd smashed his mother's favorite pitcher during a wrestling match with his brother.

He forced out the words that were somehow hard to say. "You did the right thing."

"What?"

"Speaking to Nellie like that. Telling the truth." Huskiness snuck into his voice. "You did good."

He could no longer consider Anna in the same way he did the revivalist who'd prophesied over his mother. No deceitful bone existed in Anna. She could no more lie than breathe under water. Her desire to help others, her commitment to the Lord, was as genuine as the dirt under his fingernails.

As genuine as the storm brewing in his heart.

God did heal. Yes, he'd always known that, despite what he'd told Anna.

And admitting such only made things worse. If God could heal, why had He let his mother die?

Chapter Eighteen

Tristan bowed his head as Reverend Bagley offered the prayer of invocation. Every Sunday it was the same. "We invite your presence, O Lord." Beckoning the unseen, immortal God of the universe to draw near.

Then where was He?

Are you ready for me?

The perception pricked his mind. Tristan brushed his hand across his ear. No draft blew. No bug crept.

Are you ready for me?

Tristan held his breath, straining to hear more of this nearly audible voice.

Lord? He heard nothing but the echo of his resentment. *I was ready seven years ago.*

He worked to keep the scowl from his face as he opened the hymnal and snuck a glance at Anna. Her head was bowed. Here was a woman always ready. Ready to receive, worship, heal.

Ready for miracles.

She hunched in the far corner this morning. At Reverend Bagley's amen, she opened her eyes and stared out the window. She was the strange one among them, the one who expected more from the Lord than passage into heaven. Tristan had resented her joy, mocked her expectations.

And now he envied her. Wanted to be ready. Wanted to expect more.

I'm ready. But where are you?

Something stood in the way between him and the Lord. More than the failed prophecy. He'd tried praying, but couldn't. Thoughts of Anna and her land encrusted his heart until he couldn't feel anything but confusion, anger.

As soon as he figured out what to do about Anna's land,

maybe he could find the Lord. That was, if the Lord would finally show Himself.

"Are you serious?" Tristan strained to hear Denny's words over the rain pelting the roof of Yesler Hall, where they'd sought shelter Monday morning.

Rain dripped from Denny's long coat. "Hall and Bagley think this is what we need to increase enrollment, move beyond housing public schooling and actually teach college classes."

Hall and Bagley. Denny hadn't included himself.

"However, we want you to speak with those in charge of the territory before we continue with plans. Get their blessing, advice."

There was always a stipulation, a rock that wouldn't budge from a fertile field. "I have to travel to Olympia in the midst of this?" The steady downpour had continued for two days. For all Tristan knew, the rain would last until May. He didn't do boats in rough waters or miles of horseback through mud.

"Wait as long as you like, but the trustees have agreed to move forward only after you discuss this with the territorial education committee."

"I thought they handed complete control to the trustees."

"Sure." Denny smirked. "But after the debacle with Bagley and the land claims, well . . . we'd like to respect their authority."

Tristan stifled a groan. Bagley had kept a less-than-stellar account of the claims he'd sold to fund the opening of the school, igniting suspicion. But Tristan would gather every letter he'd received, every bit of documentation from his father's days arguing with the Illinois legislature, and he'd march to Olympia and tell them how it was.

If only he had the confidence it would work.

Anna finished her tea, paid for the early lunch, and exited the Occidental with Mrs. Tolliver. The rain had finally slowed, but she kept her hood up. The triangular intersection of Skid Row, James Street, and Front Street was crowded with wagons and horses, as was custom on market day.

Mrs. Tolliver's limp seemed more pronounced after sitting for lunch.

"Are you sure you're okay?" Anna gripped Mrs. Tolliver's arm.

"Child, please."

"You look flushed." Anna reached to feel her forehead, but Mrs. Tolliver swatted her hand.

"I'm not an invalid. A little nick with an axe isn't going to keep me off my feet."

No, that wouldn't stop Mrs. Tolliver, but she might have stayed home rather than come to market and sell her preserves and honey.

Mrs. Tolliver retracted her elbow and sank down onto the bench in front of Joe's. "Where are you traveling this week?"

"You mean, this month? Since Mr. Foreman's notice to my clients, I've wondered if I should even keep freighting."

"Course you should. Time for some new clients, is all."

And where would she find those clients? "Mr. Roberts has asked me to bring a delivery out. It's due in on the steamer today."

Mrs. Tolliver frowned. "That's a man I wouldn't do business with. Shady's what he is."

"Father and I hauled things for him."

"Doesn't mean you have to."

She could hardly say no, considering the loss of clients. "It's just an afternoon trip. The steamer's even early."

The impressive white vessel bobbed next to the wharf, with a sense of command.

"He been out to your house anymore the last few weeks?"

Anna shook her head.

"Take Tristan with you."

Heat rushed her face.

The twinkle in Mrs. Tolliver's eyes betrayed her attempt to be casual. "He hangs around you like a schoolboy. Talks to you every week at church."

"He hangs around me like a wounded animal trying to distract himself by pestering another."

Mrs. Tolliver raised her brow.

"Besides, he's too busy at market."

Mrs. Tolliver cackled. "You ask him to take you, and see what happens. He'll leave his produce without a backward glance. He'd leave a plow in the middle of a field to help you."

That she could matter that much to someone was . . . well, it stirred anticipation.

Later that afternoon, the wagon jostled over the road, but for once, Anna didn't find it soothing. The rocking triggered nausea, which the tickling wind intensified. She inhaled and blew out long and slow, the visible breaths a reminder that winter still reigned. The rain had made the road a muddied mess, and each time the wheels skidded, Anna tensed. How she didn't want to go digging.

Two more miles until Mr. Roberts's homestead. Two more miles of hauling these mystery crates. Whatever their contents, each divot the wagon hit set off clattering.

"You nervous?" The tender voice beside her broke her mindless stare at the horses.

That she'd ended up asking Michael posed more than a little irony. She'd turned to Tristan the other day to avoid Michael. And today she'd turned to Michael to avoid Tristan. Any attempts to wade through her motives left her more confused.

She pushed down the rising queasiness. "Michael, do you

ever get the sensation that something's wrong? That maybe you're missing something important?"

He squinted his eyes, and she mumbled a halfhearted laugh.

A strand of hair blew into her face, and she wiped it away. "I don't know. I just feel unsettled."

"Let yourself be fine with that. You've lost your father. You've been freighting by yourself. You're wondering about your land, learning about the gift of healing God's given you. It all sounds unsettling to me."

Anna grimaced. These feelings were borne from more than grief or adjustment. Something felt wrong.

They hit a bump as they pulled into Mr. Roberts's yard, and the objects in the crates rattled again. Her stomach flopped, and bile climbed into her throat. She coughed it away.

She reined in the team as Mr. Roberts swaggered from his cabin, mud streaking his pants and shirt. Tristan wore the earth like a medal of hard work, but earth on Mr. Roberts appeared unkempt, disheveled. She covered her nose. She was sure the earth never smelled like this on Tristan.

Before she could hop down, Mr. Roberts offered a hand.

"Mr. Roberts, good day." She gritted her teeth as his pudgy fingers stroked the back of her hand. Her feet on the ground, she reclaimed her hand.

Mr. Roberts narrowed his eyes at Michael. "Don't be a preaching at me, boy."

Michael nodded and held up a hand, but she'd give him five minutes before he started in with Scripture.

"Where shall we unload your crates of . . ." Anna fished for an explanation.

"You let me and the preacher unload them over here behind the barn."

Anna led the team to the back of the barn, where a rusted plow lay. She hoisted herself into the bed and loosened the ropes.

When the crates were unloaded, Mr. Roberts threw a

blanket over them and dusted off his hands. "Come inside."

The gruff words did little to entice her. "No, thank you. I'd like to make it back by dark."

He opened the door to the tiny cabin and entered, obviously expecting them to follow. "I need to show you something that came in the mail last week."

Anna met Michael's eyes, and he shrugged. She stepped over the threshold, and the stench of mildew overpowered her. The clutter of the small interior reminded her of another messy cabin, but Mr. Roberts's disorder had a dank dirtiness to it that Tristan's had lacked.

Mr. Roberts lit a lamp and held out an envelope. Stepping around a pile of books on the floor, and she took the letter.

"The answer we've all been waiting for." A pleased look settled over his rounded features.

Michael snatched the letter from her, unfolded it, and scanned the page. He grunted. "I don't believe it."

Anna reached for the paper, but Michael held it away. He looked at her with a tenderness that streamed warning. "This letter from Mr. Wyse says that Mr. Roberts's offer on your land was accepted by your father"—Michael took a deep breath—"two weeks before your father died."

Anna faced Mr. Roberts, numbness creeping into her limbs. "You own my land?"

"I was hoping my offer had been accepted, but with my absence, and then Mr. Wyse's, I couldn't be certain until this letter from him. Only took me three months to track down Wyse."

"You bought my land?" It made no sense. Why had he come to her cabin the other week pretending to be confused?

"Your father knew he wouldn't recover, and I made an excellent offer."

This wasn't true.

She plucked the letter from Michael's hands and scanned it.

Yes, it was as Michael had said. Signed and dated by Mr. Wyse only one month ago, confirming Mr. Roberts's inquiry about his offer on the Warren homestead. Was that why Mr. Wyse had held back when she'd asked if women could own land? Was this the news behind the hesitation she'd seen in Father's eyes during his last week of life?

Mr. Roberts touched her arm, and she stiffened. "Your father didn't want you to be in need. The money I paid for the land provided a comfy account for you."

Anna stepped back and encountered Michael's solid chest. He gripped her shoulders, and all discernment drained from her. Father *had* left her more money than she'd expected.

She had to get to Olympia, but she'd missed the weekly steamer. It would have left for its return trip by now.

When she turned to the door, Mr. Roberts's oily voice chased her. "You're free to stay for the next month. I won't have use of the land until spring."

She needed to be home where she could think, needed to hear the creaking floorboard in front of the woodstove and the passel of crows that nested in the giant hemlock by her barn. Heading for the door, she tried to clear her mind, find some sense in this.

Oh, God, she needed help.

She needed Tristan.

Tristan crossed the street and entered the back of the smithy. In spite of the cold and the waning sunlight, sweat beaded on Mr. Johnson's brow as he stoked his fire. Lazarus sat in a chair reading the *Puget Sound Dispatch*, which once again had a piece written by Tristan.

Tristan approached Mr. Johnson. "You got those hinges ready?"

"Two more to go."

Tristan sat by Lazarus, who offered him a piece of the paper. Tristan pushed it away. Lazarus grunted. "You as cloudy as the sky. You told her yet?"

Tristan glared.

"Mr. Johnson?" Anna's voice sounded from the front of the smithy.

Tristan could have groaned, but he wouldn't give Lazarus the satisfaction.

Lazarus chuckled. "The Lord has sent a sign."

Tristan catapulted from his chair and snuck out the back door. Just hearing the sweetness of Anna's voice triggered such anger. The angst had gone beyond his mother's death. Beyond his disappointment in God. The anger had become alive, and he didn't know what to do about it.

Rain dripped over the brim of his hat, punctuating the dreariness of the day. Clouds mimicked the color of the washed-out Sound. Sure, as a farmer he relied on rain, but after weeks of it, all he wanted was a day of sunshine and—

He sucked in a breath as an idea slid into his mind. An idea that would make a trip to Olympia worthwhile. He'd deed the land directly to the university—anonymously—with conditions for its use, and then it wouldn't be his. She'd never need to know he'd owned her land.

Anna rounded the corner so suddenly Tristan fell back against the wall. Her hands thrashed out as she slipped in the mud and regained her balance. Wisps of hair poked from beneath her hood, their wet ends clumped together.

He reached up and wiped a smudge of mud from her cheek, surprised her skin felt so warm.

She jerked back, eyes narrowing. "Are you all right?"

"No. I'm angry."

"Always honest."

He huffed. "Don't call me honest."

"Father loved your integrity. Said he didn't know a man

who did business better than you. Of course, Father—"

"Saint."

Her eyes met his. They were red rimmed and puffy. The sight ignited the protector in him that never seemed far off when she was around.

"Is forthright a better word to use than honest?" she asked.

He growled.

She squared her shoulders, tipped her chin up, and held his gaze. He anticipated the shift of conversation and girded his heart for whatever she was about to say.

"Arthur Denny mentioned you might go to Olympia."

Not might. Would. "Yeah?"

She licked her lips. "Are you going to wait until next Monday's steamer?"

A whole week. "No."

She sighed, looked away, then brought her eyes back to his. "Please take me with you."

His heart skipped ahead four beats. "Why?" As if he didn't know.

"Jude McGrath told me to check the territorial records."

Time had run out. His idea had come too late. He should tell her now, but fear put a vice grip over his jaw.

"Tristan, please." Urgency flooded her tone.

Combined with the moisture in her eyes, it made him sick. Had something happened to her to bring on this desperation?

Her jaw shook. "This land is all I have. Julia's dying. Mr. Foreman's turned the town against me. I don't have friends—"

"You have friends." He'd never seen her flustered like this, and it sent panic through him. "And the town's not against you." They just didn't understand her. He didn't understand her.

"I can't rest until I know."

He couldn't rest at all. Not in her presence. Not with this lie suspended above his head. If she'd only wait, he could fix the situation. "Wait for Mr. Wyse."

"I've been waiting."

"Then go yourself." He left before he had to face those earnest eyes another second.

If only Peter Warren had never deeded him the land. If only he wasn't beginning to care so much for Anna. If only . . .

He could play that game forever. All the *if onlys* of life had grown thick as late summer weeds.

Anna's heart plummeted. His refusal only hurt because she cared so much for her land. The rejection only wounded because the need to know the truth had carved away part of herself.

She sighed, the deeper truth bubbling to the surface. His refusal and surly mood hurt because . . . because she'd thought they'd . . .

Because she considered him her closest friend.

How pathetic. She'd been back over four months and in that time hadn't managed to make a close girlfriend, but somehow she had managed to let Tristan twine himself around her heart. Strange to think that the person who rattled her peace with the strength of a winter gale was her closest friend. But he did more than fluster her. He overflowed her mind. She'd come to appreciate his questions, even to anticipate the challenge of them. Underneath the stringent surface, he cared for her. She knew it.

Footsteps approached from behind, rushing.

She spun, ready to confront Tristan.

But it was Lazarus. "Good day, Miz Warren."

"Is it?"

He smiled, all round cheeks and white teeth. "'Tis the day the Lord's made."

Anna's heart yielded to the invitation to praise. This was the day the Lord had made. She peered into the dark eyes of the man who'd been Tristan's lifelong friend. "I don't understand him."

He chuckled. "He don't understand himself." The deep smile disappeared. "You don't give up on him, Miz Warren."

"What?"

"You keep pestering him." Lazarus leaned forward and softened his voice. "And remember he hurting. He a good man, but he hurting."

"I know he's good."

Lazarus bid farewell and sludged through the mud back toward the smithy. The dampness of the day seeped through her clothes and traveled into her heart.

Don't give up on Tristan. She couldn't.

And she couldn't give up on her land. Mr. Roberts was scheming, and when she made it to Olympia, she'd prove it.

Chapter Nineteen

Darkness was thick over the yard by the time Anna finished supper and made her way to the barn. She pulled Father's cap farther over her ears, relishing the familiar smell. Wind off the bay pushed in a bank of clouds, the forbearer of rain, and the cold cupped her cheek with invisible fingers.

She hoisted open the wide plank doors and stepped into the dank interior. The drafts barely blinked their eyes at her as they finished their oats, but Maple moved to the end of the stall and stretched her long neck over the edge. Anna tousled the mare's golden mane and ticked down her list. Fix the back hook on the wagon, which she needed for the rain cover. Smooth the rough edge of the seat, lest her dress rip. Tighten the door on the chicken coop so that the coyotes couldn't claim another victim. And finally, tend the bruise on the back of Maple's fetlock.

With a final ruffle to Maple's head, she went in search of her hammer. Her barn didn't boast the organization of Tristan's, proven by the fact she found the hammer underneath the canvas rain cover. She set to work tapping the broken hook on the wagon.

"Anna?" The male voice sounded in between raps.

Tristan must have changed his mind. She tossed the hammer down, rushed to the door, and poked her head out. Disappointment cut into her at the sight of dark hair and an enthusiastic grin. "Hello, Michael."

"Working?" He entered and settled on the stump of a huge hazelnut tree Father had felled a year ago.

"There's always something to do." And after this afternoon's experience with Mr. Roberts, she needed her affairs in order so she could go to Olympia. She yanked the broken hook off the back corner and tapped a new hole next to the old.

With a firm twist, she wedged in another hook.

Leaning with his elbows on his knees, Michael studied her. She couldn't imagine he'd come to pay a social call. It'd hardly been two hours since she'd seen him.

"You busy this week?"

He knew she wasn't. Everyone knew of Mr. Foreman's actions. "Not particularly. Doc has a list of outposts for me to deliver medicine to, but the sleet's delayed me." She climbed on the wagon and started filing the rough edge of the seat. "You're probably going to say this opposition is a sign the Lord wants me to stop."

"No, it's not that." He stood and leaned on the wagon, peering up at her.

She paused and let herself be drawn in to his gaze.

"It's that I think there are other things you should do."

The way his eyes danced cautioned her.

"Come down a minute." He offered her a hand.

She accepted, his hand narrow and warm. Much preferable to Mr. Roberts's, but she felt nothing close to the sensation she'd experienced when Tristan had cradled her hand at church. She released her grip on Michael and sought space.

"You have a gift," he said. "Let me be straightforward."

The reason for his visit became clear—only she prayed she was mistaken.

"Our gifts fit together." He stepped toward her, and his voice turned tender. "I want to take you with me when I leave in a few months. We'll travel and do ministry. You were made for that." He reached for her hand, and she couldn't deny him, knowing what was coming. "I love you, Anna. I want to marry you."

She'd been drawn to him and the way he attacked life, but he saw her as something greater than what she was. He venerated her, and it scared her. And then there was the way he manipulated faith, and in turn, manipulated her. His liveliness that she'd labeled enthusiasm—it was pushiness, and she was done with it. "I can't leave Seattle."

"You have much to offer those who are hurting."

Were prayer and ministry all she was good for? And did she have to sacrifice what she wanted—belonging, a quiet life—in order to be used by the Lord? "I serve the community by freighting. Businesses and small towns depend on me."

"They managed all summer when you were in Portland." He shrugged. "Plenty of people can haul things in a wagon. Not everyone can pray like you. Besides, Mr. Foreman's putting an end to your freighting usefulness."

And Michael hadn't stood up for her. "You want me to be someone I can't be."

He shook his head, released her hand, and cupped her face instead. "You don't know your potential. Think of the invitation God has given his children to ask him for anything."

"Ask. Not demand."

"Ask in faith."

Anna pushed his hands from his face. "It's arrogant to think we can demand a miracle."

"It's cowardice not to. Faith is bold, Anna. It's not content to let pain have its way."

"Faith is bold when it clings to Jesus, the one who conquered sin and death, not when it clings to an idea of what a sovereign God should do."

Michael pulled a Bible from his inside coat pocket and began reading. "Then he said to him, 'Rise and go; your faith has made you well.'" He flipped to another passage. "Then he said to her, 'Daughter, your faith has healed you. Go in peace.'"

He turned more pages. Was he to read every passage that connected faith and healing? He began to read of the Roman centurion, his voice intensifying as he reached Jesus's final words. "'I tell you, I have not found such great faith even in Israel.'"

His eyes pleaded with her for agreement. Beautiful eyes

filled with love. She couldn't satisfy him spiritually. Life with Michael would be too strenuous for her spirit, no matter how much he adored her. His assertiveness drained her.

Tristan, for all his strength and intensity, had a nonchalance about him that—but this conversation wasn't about Tristan.

She thrust her hands into her coat pockets. "Michael." She couldn't tear her eyes from the pain pooling in his. "I never said faith wasn't important. It's 'by grace . . . through faith' we are saved. It's always been that way, even for Abraham, who believed and was considered righteous." Her thoughts jammed. "I can't explain it any other way: healing cannot depend on willpower. And for you, faith seems to equal willpower."

He didn't respond, not with a shake of his head, a blink of his eye, or a stuttered word. Nonetheless, she knew when he understood her rejection by the barely perceptible sag of his shoulders.

"I'm sorry, Anna. I want you to know I don't hold anything against you for believing as you do. I don't think it would be an issue."

It was an issue for her. "You're an amazing preacher. Go to seminary. Study and grow. I have no doubt God will use you. He has already."

"So you cannot marry me?"

His voice quaked. Confident, gregarious, Michael. She hated this brokenness she caused and could only answer by shaking her head.

He cupped her face again, a new fierceness in his grip, and her breathing stopped. "Is faith the issue, or is love?"

She stepped back, her elbow colliding with the wagon. Pain shot through her arm. "I don't know. It's both, I suppose." Tears threatened. "I don't love you the way a wife should love a husband."

"Does this have anything to do with Tristan?"

"No." She spit the word out as if he'd accused her of

stealing.

"You needn't be so touchy."

They were talking of faith and marriage, not of farming or Tristan.

"Michael . . ."

"All right, Anna." His posture straightened, and he tugged his coat tighter. "I've left behind what I've loved before, and I can do it again." He walked to the doors and swung them open. The wind blew them back against the walls. Michael looked over his shoulder. "You do have a gift. And . . ." He shook his head, turned, and walked into the darkness.

Tristan thrust his shovel into the ground. After a night of rain, the soil succumbed easily to his spade. Cool air caressed his sweaty forehead until he was hot and cold at the same time. In four months, this forty-by-twenty-foot plot would yield all the kitchen vegetables and herbs Conklin House would need. As if he didn't have enough things on his plate, Tristan had contracted with Mary Ann Conklin to supply a weekly delivery of produce starting in May.

The shovel dinged a rock, and Tristan reached down to toss it into the wagon. That was when he saw the visitor. Tristan's grip tightened on the wooden handle as recognition hit.

If this was an evangelistic mission, preacher man was in for more than a confession of sin.

"Tristan." Michael slid off his horse, none of the characteristic friendliness in his expression. "I'll get down to business."

Fine with him. He wasn't prepared to waste a minute of his Tuesday morning chitchatting with Michael.

"Do you own Anna's land?"

Tristan stumbled over his next breath. Someone had finally voiced the obvious. "What do you take me for?"

"I don't know." Michael stepped closer, a bold move that neglected discretion. "I just got to thinking—"

Thinking never did much good in situations like these. Tristan gripped Michael's shirt and held on tight so as not to hit him. "My business is my business."

The man kept calm. "If it's Anna's business, I take an interest in it too."

"Not sure you have the right to." He'd better not have the right to Anna's business.

"If rumor is correct, someone owns Anna's land. You knew her father. Quite well, from what I understand."

Michael didn't understand anything. He didn't know what it felt like to spend a day in the fields, earning one's survival. He didn't know what it felt like to have a secret hooked into his chest that ripped a bit more of his flesh each day.

"This conversation's over." Tristan released Michael's shirt. "I'll ask you never again to come and point a finger at me. And I know you wouldn't go spreading another rumor."

Because if this got to Anna . . . Though how she hadn't thought to come to him and ask him straight out if he owned her land, Tristan didn't know. Perhaps her mind was too wrapped up in issues of healing or grieving her father. Or maybe the obvious was hardest to see. Whatever the reason, Tristan knew his days were numbered, and he planned to do good things with those last days of secrecy.

Early tomorrow morning he'd leave for Olympia, and by Friday, his business would be complete.

If she sat at home another minute, she'd go mad. Even working through her list of things to do hadn't calmed her heart. Thinking of Michael's proposal and wondering when Tristan would find out, and if he'd even care, sent her mind into convulsions.

Anna readied Maple and rode toward town. She'd share her concerns with Doc about Mrs. Tolliver's continuing weakness from her injury and then walk the shoreline. Maybe if Jude McGrath was around, she could check about Mr. Wyse and convince him to unlock the lawyer's files.

Bright sunshine masqueraded as spring, but coolness snuck through Anna's sweater. The dreariness of winter seemed never ending. She'd been inside her cabin more this winter than ever. Still, the comfort of home hadn't allayed the loneliness.

Which didn't make sense. She had tea with Mrs. Tolliver once a week. She attended nearly every library association meeting, never missed church, and strolled in and out of Joe's as if it were a second home.

An oncoming wagon crested the incline, and she stepped Maple aside.

"Miss Warren?" Jared Simms tipped his hat, and his countenance broke into a smile. "Julia ate three pieces of bread in the past twenty-four hours, and she's wanting more."

"That's wonderful." Tension released like a slow exhale.

"Doc says it's just another pause in the cancer's growth and not to get excited, but what does he expect us to do? My little girl's eating again."

"Thank you for telling me."

He looked at his hands. "Nellie . . . she'd like you to come by."

Had Nellie asked for her? Anna couldn't read the reserved Mr. Simms, had no way to know if Nellie considered her friend or foe. "I'll do that sometime."

"She's happy at this change in Julia, really happy."

Anna nodded. She wanted to be wrong about what she'd told Nellie the other day. *Lord, let me be wrong.*

"Good day." Mr. Simms tipped his hat and called his horses to motion.

Her grin tingled down to her toes as she spurred Maple over

the rise and into town.

Joe was setting a bucket of daffodils outside his store as she passed. "Just came in from Frisco," he said. "They like to tease us with evidence of their warmer weather."

She dismounted and tied Maple out front. "I'll take a bunch."

He handed her a cluster bound by a piece of twine. She'd buy a length of ribbon and deliver the gift to Nellie. A peace offering. An encouragement.

The lively din of Joe's hit her as she entered. She wound around the shelves until she reached the spools of ribbon hanging along the back wall.

Lazarus's rich voice floated from behind the storeroom curtain. "We are climbing Jacob's ladder . . ."

Anna jerked her head around, scanning for Tristan. He wasn't in sight. Confusing relief flooded her. Not only had his gestures of tenderness intensified, but so had his crankiness over anything spiritual.

"Where is that paint?" Mrs. Foreman brushed against her from behind. She jerked around. "Ah. Miss Warren." Her smile looked forced, and her gaze flitted over Anna's shoulders, scanning the rest of the store.

No doubt in search of her husband. "How have you been, Mrs. Foreman?" Since the revival, Mrs. Foreman had avoided her, not even allowing eye contact at church services.

"I've been fine. And yourself?" Her tone seemed stilted, void of the warmth they'd shared when they'd prayed together. Without waiting for Anna to answer, Mrs. Foreman rushed on. "Joe said he had a can of white paint in the back."

"I think he meant in here." Anna led her through the curtain into the storeroom, expecting to see Lazarus, but the man had already left. She plucked a can from the near shelf and handed it to Mrs. Foreman.

"Thank you." Mrs. Foreman pushed the curtain aside but

didn't exit. "I don't approve of what my husband has done. I want you to know that." She let the fabric fall back into place. "Even if I agree with his position, he's acting out of place."

Heat stung the back of Anna's throat.

"I know he only has the best in mind for his business." Mrs. Foreman shrugged. "Though I do wonder if he has a point. You're setting others up for disappointment when you pray with them." She laughed. "I mean, how often does the Lord do a miracle?"

Mrs. Foreman should know. Hadn't she felt God's healing touch through prayer? Anna cleared her throat. "If anything about our prayer time together disappointed, I'm sorry."

"No. Not at all. Our prayer time was an encouragement." Mrs. Foreman straightened the broach at her collar. "But there've been rumors lately about your chants, and such."

Anna had no doubt who had started those rumors. "I don't chant."

"Some people say you use magic words."

Some people, as in her husband. "I don't believe in magic. I speak to Jesus. That's all." She felt her cheeks flush. "I really do seek to honor God through my prayers. I'm not trying to mislead people."

"Try or not, Anna, that's what's happening. Please keep in mind my concern."

If this was the concern of the community, Anna didn't want to belong.

Mrs. Foreman pushed through the curtain, leaving Anna alone in the dimly lit back room. She closed her eyes and tried not to think of that moment she'd shared with Tristan in this very spot. That moment she'd almost wept in his arms. Given another chance in this moment, she'd do it.

But he wasn't here. And she needed to stop pitying herself.

She exited the storeroom and selected a length of blue ribbon before heading toward the line at the counter.

The front door flung open and slammed against the wall.

"Folks, I tell you." Mr. Kellman's booming voice silenced all conversation. "I can't believe it, but I think something's finally gonna take out Mrs. Tolliver. Just rode past her place, and she's sick as a fungus-infected cedar."

Anna squeezed the cluster of flowers in her fist. "What's wrong?"

"A stew of things. Nasty infection in her limb, not to mention a terrible cough. Doc's with her now. Says it might be blood poisoning. Maybe pneumonia. I say it's both."

Anna sprang for the door. Five feet from the exit, Reverend Bagley cut her off.

"We all care about Mrs. Tolliver," he said. "Doc will do his best."

They'd not hold her prisoner. "She's my friend."

"You going to chant over her?" Mr. Foreman asked from behind.

Anna spun to face him. His glare ignited her confidence. "I'm going to pray Scripture over her, to give the comfort and aid of a friend."

Mr. Foreman raised a brow in Reverend Bagley's direction. "See, this is what I mean."

"Miss Warren, my wife will take some food out later." Reverend Bagley shifted his feet. "I can send word on how Mrs. Tolliver is."

Why were they doing this? They'd bridled her heart and were yanking around reins like they owned her. Time was slipping. With a final glance at the disgruntled men, she fled out the door.

Her pulse pounded against her wrists, her temple, her throat. They wouldn't pursue her, would they?

"Anna!" Lazarus ran up beside her. "Let Tristan take you."

No. Not him, not now.

"Tristan!"

She shrank from Lazarus's yell and struggled to pull her arm free of his grip. Tristan rounded the corner of the livery next door, a ready frown in place. "What's going on?"

"Mrs. Tolliver be ill, and Anna needs to get out there."

Tristan stared at her.

She couldn't wait for him to make a decision. "I don't want to bother you."

Tristan smirked. "You're never a bother."

She doubted the truth of that.

"I mean . . ." His voice faded as he marched over and took her arm from Lazarus.

"I put your horse at the livery, Miss Anna."

She whispered a thank-you at Lazarus while Tristan steered her around back of the livery to his wagon. "You're too busy."

"Get in." He jumped on the wagon, leaving her to clamber up herself.

Which is when she realized she still held the daffodils and ribbon in her hand.

Tristan reached down, took them from her, and tossed them down to the boardwalk. "Deal with it later."

She settled on the buckboard as far from Tristan as possible. Not far enough. What was he doing, thrusting himself into a situation she knew caused him discomfort? That day she'd dragged him to Julia's, it'd been a mistake, even if he had affirmed her. She'd seen the war in his eyes.

She shook, but not from cold, and began a tentative hum of "Fairest Lord Jesus." With her eyes closed and the soft movement of the wagon, she tried to imagine Father beside her.

Except Tristan's moodiness was palpable.

She hummed louder.

Chapter Twenty

They pulled into Mrs. Tolliver's yard as the sun dipped into the trees. One more hour of shadowed light. Tristan helped Anna down, and his gaze followed the swishing of her skirt as she walked toward the door. When she reached the entrance, she looked back. He waved her on. He'd been a fool to bring her. She was a seasoned traveler, after all. But the desperation of her eyes had been more than he could take.

He made his way to the woodshed, where a half-chopped log lay nearby. With one tug, he yanked the axe from a stump and twisted the handle around in his hands.

Forty-five minutes later Tristan had demolished the log and stacked the pieces in the woodshed. He set the axe, wiped his brow, and retrieved his jacket. Leaning against the shed, he waited for his breathing to settle. This whole situation with Anna—the healing, land, his growing affection—twisted him inside until he thought he'd snap.

She'd merely looked at a woman in church the other day, and the woman's coughing spell had ceased. Coincidence? Maybe. He wanted to understand. What gave her the courage to pray for healing when she didn't have the gall to stand up to Mr. Foreman? Maybe if he could get some answers, he would understand why his mother lay dead in a cemetery, while Amelia traipsed around town.

He strode to the cabin door to fetch her and take her home. She'd had long enough to pray.

When he opened the door, an awareness of peace rested on him as real as the warmth from the stove. Not wanting to disrupt the sense of holiness, he entered quietly. Mrs. Tolliver's mutt slept in front of the stove, but neither Anna nor the doctor were present.

An older man sat rocking in the corner. "That Anna is something, huh?" He smiled, revealing an incomplete set of teeth.

Tristan nodded at the stranger. He couldn't argue with that. She was something. Something that stirred a bitterness he'd stuffed down, but did it in such a sweet way he couldn't blame her. He'd had his light moments with Anna, but in his honest moments, he admitted the storm in his heart felt as if it were drowning him.

And Anna was the wind, the lightning, and the thunder. Couldn't she just go to church and smile like the rest of them?

"She's in there." The old man pointed to a curtain-covered doorway.

Tristan pushed the flannel aside and observed the low-lit room. Mrs. Tolliver slept, the quilt rising and falling with each breath. Doc sat in a chair reading.

Tristan frowned, unable to see Anna anywhere. The cabin only had two rooms. He began to turn, but movement stopped him. On the far side of the bed, Anna knelt, lamplight reflecting off her bowed head. With one hand around Mrs. Tolliver's, she rested her head on the bedside, her face hidden from view.

Mrs. Tolliver shifted, a sudden twitch, and her breathing quieted.

Tristan's heart squeezed. Had she died? The doctor glanced up, noticed Tristan, and offered a smile before resuming reading. Apparently, she hadn't.

Anna stirred and raised her head. He sucked in a breath and fell against the doorjamb. Her beauty stunned him, the softness of her face, closed eyes, cheeks pushed upward by the fringe of a smile. He'd teased her once about looking mature with her hair pinned up. Truth was, Anna looked young no matter what. Unpresuming, trusting. Even now, concentrated as she was in prayer, her peace filled him with a sense of loveliness so strong he ached.

He'd been so busy guarding against her kindness, and harboring the secret of her land, that her beauty had snuck up on him.

His gaze rested upon the small movements of her lips as she prayed, and her mumbled, whispered words found him.

". . . in Jesus's name . . ."

The same words he'd heard beneath the tent, his arm around his mother, her wheezing stealing his own breath.

He shifted positions, and a floorboard creaked beneath his weight.

Anna opened her eyes, and her serene smile chiseled his heart.

He let the curtain fall across the doorway and strode outside. Sitting on the chopping stump, he leaned his elbows on his lap and shoved his head into his hands. Sweat broke out across his forehead as his short, fast breaths clouded in the cold air.

With those three words, Anna had unlocked his heart, releasing all the memories he didn't want loose. That summer of '64 sifted through his mind, pounding him with images of his mother and her illness, of the preacher and his promises, and ultimately of the grave that had dismantled his faith.

He stomped his right foot and raised his head from his hands. The sun had dropped below the hill, but its tail of dusky light wagged across the ridgeline. He sat and watched the sky darken and tried to gauge the exact moment dusk surrendered to night.

Helplessness plagued him.

He couldn't stop the darkening, just as he couldn't have stopped the illness from ravaging his mother. The bullets of Gettysburg, also unstoppable as they took down his brothers and father. Nor could he stop his sister and her husband from taking over management of the family acreage.

He couldn't be the leader the association wanted. He

couldn't harbor his secret from Anna much longer. He couldn't get God to give him answers.

He couldn't.

A door clicked shut. Footsteps crunched. He knew it was Anna by her delicate tread and the alertness of his heart.

His defenses rose as lantern light flickered closer, an ugliness in him he couldn't hold back. "Did you heal her yet?"

She gasped, obviously unaware of his presence, and dropped the lantern. It sputtered but didn't go out and, thankfully, didn't break fire upon the ground.

She snatched it up. "You startled me."

"I'm sorry." Sorry he came. Sorry that this business of healing yielded more brokenness inside him.

"And no, I've not healed her. I've prayed for her."

"Same thing."

Anna didn't respond, and he wished he hadn't provoked her, because the last thing he wanted was to listen to Anna spout Scripture.

She hugged herself with her arm not clinging to the lantern, and rubbed her hand over her dress sleeve. His body flushed with the desire to hold her close and repress the chills, the vulnerability he saw in her eyes, and the foolishness brought on by her compassion.

As though sensing the direction of his thoughts, she backed up. A safe move.

"You're going to need me to pray for you someday," she said, "and I won't come. You'll wish then you hadn't been so hard hearted."

His jaw unhinged. He'd been expecting a spiritual reprimand, and Anna had dished out a threat. Her downcast gaze—and more so her character—told him she regretted her words.

"I already need prayer, and I already wish I were nicer to you." He took her hand, prying it loose from her sleeve. It trembled. Before better judgment took over, he laced his fingers through hers and felt the twining in his heart as well. "And you would come pray for me because you're generous like that."

"I hate being generous."

She tried to pull her hand back, but he kept it, rubbing his thumb over the back of it. "I hate being mean."

Her gaze snapped up. "You're not mean. Not really. You're just . . ." Her eyes squinted toward the woodshed. "You chopped all this?"

He nodded.

"That's very kind."

"I did it to avoid you."

Her brows furrowed. He let her withdraw her hand and followed her as she walked to the wagon, head down. Her shoulders shook as she raised a foot to the wheel, and without second thought, he reached around her waist and pulled her back. The wagon groaned as he jumped up to the seat and reached beneath for the coat Lazarus had handed him, a thin thing more suited for rain than cold. She should know better. He tossed it down.

She slipped into it and fingered the buttons. "I need to talk to Doc a moment."

He slumped against the wagon and watched her walk inside. If Anna was the most beautiful woman he'd ever met, if her kindness was unsurpassed, then why did he feel so much pain around her?

Either the tools in the back of Tristan's wagon were rattling or Anna's teeth were about to fall out of her head. The loose weave on her coat did nothing to stop the chill from invading. It would be a long eight miles into town and east to her cabin. She edged toward Tristan, seeking warmth, as she might have done with Father.

Except this wasn't Father.

She shifted back, aware that Tristan cocked his head her direction.

A gust of frigid air encased her body, sending a wave of shivers from head to toe. Her fingers were like iced pine needles. She knew better than to be caught without gloves in February.

She looked sideways at Tristan. He wore a grimace, an expression so familiar it had become endearing, cozying her heart the same way a smile might. If only that grimace could cozy her body.

"Why didn't you say you were cold?"

"I don't want to be a bother." And what could he do about it anyway? Flexing her toes, she willed her body to stop shaking. Even after taking Doc's elixir, Mrs. Tolliver's face had creased with each breath. In light of that discomfort, Anna could deal with cold air. "There's no use complaining about something I can't control. Others are suffering more than me right now."

"And what does their suffering have to do with you being cold?"

"I'm trying to be grateful."

"You should let yourself feel the bad things in life. It's not a sin to acknowledge negative emotion."

Her spirit rejected the suggestion, wanted to argue that peace was about fighting through the negative. But she had to admit that striving for contentment hadn't worked well for her the past months she'd been home. "I have days when I feel down."

"I'm not talking about feeling down. I'm talking about anger, sadness, frustration, despair."

"You're listing some of your favorite emotions." Her lips shook as she smiled.

She expected him to roll his eyes or ignore her. Instead, his eyes snagged hers, and he laughed, a soft sound that did more to warm her than her miserable shell of a coat did.

"Get over here before you shiver away your health." He smiled.

All she could think of was how much she wanted one minute of his body warmth. Still, she resisted the cheeky invitation, for a variety of reasons. Impropriety aside, she *wanted* to sit close to him, and that provided reason enough to stay put.

"Tristan, I don't—"

His arm snagged her waist and pulled her across the separation. He tucked her against his side, out of the wind's path. Her shivering ceased, only to be replaced by quaking of another kind. She'd huddled against Father many times, but she'd never felt warmed like this, never like her heart burned.

"Relax," he said. "You're stiff as the logs on Skid Row."

"No, I'm not."

"Cozy, then?"

She wanted to return banter, but his proximity numbed her voice. If she turned to look at him—which she so wanted to do—her face would be inches from his. She couldn't handle a face-to-face moment with a man who vacillated between grumpiness and gentleness with the unpredictability of a green horse.

"It's just . . ." She'd started to speak without a thought in mind. "So cold for February." What a dunce. February's night temperatures frequently danced in the thirties.

"Listen, Anna. I've already pulled you against me. What else am I supposed to do, put you on my lap?"

Heaven forbid, yes, that sounded nice. She straightened, but his firm grip kept her from pulling away.

"I'm teasing. Loosen up." He chuckled longer than necessary.

Anna swallowed, grateful the darkness covered her flaming face. The wagon rocked a soothing rhythm, and by the time they traveled to the outskirts of Seattle, Anna had managed to assume the appearance of relaxation, not that she'd convinced her heart to feel it.

She soaked in the beauty of the night-clothed Sound. A moonlit pathway stretched across the Sound, and Anna thought of Jesus walking to his disciples. If Jesus could walk on water so many years ago, in the presence of unbelieving disciples, why could He not heal, by His Spirit, today, in the presence of His believing disciples?

What would Tristan think of that thought? She'd not know, at least not now, when the silence had created an intimacy that rendered her speechless. Tristan's arm still rested around her for all to see. She should scoot away, but his warmth was too hard to leave.

The wagon rolled gently down Front Street, the clopping of the horses no match for the noise of Seattle's saloons. Though lumberjacks from surrounding camps only came on Saturday night, plenty of local millworkers and dockworkers came each evening to seek the pleasures of cards, drink, or . . . She looked south at the dim light of Conklin House.

"There's some healing work for you," Tristan said.

He'd noticed the direction of her gaze, of course, since the turning of her head had brushed against his shoulder. "Please stop talking about healing like it's a skill of mine."

"I know it's not. But I'm not sure everyone else knows, the way people flock to you like you're Jesus."

Anna wriggled some space between them and, turning sideways, looked up at him.

He maintained his forward gaze. "If you need an axe, go to Joe's. If you need a library book, see Mrs. Yesler. If you're sick, see Doc. Or if you'd rather, have Anna pray for you."

Her breath caught, and she wanted to deny his words, but they were true. Others saw her as an asset, not a friend.

She returned to her original place on the wagon seat, the cold air once more encasing her body. "I'm a business to them, aren't I? I'm not a friend."

Tristan huffed. "Sometimes you're blind, do you know that? Do you know what Reverend Bagley said about you the other day?"

Did she want to know? He'd not stood up for her in front of Mr. Foreman, not like a friend would.

"He said you're one of us. So stop moping about fitting in."

"I—"

"The university doesn't understand me, but I'm not groaning about it." He mumbled words she couldn't understand, an aside more for himself than her. "Some people get your gift. Some don't. But most people like you. I've said this before, and I'll say it again—you can't please everyone. And if you're going to try, you'll see only the rejections, not the relationships."

His outburst stilled her complaints. She'd deserved those words. This attitude of pity she'd adopted since returning had to stop.

Lord, let me see the relationships.

Tristan ignored her, pulling the wagon to a stop in front of Joe's, where her basket sat outside. He gave her a *stay put* look and hopped from the wagon, leaving her clouted by the sudden vacancy. He handed her basket up and then climbed back beside her. For a brief instant she anticipated him sitting close again. He didn't. At the livery, he retrieved Maple and tied her to the back of his wagon.

The dim lanterns of the city faded once they crested the hill. She had only minutes longer to endure Tristan and this cold. But *endure* seemed the wrong word concerning Tristan. As disconcerting as it'd been tucked next to him, it'd been equally enjoyable.

He reached across the several feet and put his hand on her upper back.

She stiffened, and a wave of warmth swept down her throat and into her chest.

"I don't understand much about healing," he said.

She heard the apology in his words. "It's all right."

"No."

She sensed more than emotion churning beneath that one word. She felt the closest she'd ever been to the undercurrent of his life story, the rhythm that drove him, and she wanted to know more.

"Tristan." She angled her body until she faced him.

He dropped his hand from her back, and she took it in her own before she lost courage. There were those calluses rubbing against her again, a picture of his heart. His expression softened into an unspoken question.

With sudden clarity, she knew the pain that had fissured his heart. "Who died?"

His jaw clenched like he wanted to look away, but her eyes pleaded, and he seemed to find the nerve to hold her gaze.

"My mother." His whisper slipped into the night. "The preacher promised God would heal her." He looked away then, but not before Anna saw the glistening in his eyes.

They rode the remaining minutes in silence, his hand in hers. From the rhythm of his breathing, she knew that for once Tristan was unable to handle his emotions. Good.

Let it come, Lord Jesus.

Tristan stopped the horses in front of her cabin. His breathing had evened, and he felt his heart come under control again. As if this woman didn't do enough havoc to his feelings, she had to pierce him with her perceptiveness. *Who died?* She'd reached straight into him with a pitchfork and stabbed his pain.

He set the brake and walked around to help her down. Though she looked young and vulnerable tonight, when his hands encircled her waist and lifted her down, she felt every bit a woman with the gentle curve of her hips. He never should have hauled her against him earlier. Even a fistful of rich dirt couldn't compare to the sensation of life he experienced with his hands on her.

He'd crossed a line. From one field to another.

But really, what line had she crossed? By going to Mrs. Tolliver and praying, Anna had dismissed Reverend Bagley's request, which though misdirected, had been for Anna's best interest.

"Tristan?"

Her quizzical expression seared him, and he realized he'd tightened his grip on her waist. He released her and felt the emptiness as she moved to enter her house. Lazarus's words pelted his memory. *I'd just hide in that cabin of hers and wait till she come through the door.*

"Wait." With a hand on her shoulder, he maneuvered around to enter first. Even chilly and damp, the inside of the cabin felt holier than a church. A palpable presence lived here, and he knew it was the Lord. A presence he'd felt in his childhood home. A presence he'd since pushed aside.

He lit a lantern, and a soft glow bathed the four walls. Her eyes squinted, and his heart reacted at the openness he saw in them. "Hold on. I'll be right back."

He bolted outside, knowing he'd left for more than needing to retrieve wood. He gathered as much as he could, the rough touch refreshing, pulling him back to his senses.

When he returned, Anna had lit kindling. She stared into the flames. He imagined her praying over them, willing them to burgeon. He dropped the wood, and she reached for a piece. So much for being needed. She finagled the growing fire with a poker. Again he thought of his heart, the way she probed him, and the mix of pleasure and pain she evoked.

Pulling his gaze from her was like trying to pull a workhorse from his dinner. He forced his attention to wander throughout the tidy cabin. Above the shelves and windows, red gingham fabric swagged. He recalled her comments about his barn and the way she'd been embarrassed by her chattering about his house. Maybe it was more than the Lord he sensed when he entered this place. Maybe it was the intentionality of Anna, her kindheartedness reflected in the way she cared for her home. And of course, he couldn't come here now and not remember the nights he'd spent before her return from Portland.

"Thank you."

He swung his gaze back to her. "You're welcome."

"I'm sorry about your mother."

He nodded. This was the part of his story he didn't talk about. It was simply the piece of his past he worked around, like the stump of the giant Douglas fir in his east field. He'd never been able to get the whole thing out.

But Anna was an uprooter. She'd done things in him that others hadn't been able to do.

"My mother caught pneumonia. The preacher said she'd live. He had a picture of her . . ." He shook his head. Didn't matter now what image the preacher had painted of his mama. It hadn't been true.

"I'm truly sorry, Tristan."

From the way Anna was studying him, he didn't know whether to expect a sermon or a hug. One would be more detrimental to his soul, the other to his heart. Finally she frowned, then sighed. "How did you get out here?"

Her question moved him on from the worst of his story. Thank God. "I joined a wagon team traveling to Seattle. Lazarus followed. I couldn't stop him." Tristan's mouth quivered a smile.

"And as soon as you arrived, you started farming?"

"Why not? Got to make a living."

She chuckled. Man, she looked beautiful in the lamplight.

"Farming is more than *making a living* to you." She quirked an eyebrow, a bit of mischief replacing the weariness he'd seen in her an hour ago outside Mrs. Tolliver's.

He needed to get out of here. "I'm glad you got to see Mrs. Tolliver. She loves you like a daughter."

"Yes, well . . ." Her smile faded, and a tear trickled down her cheek.

He reached his thumb up and brushed it away, then slipped his hand around the back of her neck. It was warm beneath her hair, which was softer than he expected.

Why had he never considered how Anna must miss her mother like he missed his? Only she had no memory of hers. He opened his mouth to ask a question, but a swell of affection overpowered him. He shut his mouth and withdrew his hand. What was he doing touching her again?

"Good night, Anna."

He had to get out of this place. Not just this cabin, but the place his heart was pulling him. His hand grasped for the doorknob.

"Tristan."

The tentativeness of her voice cracked his heart open. *Not now, Anna.* He fought for control the only way he knew how. "Every time I'm about to leave, you always have one more thing to say."

Her two whispered words, "I'm sorry," pierced him.

He turned to find her head down. She'd obviously missed the jest. "Anna, I was teasing."

She lifted her eyes. "Are you leaving for Olympia tomorrow?"

He answered with the slightest nod.

"Will you deliver a letter for me? About my land?"

If he said yes, this whole land issue could travel down a bad road. But if he said no, she would pester him, demand to know why, or even go herself.

"Sure."

She frowned. "I haven't written it yet. I—"

"I'll be by early tomorrow morning to pick it up."

He stepped outside, turning to pull the door shut—to her cabin and to his heart.

Chapter Twenty-One

Pacing in front of the fire last night, Anna had rehearsed her arguments, chosen her words carefully. And then packed her bag. Boldness and audacity, typically foreign to her, undergirded her energy as she rose in the wee hours, fed her chickens, and worked in the kitchen to get bread baked for the trip.

She felt almost feisty, until she opened the door and Tristan met her with a strong dose of detachment. Evidently the warmth of last night had fizzled. His brief eye contact gave way to the study of surrounding shadows, the winter sun having yet to shatter the horizon.

He would say no. She should concede before the fight left behind emotional casualties that would demand a week's recovery.

She started to hand him the letter, but he shifted his gaze back to hers, and the resistance there reignited her willpower. "Would you care for some coffee and scones? You have a long trip ahead." She'd attempt to win him through hospitality.

"Scones?"

"Nellie taught me how to make them." When they'd been friends, which seemed like seasons ago, not weeks.

"No, thanks. Is the letter ready?" He remained committed to the porch.

"Please, come in. I want to discuss something."

"I only have a moment." His eyes narrowed as he stepped around her and entered.

A direct approach might work best, though if she was too direct, she'd end up blurting out how his presence intimidated her, how every time he looked at her, her stomach tightened and remained in a knot for half a day. She wanted him to leave, but then again, she didn't. She wanted him to put his arm around her again, but if he came too close, she might grab him by the shirt and beg. Unappealing, for sure.

She shoved another log into the woodstove. Feeling as if her stomach might reject the scone she'd eaten, she spoke quickly. "I need to go with you to Olympia."

His expression remained stoic. "You can't come."

"Why?"

"Do you have to ask?" His whisper held a pinch of nervousness. When had Tristan ever been nervous around her?

"This is the only home I've known. My father and I built this cabin together—"

"I hardly think you helped. You had to have been, what, eight?"

"Seven. And I did help. A seven-year-old can work, as I'm sure you did on the farm." She had to pause because of the lump in her throat. "I need this place. Why won't you help?"

He stepped across the small room to the window and peered out to the purple haze of dawn. "I said I'd take your letter."

She grunted, not caring how unladylike it sounded. Tristan was rigid as stone when she needed him to be malleable as leather. "I won't slow you down. I have warm clothes. I've slept outside—"

"No."

Tristan grabbed the letter from her hand and turned toward the door.

Hospitality had failed. Directness had failed. She rushed around him, intercepting him before he reached the door, and placed her hands flat on his chest. His hard chest. His warm chest, like a person with a heart. She saw none of that heart at the moment.

"You are so . . ." She had no word for him, or maybe she had too many—stubborn, guarded, impersonal—but she wasn't mean enough to say them, didn't know if she actually believed them. "I could go alone, you know. I'm not some knee-high wisp of a girl who'll blow over in the breeze—"

"That's debatable."

"I asked you because I trust you, and I'd feel safer with someone."

"Safer? You're like a Native in these woods. You're out by yourself all the time"

"I've never been overnight by myself." Yet if she had to, she'd do it.

He studied her, again with that stoic expression. His jaw didn't clamp. His pulse didn't quicken, at least that she could feel with her hands still square on his chest. His mouth had even relaxed. Was he pitying her? She could work with pity.

But in the next instant, his eyebrows drew inward, and he pried her fingers from his shirt.

Perhaps she'd been a dunce to think she'd sensed care in the way he'd sheltered her from the cold last night. Tristan was living up to the aloof, intimidating person she'd first judged him to be.

"I'll not be a bother," she said. "I'll hardly talk."

That should be tempting, seeing as he'd once asked her to stop talking.

"I like your chatter." He shook his head, seemingly as shocked by his words as she was. "You will be a bother, and the reasons I say no are numerous and personal."

"List them. At least one, rational reason."

"It's not proper." He stepped past her, grabbed the door handle, and pulled.

Why couldn't he yank it? Was she the only flustered one here? That nonchalance of his begged her to pummel him, if not with fists, then words.

"You are cruel and selfish." She'd done it. She'd said something mean.

With a burst of laughter, he strode out the door.

Anna followed, stepping heavy with her boots, hoping he absorbed their punches. "I've never asked you for a favor. I even try to avoid you." She needn't mention she avoided him because of the affection that threatened to overwhelm her when he was around.

Affection, hah!

Tristan placed the letter in his saddlebag and rested his hands on the side of the saddle, bowing his head. He was an impenetrable target, and all her words were blunt arrows.

She laid her hand on his arm. "Tristan, please." *Look me in the eyes.* Then she could let her heart plead along with her voice. "I've got to get to Olympia. You don't understand. If I can't get my land back, I'll get on with my life. I won't bother you again. I promise."

"Are you trying to bargain with me?" he whispered.

She dropped her hand from his arm. As if he were willing to bargain.

He turned his head and met her gaze, and instead of Tristan the conqueror, who battled the university until they'd give him a chance, she saw Tristan the wounded. The boy who'd lost a mother.

"Anna . . ." He slapped his hands on the saddle and pulled her into his arms.

His grip contained a fierceness that drew a gasp from her. Warm breath blew on the top of her head, and for some reason, stilled her out-of-control feeling. She wanted to close her eyes and sleep, to wake and have this issue solved. The peace that had seemed elusive suddenly had arms, warmth, and a smell like sweet earth.

With one embrace, he'd lifted her heart above water and allowed her hope to breathe.

He let her go too soon, and she stepped back. His gaze downcast, he scratched behind his neck. For the first time since she'd met him, she thought she'd witness the changing of his mind. A softening.

"Sorry. I can't take you."

His husky words pushed her hope under again.

"Fine, I'll ask Michael." Oh, why had she said that?

He snapped his gaze up. "You will not."

He was right. She wouldn't.

His eyes burned as he stepped toward her. She moved back.

"Fine. Ask Michael." Tristan shot his words. "And while you're at it, marry him."

He swung up on his horse, grabbed the reins, and tore off into the new light.

She returned to the house and flopped into the rocking chair by the woodstove. The soft sizzle of the burning chestnut wood melted her spirit. She'd acted childish, foolish. Temperamental.

God, forgive me.

She leaned her head against the back of the chair and cried.

Tristan pushed his mount. The look in Anna's eyes had never disturbed him like it had this morning. She was at the end of her wits, and a desperate Anna was not an Anna with whom he was familiar. The Anna who wore peace like a garment, whose compassion sparkled like diamonds, that was the Anna he knew. She'd find a way to Olympia, he was sure of it, and when she discovered he owned her land and had planned—correction, was planning—to use it for an agricultural school, how would she feel?

He'd been a fool to let it go this far. This wasn't worth it. He'd not enjoy leading a program knowing he'd hurt Anna for the chance at it.

He grunted into the wind, a wild release of frustration. That Anna would pursue this land issue like it were her own wayward child had caught him off guard. Now that he knew her better, he wasn't surprised. She'd slept most of her days under a wagon. It was stupid of him to think she wouldn't need the physical connection to her father that the cabin provided. The cabin was part of her battle to belong. He saw the way she looked at the women at church as they huddled together after services and gabbed about whatever women gab about. Quilts, maybe. Children. *Go join the conversation*, he wanted to say to her. Instead, she had to analyze every look, every tone of voice. Had to take people's spiritual struggles with healing as a personal affront.

Then there was the issue with Julia. She'd taken Nellie's behavior like a death sentence from a judge. Add to that the withdrawal of business from her clients, and she'd sealed her belief that no one liked her.

She was so wrong.

People adored her, he was certain. They didn't understand her gift. Maybe they even pitied her past, that she'd grown up without a mother, with trees and birds for companions. But they accepted her. Many were even drawn to her. Hadn't she seen that at the revival? Or realized that people's call for her to pray was a sign of trust?

True, Mr. Foreman didn't like her. And that caused others to be cautious. No one wanted to offend Mr. Foreman or be rejected by the bank.

Rejected.

He'd thought he could keep his ownership a secret. He hadn't realized she'd crawl under his skin and make straight for his heart. When he'd left his cabin that morning, he'd committed himself to remain distant, to focus on the task ahead. Hauling her next to him in the wagon last night had been disastrous. It'd taken half the night for the sensation of her body next to his to wane enough for him to fall asleep.

He'd determined to make up for the ground she'd captured. Grab the letter and leave before he did something imprudent, again. He'd made a mistake going inside the cabin, where her presence wrapped around him as real as if she held him.

Then when he'd taken her in his arms, he'd held her very spirit. Breath and life had blown into places that had been empty for years.

And now he felt sick. Sick to have lied. Sick to do what he was about to do. But he'd trapped himself. He needed out.

Judge Rudolph Lander.

Anna stared at the name etched on the office door. This was it. The moment of truth. She wiped sweaty palms on her brown skirt and ran her fingers through her wind-blown hair. She'd made it to Olympia. On her own, or rather with a little help. Not Tristan's.

"Miss Warren?" The woman who'd greeted her as she'd entered the courthouse held out a cup of coffee.

"Thank you." Anna took the cup and leaned close, whiffing the rich scent. She wasn't sure she'd warm up for another six hours.

"Judge Lander should return shortly."

Anna settled on the red settee. The velvet cushion sank beneath her, a soft and welcome change from the splintered hardness of the boat. Praise the Lord for Pale Moon and her husband, who'd rowed into Seattle Wednesday morning with their barrels of fish and offered to take Anna to Olympia. Having many connections—with settlers and Natives—was one of the gifts of freighting. The truth would be worth the two days she'd rocked back and forth.

Drizzle spotted the windows, and Anna looked past the mist into the grayness of Friday morning, hoping for a glimpse of Tristan even though she had little desire to run into him. Anger from Wednesday morning ached like an infected sliver. Nonetheless, she looked out the window again.

Little, but *some,* desire.

The hours from Seattle to Olympia, including the cold

night camped on shore, had offered too much time to dwell on this farmer who was harvesting more from her heart than she'd been willing to yield. This fullness within her whenever he was around, the emptiness when he wasn't, and the anticipation of seeing him again—God help her—it could only mean one thing.

The door to the courthouse opened, and Anna's heart swelled. A familiar marshal walked in.

"Mr. McGrath."

He hung his hat and stripped out of his wet overcoat. "Good to see you again, Miss Warren."

The pounding of her heart eased. When that door had started to open, she'd expected Tristan. *Relax, Saint*, she could hear him say.

Mr. McGrath strode across the room and kissed the secretary on the cheek. "Mrs. Hayes, you are a welcome sight."

The older woman smiled. "Don't flatter me, Jude. Pull up a chair and chat. You're in line behind Miss Warren anyway, so we've time to catch up."

Mr. McGrath settled delicately on a small-framed chair. "Nothing new with me."

"Don't give me that line."

The door opened again, and before her heart could jump to conclusions, a tall man with a full beard entered.

"Jude. You did a magnificent job." The man strode across the room, hand held out. "Let's get this business settled, shall we?"

Mr. McGrath stood and shook the man's hand. "I believe you have another client first." He gestured to Anna.

Judge Lander turned, and his thin eyebrows arched high. "Well, pardon me." He clapped Mr. McGrath on the shoulder as the marshal settled back in his chair. "This way, miss."

He swung open the mahogany door, revealing an office filled with ornate furnishings. A burgundy rug marked off a seating area.

"Please." Judge Lander motioned toward three plush chairs arranged around a table.

Anna chose the smallest, and even then, she was dwarfed by the deep seat and cushioned arms. As if meeting with a judge weren't intimidating enough.

"What can I do for you, Miss . . ."

"Anna Warren."

Judge Lander lowered himself slowly into the chair across from Anna, though she doubted the slowness was due to age, for he'd sauntered into the office with no trouble at all. Had Tristan already delivered her letter?

"Anna Warren." Judge Lander snatched his pipe and flipped it around in his hands.

"Did you receive my letter?"

"Not that I'm aware of. I get many letters though, and I have a backlog of messages to read through."

"I need to know who owns my land."

Judge Lander frowned.

She'd been too abrupt, but now that she was here before the judge, her heart needed to plead its case. The words tumbled, unhindered. "My father died last August while we were in Portland. When I returned, Mr. Wyse showed me my inheritance, but we were interrupted. After that, he disappeared, and I have no way to find out if I inherited the cabin. I heard a rumor that my father left the land to someone else. At first I didn't believe it, but then I remembered my father wanting to speak to me. He was sick and tired. I encouraged him to nap, and then he died. I never considered he had anything drastic to tell me until—"

"As a matter of fact"—Judge Lander shifted in his chair—"I've been discussing that property recently."

"My land?"

Judge Lander nodded. He stood and paced. "The rumors are right. Your father left the land to someone else." He ran a hand over his well-trimmed beard.

The beating of her heart rushed faster than the ticking of the mantel clock, which seemed overly loud. Her mouth dried, prohibiting her swallow. She waited for the obvious, the revelation of who, but Judge Lander stared out the window.

She opened her mouth, but her breath staggered, and the whispered "Who?" went unheard.

She knew Father loved her, but why would he do such a thing?

"Miss Warren?"

Anna gasped from her stupor and raised her gaze to Judge Lander. He stared down at her before kneeling and taking her hand. Something like a father would do. "This is difficult, I know. It's difficult for me too, because . . ." He sighed. "This is more complicated than you realize."

No matter how complicated, she had a right to know. "Tell me. Please."

She sensed compassion in his brown eyes, but he shook his head. "I need you to trust me." He stood and walked to his desk. A stack of papers fell to the floor as he rumbled through piles. "Ah, here." He brought over a newspaper and held it in front of her.

Seattle Lawyer Arrested for Fraud.

"Mr. Wyse?" she asked.

"Yes. Jude's the one who brought him in."

"What does this have to do with my land? And please, who owns it?"

"Mr. Wyse was arrested on charges of tampering with documents. Until we know if your father's will was one of those documents, I'd like to keep it a secret."

"You won't tell me?"

"Trust me, Miss Warren."

"But how can I stay at a place when—does this person who owns my land know?"

When Judge Lander held her eyes but did not answer, Anna knew the answer.

"I'm sorry, Miss Warren, but trust me when I tell you that you may stay at your cabin without fear of this person interfering."

Trust me. If she heard those words again, she might scream. Anna clung to Judge Lander's gaze. Seeing only tenderness and a fatherly concern, she nodded. "How long will I have to wait?"

"Hopefully not long."

"What does that mean?"

Judge Lander chuckled. "Let's say"—he scrunched his brow—"a month. Two at the most."

Anna cringed. "Will someone let me know, or do I need to return to Olympia?"

"We'll get in touch with you."

Anna stumbled to her feet, the weight of defeat pushing her down. She'd been sure this would be the day of freedom, the day the unknown would become known. And now what? She'd head to the wharf and attempt to find passage on a private steamer heading north out of the Sound. Olympia had nothing to offer her, and though she now knew the truth about the rumor, she only wanted to be in her cabin. Even if it weren't hers. To savor the smell and memorize the chinks in the walls.

Anna cleared her throat, summoning her voice and the courage to accept the unchangeable. "Thank you for your time, Judge Lander."

He smiled as he took her hands in his. "I'm sorry it has to be this way, Miss Warren. Thank you for understanding."

But she didn't understand. Not at all.

He'd come all this way to be told no.

Tristan wound around the clumps of rhododendrons flanking the capital building. The stone path led to the road, and that road rose to the top of the bluff, where Capital Inn overlooked the town. His stomach growled. They'd kept him waiting all day before taking only five minutes to hear him and reject him.

I'm sorry, but we won't support such a program.

President Hall wouldn't move forward without legislative support. Nor Denny. Certainly not Bagley, who'd already upset the politicians.

The issue with Anna's land pressed on him as much as his failure with the legislature. Judge Lander had refused to allow him to sign the land over to the university. And perhaps that was good, since he'd been presumptuous to visit with the judge first thing yesterday evening when he'd arrived in town—before meeting with the legislature.

Things were going about as well as plowing in a hailstorm.

He'd give anything to be home now. He missed his bed and the way the moon shone across his floor. He missed working in the barn as the sun rose. He missed walking across his fields, feet sinking into soft earth.

He missed Anna. Or at least the chance of seeing her when he made up an excuse to wander to town.

He glanced sideways and quickened his pace. Catching a glimpse of her long hair blowing as she marched the streets of Olympia wouldn't come as a surprise, seeing how everything else had fallen apart. At least he'd delivered her letter. Surprising how good that honesty felt.

He entered Capital Inn and trudged the stairs to his room. Perched on the bed, he unlaced his boots. The room smelled of a strange mix of soap and body odor, and a sense of barrenness filled the small space. Other than a mirror and several clothes hooks, the whitewashed walls were naked. How did Anna do it for so many years? The travel, the homelessness, the unceasing change.

A knock sounded.

"Come in."

"Tristan Porter?"

A broad man with fluffy gray hair and an angular nose stood in the doorway. He held out his hand. "I'm Professor Willard Polk."

Impossible.

Tristan dropped his boot on the floor. "*The* Professor Polk?" Tristan sprung to his feet, one boot on and one off, and shook the man's hand. "It's a pleasure to meet you."

"I overheard your name spoken at the front desk, and I thought, *the* Tristan Porter?" A full-fledged grin stretched across the man's wrinkled face. "The same Tristan who wrote to me three months ago? The man who's giving the TU an earful?" Polk chuckled. "You've earned a reputation. Not everyone has vision like you."

"I can't believe it."

"It's not hard to get a reputation, son."

"I mean—"

"I know. You can't believe it's me in the flesh." Polk chuckled again and patted his belly. "And there's a bit of flesh here."

"Have you eaten yet . . . sir?"

Polk's eyes twinkled. "No. I suppose you want to question me until I can't get any food in my mouth."

Tristan smiled. "Sounds like a plan to me."

"Meet you in the lobby in half an hour." Professor Polk left the doorway and continued down the hallway.

Tristan stared at the empty space, resisting the urge to stick his head out the door and see which room was Polk's. Amazing that one of the men who'd assisted in the running of the first Morrill program now showed up on the doorstep of his temporary home.

Surely this was a sign that all hope was not lost with the Territorial University.

The dining room had long cleared, but Tristan sat across from the professor, his napkin still tucked in his shirt. "Say that again." Tristan hunched over his paper, hardly any room left between his scribbles, and filled in the part he'd missed as Polk repeated himself.

"I appreciate a man with your appetite."

Tristan surveyed the dirty plates. He'd eaten a feast while Polk had talked and talked about the Morrill Act.

"I didn't mean supper." Polk laughed. "Though you did put down an impressive amount. I referred to your ambition for farming. It's delightful."

Delightful. The same word Polk had used to describe the chocolate cake. But it was a compliment nonetheless. "Thanks. There's much to learn, and the industry's changing fast."

"Exactly."

"That's why I need this program. After hearing about the program you ran at Ohio, I feel even more strongly that education is the only way to improve farming and keep pace with the demands across this growing country."

Polk tossed his napkin on the table and leaned back. Moments passed while the professor stared. Tristan squirmed under the unexpected scrutiny.

Finally, Polk cleared his throat. "I'm not sure I agree."

Tristan frowned. They'd discussed Polk's former Morrill program for the last hour. How could Polk change his mind now?

"You've asked questions about my years in Ohio, but you haven't asked what I do now in Portland."

"All right. What are you doing?"

"Mentoring other farmers."

Tristan reached for his water glass. He'd expect nothing less from a man like Polk.

"I teach a couple college classes, but primarily, I lead the Portland Agricultural Association."

Tristan choked on his water and coughed. "An association?"

"Sure."

"You pass out new copies of *American Agriculturalist* and preside over long, boring meetings?"

Polk shook his head. "Where did you get the idea that leading an association is nothing more than a social endeavor? I lobby with politicians. I keep records of crops, and I give lectures." Folding his hands before him, Polk leaned on the table. "If you think about it, the percentage of farmers who can attend an agricultural program is low. You reach more people through an association."

"You put up with a lot more too."

"Like what?"

"At our first meeting, I had to hold court between neighbors who were arguing about escaped animals."

Polk laughed. "You don't have to put up with that. Ask them to discuss it later. When you're in charge, you run the meetings. You delegate those issues to others."

Fine. Next time he'd hand all escaped-animal matters to Jimmy. That was, if there was a next time.

"I tell you, I've not had such close relationships." Polk sipped his coffee. "I've signaled out those who have an interest to learn, and I've put effort into training them. Tristan, if you've been asked to help with an association, do it. You'll make connections which will someday make it easier for you to run a program. You'll prove your leadership and skill."

The truth of Polk's words frustrated Tristan. "They already believe in my abilities. That's why they've asked me to lead this thing."

"With a program, you'll be forced to meet government regulations and comply with school authority. And your students are as likely as association members to bicker, be lazy, and have ulterior motives. That's human nature. With an association, you'll have broader connections, more flexibility, and you'll still have time to work your own fields like you desire." Polk stood and pushed in his chair. "Think about it before you dismiss it so quickly."

Think about it? Tristan had done that. He didn't have time to think about it more. But this was Professor Willard Polk, so Tristan nodded.

"Don't just give me the nod. Do it. Think about it. Perhaps the good Lord has something for you which you've not recognized."

The good Lord? Polk didn't know what all the good Lord had already given him, or rather, taken from him. Tristan swallowed the cynicism and forced himself to be gracious. "Thanks, Professor, for your time and suggestions. I do appreciate them."

Polk pursed his lips. "You've got passion. You've got talent. Don't narrow your dreams." He stood and clapped Tristan on the back. "Write to me, and tell me how things go." He winked and strolled from the dining room, leaving Tristan more confused than ever.

Chapter Twenty-Two

The pitter-patter of rain called her from sleep. How sweet to be home—at least the place that would be home for a bit longer. Anna turned onto her back, the weight of the quilts pressing snug and cozy around her. Early light crept between the curtain and the wall, casting a bluish haze in the room. How she longed for someone to stock the woodstove, but she'd have to roll from the warmth of bed and shuffle across the cold floor herself.

Taste and see that the Lord is good. She prayed the words of Psalm 34. *Lord, let me experience that goodness today.*

Before she lost courage, she jumped from bed, wrapped herself in her robe, and hastened to the woodstove. The woodpile was nearing its end. She'd brought four loads in last night upon returning from Olympia soaked and chilled. After five months, Tristan's supply would be gone within a few weeks.

The depletion went beyond the woodpile.

But this was the Sabbath. She would taste and see that the Lord was good. For today, that meant shelving thoughts of Tristan, the land, and her trip to Olympia. Four days of travel for a mere ten minutes with Judge Lander.

She ate her breakfast of eggs and cheese, listening to the quiet splatter of rain. When she'd donned her brown skirt, yellow calico top, and wool cloak, she paused at the window. Her hand traced the moisture beaded on the pane. How had she not minded the days of travel through gloomy weather?

"I don't want to go out in this." The warm breath of her whisper clouded the pain and sent the condensation dribbling down. She groaned, feeling the frustration of not only the weather but her ungrateful attitude.

She hummed as she laced her boots, a simple tune she and Father had created to go with Paul's passage in Philippians:

Whatever is true, whatever is noble, whatever is right, whatever is pure, whatever is lovely, whatever is admirable —think about such things.

However, by the time she arrived at church, water dripping off her hood, face numb, her list of thoughts looked more like an admonition of what not to dwell on: whatever is fearful, whatever is uncertain, whatever is exasperating.

She clomped up the steps, shaking the dirt off her boots, and through the door.

Few pews were occupied, and the hush of the sanctuary was unprecedented. Apparently, others had not wanted to go out in the rain. Lazarus sat by himself, and another couple spoke quietly to each other.

Something else wasn't right. Reverend Bagley was nowhere to be seen. She approached Lazarus to sit by him, but hesitated. A sheet of paper was next to him on the bench. "May I sit by you?"

He looked up, the shine of tears in his dark eyes.

Panic chased through her heart. "What's wrong? Where is everyone?" Had something happened to Tristan? Mrs. Tolliver?

"Sit." Lazarus moved the paper to his other side. "Oh, Lawd." His sigh heaved slow and deep as he looked at the ceiling. When his gaze returned to hers, Anna shivered.

"What, Lazarus?" Her heartbeat shook her throat, and heat rushed into her belly. "Tristan?" she whispered.

"No, child." The faintest smile tilted the corner of Lazarus's mouth as he shook his head. "Miz Julia be with the Lord as of this morning."

"Dead?"

Lazarus nodded.

A chalky taste coated her mouth. "I . . ." She buried her head in her lap, her breath quickening. Julia gone. Nellie . . . Anna had to be with Nellie. No. Nellie wouldn't want to see her.

You should go anyway.

"Lazarus . . ."

"It be a mystery, but it ain't your fault." Lazarus took her hand, and his calluses reminded her of another farmer's hand, a farmer she needed now. Lazarus patted her fingers with his other hand. "No, no. Don't go blaming yourself."

She knew it wasn't her fault. Then again, she didn't know. She'd disappointed the whole town. She should have stayed instead of gone to Olympia. But no, she'd been selfish. "Excuse me."

She rushed outside, and with shaky hands, grabbed Maple's reins. Her fingers weren't working. The ropes twisted in her hand until she somehow tugged them free.

Taste and see that the Lord is good.

The only thing she tasted was the drop of blood from where her teeth had bit her tongue. And the only thing she saw, beyond the tears, was a figure hastening down the church steps.

"Miz Anna." Lazarus crossed the churchyard. "This be a hard time, I know, but I found something yesterday and . . ." Lazarus sighed. "I hope I'm doing right, but I think you should have it."

Anna wiped her tears and frowned at the folded piece of paper Lazarus held out. Smudged with dirt, it looked worn around the edges, like it'd been fingered, but the seal remained.

"It's . . . well, you'll see."

She shoved it in her pocket, the stupor of Julia's death enough burden for the present moment.

Lazarus put his hand on her shoulder and squeezed. He returned to the church, leaving the cold ache of grief to settle like a mantle on her soul.

Anna stared at the gray waters. Waves rolled toward the rocky shore, and the low clouds blocked the mountains across the sound. The breeze spat raindrops at her face. Everything appeared as usual, except nothing would be the same again.

Her knees wobbled, and she sought relief from the weakness

by sitting on a tree stump. The wetness soaked through her dress. She tried to pray, but the only prayer she managed was the thrust of her heart up to heaven. An inner cry. She wrapped her arms about herself. The letter inside her cloak crinkled. She reached inside, but voices interrupted.

Oh, Lord. The Foremans, Johnsons, and Bagleys walked up Madison. When they reached the churchyard, their conversation hushed.

Mrs. Foreman stared at the ground, hands picking at the rouching in front of her dress, but Mr. Foreman wasted no time in approaching Anna and meeting her gaze. Condemnation heaved from his eyes. "Are you satisfied?"

Something burst in her. She'd had enough of his bullying.

Reverend Bagley pulled Mr. Foreman back. "Not now, Clyde."

"Then when? When will you confront this foolishness?" Mr. Foreman jabbed a finger at her. "You promised Nellie that Julia would live."

She didn't blink or flinch. "I did no such thing. You lie."

Reverend Bagley stepped between her and Mr. Foreman. "This is not the time. Let's go inside, read Scripture, and sing. This is a time for prayer, not argument."

Anna stared at Mr. Foreman, refusing to be the first to look away. She'd lost a friend through this ordeal with Julia, and now that friend had lost a child. She was hurting like the rest of them, and yet they thought her the perpetrator.

Mr. Foreman finally turned and stalked off toward the others, and with his absence, Anna's anger collapsed. In its place, sorrow burrowed and expanded.

"I'm sorry."

Anna jerked her head around. Mrs. Foreman stood, gaze skirting the woods.

Before Anna could respond, Mrs. Foreman rushed after her husband. Anna knew she should follow and attend the service, but the pain in her stomach and head made the thought of sitting among her condemners unbearable.

You're likeable, Saint. They don't understand your gift.

Tristan's words offered comfort, and she rose and twined Maple's reins around her hand. The mud of Second Street squished under her boots as she walked south. If anyone looked out the church now and saw her leaving, well, it'd only confirm what they already thought of her. A fraud. A self-glorifying—

Her ankle slipped on a wet rock and twisted. She groaned, grasping her foot. Her hand fisted until her fingers could squeeze no longer and weakness forced her to let go. "Lord, help." She turned to Maple and rested her forehead against the horse's damp mane.

Julia with Jesus.

Picture it, Anna. No more pain. The arms of her Savior.

A touch of joy trespassed upon her anguish. The moments of faith she'd had since returning in September glistened in her mind: surrender at Tristan's lookout, God's words *all things new*, the silent peace of sleeping on her porch, the thrill of praying for others at the revival.

But the ache of Julia's death remained.

"I hurt, Lord." She whispered into Maple's mane, the warmth of her breath emphasizing how alive she was. And how gone Julia was. "In this hurt, all things new. In this hurt, your presence is enough."

She lifted her head.

"Come on, girl." Anna led Maple along the road until she reached James Street.

The curtains of the Simms' residence were drawn. Several wagons crowded the street in front. Determination fought back doubt. She had to see Nellie. She wouldn't hide and pity herself or fear the responses of others.

She raised her hand to knock on the door, but it opened. Jared Simms stepped out with mouth drawn tight. "Nellie's not ready to see you."

"Mr. Simms, I can't express how sorry I am for your loss."

He didn't look at her, and when he spoke, his mouth hardly moved. "I know." He crossed his arms and remained in front of the door.

A head poked around a curtain and pressed against the front glass. Britton. A few seconds later the door flung wide, and Britton thrust himself into her arms.

"I'd like to see Nellie, please," Anna said.

"She doesn't want to see you."

"I know she's upset, but I need to see her. I still love her."

Mr. Simms sighed. He backed through the open door. "She's in the parlor with Mrs. Mercer."

Anna followed Mr. Simms inside, with Britton's arms wrapped around her middle. The aroma of bread and smoldering wood contradicted the empty feeling.

Anna put her mouth near Britton's ear. "Are you all right?" She felt his nod against her side.

Nellie turned from the fireplace as Anna entered, and for an instant Anna thought she saw gratefulness in Nellie's eyes, but when Nellie looked back to the flames without acknowledging her, Anna's calm crumpled. Mrs. Mercer rose and left the room. Anna reached to unwrap Britton's arms, but they locked around her waist.

Anna whispered again in his ear. "Give me a moment with your mama?"

Slowly, he released her and left the room. Wringing her hands, Anna studied Nellie. Her rumpled dress evidenced a long, sleepless night.

Anna approached and put her hand on Nellie's shoulder. Nellie startled, jerking from Anna's touch.

"I'm sorry, Nellie." The fire popped and sparks danced. Anna prayed for wisdom. "This is difficult. I'm hurting for you and Jared."

Still no response.

"How can I help?"

Silence. Anna reached around and jacketed Nellie with her arms. Nellie didn't respond, but neither did she withdraw. Anna tightened her grip, prayers for Nellie's comfort streaming through her mind.

"Nellie?" Mrs. Mercer poked her head around the doorway. "Mr. Simms needs you upstairs."

Anna sighed.

Nellie pulled back and nodded at Mrs. Mercer. And then she left, without looking back.

Sorrow seamed the day in on all sides, and the cabin felt empty as an abandoned seashell. Anna curled her toes under her nightgown and closed *Aesop's Fables*. A mere hint of pain remained from her tweaked ankle. Wood sizzled in the stove, and the hot tea she'd made cozied her throat. Her heart remained numb.

Here she sat in her cabin, and yet it wasn't hers. The disconnect tore the comfort of home from her.

She fingered the letter she'd been holding the past fifteen minutes. A letter she'd yet to read. She shuddered at the sight of one word scribbled on the outside: Anna. Father's shaky scrawl took her back six months to that room at Mrs. Ford's when feelings of hope had tangled with devastation.

Her finger ran in a steady circle around the *A* of her name. The paper was worn like a page from his Bible. Soft. How had Lazarus come by it? She was tired of mystery. Of unanswered questions.

Finally, the need to connect with Father overrode the fear of what she'd find inside, and she unfolded and read:

Daughter,

My time is short—not only in this life, but the time I

have to write this while you are walking. I will write this letter and enclose it with the letter I am sending to Tristan.

The sight of that name . . . An awfulness sank into her being.

I know it will be difficult for you to stay in Portland, and so I write this letter in case you journey home. You are brave to stay and try working for Mrs. Ford—for I really think you would enjoy it here—but I do not know where your heart will lead you. If back to Seattle . . . that is the purpose of this letter.

I have tried to find the courage and the perfect time to tell you of the important decision I've made, and so far, I haven't found it. And while I know a letter may be the coward's way, I know you'll forgive me. Through the years, we've had numerous people interested in our land. I've never been drawn in by their monetary offers. But I've been drawn in by Tristan. More than I know how to express, or even understand. His passion for farming is unsurpassed. I'd like him to have the opportunity to pioneer an agricultural program, but with the financial situation of the university, I know it would be difficult. I've sent a letter to Mr. Wyse stating that our land is to go to Tristan. I hope a sizeable chunk of acreage near the university eases his obstacles.

Let me assure you, we have saved a good amount of money. I couldn't have left Tristan the land if we'd not had so much success. Please know I believe my inspiration is from the Lord. That boy feels like a son to me.

And she felt much like the disinherited daughter, no matter of Father's reassurances. It didn't make sense. And yet, it did. Knowing Father's affection for Tristan, Father's generous spirit—it seemed obvious now.

But hadn't she asked Tristan if he'd owned the land? They

were standing by the livery, the day before the revival began. She strained to recall the conversation. No. She hadn't asked him if he owned it, only if he'd thought leaving the land to another sounded like something Father would do.

And he'd said no.

Her fingers tightened on the page, and she forced her mind to slow its frantic whirring so she could finish the last paragraphs.

> *Please do not misunderstand my next lines, for you know how my parents tried to push me into a marriage before I met your mama.*

He wouldn't. Father surely wasn't going to suggest . . .

> *That's not what I want to do to you, so I'll say it simply: I approve of Tristan, should you ever desire to marry him. I mention this only to give a blessing, should the need arise. I trust the Spirit of the Lord in you when it comes to making decisions.*
>
> *You will return soon from your walk, and my eyes are growing heavy. No time to write the accolades of Tristan, though if you'd talk an hour with him instead of shuffling off with your book, you could see for yourself. I'm smiling as I write that. Know that I love you. Know that I only want the best for you.*

> *Father*

Anna couldn't breathe. In the stillness, the audible thud of her heart shook her chest. If she understood Father's intentions correctly, he'd sent both letters to Tristan, with hers to be given to her if she returned. Yet Tristan had kept it. Kept the truth from her.

Marry him? Marry a man who lacked the courage to be honest? A man who'd selfishly held back information he knew she longed for?

Every conversation she'd had with Tristan rushed her

senses—the emotions, the words, his facial expressions.

She sprang from the chair, sending the book and letter to the floor, and paced to the window. Her hand trembled, drawing back the curtain. She peeked at the black night as if it had an answer for her distorted feelings.

Tristan's deception scarred deep and cut away the fleeting relief at knowing who owned her land.

Her thoughts raced, and with it, her feet. Back and forth between rooms. She tripped and caught herself on the four-posted bed. Looking down, she noticed the corner of her satchel jutting from beneath. She tossed it onto the quilt. It didn't take long to stuff in clothes. She searched for Father's satchel, and when that was full, she went into the main room. She packed the dishes in her trunk, and after that, books. She hunted for more containers. Old crates lingering in the barn would work fine.

She dragged them inside and continued to pack.

Tristan might not be bold enough to tell her he owned her land, so she'd help him out. When he returned from Olympia, he could move right in.

She'd be gone. From his cabin and his life. Like he'd wanted but hadn't had the guts to request.

A cold front of air had wafted in overnight from the Sound, and now it squeezed around the mourners gathered by the small headstone. Anna shivered beneath her cloak.

She'd laid her father to rest in Portland, having acquired the services of a minister she'd hardly known. Mrs. Ford, bless her mothering heart, had stood beside Anna and held her hand. Yet not even the grip of a strong-spirited woman had made Anna feel any less alone.

She yearned for Mrs. Tolliver's grip now. But that friendship too had been stripped from her. At least during this season of illness. Thank God for the news that she was recovering slowly.

Reverend Bagley's voice rose above the muffled sobs, proclaiming God's resurrection promises. Anna received the beautiful words from First Corinthians with her eyes closed, afraid that if she opened them the sight of the Simms would destroy what semblance of peace she'd garnered for this service.

To close the service, Lorna sang Psalm 23. "The Lord is my shepherd, I shall not be in want . . ."

Anna found the courage to let her eyes wander the sterile, frozen expressions on the faces of those gathered. Lorna's silky voice superseded the crows' ruckus, a baby's wail, and the rough waters of the Sound. Anna met Britton's eyes, and he smiled just as Lorna proclaimed, "Surely goodness and mercy will follow me." Biting her wobbling lip, Anna nodded. Her fingers dug into her cloak and tensed around folds of material.

Reverend Bagley pronounced the benediction when Lorna had finished. While townsfolk hugged the Simms family and dispersed, Anna lingered near the gate. Families ushered silently by. The Johnsons neared, and she prepared to greet them, but they passed without looking up, as if she wasn't present. The Webbs circled the long way around the group before slipping out the gate furthest from Anna. She backed against the railing, and a spire jabbed her spine.

She'd become an outcast. Or was she reading too much into these actions? This was a funeral, not a social event. She feared she'd lost the ability to think objectively.

Mr. Foreman met her glance with a searing frown, and clinched the elbow of Mrs. Foreman as he guided her through the gate.

Anna moved heavy legs toward Nellie, doing what had to be done. As she neared the Simms, Britton broke away and ran to her. His arms around her felt like a divine rescue, but she released him and focused on Nellie.

"Nellie?" Anna spoke gently.

Nellie turned around, her dark skirts swishing. Her bloodshot eyes appeared empty.

"I'm sorry," Anna said.

Nellie pursed her lips and stared at the ground.

"Please, talk to me." Anna's whispered words sounded too much like a plea for attention. She grimaced and glanced away. Today was Nellie's day to hurt; Anna had to offer grace, not desperation.

When Anna looked back, Nellie's eyes had filled with tears, and her balled fists hung by her skirts. Jerking her head to the side, she let out a gut-wrenching sigh. "I'm so angry."

Anna startled.

"You can't understand." Nellie wiped her sleeve across her nose.

Reverend Bagley, Jared, Britton, and Julia's older sisters stood motionless. Fear paralyzed Anna's mind and body. She struggled for a response, but everything in her mind seemed like a platitude.

Nellie stalked to the gate. Slamming the picketed wood behind her, she looked back at Anna, her eyes narrow and her face red. And then she turned and left.

Anna stared, not wanting to acknowledge the anger cropping up in her heart and hating the selfish thoughts. What gave Nellie the right to say Anna didn't understand? Anna knew pain. She knew rejection and loss.

Looking at the others, her breathing quickened.

Reverend Bagley clasped his Bible to his chest. "Nellie needs time and space to grieve."

Without a word, Jared led the other children to their wagon. Britton looked back and waved, and it took all Anna's strength to lift her arm in response. At least she had one friend left, even if he was ten years old.

Arthur Denny's office was as straightforward as the man himself. Anna sat in a wood chair and stared across the spotless desk. "I need a place to rent."

He rubbed his hands across his face. "Would you at least tell me what this is about?"

Anna opened her mouth, then shut it again. Two hours ago the town had all but rejected her at Julia's graveside. She didn't want to add fodder to the gossip. "Well, I . . ."

"This doesn't have to do with Julia dying, does it?"

"What? No." His earnest expression pulled the truth from her. This was Arthur Denny, the trustworthy, reticent founder of Seattle. "I found out who owns my land."

Mr. Denny's brows arched. "Who?"

"It's personal."

Mr. Denny frowned again. "All right. That's your business, I suppose. You can rent the house on Cherry Street for a month, but then I've promised it to another family."

Mr. Denny's old house. The first home she'd entered as a shy four-year-old when she and Father had stepped off the ship from New York. Mrs. Denny had fed them sugar cookies and fresh milk. Time would never erase the memory of that afternoon when Father had struck a deal with Arthur for the land Tristan now owned.

"Thank you." Anna stood and held out her hand, as Father had taught her.

Mr. Denny shook firm. No wonder Tristan respected this man.

Anna left the office, slumped against the rough wall, and bowed her head. "Lord, am I doing the right thing?"

Maybe she was overreacting. Maybe Tristan deserved grace.

No, she had deserved the truth.

Anna looked up in time to see Nellie cross the street. Anna followed her progress around the corner. How she wanted to chase Nellie down and wrap her arms around her.

She stamped her booted foot on the wooden walkway. Tristan should be chasing her down, wrapping his arms around her, telling her he'd been wrong, a fool blinded by a pigheaded pursuit of a dream.

He'd put his arms around her for the last time a week ago when she'd implored him to take her to Olympia. To think, he'd tried to comfort her with his arms when his lips were what he should have offered.

A confession, that is.

Her hands cupped her heating face, and she sucked in a lungful of sea air. The air of her Seattle. It didn't feel right here anymore, but neither did leaving. New fury bristled.

That farmer.

She could board the drafts at the livery, find a place to park the wagon, but the thought of freighting no longer brought feelings of freedom. She'd been chained too long to the demands of travel. So what if she'd cut down her schedule, tried to weave between the tight-threaded fabric of this pioneer town. It hadn't worked.

Anna crossed the street to Joe's. The bells above the door failed to elicit a warm greeting from him. Boards creaked beneath her feet as she wandered up and down the narrow rows. Noises from the back indicated Joe's presence, but other than him and her, the store was as empty as her heart.

She swiped a finger across a dusty shelf. Frowning, she glanced around, noting the haphazardly stacked blankets, tipped over container of hinges, and overly crowded bin of rakes. The store was a mess. Joe might hire her and let her clean and stock. He'd had helpers before, but didn't now, as far as she knew.

When she reached the end of the aisle, she rounded the shelf of canned vegetables and stopped. A pair of booted feet stood in her floorward gaze.

"Anna." Joe stepped around her, carrying two crates of fabric bolts down the row.

He'd never been so sparse in his greeting. Forget working for Joe.

She'd never been so sparse in her joy.

Chapter Twenty-Three

Tuesday afternoon, as the sun slanted low in the west, Tristan rode into his yard cold, hungry, and as unsettled as the swift-moving clouds above. He hadn't felt this antsy since he'd planted his first field after arriving in Seattle. That March had seemed like a year, each day slowed by the anticipation of sprouting seedlings. The fear he'd fail, that the Northwest earth wouldn't yield to his touch, had cramped his appetite.

He was like that novice again. Uptight. Expectant. Except it wasn't the soil that roused the unease, it was life. Failure. Secrets wrongfully kept.

With each beat of Ember's hoof between Olympia and home, Anna's voice had lilted through his head, words she'd spoken, words he imagined her speaking. He'd just about come to the end of his field with her. There was nothing more to plant in this relationship unless he could spit out a confession and she could forgive him.

But no, Scripture said a man reaped what he sowed. He understood that better than most because he lived it. And he'd sowed deceit with Anna for a chance at what he thought he'd wanted.

Don't narrow your dreams, boy. Those words vied with Anna's voice for space in his thoughts. Is that what he'd done? His deceit against Anna had scraped against his soul and turned him raw from the inside out, so much so he almost didn't care about those dreams anymore. Almost. He couldn't help it. He cared for a program. He'd do anything for a program.

Like lie?

There was that soul scraping again. His next step . . . He didn't know what it was, but it had to do with honesty. The shame of it all stung, made the confession too difficult.

He slipped off Ember, and his legs buckled. Too long in the saddle. He rubbed his hind side. Everything ached. Head to rear to heart.

The barn doors stood open. Ember entered without his prompting, but Tristan hung back. Lazarus's smooth voice echoed as he greeted the mare. Sounds of the oat bin opening and hay being forked let Tristan know Lazarus was caring for Ember. Lazarus always cared, without grumbling, without expectation, and often without Tristan's gratitude. Not that Tristan intentionally ignored the man's hard work. But hard work was the foundation of this operation. He and Lazarus offered hard work to each other. It was a given.

Tristan stared at his hard work: the barn he'd raised with Lazarus and two other traveling helps, the cabin he'd constructed, which he'd faithfully added to as if five children and a wife depended on him. His fields, yeah, he was most proud about them. Even fallow, like now, they burgeoned with the potential for life.

But for all the hard work, he'd reaped nothing good inside.

A sack of potatoes sagged against the barn wall. Tristan knelt and palmed one of the root vegetables. The sting of earth touched his nostrils, but instead of joy, anger surged. He dropped the potato into the sack, but it rolled onto the ground. Tristan kicked it, sending it thudding against the wall.

Lazarus strode from the barn. "Welcome back."

Tristan brushed past, but reconsidered, turned, and met Lazarus's dark eyes. "Thanks."

Those eyes smiled, and Tristan could have dumped a barrel of corn over Lazarus's head.

"Well?" Lazarus waited.

"It's not happening."

"Tristan, I—"

"Where have I gone wrong, huh? Tell me?" Tristan paced to the end of the barn. "Honestly, Laz. You see the need for a program, don't you?"

"Sure do."

"It's feasible, isn't it?"

"It's a stretch, but yes."

"So what's the issue with these people?" Tristan kicked the post of Ember's stall, but the horse didn't lift her head from her feed.

"It's not the people. You know that."

Tristan stepped into the stall and began to brush Ember. "I don't know anything, apparently."

"That be a plain lie."

"Guess who I met in Olympia?"

"Anna?"

"What? No." Tristan narrowed his eyes. "Professor Willard Polk, one of the original Morrill Act men. And do you know what he said to me?"

Lazarus held up his hands.

"He went on and on about the joy of working with farmers in the Portland area as the leader of their association."

"Ah." Lazarus's eyes sparkled.

"You know about that?"

Lazarus shrugged.

"If you somehow wrote to him—"

"Nah."

Tristan swallowed, his throat thick. "Polk said, 'Don't narrow your dreams.'" Tristan ran the brush over Ember's shoulder. "You think I've narrowed my dreams?"

"Maybe." Lazarus leaned his forearms on the edge of the stall. "You haven't so much narrowed your dreams as your heart."

"What's that supposed to mean?"

"You closed yourself when you lost your father, brother, and mother."

Tristan stopped brushing. "And do you blame me?"

Lazarus stared at him.

"For God's sake, Lazarus, that was my family!"

"I know. They was my family too."

Such simple words. Tristan hung his head. Yeah, Lazarus knew.

"It's time to let go, boy."

Tristan's hand clenched the brush until the wood dug into his palm and sent pain nerving up his finger. The deep-brown eyes before him surged conviction with the strength of a flooding river.

"I'm doing fine."

"When's the last time God needed counsel?" Lazarus dragged him by the arm to the edge of the barn. The red horizon gave way to the deep-blue of a darkening sky above. "Look at those first stars. I'm sure glad you thought of stars, Tristan. Sky wouldn't be the same without them."

Tristan closed his eyes.

In the following silence, Tristan thought he'd escape this unexpected sermon. Then Lazarus shifted his feet, and Tristan tensed. *Go home, Laz.*

"I'd like some good rest tonight, Tristan. Can you promise me that?"

Tristan blew out a breath of air. "I get your point. I'm not God."

"Nice to finally hear that confession. But I don't think you believe it."

God, let this man be silent!

His pain had been buried so long it had petrified. He hauled that heaviness around like a gravestone, a constant memorial to the day that had changed his life. Even if he wanted to heal—which he now did, God help him—he couldn't undo the past. It was like planting. If disease invaded the crops, the whole field had to be uprooted. But he couldn't rip his heart out. No, the seed that had settled in the bottom was there to stay. He'd just have to work around it and hope for the best.

Tristan swiveled and strode back to Ember. He brushed fast and strong across her back.

"One more thing." Hesitancy rang in Lazarus's voice.

Tristan growled beneath his breath. "What?"

"I found a letter with Anna's name on it inside the drawer of the worktable."

His every nerve screamed for mercy.

"I gave it to her."

"You did what?" Tristan shoved the stall door open. It slammed against the outside wall. He could retch his stomach.

"Gave it to her. Felt like it was the thing to do."

"That wasn't yours to give her."

"Wasn't yours to keep."

"How do you know?"

"Weren't your handwriting."

"That's right." Tristan yanked open the drawer as if he'd still see the letter.

"Why you have it?"

Tristan stared fire at Lazarus.

"Tells the truth about her land, huh?"

Of course it did. "I didn't read it."

"You know what it says."

Tristan paced across the earth floor.

The musty smell of hay choked him. He couldn't breathe as he let the news sink in. Anna knew. He didn't even get the dignity of revealing his own shame. His fingers coiled in his hair. "Arggh!" The growl startled the animals, who stomped and banged against their stall doors.

Lazarus leaned back on a post.

Tristan hated his calm. "Why, Lazarus, why?"

"The Lord told me."

Great. And who could argue with the Lord? Tristan had been trying for years, and evidently, it was all going down tonight, and not in a way of his choosing. "The Lord has it in for me."

"You don't know what the Lord has for you. He's been waiting for you to let it all go. But you got to cling to this program thing. You got to cling to your secrets. Cling, cling, cling. I'd think the knuckles of your heart be white and weak by now."

"How poetic, Lazarus."

Lazarus walked to the door and stepped into the waning light of evening. "Oh, I almost forgot."

Something else? It couldn't get worse.

"Julia died."

Tristan marched down the path to where the Duwamish sliced through the corner of his land. The gentle sound of the current mocked his agitation.

Rage. Pain. Regret. He was reaping it all right now.

He heaved the sack of potatoes from his shoulder and dropped it on the ground. It landed with a thud. Picking up a thick, round potato, he studied it. He'd grown this. He'd toiled to bring these roots from the ground. And for what? He'd have no program with the university.

Worse, he'd lost Anna through his own humiliation.

Yes, worse, you fool.

Tristan hurled the potato at a hazelnut tree. The potato split, leaving a trail of juice on the trunk. He reached into the sack again, this time drawing out as many potatoes as he could hold. One after the other, he smashed them against the trunk. Then more potatoes. And more. Sweat dripped down his back. Darkness hunkered around as the last light drained from the sky. The trunk was no longer visible, but still, his aim rang true, as witnessed by the splatting sound of potato flesh.

Breathing hard, he stomped to the tree and ran his hand

through the mess. The pulp oozed over the bark. Needing to inhale the rank odor, he pressed his hand against his face. Dampness. He looked upward expecting drops of rain to spit down at him. Stars cried out from the black backdrop, and the cold air stung against the moistness of his cheek.

He was crying.

His shoulders shook as he sank to the ground and squeezed the potato remnants in his palm, the mush slipping between his fingers. He laid his forehead against the ground.

Sobs weakened his body. The verse *Jesus wept* echoed amidst his internal storm, each cry of his reinforcing the humanity of Jesus. He felt the breaking open of the seed, like Lazarus had spoken of, and this time, the resistance wasn't there.

He pictured Jesus weeping at the house of Mary, Martha, and Lazarus. Then the image of the house shifted, and Jesus entered Tristan's boyhood home and walked down the hallway toward his mother's room, where her body waited, laid out for burial. And Jesus wept. Wept for Tristan's mother. Wept for him, the fifteen-year-old boy sitting in the corner of the kitchen, staring at a bowl of potato peelings.

Tristan couldn't stop the throbbing of his heart, the slow emptying of all the bitterness he'd stored from that moment the doctor had pronounced his mother gone. So this was what surrender felt like. The mucking out of anger and pain like manure from a stall. The digging work of grace.

And he was helpless to resist.

An hour later, or maybe only minutes, when the tears ceased, he turned to his back and looked at the stars. Questions still roamed his heart, but the pain was gone. His weeping—no, the weeping of Jesus—had transfigured the pain into peace.

He rose from the ground and ran down the path into his field. The pale moon glowed on the horizon, illuminating the plane of his rooftop. He bolted to the cabin, not bothering to shut the door behind him, and rushed into his bedroom. He snatched the quilt his sister had made. Tomorrow, he'd write to her. Tomorrow, he'd . . .

Tomorrow could wait. Tonight he wanted the field beneath him and the sky above him. He wanted to live like Anna, not only in surrender and peace, but with that beautiful openness. And what was more open than sleeping exposed to heaven?

The dirt gave beneath his footsteps as he walked to the middle of his oat field. That first softening of the ground meant he'd be planting soon. Sowing new life. He wrapped up in the quilt and lay down, still clothed and dirty from his trip.

But as the sound of the river whispered in the distance, he'd never felt cleaner.

Chapter Twenty-Four

Four days of coming and going from Mr. Denny's old house, and the entire town seemed to know her every move. They glanced at her with cautious eyes. Some looked away. Their stilted greetings and curt nods confirmed Anna's fear: Seattle was disappointed in her. Maybe they'd heard about Tristan's ownership and pitied her.

Anna grasped the door of the church, ready to seek sanctuary from the disapproval, but scuffing footsteps halted her.

She smelled him before she turned. "Mr. Roberts?"

"Miss Warren." He raised his hat. Even the thin veil of politeness couldn't mask the mischief of his eyes.

She had no time for schemes. "I've received a letter my father wrote before he passed, which reveals the owner of my land, and it is not you."

"I—"

"Good day." Ignoring his questions, she yanked open the door, entered, and shut it behind her. The cedar door felt thick on her back as she leaned into it and waited in the darkened room until she heard footsteps retreat.

Whatever Mr. Roberts had in mind concerning the land, she no longer cared. Tristan could deal with his conniving.

In the quiet of the empty church, she not only felt her steady heartbeat but heard its voice. Her eyes strayed to her and Father's spot, and a smile formed on her face, drawn out by the memory of his robust singing.

A smile—amidst the grieving and changing and wondering. The joy soothed away the past few days of shadowed glances.

Her gaze drifted to Tristan's pew, and her smile faded. How easily pain eclipsed affection.

The door rattled against her back. Had Mr. Roberts not left after all?

She spun and stuck her head out. "Please go—"

A wide grin silenced her entreaty.

"Michael, come in." She moved and let him enter.

"What a week," he said. "How are you holding up?"

"I'm trying to be all right." She walked to the front pew.

He sauntered up the aisle after her. "I'm sorry I wasn't around to comfort you."

That might have been disastrous. His presence required more effort from her than it gave comfort.

He clasped his hands behind his back, that authoritative gaze of his arresting her attention. "It's all right to embrace the pain."

Her eyes narrowed. She'd expected a homily on victorious living, not permission to hurt. "You're sounding like Tristan."

Michael grunted. "Nice."

"He said I should let myself feel bad."

"He wants you to feel bad?" Michael's voice carried an ache.

"Not like you think."

"If he didn't want you to feel bad, why did he lie to you?"

So Michael had heard. "He didn't lie. He held something back, probably for a good reason." Her defense sounded weak and went against the pain inside.

"All the same. He deceived you."

Yes, and no amount of convincing herself otherwise overcame the sense of betrayal. The tears bulging her eyes leaked out. She inhaled slowly, but that only caused the sobs to start. She sank to the front pew and bowed her head in her hands.

"Ah, Anna." Michael knelt. "Why can't you feel this way about me?"

Anna raised her head, took the hanky Michael offered, and wiped her face. "Pardon?"

"Never mind." Michael took the hanky she gave back and

shoved it in his pocket. "Listen. You obviously feel strongly about Tristan. You have to forgive him and move on."

"I have forgiven him." She'd prayed, at least. Out loud. She'd spoken the words, *Lord, I forgive him.*

"Oh?"

"Of course." She held his gaze, even when fresh tears blurred her vision. "Forgiveness is a choice."

Michael shrugged. "Ultimately, I guess. But if you're still this broken about it, maybe you need to ask the Lord to strengthen that forgiveness in you."

Still this broken. It'd been four days. This shattering would take much more time to mend.

Michael rose from his knees and resituated himself on the pew a few feet from her. "How did Tristan act when he apologized? Was it sincere?"

Anna stared at the cross on the wall behind the pulpit.

"He has apologized, hasn't he?"

She shook her head.

"Good heavens. And still you care for him?"

The cross stared back at her, and her imagined vision of Jesus hanging there bloodied and beaten was so strong she could almost hear his voice—*Father, forgive them for they know not what they do.*

She wasn't sure where she was in forgiving Tristan—even her father—but caring was not the issue. She couldn't not care. She smiled as a salty tear slipped into her mouth. "Yes, I care."

Michael walked to the pulpit and ran his hand across the top. "I was wrong about you."

"Huh?"

"Your faith." He gripped both sides of the pulpit as if facing his congregation. "At first I thought it timid, in spite of your gumption when it came to healing prayer."

"Timid? Why?" Anna stood and walked into the aisle, peering up at Michael.

"I don't know. Maybe because of your sweetness. You have a gullibility about you." He knocked his fist on the pulpit before stepping down and joining her. Placing his hands on her shoulders, he bent his head down and met her eyes. "Seeing how you persevere in situations of doubt, I realize just how strong your faith is. That you could hold your head high even though Julia died, or believe in Tristan like you do, shows how sure you are of the redeeming work of Jesus."

Anna gaped. "Michael . . ." She wiped her eyes. "Thank you."

He squeezed her shoulders, and for a moment she worried he might kiss her, but he backed away. "You're a good woman, Anna."

On Thursday afternoon, Tristan rode to Anna's cabin. He'd hardly slept Tuesday night in that field, thinking of Anna, how he'd make things right, searching for the words to convey his remorse.

Nothing. He had no excuse.

Since he'd wept himself to the foot of the cross and emptied the anger, he'd not been able to stop praying. God had reached down and planted a seed of prayer within him, he was certain. Nothing else explained this unceasing flow of conversation heavenward.

He'd about worked up the confidence to see Anna, when Jimmy had whistled himself into the yard to talk about the association. The energy within that youth could have plowed three fields, so excited he was of Tristan's renewed interest.

And now Thursday, here he was. Still without words, without excuse. His hope lay in Anna's gentle spirit, in the care he'd seen in her eyes when he'd ripped back the secrecy from his wounds, revealing the broken fifteen-year-old boy still in charge of his heart. Maybe she didn't feel for him that wild pull he felt toward her, but at least her compassion should lead to forgiveness.

Please, Lord.

Yet in spite of the prayer and the hopes he had in Anna's character, when he rounded the drive and saw her cabin, his heart thundered. Fool. He'd been a plain and selfish fool. He wanted to feel her anger, needed to feel it.

He dismounted, his deep breath triggering an ache in his side. Every part of him stood guard for movement—a wisp of brown hair, a swish of skirts. Even the few chickens she'd kept next to the barn were quiet. In fact—strange—they weren't even in their run. He tied Ember to a post. The creak of wood screamed his presence as he stepped onto the porch, and he braced himself for her to swing the door open. He could picture her with that gun she'd pointed at him right in this yard. Maybe this time she'd pull the trigger.

Still no movement, no sign of presence. Sweat coated his palms. He knocked on the door. *Settle down. This is Anna.* Peaceful, chatty, Anna. Intense, honest, Anna.

He was in for it.

Tristan knocked again. "Anna?"

When she didn't come, he walked to the front window and put his face to the glass. Empty? He strode back to the door and threw it open. All her stuff, gone. A piece of paper lay in the center of the room. He didn't need to enter to see the large lettering: *Welcome home, Tristan.*

Frustration pushed him across the yard to the barn. Empty. Another piece of paper fluttered in the breeze, attached by a nail to the front post. He turned it over: *Welcome home, Ember.*

Seriously, Saint? What sort of a joke was this? He slammed the barn doors. He was no ordinary fool. A dimwitted, scoundrel of a fool's what he'd been.

And oh, the shame. How could he face her?

How can you wait any longer?

"We got work to do, girl." He slapped Ember on the shoulder. Apologizing to Anna might clear his conscience before the Lord, but he had months of work ahead if this friendship would be restored.

Tristan kept Ember at a canter as he rode to town. It wouldn't be hard to locate Anna in a place where everyone knew everyone else. Unless she'd gone to Portland. Panic threatened to push his heart out his chest.

"Easy there." Ember minded his command. His heart didn't.

He entered Joe's, gaze racing over the rows.

Arthur Denny turned from the counter and motioned him aside, a scowl darkening his face. "You've got some explaining to do."

Tristan's face heated beneath the less-than-friendly expressions on customers' faces. He leaned closer to Denny. "I've been a fool."

Denny smiled, a rare full-cheeked grin. A chuckle escaped before his expression sobered. "We all make mistakes, but not all of us know how to remedy them." Denny placed a hand on Tristan's shoulder and nudged him to the door. "Follow me."

Denny walked down Front Street to Cherry. He crossed his arms and faced Tristan. "I don't know why you chose to keep secret what you did—"

"I—"

"I'm not asking for reasons or excuses." Denny motioned up Cherry Street. "She's up there." He walked away.

"Up where?" Tristan's call went unanswered.

He returned his gaze to Cherry Street. At Denny's old house? She'd gone to him for help? Frowning, he walked up the incline and stopped in front of the square house. Red gingham hung in the front window, the same gingham from Anna's cabin.

Lord, help.

He swung open the gate, stepped onto the walk, and closed

the white-picketed entrance behind him. The rusted latch refused to fasten. He'd take the latch down to the smithy later, but for now, he pushed harder. It still didn't catch.

"It's broken."

His fingers clammed as he released the latch. Broken. "I see."

He turned and met her gaze, not knowing what he'd find, but certainly not prepared for the barrier he saw. A wall he'd put there. "Anna . . ."

She stepped around him, and her basket brushed against his forearm. He reached out and grabbed it. She twirled, eyes wide as if keeping them so would hold the wall in place. The pain breeched it.

Her gaze flitted up to the blues and grays above. "Nice patchy sky, today. Planting time soon, I suppose."

Erecting a front of sweetness couldn't veil the anger he sensed beneath.

"Do you have students already?" she asked

"Anna—"

"I guess Jimmy will be one. I'm sure many are interested. Maybe even some lumberjacks who'd rather farm but don't know how to start. You'll do—"

"Saint." He took hold of her elbow. She stared at her hands, her body so still he wasn't sure she breathed. Her nearness overwhelmed him, and he scanned the small yard. "Where are your chickens?"

"What?"

He looked back to her softened expression and smiled at the way he'd brought down her defenses, even if for a moment.

"I gave them away," she said.

He lifted her chin with his finger, but she wrenched back and threw open the gate. It banged against his leg.

"Anna." He lunged around the white slats and snagged her basket. "We need to talk."

She was shaking her head before he'd finished his sentence.

Her pulse throbbed against her temple, and he wanted to reach out and touch it. But he wouldn't be more of a fool than he'd already been.

She gripped the basket against her belly like a shield, and when he moved to pry her hands from it, she tugged it closer and stepped back.

Inadequacy attacked him. His nickname for her might have started in jest, but now it meant so much more. Her faith humbled him. He didn't know where to start with an apology— by acknowledging Julia's death or simply saying he was sorry.

He spit out the first words that came to him. "Please come back to your house."

"It's not mine anymore, and I like being in town."

Sure she did.

She practically preferred sleeping under the stars rather than in a bed. No way did she like living blocks from Conklin House, Yesler Hall, or Skid Row with all their liveliness.

"I'm signing the land back to you."

"My father gave it to you." She kept her gaze far from his.

"I don't need it." He needed her, not her land, but he couldn't say it. Not when he'd already disappointed her. Not when she stood, a casual air roosting about her, pretending to hold it together. He ached to reach past the facade.

"I'm sorry." He poured all his regret into those two words.

"I forgive you."

She'd uttered the response as if she were doing recitations, as if it was the answer she knew he wanted to hear. And he did want to hear it—from her heart.

But what he really wanted to hear first was her anger. He wanted more than calm words or forced friendliness. Just once he wanted to see her lose it. He wanted to experience her fury. He deserved wrath, not an absentminded acquittal.

"I was wrong." He crossed his arms and sighed. "Look at me, please."

"I don't want to look at you. I don't want to speak to you. And I don't want you signing the land back."

Agitation. Finally.

"Did you know Mr. Roberts told me he owned my land? I came home to him sitting on my porch in the dark."

Tristan felt like someone knocked the wind out of him.

"How could you look me in the eyes, see my pain, and not say anything? It was heartless. Gutless. And I never thought you were capable of being gutless."

She held up her hands, closed her eyes, and breathed with obvious effort. "I'm sorry. I'm still working through this. The surprise . . . I've forgiven you, really, I have. I know you had good reasons not to say anything."

He had no excuse. "Saint, look at me." He didn't care how desperate he sounded.

She lifted her eyes.

"I . . ." He lost his thoughts. "I hurled potatoes at a tree."

Confusion wrinkled her brow. How did one express an experience so intimate as the night he'd buried his past by sleeping openhearted in his field. "I mean, I found peace." When she didn't respond, he added, "with Jesus."

"That's nice, Tristan."

That's nice? All she could offer was a relaxed, unexcited, *that's nice?* It was glorious. A miracle, and she knew it. She had to know. This detachment drove him crazy.

Maybe if he pulled her into his arms and kissed her he'd open the vault to her heart.

"Tristan." A male voice hailed him from behind, on top of the hill.

Anna startled, and Tristan hauled his gaze from her lips to peer behind him. Jared Simms drove down the hill. When Tristan looked back to Anna, she was already scuttling down Cherry Street. He'd let her go—for now.

Chapter Twenty-Five

Anna dropped her basket off at Joe's, told him she'd be back to pick up her order, then walked toward the livery. The image of Tristan as he'd confessed to hammering a tree with potatoes and surrendering to Jesus hovered in her mind. Thanks to that bit of news, nervousness had joined the swell of competing emotions, mingling with the anger and grief, forgiveness and grace.

Tristan at peace with Jesus. This changed things. Made everything more complicated.

Bless Jared Simms for appearing like an angel from above. Tristan had been about to beg forgiveness, despite her already offering it. He'd seen through her halfhearted *I forgive you.* She'd have crumbled like gingerbread if he'd begged, and she couldn't crumble yet. Not before she sorted through the feelings of disappointment. In Tristan. In Father.

In herself.

She entered the livery in pursuit of Maple, and the mere presence of horses, hay, and wagons—a reminder of her entire life—plummeted her spirit. And now what would the future hold?

"Just about got her saddled," Mr. Johnson said from behind Maple. "You like living in town?"

"I'll get used to it."

Mr. Johnson held Maple while Anna mounted, then handed Anna the reins.

He fiddled with the leather clasp on the bridle. "My nephew can move his fingers now." The lines around his mouth wobbled as he smiled. "I might not understand all this healing stuff, but I believe it. I guess that's how the Lord uses you." He gave a final tug on the bridle and released it. "Give my best to Mrs. Tolliver."

He wiped his hands on a cloth before picking up his hammer. "Take care of yourself now."

Gratitude thickened in her heart. "Thank you. I will."

God had snuck his grace gifts into her week, like the afternoons she'd been spending with Mrs. Tolliver, whose recovery was grace upon grace for Anna. Now here at the livery, unexpected affirmation.

Since God's miracle with Michael, she'd read the response of the community as critical. She was beginning to doubt her perception. Maybe they didn't know how else to act, as Mrs. Tolliver had suggested. Maybe their responses were less from disapproval and more from discomfort, a lack of understanding, as Tristan had told her. Because when God moved beyond understanding, things got uncomfortable. It was safer to hide from intimacy than consider that God might be closer than one expected.

Hadn't she hid behind her perception of the community? Felt it safer to feel victimized by others' opinions than to open up and invite them to be part of the Lord's work in her?

Crisp air blew her hair back as she rode to Mrs. Tolliver's, eager to share her new thoughts.

Mrs. Tolliver was standing at the door as Anna pulled into the yard. Anna dismounted, her eyes drawn to the axe by the woodpile, where she imagined Tristan sitting on the chopping stump. What a mess that relationship was.

She turned to Mrs. Tolliver and forced a smile. "Are you supposed to be out of bed?"

"How else am I supposed to get my strength back?" She hobbled aside and let Anna enter.

Warmth from the woodstove burned her cool cheeks, and she paused, enjoying the peace.

Mrs. Tolliver nudged Anna's lower back. "What's bothering you?"

Anna shrugged out of her coat, hung it on the hook, and let

Mrs. Tolliver lead her to the table. Steam swirled from the spout of a teapot, and the aroma of warm biscuits stirred her hunger.

Tears gathered in Anna's eyes. "You didn't have to do this. It's too much work, too soon."

"You've been to visit every day this week, and I haven't fed you a morsel. Just because I've been ill a spell doesn't mean I can't serve a friend." Mrs. Tolliver sank into her chair. "And you need a friend right now."

"Is it that obvious?"

"This year has been tumultuous for you."

She frowned and bit her lip, willing herself not to cry. She'd cried two days ago with Mrs. Tolliver, the tears streaming as she'd pondered why Father had done what he'd done. This was supposed to be afternoon tea, not afternoon cry her eyes out.

"You've seen Tristan?"

Anna poured the tea for them both. "Sort of."

"How do you sort of see someone?"

"I saw him. But not for long." The pleading of Tristan's eyes had scorched her heart. He'd been different, and she'd been unprepared. "I'm not ready to face him."

"How long until you're ready?" Mrs. Tolliver hooked her finger through her teacup.

"Until I forgive myself for being so stupid."

Mrs. Tolliver took a drink, gaze not wavering from Anna. This woman stripped Anna's heart bare with eyes that pried deep. Anna's jaw trembled.

"It's fine to be angry." Mrs. Tolliver set her cup down. "In fact, if you weren't angry, I'd think you were out of touch with reality."

"It's more than anger. It's . . . I'm so confused."

Mrs. Tolliver reached over and stilled Anna's hands. "It's simple, really. When you care for someone and he hurts you, the heart closes. Snaps right shut like a coon trap. But that doesn't stop the yearning. It only shoves it down and makes it stronger."

Mrs. Tolliver released her hand and buttered a biscuit. "Still, you can't avoid him. You have to let him have his say. God will give grace when you need it."

Anna sipped the hot tea, the liquid warming a path down her chest. A grace path. She held the cup close and inhaled the vanilla fragrance. This incident with her land might be part of God's grace path for Tristan. Regret was a powerful teacher.

If only she weren't so embarrassed. Those times she'd bared her frustration to him, let him see the way the unknowing about her land churned her up. And he'd known all along. He'd had the power to put her anxiety to rest. God may give grace for the moment when she faced him, but that didn't mean it wouldn't still be awkward.

Anna swigged her last drops of tea. "I can't think around him. He's got this consuming intensity. Like a storm you can't take shelter from."

"He probably can't think around you." Mrs. Tolliver's eyes sparkled. "You've got that same intensity. He sees that in you. I'll bet that's what's drawn him."

"Oh, I doubt it." He was drawn to keep her from figuring out his secret. Drawn to helping the daughter of his friend. Duty drawn.

Spirit drawn. The simple whisper quickened her heart.

Mrs. Tolliver raised her brows. "I think God's work in you and Tristan is just beginning. I look forward to watching it unfold."

Anna raised a hand to her heated cheeks. She'd love to watch it too. But she was in the middle of it, and the only way she'd get to see it was to allow God to do it through her.

Nausea stirred in Anna's stomach as she read the note tacked to her door.

Miss Warren, when you arrive home, please come to Yesler

Hall for a called meeting to discuss your behavior. Signed by Mr. Foreman and *others*, whatever that meant.

Anna sank to the front step and stared across the sun-kissed water. The time had come for her to offer grace to the community, withstand their discomfort, and throw off the pity she'd too easily turned to when discouraged by the responses of others.

Through the hazy light of dusk, she saw wagons gathering a block south near the meeting hall, heard voices call greetings. She made herself rise and move toward the meeting. How she wanted Mrs. Tolliver to be there. And Tristan.

For sure, he would be.

When she walked into the soft light of Yesler's, conversation ceased. She scanned the people, many who avoided her eyes.

They're as uncomfortable as you. Don't take it personally.

Amelia crouched in a corner, knitting, with Jimmy perched a few feet from her trying to engage her in conversation. The Webbs, Mercers, and Johnsons sat toward the front. The Simms family was absent—wait, Britton huddled next to a window. Michael was absent, but she wasn't surprised. For all she knew, he'd traveled to a neighboring town to preach.

But the realization of Tristan's absence cut off her willpower to stay calm. So what if she'd not been ready to face him this afternoon. She needed him here. Because in spite of how he'd hurt her, he was for her. In spite of the struggle to forgive him, she'd already conquered the struggle of loving him.

She loved him. No more rolling the idea around in her heart, hiding the emotion behind the other distractions in her life. God had thrust the love to the forefront, hand in hand with the pain of losing her land.

Tears warmed the back of her eyes, and she gritted her teeth to keep them at bay. What a strange moment to realize she loved him. Here, when she needed him, and he'd failed her again.

She fidgeted with her skirt, waiting at the back and

wondering if she should move forward. Mr. Foreman and Reverend Bagley discussed something, apparently disagreeing, considering the way Reverend Bagley shifted his eyes between her and Mr. Foreman. Directing a scowl at Mr. Foreman, Reverend Bagley hustled down the aisle. He took Anna's arm and ushered her outside. Though she'd only been inside a minute, she drank in the fresh air as if she'd been held underwater five minutes.

"I only learned this evening of the meeting. I didn't want to handle the situation this way," Reverend Bagley said.

"What situation?" Her fingers knotted together.

"Everything—I mean, the healings, your work with Michael, and now Julia's death."

Was this to be some sort of court where they found her guilty, took her out, and stoned her? "But I—"

"I know you're not at fault." He must have seen something wild in her eyes, for he gripped her shoulders. "Anna, I'm not against you. I know you mean well."

"What's going to happen?"

"I need to let Foreman have his say. With his position in town, we need to be careful about how we handle things. We'll use this meeting for conversation. Let people express their thoughts." He looked out at the dusky water. "I won't let things get out of control."

That wasn't much consolation, considering she felt lightheaded, her heart beat rapidly, and fear attacked her commitment to give the community the benefit of the doubt. Things already seemed out of control.

He opened the door, motioned her inside, and she found a seat next to the Johnsons.

Reverend Bagley addressed the community. "Friends, this meeting is to be a discussion about recent events concerning Anna and prayers for healing. This is not a time for blame or underhanded remarks." He glanced at Mr. Foreman, who took the look as a cue to stand. "Let's use this as a time for healthy discussion."

The banker put his hands behind his back and paced before the sixty-some people crammed into Yesler's. "Many of us have been concerned about the presumptuous actions of Miss Warren. Through private conversations with you, I've discerned the need for us to deal with Miss Warren corporately."

The creaking of the door interrupted the gathering and sent Anna's heart hammering. *Please let it be Tristan.* When Doc Maynard slipped in, disappointment slapped her hard.

Tristan had chosen not to come. Was it because she'd rushed from him earlier in the week, not letting him finish his apology?

Mr. Foreman continued. "The audacious visits to sick people, the promises of healing. Look what it's done to the Simms family."

A throat cleared, and attention shifted to Doc. He pushed from the wall. "Julia Simms had an aggressive tumor in her stomach. Treatment is limited. Anna showed kindness to that family."

"Kindness?" Mr. Foreman strode halfway down the center aisle. "Julia died."

"We are not assigning blame." Reverend Bagley rose. "Julia's death is not Anna's fault."

"I must agree," Doc said.

Anna breathed relief over the two voices of support. As if one could murder someone with prayer.

"Fine." Mr. Foreman glowered. "But Miss Warren has still planted false ideas of miracles inside the minds of these people. My wife, for example."

Anna turned and sought out Mrs. Foreman. Three rows back and on the other side, the banker's wife smoothed the front of her vest and then twisted her hands together in her lap.

"I wouldn't be surprised if Miss Warren and Mr. Riley are

in cahoots and the Irishman faked his injury."

Gasps waved through the room. Anna had reached the end of her ability to be shocked.

"I examined Mr. Riley," Doc said. "He was unconscious and bloody. His pulse on the fringe of nonexistent. Are you calling into question my medical expertise?"

Mr. Foreman ignored Doc. "I suggest excommunication."

Silence followed the proposal, during which blood pounded in Anna's ears, an aching warmth.

Mr. Kellman raised his hand. "This is ridiculous. This meeting, all the hullabaloo. I was told we were voting on an important town issue, but I wasn't told what. This has been a waste of my time." He stood, marched down the aisle, and pushed through the door.

Amens and uttered agreements rippled through the crowd.

"Anna has not done anything unbiblical to warrant excommunication," Reverend Bagley said.

"Posing as God is biblical?"

"Ease up, Foreman." Amelia's voice rose above the others.

Anna stepped over Mr. and Mrs. Johnson into the aisle. She'd not accept being a victim, but neither would she accept accusations without speaking her peace. "I have never claimed to be God. I've never forced prayer on anyone. Everything I've done has been for God's glory, an outpouring of the prayer 'your kingdom come, your will be done, on earth as it is in heaven.'"

A few nods caught her eye, strengthened her courage.

"I say we take a vote," Mr. Foreman said.

Reverend Bagley thrust one hand up. "No. This is not a church disciplinary meeting. This is a time for the community to express opinions."

"And I've expressed mine quite clearly." Mr. Foreman's eyes hardened as he toed off with Reverend Bagley.

"I've got a clear opinion too." Amelia walked to the front. The scar from her knife injury jutted above the collar of her pale-yellow blouse. "Anna's done nothing wrong. You all ought to be ashamed of yourselves for looking down on someone for praying. Praying, for heaven's sake!" Amelia fled back to her seat and resumed knitting.

"Thank you, Amelia." Reverend Bagley turned to Mr. Foreman. "We'll talk privately. If I deem it necessary, we'll take a vote Sunday after church." He faced the people and held out both hands. "Dismissed."

Mr. Foreman coursed down the aisle and out the door without looking at Anna. Compassion stitched Anna as she tried to catch Mrs. Foreman's eyes, but the woman's gaze remained down as she followed her husband.

After the door closed on the Foremans, Reverend Bagley sighed, a soft sound nearly swallowed by the chitchat and rustling of people as they left. "Why didn't anyone notify me sooner about this meeting?"

Mr. Johnson shrugged. "Mr. Foreman sent errand boys around this morning saying all bank customers had to attend this meeting."

"This isn't right." Reverend Bagley shook his head.

Tristan. He was a bank customer, meaning he should have been here. She waited for the rush of anger, but instead, sadness stung her heart. Heavy, solid sadness.

Chapter Twenty-Six

Anna walked up James Street, intent on seeing Nellie. Footsteps chased her, but she didn't turn. Didn't want to dare think—

"Where are you rushing off to?" Tristan's voice pulled her to a stop.

Anna spun to see the morning sun reflected in his eyes, and despite her sorrow, she couldn't help enjoying the sight of him. She cleared her throat, but it remained tight. "I'm going to see Nellie. I can't take her silence any longer."

"Saint, it's not even been a week. She needs time."

He tucked a wisp of hair behind her ears. Longing ambushed her, and she leaned her cheek into his hand, her jaw trembling.

Anna stepped back. "I need to go," she whispered.

He nodded, and she didn't wait for his reply but fled up the street.

"Anna Warren."

The way he spoke her name tugged violently at her heart. She glanced over her shoulder.

He raked his fingers through his hair and looked away before circling his eyes back to hers. She enjoyed his discomfort as much as she'd enjoyed the sun in his eyes.

He stepped forward, and her heart sped up. "We need to talk."

Anna faced away. "I'm not ready." She looked over her shoulder. "It's not even been a week, after all. I need time."

Her slight smile drew a grin from him, and that grin elicited fresh pain. He looked at her like he loved her. Then why had he lied? Why hadn't he been there last night?

She raced down James Street and crossed to the livery. The

encounter with Tristan had sapped her hope. It was foolish to think Nellie would talk with her. Tristan was right. It was too soon.

Tristan sat in the same rickety chair in President Hall's office as he'd sat in last August. This time, instead of confining heat and frustration, peace filled his heart as he waited for the president to finish teaching his class.

Jimmy leaned against the wall, whistling. "They sure built this place to be the next Princeton, huh?"

"Academia lends itself to fancy, I guess."

"Too bad you're giving up on the program. They could use something to draw students to fill this place."

"I'm not giving up. I'm postponing."

"What about using your gifts?"

"Sometimes God has different ways for you to use your talents than you think."

Jimmy shrugged. "I'm not complaining. Leading this association with you is going to be great."

Tristan smirked. The boy had maintained he was coleader, since McRedmond had asked him last Christmas. Fine. Tristan would put him in charge of petty arguments. And animal husbandry. And anything else he didn't want to deal with.

Footsteps sounded outside the door moments before Hall burst into the room. "Ah, Latin. Nothing like it to brighten your morning." He plunked into his chair and crossed his arms.

"I'm withdrawing interest in a program," Tristan said. "For now."

Hall sighed. "Tristan, I never meant to be difficult. Things with the university have been so up and down. You'll do better in an association. You'll be more satisfied. For now." Hall drummed his fingers on the desk. "But keep dreaming. It's people like you who make names for themselves in academia.

You've got vision."

Impaired vision, apparently, since he'd been wrong to hoard Anna's land and push headstrong for a program without the Lord's blessing or guidance. Tristan stood and held out his hand. "Thank you. Maybe we'll have a chance to work together. You know, a partnership between the association and university."

Hall laughed. "Perhaps. After a while."

"I know. A long while." Tristan smiled and walked to the door. "But I'll be back."

Tristan left, leaving Jimmy to close the door behind them as Hall's laughter followed them out the building.

"He took it well," Jimmy said. "Maybe Anna will take it as well."

Tristan's smile faded, not sure how to discern Anna's responses to him. "Let's stop in at the paper and see if they'll advertise the association." He spoke over his shoulder to Jimmy, hoping Jimmy'd figure out that Anna wasn't open for discussion.

Smells of ink and oil stung his nose when he entered the office at the corner of James Street. Charles Larrabee scribbled notes at a desk, not looking up until the door slammed. "Tristan and Jimmy. I suppose you want to run something." He jotted more notes. "Give me a minute."

Jimmy whistled a tune he must have learned from Lazarus. The boy had been whistling nonstop lately. Must be the onslaught of planting season. Nothing like plunging seeds into soil to boost a man's spirit. Since Tristan had exchanged his pain for peace, it hadn't taken much to raise his morale. Just looking across his field gave him great hope that perhaps he could tend Anna's heart like he did his land. Slow and careful, with a lot of work. And maybe she'd forgive him, truly.

If he had the patience to wait for her, like he waited for his seeds. After this morning, the way she'd leaned into his touch, he doubted his reservoir of patience would last much longer.

"We'll plant oats next Wednesday," Tristan said. "I've been working to prepare the field. Probably need a few more days."

Jimmy stopped whistling. "You want me to stay on?"

Why would he think otherwise? They had something going.

"Sure. If you want." Tristan studied Jimmy, seeing him in new ways. The angular jaw that had looked rigid and surly at first impression now looked only strong, determined. "When I met you last fall you seemed . . . angry, or something."

"I could say the same about you."

"True."

"I was adjusting. You know, getting used to the west, letting go of the old life." Jimmy shrugged. "I'm good now."

Tristan gripped Jimmy's shoulder. "I want you to work for me. Year round."

Jimmy looked beyond Tristan, out the front window, and frowned. Tristan turned.

Anna and Amelia stood across James Street, talking. Even from this distance, Tristan admired Anna's composure. She held herself with a grace that couldn't be easy, what with the death of Julia and loss of friendship with Nellie. Not to mention her land and his idiocy.

"She's beautiful, huh?" Jimmy's voice carried a quiet admiration.

Jealousy shot straight up Tristan's spine. "She's mine."

Jimmy laughed. "Not Anna. Amelia."

Tristan's face heated. Since when had Jimmy been interested in Amelia? That strange woman was intimidating at best. "You care for Amelia?"

"Is there a problem?"

"No. It's just . . ."

"She's got grit, I know. But it's a cover for fear or something. I'll figure it out."

"Good luck with that. You even figured out her last name yet?"

"I'm working on that too."

Mr. Larrabee scraped his chair across the floor and rose. "Sorry about that. Tell me your business."

Tristan laid out the terms of the association and the dates for the first three meetings.

"It's going to take half a page to get all that in, and it's going to cost," Mr. Larrabee said.

"That's not a problem." Tristan pulled out money.

"I'll run it first of the week." Larrabee sighed. "Getting to be a full paper."

Tristan scanned the notes and scraps of paper littering Larrabee's desk. "What's this?" He picked up a page with *CF* inscribed at the top.

"Something Clyde wants printed."

Tristan scanned the letter to the editor. "You can't print this." He wanted to rip the paper to shreds, burn it, conceal it. Anything to keep it from going to print, to keep Anna from seeing it. Jimmy plucked the page from his hands.

"It's a free country, Tristan," Mr. Larrabee said.

"Then use your freedom and don't print this." Anna had to endured enough at the hand of Foreman. "There's got to be some sort of rule against this type of thing."

"Witchcraft?" Jimmy scoffed, eyes roving back and forth over the letter. "This man needs to be put in his place."

Tristan retrieved the paper from Jimmy.

Larrabee chuckled. "And who's going to do it?"

Tristan took one last glance at the embossed page before crumpling it and throwing it across the room. Time to do what he should have done months ago, and would have, if he hadn't been so self-absorbed.

Tristan shoved open the door to the bank and strode up to the secretary's desk. The young clerk put down his book and removed his spectacles with far too much nonchalance for Tristan.

Tristan placed both hands on the desk and leaned in. "Tristan Porter for Clyde Foreman."

"Mr. Foreman is with someone at present. If you'd like to schedule—"

"I'll wait." Tristan crossed his arms.

"If you'd care to have a seat—"

"I'll stand." Tristan noted the empty waiting room. Jimmy hadn't followed. Good intuition from him. This conversation would get personal.

"Can I get you some coffee or tea?"

"All I need is an audience with Mr. Foreman."

The clerk coughed. "That will be soon, I hope." He rose from the desk, took a rag, and began dusting the bookshelves lining the far wall.

A door opened down the hall, and voices announced the presence of Mr. Foreman and—Tristan's eyes widened—his guest.

Mr. Roberts handed Mr. Foreman a file.

"We're set to go, then?" Mr. Foreman spoke to Mr. Roberts, not having noticed Tristan.

"Should take about a week," Mr. Roberts said.

"No longer, please."

Tristan stomped his boot. The men glanced up, and for a moment, Mr. Roberts looked as if he would lose the contents of his last meal. Clyde Foreman, as always, appeared professional, even austere with his narrow eyes staring down his hawk nose. Little did Foreman know his days as predator were about to end.

Mr. Foreman nodded to Mr. Roberts, who headed for the door.

Tristan cut him off. "Since you're here, how about we make this conversation three-way?" He gestured to the office down the hall.

Mr. Roberts glanced at Mr. Foreman, a look Tristan interpreted as a request for permission. Interesting that Foreman seemed to be in charge of Roberts.

"I'm sure I can help you with what you need." Mr. Foreman nodded at Mr. Roberts to leave.

Tristan refused to move from Roberts's path even as he directed his words to Foreman. "I expect you to." He met Roberts's gaze. "But I'd still like a conference with both of you."

Mr. Foreman shrugged. "Well then, I'm sure Mr. Roberts would be glad to join us." The banker smiled, but Tristan didn't buy the friendly gesture.

Tristan waited for Mr. Roberts to follow Mr. Foreman. He wasn't going to turn his back and let Roberts slip out the front door. Mr. Roberts glared and strode past Tristan.

Walking into Mr. Foreman's office was like walking into an art gallery. Paintings covered one of the walls, and vases lined a shelf. Thick curtains framed the window looking out the back of the bank. A miniature *David* statue rested on a table next to a velvet settee. Foreman evidently thought he deserved an office worthy of the US president.

Mr. Foreman sat behind his desk and gestured for Tristan to sit on the settee.

Mr. Roberts ambled over to a wingback chair, sank down, and stretched out his legs. "Porter, what game you playing?"

"I should be asking you. Both of you." Tristan remained standing, refusing to sit on velvet or position himself across the desk from Foreman as if he were a client begging for mercy.

"Is this about her?" Mr. Foreman smiled.

Yes, it was about her. The *her* that had not only tipped the wagon and spilled his plow down the hillside but had capsized his heart. "I was just at Larrabee's. You can't print that slanderous letter."

Mr. Roberts sneered. "She's all that and more."

"It's not slanderous." Mr. Foreman stared at Tristan.

Tristan slammed his fist on the desk. "You know it is. I don't think you even believe what you say about her. The only thing I don't understand is what you seek to gain by picking on her. Is this about her land? Her inheritance?"

Mr. Roberts laughed. "You mean your land? Your inheritance?"

Tristan turned on the man behind him. "Peter left that land to me because he thought it would help my chances with the university. Anna's inheritance is her own."

"Too bad you failed with the university."

Tristan ignored the barb. "I don't like how you've been threatening Anna." Tristan stepped close to Roberts, forcing the man to draw back his extended legs. "Why did you tell her you owned her land?"

"I had my reasons."

Tristan fought the urge to pummel him. "Did you think she'd marry you because you owned her land?"

"A man can hope, can't he? Only now it looks like you're the one with that hope."

Muffled voices sounded from down the hall. Mr. Roberts sat straighter, hands on the arms of his chair. Mr. Foreman stood just as Jude McGrath swung the door open and marched in with two deputies behind.

Tristan stepped from the line of McGrath's pulled gun and pressed himself against the wall.

"Clyde Foreman and George Roberts, hands in the air. You're under arrest." McGrath's gaze flickered over Tristan, his eyes hinting at surprise.

"What's the purpose of this?" Mr. Foreman glowered and moved from behind his desk. "I'll have my lawyer after you."

"He's already been arrested, as you know." McGrath kept his gun on Mr. Foreman and Mr. Roberts as the deputies moved to take them into custody. "Mr. Wyse, along with the two of you, are charged with the tampering of legal documents, the swindling of land, and the laundering of funds." McGrath nodded toward Foreman. "And you're also being charged with blackmail."

"That's not an offense."

"Should be," Tristan said. It'd destroyed Anna's business, after all.

McGrath faced his deputies. "Lock them up. Feed them some dinner. I'll be by shortly to finish the paper work." McGrath moved around Foreman's desk and started opening drawers as the deputies handcuffed the men and led them out.

Tristan stepped to the door. He'd hoped to put Foreman in his place, but he'd not expected that place to be jail.

"Tristan, wait, please."

Tristan palmed the doorjamb and looked at McGrath.

"I've received word that Peter's will stands. The land is yours."

The gift Peter had intended for blessing had caused him angst. He'd prayed the will wouldn't stand. Now he'd have to deal with every last consequence of his deceit.

McGrath grabbed a stack of papers from Mr. Foreman's desk and walked to the door. "With the arrest, I guess there'll be no need for a second meeting on Sunday."

"Second meeting?"

"Weren't you there last night?"

"Where?"

"Foreman organized a meeting. Mr. Johnson told me about it this morning. He called for a vote to excommunicate Anna."

Tristan's sweaty hands curled into fists. Had he known about this fifteen minutes ago before McGrath burst on the scene, he would have excommunicated Foreman's nose from his face.

"Bagley dismissed the meeting and said they'd meet again Sunday, if necessary. Which it's not, thank God. That poor girl."

Everything in Tristan leapt to life. Enough games. He had to see Anna. He surged from the building and ran toward Cherry Street. She wasn't walking away from him anymore. He might have been a fool these past months, but he was a repentant fool, a fool in love. He'd get on his knees and beg forgiveness.

He jogged up the hill to her house and pushed through the broken gate. His hand shook as he banged on the door. No answer. His stomach growled as he headed down to Front Street, past Matthias's. He peeked in the window. No Anna, and no time for food. He entered Joe's with such force that the door banged against the wall and customers paused their shopping. Up and down the aisles he searched. No Anna.

"Joe?" Tristan's voice shook the store.

"Tristan?" Jimmy walked through the curtain at the back.

"Have you seen Anna?"

Mrs. Johnson looked up from the fabric table. "I saw her leave the livery on Maple about half an hour ago."

Tristan tore from the store.

"Tristan, wait." Jimmy ran up and pulled on his arm. "You don't know where she is. You'll waste your time galloping the countryside. Wait at her house."

Tristan narrowed his eyes. "How come you didn't tell me about last night?"

Jimmy opened his mouth, then shut it. "I guess I got distracted by your asking me to work with you."

"You got distracted all right. But it probably had more to do with a woman."

Color rose up Jimmy's neck.

"If this were Amelia and you were desperate to talk to her, what would you do, sit and twiddle your thumbs?"

"I'd gallop around the countryside."

"Thought so." He swatted Jimmy on the shoulder, then crossed the street and entered the livery.

"Ben?" Tristan searched the tack room. "Ben?" He paced between the stalls, fingering his hat.

"What's the hollering about?" Ben emerged through the back door, leading a chestnut roan.

"Anna. Where is she?"

"She's been heading to Mrs. Tolliver's every day this week. That'd be my guess."

Good enough. Tristan slammed his hat on his head and raced out the front and down the street. When he reached the corner, he skidded to a stop. He was running helter skelter like a panicked squirrel.

Think. Where did you leave your horse?

He relived the morning: riding in, clashing with Anna, meeting Jimmy, inviting him—ah! The university. He jogged up Front Street and turned west at University.

Ember munched happily on grass. Tristan's hands fumbled with the reins.

Wait.

Tristan paused, foot in stirrup. The sense came again, stronger.

Wait.

Was this how Anna heard the Lord? He pounded his hands on the saddle. "Why, Lord?"

No answer.

Tristan leaned his forehead against Ember. "I don't want to wait." He breathed deep, the scent of leather and horse choking his thoughts. Why couldn't he go to her now? He'd ride out to Mrs. Tolliver's, kiss her first, apologize later.

Wait.

Tristan counted to ten and surrendered. Biting his lip, he stared up at the sky. He recalled Tuesday night. The smell of potatoes, the comfort of the earth beneath him as he'd slept.

"All right, Lord, I'll wait."

Chapter Twenty-Seven

Tristan knocked on Anna's door, a little too hard, thanks to the energy rushing through him. The urge to wait had lifted that morning. After forcing himself to get some work done and not letting Lazarus see what a schoolboy he'd turned into, he'd made an excuse, gone into town, dined at Matthias's, sold some more potatoes to Joe. And now here he was, on the threshold of heaven. Figuratively speaking, as long as she offered true forgiveness this time.

Tristan knocked again. From the other side of the door came a crash, then an exclamation.

"Anna?"

She flung the door open. Her cheeks were flushed, and her breathing labored. He perused the small living room, noting the open trunk. No way. She wasn't going anywhere.

He waited for her to invite him in, but she stared at him, unmoving. He took his hat off. "May I come in, please?"

She stepped back, her features guarded. That's when he noticed the rag in her hand.

He gestured with his hat. "I see you've been exercising your instinct for tidiness."

His comment drew a trace smile.

Keep it simple. Apologize. Explain the truth. He debriefed himself as he hung his hat and coat on the peg inside the door.

She twisted the rag and then snapped from her reticence. "Let me start some coffee." She pounded across the room and set the kettle on the stove, threw open the iron door, and stoked the fire. "Have a seat."

He didn't know if he could still his anxious legs, but he folded himself into one of the chairs at the table anyhow. While she fiddled with a tray, he took in the sparse furnishings of her new home. A washstand with a broken drawer handle, several small shelves, a chipped mirror. She'd put out a picture, laid a quilt over the one padded chair in the room, and stacked a pile of books on the stand next to it.

"Cookie?" She held a tin before him. "They're molasses. But no, I didn't make them. I can cook biscuits over a fire and potato stew. That's about it. I was getting good at scrambled eggs until . . ."

Until he'd taken away her land and she'd gotten rid of the chickens.

He munched cookies while she stood in front of the stove facing him, hands clasped behind her back.

Brushing crumbs from his mouth, he set his last bite on the table. "I've been in agony, not knowing how to apologize to you," he said. "Ashamed—"

She lunged across the small space and reached for his hand. The warm pressure silenced his thoughts.

"Everyone makes bad choices." The inflexibility of her gaze sent a tremor down his throat to unnamed places. "I've already forgiven you. I'm sorry if I didn't sound sincere the other day." She released his hand with the same suddenness she'd taken it and stood.

The sound of percolating coffee filtered through his mind with the rest of his questions. "I kept your letter from you."

She moved to the stove and fiddled with the coffee. "You made choices. And so did I. I'm choosing to forgive you now."

"I don't deserve it."

"No, you don't." She turned and smiled. "But forgiveness isn't about deserving, is it?"

Unlike the other afternoon, today she spoke with resolve. "That may be true—"

"It *is* true."

"—but I still need to say some things."

The anticipation in her eyes focused him, made him want to

do his best to show her she could trust him.

"Your father and I . . . I don't know what he saw in me. I liked him the moment we met. He had such integrity." Her father had had the Spirit, though Tristan wouldn't have labeled it such at the time. The same Spirit he'd seen in Anna. The Spirit he now felt making a way between him and Anna. "We talked about my past. We talked about my dreams for the future. Your father listened. When I got that letter from him, I couldn't believe he'd left me your land. I never asked for it, never even hinted about it. I would have resisted the offer had he made it in person." He stood. "I could never have willingly taken your home from you."

She pursed her lips and nodded.

"I wanted to tell you. I wanted to give you his letter, in time. I thought if I could—"

"I know. You don't need to make excuses."

No, he didn't. And yet his mouth was moving ahead of his mind. "When you found me at your cabin and I realized you weren't aware I owned it, I didn't know how to tell you. And then the healings began . . ."

"Tristan, I forgive you."

"Arthur said you weren't coming back. I'd only stayed at your cabin several times."

"Enough."

The gently spoken word cut off his rambling, and he stared across the table at the woman he loved.

Her gaze broke from his. "I was angry at first, but that anger wasn't just at you. It was at my father, at God, at . . ." She took off her apron and hung it on a hook. ". . . myself."

With four steps, he was at her side, gripping her shoulders, seeking her eyes. "You have no reason to be angry at yourself. I've never admired anyone's faith more."

She stared up at him, eyes full of emotion he couldn't read. "Thank you, Tristan, but I don't deserve that admiration."

"You're not at fault for Julia's death. You didn't fail Nellie or Julia. You didn't fail God." He waited for her gaze to find his and spoke the words she'd uttered months ago. "He extends his hand to heal, or He doesn't. We don't always understand."

She gasped. "I know."

"Do you?"

She paced from him, plucked a dishcloth from the dry sink, and fiddled with the frayed edges. Several times she glanced at him, motioned with her hand, and opened her mouth to speak, but no words came out. Tears traced the soft lines of her cheeks, a course he wanted to follow with his finger. Was this about her land, Julia's death, or something else? He'd never seen such uncertainty from her. It caught him off guard. It halted him.

And at last, it propelled him.

"Anna, honey." He took her in his arms.

She trembled, which only strengthened his hold. He rested his chin on the top of her head and fingered her hair until, finally, her arms wrapped around him and she dug her hands into the back of his shirt. He'd gladly stand still and let her cling to him all night if that was what it took to settle her.

But in another minute her crying ceased, and she stirred against him. He tightened his grasp, not wanting to let her go, but instead of stepping back, she turned her head sideways so it rested against his chest. "Why weren't you there?"

He didn't need to ask where. "I didn't know."

A pause. "Really?"

"Really." He kept running his hand over her hair, holding her head against his heart, hoping her loosened fingers would grasp his shirt again.

"I've been so selfish." She moved from his embrace. "It felt good to be needed by people, sought out. I wanted to prove myself worthy of their friendship."

She picked up the kettle and searched for cups. He disliked the emptiness of his arms, already forgetting the feel of her, needing to hold her again to remember. He took two steps forward and cupped her face in his hands. He didn't know why, but he knew the words she needed to hear. Whether from God, or him, or both.

"You're forgiven."

Her lips parted, and guilt ebbed from her eyes. Beneath his hands, her face warmed. She reached up and drew his face inches from her own. His heart took off like a hound on the hunt, thoughts of *keep it simple* having long fled.

She spoke softly. "Remember when your plow tumbled over the edge of the wagon and down into the ravine?"

He couldn't remember anything with her this close, but she seemed at ease, so he went with it. "I had two fields waiting to be turned up, but I had to forgive you when you begged."

A hint of tease poked through her solemn expression. "I've been intimidated by you ever since."

He straightened and pushed her back at arm's length. "Intimidated?" He couldn't check his laughter. She'd been the one healing. The one whose prayer life had rivaled the holiest of saints. He'd been called many things, but not intimidating. "What's so intimidating about me?"

She felt a blush creep up the side of her neck.

What was so intimidating about him? That was like asking what was so dangerous about a mountain lion. What was so beautiful about Elliot Bay in first light?

Anna nearly choked on her exasperation. At first it had been his intensity, his work ethic, and his impressive homesteading operation despite his youthfulness. Then it had been his aloofness, his hard questions, his penetrating gaze. The expectation she felt to provide answers. She could think for an hour about the intimidating traits of Tristan Porter.

"You're intense." She started with the obvious. "And I feel

pressure around you."

"Pressure?" He spit out the word as if he'd bitten a sour cherry.

"Yes, pressure. For one thing, my chatter wears you out, and you took to escorting me home as if it were a jail sentence. And do you deny asking me all those theological questions? You put me on guard, not wanting to turn you from God by my failure to provide the answers you needed. I used to imagine you lying in bed thinking up difficult things to ask me."

He raised an eyebrow.

Heat invaded every pore of her face as she realized what she'd spoken.

"If I thought about you while laying in bed, it wasn't in regard to theology," he said.

She punished his boldness with a scowl. His smile held steady, but in spite of her embarrassment, she refused to glance away first.

He must have sensed her resolve and decided mercy was the duty of a gentleman, for he walked across the room. He patted a stack of linens. "Are you packing or unpacking?"

"I'd been packing, but now I'm unpacking."

Again, the silent question of the raised brow. Yes, that was also intimidating, the way he could speak to her without words.

"I was planning to return to Portland, but I realized that would be running from my problems. Despite the adversity, I'd rather be in Seattle." Next to this man.

Tristan walked the perimeter of the small cabin, surveying Denny's paintings of early blockhouses, Chief Sealth, and Elliot Bay.

When he returned to where he'd started, he faced her, hands on hips. "I'm not wrestling anymore."

Even if he hadn't mentioned it Wednesday, she would have noticed. This was not the same man who'd stood in the same pose months ago telling her he was checking on things at her cabin. The aloofness was gone. The skepticism absent. The only thing that seemed unchanged was that dogged intensity, on full display as his deep eyes sowed into hers. Her stomach quivered as if a dozen butterflies had shed their cocoons.

She mustered a smile. "I'm delighted for you."

"What else?"

What else did she feel?

"What else is intimidating about me?" That provoking smile again.

"Oh . . . things." Things to remain unnamed.

Anna looked for something to do to ease the awkwardness of standing in a cramped space with Tristan acting . . . what? Peaceful, yes. But also tender. He'd clung to her and let her wash his shirt with tears. And had he called her *honey*? Words of endearment from Tristan—he definitely was not wrestling anymore.

She lifted the kettle and poured herself a cup of coffee. "Coffee?"

He nodded his head, and she turned and reached for another cup. Her arm swung down, and her elbow met the wall of muscle that was Tristan's gut.

"See? *That's* intimidating, you sneaking up on me." Her voice sounded too loud.

He placed his hands on her shoulders and turned her toward him. They had the entire stretch of the cabin, but he stood close enough the hem of her skirt brushed his trousers.

"I'm sorry I wasn't around when Julia died," he said.

"It's not your fault." She cringed at the way her whispered words made her sound fragile, and intimidated, of all things.

"I know, but I'm still sorry. I wish I could have been there when you found out. To hold you."

He picked up a strand of her hair, ran it between his fingers, and thumbed the end. "Why don't you wear your hair up?"

"Sometimes I do." Hardly. She couldn't remember the last

time. She couldn't remember much of anything with Tristan this close.

"I've only seen it up once, and you said it wasn't by choice."

"Oh." She tried to breathe without looking like an out-of-breath ninny. "Nellie bought me a ribbon and tied it up." Yes, that had been the last time. "It made my neck cold." Not like now. The heat coursing through her body could warm this cabin through a winter's night.

His eyes danced, and she felt her eyes light in response. She'd never seen him look like this, and she had no word to describe it. But her heart understood. Her heart spoke the same language.

"You suffer from a cold neck? That's why you keep it down?" He moved his hand beneath her hair, his finger running circles on her neck.

She shook her head, not trusting her voice. Her limits of control neared their end. Although she'd known the Lord would eventually win the wrestling match with Tristan, she hadn't expected for Tristan's demeanor to change like this. From skepticism to belief, yes, but not from detachment to fondness—and seemingly overnight. Nor had she expected to be overrun by the intensity of her attraction to him.

If he didn't get his hands off her, she would kiss him. Heat flooded her face at the brash thought. Now she *had* to kiss him, or he would notice her blushing yet again.

He smiled.

Too late.

She loosened her hands, which had at some unknown time gripped his shirtfront, and brushed a finger across his lips. They were warm, and a current coursed from her throat to her belly. Before she could change her mind, she grasped his neck and pulled his head down.

She meant only to press her lips to his, but between the softness of his mouth and the firmness of his arms around her, she found herself unable to pull back. He tasted like molasses, smelled like earth, and the stubble of his chin scratched away any sense of unbelonging.

He pushed his body tighter against hers, and those farmer hands journeyed down to the small of her back and tended there. When his lips moved around below her ear, she wrenched back.

"Ah, Saint." The breath from his words tickled her cheek, and he held her soul with the strength of his gaze. "Bold move."

She let out a rush of air. "Were you surprised?"

"Yeah." He grazed his lips across her forehead and rested his cheek against her hair. "But not as surprised as I've been by how much I love you."

She settled her arms around his waist, noticing the way his muscles trembled at her touch. She could face anything now, with Tristan loving her like this. Mr. Foreman could threaten her character and her business, and she'd shrug it off. Tristan could do what he wanted with her land. She had her home. Here, wrapped in the promise of these two strong arms.

She lifted her head to see his face, and her nose brushed against his neck. He shuddered, and she wanted to kiss him again, to see if a second kiss could match the sweetness of the first.

He smiled, and as if reading her thoughts, lowered his head, but she pulled back.

"What?"

She ran her finger over his smile. "I want to enjoy this rare sight, you smiling like the university said yes to you."

He shook his head. "I've chosen to lead the association like God wants me to. And this smile isn't a university smile. It's your smile."

She tipped her chin up and brushed her lips across that smile. Joy had a taste, a decidedly Tristan-like taste.

"Anna?" His lips moved against her cheek as he spoke her name.

"Mmm?"

He spoke into her hair, half kissing her ear. "You can't stay on Cherry Street."

Anna pulled back and sought his eyes. "Tristan, I told you. Don't sign the land back. I'm content in town. My father—"

He put his finger on her lips. "I don't want you to move back to your cabin either." The glow of intimacy brightened his eyes. "I want you to move to mine."

She raised a brow. "Bold move."

He sat down and pulled her into his lap, snuggling her close. "Again, bold move."

His arm rested around her waist, and his other hand reached up and traced a path around the neckline of her dress, stopping at the top button. He flicked it, an easy grin on his face, and her breath swelled.

"I love you, Anna. Marry me, please. I'll beg. I'll do anything, even quit farming."

"I'd never ask that of you." She brushed his hand off the soft spot of her neck. "I'll marry you because I love you and I want to."

He leaned his forehead on hers. "I think I could kiss you all night."

She bolted from his lap. "Not yet, plow boy."

"Next week?"

She stared at him, trying to get used to the new Tristan. He'd exchanged detachment for a playful, almost giddy disposition, giving her a glimpse into a future that looked to be more entertaining than she'd imagined a life with Tristan could be.

She smoothed his hair back from his face and traced his ear with her finger. The liveliness fled from his face, replaced by an open gaze that made her weak in the knees.

He stood abruptly. "I need to leave." Swiping his coat from the hook, he didn't look at her. "Unless you want to stop by the reverend's right now."

She released a breathy laugh. "I think I'd at least like to wear a wedding dress. Pin my hair up for once so I won't look like a child." She swallowed. "That is, if people would come to my wedding. Mr. Foreman will probably stand at the entrance of the church and shoo people away."

Tristan dropped his coat on the floor and grasped her face in his hands. His eyes burned. "Anna, I . . ."

"What?" Had she said something wrong?

"I completely forgot." Gentleness softened his expression. "First, you don't look like a child, and I don't want you to wear your hair up." He stroked his hand down the back of her hair. "But also, Mr. Foreman was arrested yesterday, along with Mr. Roberts."

How had she not heard? Because she'd not been in public since yesterday morning. "Why?"

"They were working with Mr. Wyse to manipulate documents, buy up land, and profit from it."

Anna turned from him. Too much deception had happened too fast. Her father. Tristan. Mr. Foreman. Mr. Wyse. Where was the integrity? She rubbed her hands over her face.

Arms wrapped around her from behind, and she collapsed her weight against Tristan.

"Are you all right?"

She twisted and buried her face in his chest. "I'm not happy things turned out this way, especially for Mrs. Foreman's sake, but I'm relieved the opposition will stop. I only wanted to be obedient to the Lord, not cause problems in the community."

Tristan chuckled. "You weren't the problem maker. You have a beautiful gift."

She tipped her head back, searching his gaze.

"It's not healing. It's not prayer," he said. "It's yourself, your spirit, a spirit filled with His Spirit. You have a richness of faith I need. Others need."

She pressed her lips to his chin, wanting more of his kisses, but he cupped her head and snuggled her against his chest.

"Not everyone has such intimacy with the heavenly Father."

She breathed in the faint aroma of earth and sighed.

"I criticized the healings, but that didn't stop me from falling in love with you." His thumb rubbed down her jaw. "You've got a spirit that draws people. Yet sometimes, in a strange sense, when people don't know how to respond to something, they withdraw from the very thing that captivates them."

His affirmation strengthened her conviction that she'd misread the responses of others. She'd been so focused on her own need for acceptance that she'd taken the bewilderment of others as rejection. "Thank you, Tristan."

He pushed her head off his chest. "For what? I've not done much worthy of your thanks."

"Not true. You've loved me and supported me, despite your questions."

She soaked in the tenderness of his eyes. And just when she thought he'd kiss her again, he set her back and retrieved his coat. "Time for me to go."

She smiled, thankful Tristan was a gentleman. She wasn't sure she could deny him anything when he looked at her like that.

Chapter Twenty-Eight

Anna approached Nellie from behind, not wanting to interrupt the intimate moment. Her friend knelt by Julia's grave and traced the stone etching. When she straightened and sat back, Anna stepped forward, into Nellie's line of vision.

"You hear those birds?" Nellie spoke without looking at her.

"Yes." The dancing chirps of chickadees mingled with the melodies of song sparrows and the gutturals of swallows. Nature's symphony.

"How come the world goes on, but I'm locked into this horrid moment?" Nellie's shoulders shook. "I can't get the sound of Julia's last breath out of my head. That rattled release of air, and then nothing but silence."

Anna deliberated only a moment before plunging toward Nellie and sheltering her in her arms.

Nellie's hands dug into Anna's back as sobs shook her body. "I can't do this. It's too much."

"I know, Nellie. I know."

Anna shifted in her rocking chair. Her copy of *Grimm's Fairy Tales* hung over the arm, a reminder of her failure to concentrate. She'd read three pages in an hour, not even finishing one tale. From her position, she could look out the front window and watch the steamers at Yesler's mill.

On Sunday, she'd spent the afternoon with Tristan. They'd talked about the land but had come to no decisions.

On Monday, she'd done the wash, had lunch with Nellie . . . and yearned to see Tristan. On Tuesday, she'd baked the week's bread, helped Joe organize his stockroom . . . and yearned to see Tristan. Today, Wednesday . . .

Her book slid to the floor, and she jumped. Snatching it up, she determined to finish the tale of *Little Snow White*, then take Maple for a long ride. If she happened south toward a certain farmer, she happened south.

She stood with the intention to make tea, but the sight outside her window stilled her. A crowd of women walked up the street, armloads of stuff weighing them down. She thrust the door open before they had opportunity to knock.

"Good morning, dear." Mrs. Johnson pushed the door wider and entered. "After the excommunication vote was cancelled Sunday, we wanted to make sure there'd be no doubt you knew you're an important part of this community." She looked over her shoulder at the others, who seemed more hesitant about barging in.

Mrs. Bagley stepped forward. "It's sewing-bee time. Three new dresses."

On a Wednesday?

"Thank you." Anna extended her arm, inviting them inside. The house filled with the aroma of fresh bread, cinnamon, and nutmeg.

Mrs. Denny carried a cast-iron pot to the stove. "David shot a deer yesterday and brought some to Arthur. This stew will make your insides burst with goodness."

Anna felt the worries and the striving to belong uncoiling from her as the room bustled with activity.

"We've been so dimwitted." Mrs. Webb unloaded her armful of material on the table. "We've tried to give you space to heal from losing your father. And we know how much you adore the open road. We didn't want to crowd you."

"But now we do." Mrs. Johnson set an apple pie on the table and reached for Anna's apron hanging nearby. "Ready for business."

The women set their sewing baskets on the floor in the middle of the room while Anna tried to see through the throng to complete a head count. An elbow jammed into her side, and she stepped back.

"Pardon me."

"Mrs. Foreman." Anna drew the woman into her arms. "Thank you for coming. I was sad to hear about your husband."

Mrs. Foreman's gaze flitted the room, and she spoke quietly. "No one's mentioned much. I suppose they don't know what to say."

"I hope you'll stop by often for tea." Anna squeezed Mrs. Foreman's hand.

Tears pooled in Mrs. Foreman's eyes.

Excusing herself, Anna wove through several women to the far wall. She leaned against the curve of the logs next to Mrs. Tolliver and enjoyed the laughter and fellowship unfolding through the cabin. "When did you slip in?"

"A moment ago. Takes me longer to get around these days. At least for a few more weeks, until I'm fully recovered. It's hard to chop wood while holding a cane." The older woman tapped the cane on the floor, then patted Anna's cheek. "See, these women do care."

"Anna." Mrs. Mercer hailed her from her seat in the middle of the room, piled cloth around her. "What colors would you like your new dresses?"

"I say yellow." Mrs. Webb tapped Anna's arms. "Up."

Anna lifted her arms as Mrs. Webb encircled her waist with a measuring tape.

"Sky blue would bring out the cream in her skin," Amelia said.

Anna stammered. "I . . . your kindness is a blessing. But I don't need three dresses."

"Every girl needs new dresses when it's time to go courting," Mrs. Tolliver said.

Movement ceased, and the room fell silent, except for the clattering of Mrs. Johnson's scissors as they slipped from her hands to the floor.

Smiles adorned the faces surrounding Anna, and her own blossomed. "I don't need dresses, but I could use help with a wedding dress."

The women gasped, and the room erupted in a flurry of activity. Fabric scraps were thrust back into baskets. Ribbons wound up. Patterns folded.

"Clear the table," Mrs. Mercer said and swiped the remaining scraps off the surface and into the lap of Mrs. Bagley.

"Lands, that was fast." Mrs. Tolliver's laugh ended in a shaky cough.

Anna scrunched her brow. "Should you have come?"

"No one could keep me away."

"You are marrying Tristan, aren't you?" Amelia's voice carried across the room from the stove, where she stirred Mrs. Denny's pot of stew.

The room quieted again.

Mrs. Tolliver frowned. "Of course she is. Who else?"

"Well, I . . ."

"You get your eyes off Jimmy long enough, and you'd know that." Mrs. Tolliver laughed again.

Amelia's stirring quickened. "James Jorgensen? I don't think so."

"I'm going to Joe's," Mrs. Yesler said. "If he doesn't have enough white satin, I'll search every store until I find enough."

"Actually"—Anna strode over to the chest in the corner and pulled out her mother's wedding dress—"this was my mama's. It's not exactly my size, and some of the rouching has ripped, but—"

"Lay it out here in the middle of the room." Mrs. Johnson cleared a space on the table.

And while the women inspected the dress and threw out ideas for amendments, Anna sidled up beside Amelia at the stove. "Really?"

"James is a boy, Anna."

Oh, and Amelia was all of three years older than him? "And you're a girl." Anna took the spoon from her.

A knock rose above the happy prattle of women, and someone said, "I'll get it."

Anna returned her focus to the food. The apple pie emitted a heavenly smell, the embodiment of home, family, and friends. All of which seemed to be resting immediately around the corner of her future, thanks be to God. She set the spoon aside and reached for a towel to wipe the drips she'd spilled.

Her humming started quiet and then swelled until the silence of the room broke into her worship. Now what?

"Wow."

Tristan's voice. Anna jerked around. Wow, indeed. Not only because these women cared for her, but because this man stood before her as glorious as the king's son from *Little Snow White*, looking like he wanted to take her away, rags and all.

And all these women were the dwarves? Anna shook the nonsense from her head and greeted Tristan with a smile. "Good morning."

The words came out more breathless than she'd intended.

Tristan perused the room, and his lips twitched. "Good morning to you all." He seemed to measure their smiles. "I'll come back."

Anna followed him out and shut the door. "It's a sewing bee."

"I told you they cared." He smiled. "And you must have told them I cared. They about pried me open with their grins."

Pleasure knotted her stomach. Three days since she'd seen him, and it seemed like three years. "They're going to fix up my mama's wedding dress."

"That's wonderful."

"With their determination and expertise, we'll be able to marry this Sunday after church."

"I need to sow potatoes next week."

"Oh." Her heart dropped. What did sowing potatoes have to do with getting married? He'd be plowing, sowing, weeding, and reaping the rest of their lives. He hadn't changed his mind about marrying her, had he?

He gripped her face in her hands and kissed her. His mouth was warm, delicious, and assertive, and his kiss way too short.

No, he hadn't changed his mind.

"I want to take you somewhere," he said.

She wanted to go somewhere—anywhere—with him. "Let me tell the women and grab my coat."

He shook his head and laughed. "Not now. After we get married. That's why I don't want to marry this Sunday. I want to plant potatoes next week, and marry you the last Sunday of March." He grinned. "Then take you on a trip for several weeks."

Anna rubbed her arms, the new spring air feeling more like winter. Good thing Tristan's kiss had raised her body temperature. "You haven't left the farm in six years. Can you?"

"For you, yes." He raised her hands to his mouth and kissed her palms. "I can't wait to smell potatoes on these hands."

Oh my. She loved this crazy farmer who thrilled at the smell of anything earth, root, or plant. He wrapped his arms around her, but she pulled back. "The women." Had probably seen him kiss her.

"Yes, they're looking out the window."

She turned and received waves from her guests. Meeting eyes with Tristan again, she laughed. "A week from Sunday, then. I'll be ready."

He fingered her hair. "I *am* ready." He backed away, never taking his gaze from hers. "Ready to show you what hospitality looks like in marriage. See ya, Saint."

She stared after him, desire burgeoning in her chest. Not until one of the women opened the door, gripped her elbow, and tugged did her feet land back on the ground.

Epilogue

Portland, Oregon Territory

Noise saturated the spring morning. Robins sang a greeting. Horses clopped along the road. A squirrel scampered across a headstone and up a large oak. Tristan held tight to Anna's hand and braced himself for what would come next. He hadn't been in a cemetery since his mother's death. He was here for Anna, had planned this trip for her. Then why did he cling to her hand as if she were supporting him?

Anna's steps hastened as she pulled him between the grave markers. She stopped in front of a smooth stone. A daffodil grew beside it and leaned its yellow head against the *P* of her father's name.

His wife hummed a peaceful melody. He wanted to speak but didn't want to thrust his voice into the holy stillness of her music, which had now transformed into words.

"Immortal, invisible, God only wise. In light inaccessible, hid from our eyes. Most blessed, most glorious, the ancient of days; almighty, victorious, thy great name we praise."

A song sparrow added its amen in the following silence. Anna kept her eyes pasted to the headstone, but Tristan couldn't unfasten his gaze from her face. "You're beautiful, you know that?"

Her lips turned up, and she nodded. He liked that about her. She didn't deny his compliments. True humility was gracious and accepting of favor.

She knelt on the ground and held her hands open in her lap. When her eyes slipped closed, he knelt too, joining in her unspoken prayer. At the sound of her whimper, he opened his eyes. A tear slipped down her cheek.

He brushed it away and cradled her head against his

shoulder. "Heavenly Father, we thank you for Peter's life and the witness that he bore to you. We thank you for the father he was to Anna and the godly example he was to me. We praise you that he is forever in your presence, and though we may grieve, we celebrate the power of your eternal life. Amen."

"Amen." Anna tore her attention from the gravestone and kissed him, unmeasured and deliberate. "I love you."

He struggled to find his voice.

She stood and brushed the dirt from her skirt. "Thank you for bringing me here." She took his hand as he stood, and they began to walk toward the gate. "And thank you for loving me."

He pulled her to a stop. When he tucked her against him, she sighed.

"You're easy to love—at least when you're not pointing a gun at me."

Her body vibrated against him as she chuckled.

"Though you were adorable."

"I wasn't expecting my home to have been invaded."

"You're the one who's invaded me. I haven't gotten you out of my heart since I found that note on my kitchen table thanking me for my hospitability."

"It's how we do things out here, right?"

The intensity in her eyes burned him, and if they hadn't been standing in the middle of a cemetery, he'd have taken every advantage of her wifely hospitability. "Come on." He took her hand and resumed walking. If they took a shortcut through the park, they could be back at Mrs. Ford's in ten minutes, and they still had an hour before meeting Professor Polk.

Plenty of time for hospitality.

Did you enjoy Such a Hope? A short review on Amazon.com would be a huge blessing.

Dear Reader

You are a precious part of my ministry at Trails of Love and Grace! This book you've just finished is my third published, but it was the first book I wrote, which is perhaps why Tristan and Anna are so close to my heart.

My prayer is that you experienced the presence of Jesus Christ as you journeyed with Tristan and Anna. Every one of us has wounds from being sinned against and from the wrong choices we've made. Perhaps this book has stirred a longing in you to know the healing touch of Jesus. If so, I want to encourage you to invite the Holy Spirit to come into that woundedness and bring the touch of Jesus to your heart. Wait on the Lord in prayer and see what verses He might bring to mind. It's also good to invite others to pray for you . . . And then will you drop me a note to let me know what happened? You can find me at one of these places:

www.sondrakraak.com
Facebook: Sondra Kraak Author
Instagram: SondraKraakAuthor

If you have a passion for Christian historical romance and love to gab on social media, would consider joining my Trek Team? I need you! You'll have the opportunity to receive advanced reader copies of my upcoming releases as well as join me in promoting my stories. Let me know through a Facebook message, or e-mail me at Sondra@sondrakraak.com.

Also by Sondra Kraak

Acknowledgements

My utmost gratitude to the Creator of story who birthed this in me years ago—the idea that started me on the journey of storytelling.

Thank you to my editor Dori Harrell. You were gracious, encouraging, and proficient. I have confidence in this story because of your attention to each detail.

Once again Roseanna White has created a beautiful cover. You perfectly captured Anna's gentle spirit and the hope of this story. Thank you!

Author Jennifer Rodewald, this is the story that brought us together! You've championed it from the start and been such an encouragement.

Amy Drown, Janette Foreman, and Gwendolyn Gage, the day I joined up with you critiquers my life became so much richer. Thank you for friendship, encouragement, endless ideas, and honest opinions.

To family . . . mounds of gratitude. Thank you for being excited over the little things.

And to Nate, who never stops loving and encouraging me, thank you.

About the Author

A native of Washington State, Sondra Kraak grew up playing in the rain, hammering out Chopin at the piano, and running up and down the basketball court. After attending Whitworth University in Spokane, Washington, she moved to North Carolina to work for a small non-profit ministry. It was in the backroom of that office, amidst the clamor of copy machines and printers, that love blossomed. She married her mountain man in 2004, and they spent the first season of their marriage in New England where Sondra attended Gordon-Conwell Theological Seminary.

Now settled in the foothills of the Blue Ridge Mountains, she works part-time at her church doing worship ministry and leading Bible studies. Life at home with her husband and children is full of Yahtzee, backyard football and baseball, reading parties, activities involving food, and magically multiplying loads of laundry. She writes historical romance set in the beautiful Pacific Northwest through which her passion and delight is to provide readers with stories that not only entertain, but nourish the soul.

Her debut novel, *One Plus One Equals Trouble*, was an ACFW Genesis semi-finalist and the winner of the Blue Ridge Mountains Christian Writers Conference Unpublished Women's Fiction Award.

37560065R00215